ISLAND OF THIEVES

ALSO BY GLEN ERIK HAMILTON

Past Crimes

Hard Cold Winter

Every Day Above Ground

Mercy River

A Dangerous Breed

ISLAND OF THIEVES

A NOVEL

GLEN ERIK HAMILTON

wm
WILLIAM MORROW
An Imprint of HarperCollins*Publishers*

ISLAND OF THIEVES. Copyright © 2021 by Glen Erik Hamilton. All rights reserved. Printed in the United States of America. No part of this book may be used or reproduced in any manner whatsoever without written permission except in the case of brief quotations embodied in critical articles and reviews. For information, address HarperCollins Publishers, 195 Broadway, New York, NY 10007.

HarperCollins books may be purchased for educational, business, or sales promotional use. For information, please email the Special Markets Department at SPsales@harpercollins.com.

FIRST EDITION

Designed by Nancy Singer

Library of Congress Cataloging-in-Publication Data has been applied for.

ISBN 978-0-06-297854-7

21 22 23 24 25 LSC 10 9 8 7 6 5 4 3 2 1

For the woman from Kansas. No sunset so wondrous.

PROLOGUE

Kelvin Welch leaned against a lamppost at the intersection of Dauphine and St. Peter, taking a moment to stop and admire the mayhem. A juggler costumed as the top-hatted voodoo spirit Baron Samedi swerved his six-foot-tall unicycle around a jazz quartet in the middle of the street, avoiding collision by a cat's whisker. The combo's double bass boomed applause. The reverb seemed to shake the plastic beads dangling from the necks of stragglers at the end of a second-line parade disappearing around the corner. A gal in a straw cowboy hat and a lacy sundress caught Welch looking. She shot him a big ol' inviting grin before the endless river of tourists swept her away. The band caught the chatter and the drunken laughs and the occasional shriek that floated by and mixed them right into the jam, the crowd just one more instrument.

Welch smiled around the foot-long straw of his brandy milk punch. This trip had been a long time coming. So far it was meeting all expectations.

Then he saw the dude with the red mask. Again. His smile vanished.

The dude wasn't looking at him. Not this time. He seemed to be ogling a couple of honeys in jean shorts and halter tops making their unsteady way up the block. But this was the third time Welch had spotted that same mask in as many hours.

Two times too many, he thought.

Welch had been sliding up one block and down the next since nine o'clock that night. Long enough after sundown that being outside was bearable. The heat now was from the people. Surging, jostling, the tourists like himself so easy to spot that they might as well have state license plates hung around their necks as jewelry. You had to stay sharp. A husband and wife with matching OK State T-shirts tripped off the curb, recovered, stumbled back onto the redbrick sidewalk, arms still draped around one another like a team in some boozy three-legged race. Welch had toasted their success with his plastic flute of frappé. As he raised the glass, he'd met the eyes of the guy in the red mask across the street.

The guy had looked away and Welch had done the same, barely registering the moment. Masks were common enough, even after the vaccine, even in the crush of the French Quarter where people tossed away all inhibitions along with their plastic doubloons.

An hour and three blocks later, Welch saw the man again. He'd swung through a cypress-paneled joint for another drink, becoming momentarily distracted by a waitress with a skirt so tight that Welch had been trying to make out which cheek had the tattoo. Red Mask had been outside, walking slowly up the sidewalk across the way. Welch had gotten a better look at the dude that time. White, medium height, brown hair slicked down by either gel or the heat. A black polo shirt and jeans. Nothing weird. But Welch had watched from the corner of his eye until the dude was out of sight.

He knew to pay attention to those negative vibes. Coming off three tense months in Dallas, Welch's radar was extra sensitive to any shift in the patterns around him. Any sign that his cover might be in jeopardy, and his safety along with it.

Not that the Dallas assignment had been dangerous. Playing the fool during the day, pretending to be interested in whatever idiot TV show the other guys in Data Services had watched the evening before. Welch had been too busy probing the company's internal safeguards and network traps every night to watch shit. Even after he'd cracked their system and stripped the intel he'd been sent to get, he'd had to stick around for two more anxious weeks until the contract was up and he could do the So Sorry, Got Another Offer jig before catching the next plane.

Now, with a thick roll in his pocket and a hundred times that much money coming soon for a job well done, Welch had been more than ready to relax and enjoy his vacation in New Orleans.

And if it weren't for the guy in the mask, he would be. He resented the man for spoiling his fun.

Could be a mugger, he reflected as he sauntered down Toulouse. A scavenger who had flagged him for carrying cash earlier in the night. Welch felt he could handle a robber, or at least give the asshole the slip. He kept track of the people behind him as he strolled seemingly without care. Using the windows, car windshields, his phone screen to see if the man in the mask was on his tail. Welch turned one corner, then another. The guy didn't reappear.

After ten blocks of trolling without a bite, Welch shook his head in frustration. Twitchy. That's what he was. Three months of guarding his every move and utterance had worn him raw. The booze and the humidity probably didn't help.

Crossing paths with another tourist a few times didn't even qualify as unusual. Welch knew how the *bon temps* rolled around here. Everyone seeing the same sights, the same bars and their signature drinks from the guidebooks. Look, there was the cowgirl who'd smiled at him back on St. Pete. She was shimmying her way into a saloon with purple neon and fake Spanish moss on every wall. Hot zydeco—from a jukebox, not the sweet live stuff—pulsed from the open doorway.

Welch followed, sidestepping a voodoo crone and her sidewalk table strewn with cards and fetishes. The old woman's outstretched claw brushed Welch's wrist as he passed. He ignored her sales pitch disguised as an urgent plea. He'd make his own fortune, thank you very kindly.

The cowgirl had disappeared into the crowd somehow. Welch looked for her while waiting in the crush at the bar for a replacement beverage. Something with rum and pineapple bits on a skewer. By the time he had the drink in his hand, he needed relief. He went looking for the men's room. The first door was the kitchen and the second—

Shit, he was outside. From the smell, plenty of dudes had made the same mistake and decided the alley would do just fine for their urgent appointment. The door had locked behind him. Welch edged around the Dumpster and wandered toward the fence at the end of the alley. Had to be a gate somewhere.

He heard the door to the bar open again and turned around. His eyes widened in recognition and he began to return the warm smile, an instant before a sound like a celery stalk snapping coincided with a massive blow to his chest. The drink dropped from his hand, the plastic cup bouncing and splashing pink rum over his shoes and shins. He tried to speak. There was no breath to carry the words. A second explosion of pain knocked him to his knees. Welch looked down toward the agony in his body, way down, sinking until he was lying on his side on the reeking bricks.

Hands were going over him, through his pockets. His body shivered despite a warmth that had spread all down his chest and stomach. He heard steps running until they faded into the brass blare of the trumpeter on the street beyond.

Kelvin Welch listened as the note rose, fell, smoothed into a drawn-out wail.

Long time coming, this trip, he thought.

He closed his eyes and let the music take him.

ONE

Van Shaw crouched in the shadows, as natural a home to him as the warm Gulf waters to a tiger shark. He watched as the guard with the charcoal gray uniform and company-issued Smith & Wesson completed his circuit of the dim warehouse. The guard's eyes passed over the upper level of the hangarlike building and Shaw's hiding place without pause. In his black clothes and balaclava, Shaw was next door to invisible. His relaxed breathing made no sound through the fabric of the mask.

The guard continued his patrol down Row G. One of a dozen rows of industrial-capacity cargo shelves stacked four levels high. The top shelves were forty feet above the smooth concrete floor, the same height as the catwalk where Shaw waited outside the warehouse's small offices. When the warehouse was built thirty years before, its offices had been elevated to allow foremen to supervise activity around the huge building without having to walk the rows themselves.

Shaw had spent a quiet evening earlier in the week studying the blueprints and other building schematics on file with the Port of Seattle. The plans had been updated eight years previously, when the warehouse was modified to comply with accessibility laws. The catwalk had stairs and a new elevator at one end and a fire-escape door at the other, which had provided Shaw with a convenient entry point once he'd disabled the alarm.

The offices were empty now. So were most of the shelves and the steel cages just below the catwalk, where especially valuable or confidential goods would have been stored when the building was a working bonded warehouse. The guard's patrol was perfunctory. His company protected each of the ten warehouses in the yard off Pier 90.

Just because this one was under new management, and largely vacant, that didn't mean the building was left out of the nightly rounds.

But few goods meant little heed. Shaw heard the door click as the guard left.

He waited for two minutes. He had watched the shipping yard for two nights and a day from a variety of vantage points. The guards on the midnight-to-eight shift made overlapping circuits once every ninety minutes, their routes tracing a latticework around the buildings. When he was confident that both men would be headed away from this end of the yard, he stole down the flights of metal steps to the main floor.

As quiet as Shaw's footfall was, it still seemed to carry in the cavernous space. He could hear the rasp of each strap of his rucksack against his shoulders as he moved.

The cage he wanted was at the far end. Shaw didn't approach it. Not yet. He'd spotted the cameras from the catwalk. Every row of shelves had one of the glossy black bubbles at each end, mounted twelve feet high and positioned to monitor activity on the main floor, including the secure steel cages.

He'd seen identical cameras the day before, while walking past two other active warehouses in the yard. Shaw had sent himself a box of packing materials through a freight company using Warehouse 7, which granted him access to the yard. He'd parked his truck far enough away for a long stroll and an equally long look through the open hangar doors. The security service had installed the same electronics in each facility. Closed-circuit, and running off the main power.

Shaw could have cut the power and disabled the camera watching the cage, but he had a more elegant solution in mind. He skirted the wall of the warehouse to where he could risk a dash to the first monolith of empty cargo shelves. He jumped to catch the edge of the first level, ten feet above the floor, and pulled himself up. The shelf was formed of solid metal slats. Shaw stepped lightly down the row, like walking down a train track on railroad ties, until he came up behind the camera.

He was familiar with the brand and had the necessary gear to grease it in his ruck. It took three minutes for him to tap into the camera's circuit and copy the still image of the empty floor to a customized smartphone. He bypassed the feed so that the image would be the only thing seen on the monitor screens at the guard's office, two hundred forty yards away at the eastern side of the freight area. When he was done, he lowered himself to the floor and walked without hurry to the cage.

It was a solid piece of construction. A ten-by-ten enclosure of cut-resistant wire in a tight mesh. Each wall bolted into the concrete floor. Its interior covered with hard black plastic sheeting to shield the cage's contents from view. A big RR Brink mechanical lock secured the rolling door.

The Brink was serious hardware, but he could defeat it. His concern was for what might happen once he swung the door open.

In one compartment of his ruck was a glass spray bottle. He put an extra set of leather gauntlets over his nitrile gloves and turned his face away as he sprayed a thick layer of the liquid in the bottle through the metal mesh onto the plastic screen that hid the cage's interior.

The corrosive worked quickly. Within two minutes the plastic had softened enough for Shaw to cut a hole by working the blade of a jackknife through the mesh. Careful not to inhale the last of the acidic fumes, he leaned close and shone his flashlight into the dark space beyond.

A white pedestal stood in the center of the floor. And on the pedestal the item Shaw had come for.

The cage's alarm sensor was right out in the open, like a dare. Suspended at the far corner of the ceiling. Passive infrared to measure changes in temperature. An off-the-shelf security measure any business might use.

Shaw had expected something . . . more unusual.

This is a weird score, he thought, and not for the first time.

A fast break? He could open the Brink lock, rush inside, and be out of the building long before the guards responded in any effective manner.

No, he decided. It was an avoidable risk, putting himself in a position where he had no alternative but to escape at a run. Plus, smash-and-grabs had no style. Shaw wanted to beat the system, not just bulldoze his way through it.

Shaw's grandfather, the original Donovan Shaw, would have scoffed. The iron-willed bastard had trained his daughter's son to be entirely unprecious about their profession. Getting away clean was all that mattered. Most of the time, Shaw still followed the old thief's precepts.

But this job was different. Special. The papers in the inside pocket of Shaw's fleece vest, paper-clipped and folded in precise thirds as if still in the original envelope, were enough to verify that.

He climbed up on top of the cage's roof and got to work. Cordless power shears served to slice through the wire mesh and the plastic underneath as well. The shears made an unholy whine in the open warehouse, but within thirty seconds the last echo had vanished.

Shaw removed a mottled sheet of flexible acrylic from his ruck and slid it down through the slit he'd cut in the roof, covering the IR sensor. The sensor's lens was designed to break the protected area into sections, to allow the alarm to detect changes as a heat source moved from one section to another. Shaw's acrylic sheet muddied the received signal, like smearing oil on a camera lens.

He jumped down to the floor. His lockpicks were tucked into a leather sheath around his wrist for quick access. He made the Brink lock confess its secrets in less time than it would have taken to cut a spare key.

Shaw opened the door to shine his flashlight on the object occupying the pedestal.

A figure carved in black stone. An ape, or how someone in ancient times might have imagined an ape if they'd never seen one for themselves. Maybe a baboon, given the statue's squarish snout. Whatever it was, it was happy. An erect phallus protruded two inches from between its squatting haunches.

Somebody had a sense of humor, Shaw thought.

Before he left, Shaw set a business card on the pedestal. The card wasn't his. None of the professions in his life, not thief or soldier or whatever he was now, had required such accessories. The slanted orange letter D at the center of the pristine white card looked almost fluorescent in the gloom.

The card might not have his name and number, but the owner of the stone primate would be calling him soon enough. Shaw had no doubt of that.

AT THE ANTIQUE DESK IN the study of his apartment in South Lake Union, Olen Anders worked by the light of a single lamp. Anders preferred the room this way. The darkness surrounding the pool of illumination improved his focus. He was completing his final notes on a report sent to him by Droma International's chief marketing officer. He had just added his initials next to the orange D on the report's cover when his phone rang.

Anders let it ring twice more before setting his pen aside. He hadn't expected Kilbane's call for at least another thirty minutes. He put the phone on speaker.

"Yes, Warren?" he said.

"I'm on Alaskan Way, sir. Shaw has left the cargo yard and is heading east."

Kilbane's voice sounded tense to Anders. But then the man was rigid by nature. One of the reasons Warren Kilbane made an effective head of security. A fervent belief in regulation.

"Does he have the statue?" Anders said.

"He may. He was inside the warehouse for twenty-eight minutes. The alarms didn't go off. The guards look oblivious."

Intriguing, Anders thought. And unfortunate.

"We'll have to assume he was successful," he said to Kilbane.

"Should I reacquire the item? We can intercept him before he reaches his car."

Anders could imagine Kilbane sitting in his car trying, like a well-trained watchdog, not to strain against the leash. Kilbane had likely armed himself tonight in the event that action would be required. Perhaps even hoping it would be.

"No, don't interfere," Anders said. "It's enough that we're aware Shaw completed the task."

"What if he decides to keep the statue for himself?"

"I don't believe he will." Though Shaw proving to be unreliable at this stage might be for the best.

"Sir," said Kilbane. "Hiring Shaw is . . . strange."

Even for Sebastien is what he meant, Anders knew.

"I don't think it's a good idea," Kilbane finished. "A professional thief."

Kilbane must feel strongly about the matter to challenge the will of their mutual employer. Anders supposed having someone like Shaw within his sphere of operations would feel like sandpaper against Kilbane's desire for order.

Anders also agreed with his security chief's assessment. Employing Shaw was a risk he would prefer not to take. Still, better to present a united front.

"Ours is not to reason why, Warren. Thank you for your attention to this. You and your men."

"Yes, sir. I'll send them home if that's all."

Anders said it would be.

He rose and went to the sideboard to pour himself a modest glass of the Sandeman port that Greta had set out. It was late for alcohol, but he would be awake for some time yet.

Shaw was a concern. Anders now wished he had made security at the warehouse even tighter. Impossible, even. Though Sebastien would have countered that move by saying any reasonable test for Shaw had to offer a chance at success.

Sebastien Rohner was bold. He'd often told Anders that his confidence was one-half of their success, Anders's scrutiny combined with Sebastien's daring. A kind way of saying that he sometimes found Anders's meticulous methods tiresome. Ultimately Sebastien was in charge. If he were truly determined, there was no argument Anders might mount that would be capable of diverting him.

The Rohner wealth had been built on such courage. Enough accumulated capital that even the twin blows of overextending themselves in new markets followed by the crash of the pandemic had been a survivable situation. Nearly.

Now, if Droma International were to remain solvent, Sebastien viewed his scheme as the only means to victory. He would not be denied. The most Anders could do was prepare for every eventuality.

Including an unknown factor like Shaw. On the surface Shaw was perfect for what Sebastien had in mind. The criminal expertise, the scars that spoke of a violent past. The man looked like what he was. And Shaw had proved his skill tonight. Sebastien would interpret that as a good omen.

In mathematics, to solve for a variable, one surrounded it with as many known values as possible. Anders would do the same for Shaw. Isolate him. Have Kilbane and his men keep a close watch.

Before long, if Sebastien's gamble paid off, the thief would become a solution instead of a problem.

TWO

Shaw released the trigger on the eight-pound grinder in his hands. The spinning wheel's insectoid whine quickly dimmed and ceased. He removed his earplugs and set the tool aside to brush a sheet of fine dust off the fiberglass speedboat hull in front of his chest.

To his left, the hull was still matte gray, the color of clouds biding their time before a rain shower, dotted with pits and salt corrosion and the empty carapaces of long-dead barnacles. To his right, where the grinder had done its work, a smooth and dusty mottling of the same gray paint and the white of the raw hull beneath.

His twenty-foot boat stood on drydock jack stands. Four stands on either side and each stand with four slim legs. Lending the speedboat the impression of a centipede with an especially pointed head, grown too fat for its scrabbling limbs.

Halfway done, Shaw judged, after two hours on the port side. His arms were feeling it. He knew some of that soreness was residual fatigue from the action at the warehouse the previous night. Even when he was a teenager and indestructible, he had always felt a mild ache in his muscles the day after a job. As if his body experienced a delayed reaction to the tension and the focus of his mind.

He'd once asked Dono if he felt the same way, after the two of them had relieved a mansion in Medina of a coin collection large enough to fill three albums the size of couch cushions. His grandfather's only reply had been a surprised grunt. Shaw had guessed that the older man had recognized the truth of it, even if he'd never noticed the ache for himself.

He flipped a drink coaster off the top of a can of Fremont stout— the coaster keeping the swirling fiberglass dust out of the brew—and removed his painter's mask to take a long pull. The beer had warmed during the past hour. Shaw still thought it tasted like ambrosia. Around him the boatyard hummed with the kind of frenzy only the fickle promise of early summer could bring. The whirs of half a dozen power tools competed with friendly shouts between families on the docks of the adjoining marina and the revving diesels of boats headed out on the Sound for the afternoon.

Shaw laced his fingers and stretched his arms skyward to loosen his shoulders. Finish this side of the hull and the transom and knock off for the day. He could grind the starboard side early tomorrow and have the first coat of bottom paint drying in time for the noon sun.

He indulged in one more drink before replacing the coaster hat on the can and hefting the grinder. His phone buzzed in his back pocket. He set the tool aside once more.

The screen said WREN. Shaw grinned and hit Accept.

"You're back," he said.

"I'm back. At last. Where are you?" said Wren Marchand. Her voice, which was normally a touch husky, coming at a higher pitch through a speaker on her end. In the background Shaw could hear the steady rumble of a car engine.

"Shilshole. At the marina."

"With Hollis?"

Shaw's friend Hollis Brant lived aboard his fifty-foot cruiser, the *Francesca*, in the same marina where Shaw moored his speedboat. The smaller craft had once belonged to Shaw's grandfather, and Hollis felt protective toward it. Dono and Hollis had been close friends and even better criminal accomplices at times. Dono Shaw's expertise in burglary had paired well with Hollis's smuggling and the contacts he seemed to have in every port and shipping company.

"I'm refinishing the boat hull," Shaw explained. "Hollis is off carousing with his girlfriend, I think."

"Wise man. Want to follow his example?"

Shaw most definitely did. Wren had been visiting family in Colorado and then in Arizona for more than two weeks. The memory of their last night together before she left had both sustained him and made him count the days.

"Let me hose the dust off myself and I'll pick you up," he said.

"Or you could race me to your place. I just passed the sign into King County. Leave showering until we're both there."

Shaw was already unplugging the grinder from its extension cord. "Floor it. I'll pay for any speeding tickets."

Wren's laughter stayed with him as he packed up his gear.

LATER THE TWO OF THEM lay tangled, their breaths slowing as the air pushed by the ceiling fan in Shaw's bedroom gradually cooled the damp heat on their limbs.

"I missed you," Wren said.

"Huh. Felt like you were right on target."

She swatted his hip. He took her hand and placed her index finger between his teeth for a gentle bite.

"I missed you, too," said Shaw. "Easy trip home?"

"Yes. I like long drives. Even the dull parts, when my back is sore and all I can do is look forward to getting wherever I'm going." Wren stretched. "Especially today."

"All the way from Ashland. You must have checked out of the motel before sunrise."

"I stayed with a friend."

She didn't elaborate, which was clue enough. Wren had made it clear when she and Shaw had started dating that she didn't want or expect exclusivity. He'd gleaned that Wren had a long-standing thing with a woman in San Francisco and another lover named Terry, gender unknown to Shaw, in the Ashland area.

Wren had told Shaw he could ask her anything. He thought it easier to leave well enough alone. Best not to get too attached. Wren wasn't even sure how much longer she'd be living in Seattle, having already been there three years, the longest of any home since she was a kid.

"How's the garden?" he said instead.

"Thriving, I hope. Lettie's been looking after it while I was away." Like Shaw, Wren had a few different hustles. Her calling was herbalism. Tending her plot of land with its various tiny crops required nearly as many hours as seeing clients. "Have you been working at the bar?"

"Not this week," said Shaw. "I had something else to do."

He got out of bed with some reluctance and went to open the bottom drawer of his dresser, the only other piece of furniture in the room. He had been living in the apartment less than five months. Its prepaid lease in the icily elegant Empyrea Tower in Belltown had been an unexpected acquisition. There was far more open floor space in the high-rise than seemed natural. Dating Wren had been Shaw's impetus to buy a proper bed frame, king-size.

From the drawer he retrieved the figurine of the baboon, swathed in two bath towels. He brought the ovoid mass back to the bed to unwrap it and show Wren.

"I'm up to try almost anything," she said, "but whatever you have in mind with the monkey might be a hard limit."

He laughed. "It's a score. Sort of."

She cocked one dark eyebrow. "I thought you didn't rob places anymore."

Wren knew his background, or most of it. Raised by a professional thief and a damned prodigy at the work, until he and Dono had had one fight too many. Eighteen-year-old Shaw had escaped into the Army, where to his surprise he had excelled. After surviving the hellish selection process, he had taken to life in the 75th Ranger Regiment like a pit bull to raw meat. Even getting his face half shredded on his first deployment with his new battalion hadn't dissuaded him.

But after he'd spent a decade overseas and on bases, his world had tilted on its axis once again. Shaw had become a civilian. Bearing a multitude of talents, most of them unacceptable to a polite and lawful society. And his moral compass, while still admittedly skewed, wouldn't permit him to make his fortune through thievery anymore.

Under most circumstances.

"It's not what you think," he said to Wren, hefting the baboon sculpture in his hand. "I obtained this little guy without risking prison."

Wren rescued one of the pillows, thrown to the floor in haste earlier, and propped herself up on the headboard. "But you took it."

"Taking isn't always stealing," said Shaw. "Not if you've got permission."

THREE

Shaw's arrangement with Droma International Solutions had been strange from the very start.

The first oddity had been a phone call from Ephraim Ganz. Ganz was once his grandfather's criminal attorney, as savvy at manipulating the justice system as Dono had been at combination-safe locks. Shaw hadn't spoken to Ganz in the better part of a year. The two men had parted with some acrimony, as the lawyer might have put it.

Shaw had been in Addy Proctor's kitchen, washing dishes, when the call came in. Addy and her foster kid, Cyndra, were choosing a show for the three of them to watch that night. Addy preferred *The Great British Baking Show*, while Cyn argued for a new series about vampires and the mortals who had a lot of sex with them. With sixty-five years separating the two women, finding common ground seemed unlikely. Shaw had opted for KP duty to stay out of the line of fire.

When his phone screen lit up with Ganz's name, Shaw had assumed it meant trouble. He might not be a thief anymore, but since leaving the Army, he'd racked up a list of felonies that would make a DA salivate. Had he made some misstep, left some trail leading to him?

He left Addy and Cyndra to their debate and went to the back porch. Addy's dog, Stanley, ever alert for a chance at adventure, followed him outside.

"Hello, Ephraim," Shaw said into the phone.

"Van," Ganz said. "Glad you picked up. What's your schedule like these days? Got time for lunch tomorrow?"

"I'm not at the bar until six." Shaw worked a variety of jobs at a place called Bully Betty's on Capitol Hill and had become something of a silent partner to Betty of late. Saturday nights on the Hill required all hands on deck.

"Good. Excellent, even. I want you to meet somebody. If it works out, this might be a lucrative thing for you."

Ganz's preternatural levels of energy somehow translated through the open line. Shaw could swear his phone's battery was charging the more they talked.

He picked up a hard rubber ball—solid enough that even Stanley's massive jaws wouldn't break it—and tossed it across the small yard for the dog to chase.

"Are you branching out, Ephraim? Placing temp workers?" Shaw said.

"Funny. No, this is a favor."

Shaw grunted.

"Not a favor to you," Ganz clarified. "In case you were worried you might owe me something for the trouble."

"I was wondering who could be this eager to make my acquaintance."

"A friend of mine from way back. You like seafood? The crab cakes at Canlis are going to knock you sideways. One o'clock tomorrow."

Canlis, thought Shaw. Whoever Ganz was trying to impress, it wasn't a client who'd brought him more grief than money.

"All right," Shaw said. "I'll wash my best shirt. The one with sleeves."

It was Ganz's turn to grumble. "Most people would think you were joking."

"I'll borrow some pants, too."

"Go to hell," Ganz said without rancor, and hung up.

Shaw sat down on the steps to lean against the porch rail. He waited until Stanley dropped the soggy ball at his feet for him to throw again. The night was warm and windless. The vanguard of insects that accompanied dusk had stuck around. A cloud of gnats made its slow way between Shaw and one of the solar-powered lights he'd installed over the winter along the edge of Addy's lawn. The bugs were too tiny to cast anything resembling shadows. Instead it seemed like the air itself was rippling, shifting direction based on the whim of each second.

The promise of a fine lunch and even Ganz's display of pique had been bits of distraction. The flourishes a magician makes to keep the audience from seeing the cards move. Or in this case to keep the audience from asking questions that might end the show before it started. It had seemed crucial to Ganz that Shaw make an appearance.

The wily attorney knew exactly who Shaw was. So the only real questions were, who was this old friend of Ephraim Ganz's and why did they need a thief?

THE HOSTESS AT CANLIS HAD begun nodding appreciatively before Shaw finished telling her which party he was joining. She led him with cheerfully quick strides to a window table, where Ganz and a woman in a royal-blue business suit were deep in conversation.

Ganz saw Shaw approaching. "And there he is. Linda Edgemont, Donovan Shaw."

"I'm delighted you could make it, Mr. Shaw," Edgemont said, shaking Shaw's hand.

"Ephraim set the hook pretty well," said Shaw, taking the seat next to Ganz.

Edgemont looked to be in her midfifties, a few years younger than Ganz. They were a study in contrasts. Ganz was short and angular, with eyebrows and hair that defied taming. Edgemont's height was obvious even when seated. An emphatic figure that anyone with half an eye would call curvaceous rather than heavy. And she was immaculately styled, from her champagne-blond hair unsullied by any strand of gray down to, Shaw presumed, the shoes out of sight under the tablecloth.

The server came and proffered menus and asked about drinks. Ganz followed Edgemont's lead and ordered an iced tea. Shaw requested water and had to specify uncarbonated, which in turn required him to select a brand. He had the impression the server might have fainted if he'd said tap.

"The secrecy is my fault," Edgemont said once they were alone again. "I asked Ephraim if he wouldn't mind being circumspect until we could meet in person."

"Linda and I were associates at the same firm when I first moved to Seattle," Ganz said. "She was destined for greatness even then."

Edgemont smiled warmly. "That's rose-colored hindsight. But I appreciate it anyway."

"What greatness occupies you now?" Shaw said.

"How familiar are you with Droma International Solutions?" Edgemont asked. "Or with Sebastien Rohner?"

"There's a Droma sign on a building on 6th downtown. Beyond that I'm tapped."

Edgemont nodded. "Mr. Rohner is the founder of Droma, and my employer. Droma is a privately held company. It doesn't appear in many headlines outside those of industry journals."

"Which industry?"

"Consulting services make up our primary revenue stream."

The server returned with drinks and launched into a litany describing the courses on the prix-fixe menu. This time it was Edgemont who was the odd one out, opting for an entrée of the black cod while Ganz and Shaw chose the steak. Shaw had noted the three-digit prix at the top of the menu. At least now he had a clue why Ganz was showing off. Edgemont must have been an absolute bombshell when the two of them had been legal eaglets. Middle age hadn't stolen much of the woman's luster.

"Consulting for what?" Shaw prompted.

"Ephraim has been kind enough to share some of your background. The high points, at any rate. You served in special operations for the army?"

"The Rangers. That's light infantry. Is Droma a PMC?"

"Private military?" Edgemont showed that warm smile again. "No. Our leading areas of expertise are business management, technology, and finance. But if we discover a role that's a potential growth area, we'll proactively seek out subject-matter specialists. We hire the very best and offer their services worldwide."

Shaw sipped his mineral water. It went well with the implied flattery.

"Your training is an excellent marketing hook," Edgemont said, "but it's not what brought me here. Before the army you had another occupation."

Shaw looked at Ganz. The attorney's restlessness broke into words.

"As I explained to Linda, your grandfather Dono was the one with the past." Ganz turned back to Edgemont. "Van here has no charges or convictions on his record."

"I'm glad for that," Edgemont said.

"Glad because I'm not a criminal or glad because I haven't been caught?" said Shaw.

"Either might be a point in your favor. Let me describe what we're looking for." She leaned forward. "We need someone to beta-test the security at one of our recently acquired facilities. A warehouse where we intend to hold goods on behalf of import clients on the Pacific Rim. The contract with the firm who currently provides guards and alarm maintenance is up for renewal. Mr. Rohner believes strongly in stress-testing any prospective system, physical or technological, before we invest."

"And I would be providing the stress."

"Exactly."

"Van is especially good at that," Ganz said. "I can vouch."

"Why me?" said Shaw. "There must be a dozen security companies who'd be salivating to take potshots at a competitor's work."

Edgemont shrugged minutely. Shaw thought he glimpsed something like resignation behind her polite smile.

"You said you haven't heard of Sebastien Rohner. He wouldn't be what you'd call a celebrity in Europe, but he's certainly better known there than in the States."

"'Rampage' Rohner, the British tabloids call him." Ganz smirked.

"He's an enthusiast," Edgemont said. "Sebastien made his first fortune at nineteen and founded Droma Solutions when he was twenty-six. The company's growth was unprecedented. In the past three decades, he's guided it through countless recessions and political upheavals to establish offices in fifteen nations. We've employed people in three times that number of countries."

Shaw nodded. It was a speech Edgemont had given before. She lent it just the right amount of reverence.

"So Rohner can be excused a few eccentricities," Ganz said, "like expeditions to recover sunken treasure."

"Sebastien admires individualism," said Edgemont. "His direct quote was, 'Find me someone with the proper mind-set.'"

"Which you believe is a guy with my history," Shaw said.

"And to find you I called the best criminal attorney in the city." Edgemont touched her fingers to the back of Ganz's hand. Ganz flushed lightly. "Ephraim says your grandfather was extremely skilled. And that you might be even better."

Shaw looked out the window. Across a narrow stretch of Lake Union, the beautifully rusted silos of Gas Works Park were surrounded by families enjoying the first bright weekend in recent memory. Grass covered the slopes outside the fenced silos, the lawn so lush after the wet spring that the green hills shimmered as if lit from within.

"I've got the knack," he said. "What's the job?"

"The proposition is simple. A small piece of art from Mr. Rohner's private collection will be placed in the warehouse. You'll be told where, but no more than that. Mr. Rohner insists on real-world conditions."

"Your real conditions sound like they'll lead to a real jail cell."

"We thought you might have that concern. This trial will be fully legal and documented. I have a contract drafted, and I've engaged Ephraim not only to find you but to be a witness as to why Droma is employing you."

Ganz nodded. "If you want, we can also record Linda on video making a statement to that effect."

"I'd be happy to," she said. "Mr. Rohner decided your incentive should be on a sliding scale. Your fee for taking the job and providing a summary analysis of the system's potential weaknesses is three thousand dollars. If you can lay hands on the art yourself, regardless of what happens after, that's an additional fee of the same amount. And if you manage to take the artwork without setting off the alarm or being caught by any security staff on-site, add another four thousand to the total. Ten in all."

"If the guards know I'm coming, the job's over before it starts," said Shaw. "They can sit on the art and nail me the second I show."

"They won't be told," Edgemont said. "That wouldn't be a proper test. None of the staff will know that anything is out of the ordinary in their usual routine."

"What's the time frame?"

"We'd like your analysis, at a minimum, within one week."

"That's very tight."

"Mr. Rohner is very driven," she said.

Corporate speak for impatient, Shaw mused. Normally he'd want twice that much time for casing a target and prepping a job. But he could use the money. He had some eccentric ventures of his own.

And if Edgemont was on the level, Shaw wasn't risking prison. That was practically a bonus in itself.

"The pay structure's off," he said. "You want a rush job. I'll have to devote all my time and purchase gear. Five thousand up front. Another ten if I get away clean. You can forget that stuff about counting coup with the art. If I don't manage to escape with the prize, what's the point? Your security team still caught me."

"That's a two-thirds increase on the initial payment and half again on the final total. Fifteen thousand is too expensive."

Shaw smiled. "What's the billing rate for a top attorney? Eight hundred an hour? You want an expert, you pay in arrears for the time acquiring the expertise. Plus, I'm betting on myself. If the vendor is worth your investment, you'll have saved yourself five grand."

Edgemont gave a polite chuckle. "Mr. Rohner might appreciate your confidence."

"Does the new system have aggressive countermeasures?" Shaw asked.

"Pardon?"

"Shock plates. Tear gas. A bear trap that will cut my hand off. Anything like that."

The personal attorney looked as if Shaw had suddenly spit on the table. "I don't know the particulars of the system myself, but no. Certainly not. We wouldn't endorse something of that nature."

"I'll want that in writing," Shaw said. "I'll want it all in writing, including the fact that this conversation took place. The full details of how Rohner or Droma or whoever is asking me to break into their property and take something of value all while avoiding company personnel. With an exemption from property damage."

"Within reason," Edgemont countered. "You can't burn down one of our buildings, to cite a random example."

"Shucks. That was my plan."

"He's joking," Ganz said quickly. "He does that."

Edgemont nodded. "I have an agreement drafted. I'll confirm that the proof-of-concept has no . . . countermeasures, you said? that might cause harm and add a clause to that effect. And that so long as you abide by the terms, you'll be exempt from all suits or action, now or in the future."

Shaw had met a few lawyers and was always amazed by their ability to make jargon sound like an actual conversation.

He turned to Ganz. "You'll review the contract?"

"Why not?" Ganz said. "Since you're the one taking all the risks."

Shaw saw Edgemont's gaze flick to his facial scars before smoothly moving on, down to her clutch purse. She drew a business card from a slim case made of sterling silver with a floral design of pavé diamonds.

"I'll have the papers to you by tonight," she said, handing Shaw the card. "Call me if you have any questions. Assuming everything in writing meets with your approval, may I tell Mr. Rohner we have an agreement?"

Shaw shrugged. "Like Ephraim said, why not?"

Halfway through the meal, Edgemont set down her fork to take a sip of tea. She considered Van over the rim of the glass.

"If the prototype *had* included a bear trap, or something that lethal," she said, "would you have turned us down?"

Shaw finished his bite of filet mignon and smiled.

"No," he said. "I would have demanded hazard pay."

FOUR

Wren looked at the black statue of the baboon in Shaw's hands. "A legal theft. That's bizarre. And they paid you?"

"The first installment. I'll get ten grand more when I return this fellow."

"It looks old. Is it North African?" Wren was born in Morocco, spent most of her childhood in France, and had lived in more places in the United States than Shaw had probably visited.

"Egyptian." Shaw nodded. "I Googled this boy after I brought him home. An underworld god, eating the entrails and souls of the unrighteous. Nasty fellow."

"How old is it?"

"Beats the hell out of me. An authentic statue of the baboon was auctioned at Christie's three years ago. That one was dated around 2400 B.C., a couple hundred years after the pyramids were built. It went for a million-two." Shaw hefted the granite figurine, feeling its solidity. "But I think our primate friend here is just a replica, a very old one. See in the cracks? That's probably bitumen for sealant and some gold leaf. Based on my shaky Internet research, I'd guess this piece is around a thousand years old."

"I suppose they wouldn't ask you to steal something priceless." Wren traced a finger over the markings carved into the cloak around the baboon's shoulders. "Still, it must be worth much more than they're paying you."

That had occurred to Shaw, too. If he'd stolen the figurine outright, he might have sold it for forty or fifty grand to a fence he knew who dealt in antiquities. The baboon might not date back to the time of the pharaohs, but it was in fine shape for a piece of art that had seen a millennium. Even the thing's stubby phallus was intact.

Wren began retrieving her clothes from where they'd been flung, folding each piece in turn neatly on the dresser. "Did you enjoy the work? Taking the statue?"

"Yeah. I'm good at the job. And I like the challenge."

"Pitting your wits against others' precautions."

"I suppose. The money doesn't hurt. If I'm going to get the foundation rolling in any significant way, we'll need capital."

Shaw had survived a strange and brutal start to the year. He'd come out of that time with a few unexpected life changes and a new purpose: carrying on the work of his mother, Moira. Moira had died when Shaw was six and she only twenty-two. Before her life was cut short, the young woman had been building toward a career in social work, helping kids whose parents were incarcerated.

Shaw sympathized. He'd been thrown into the beleaguered foster system himself for a couple years, when his grandfather Dono was convicted on a weapons charge.

A lifeline for children without other support. Therapy and tutoring and maybe more. That was the aim of the charity he wanted to create. It wouldn't fix everything, Shaw knew. But it could fix some things for some kids, and that was enough for him.

"I wonder if this might be a new vocation for you," Wren said. "This testing of security alarms for businesses."

Wren had no accent aside from the leveled tones of the western U.S., but occasionally the rhythms of her speech reminded Shaw that English wasn't her first language, or even her third.

He set the statue on the dresser and touched Wren's arm, where a spiral of small flying birds in different tattooing styles ran from her wrist up and over her shoulder. The line had lengthened gradually during her travels. He drew her to him.

"You like it when I talk about thievery," he said, their lips a quarter inch apart.

"No. I like it when you're so clearly enthused by someone throwing down the gauntlet. And"—she tugged him toward the bed, the sheets still twisted from before—"I like that you're very good at what you do."

"Inspiration," he said. "That's the key."

THEY WERE DRESSING TO GO to dinner when his phone rang. Linda Edgemont's mobile number, copied from her business card.

"It's Shaw," he answered.

"You don't disappoint, Mr. Shaw."

"Van. People who pay me five figures get to use my first name." Wren looked at him with amusement.

"Van it is," Edgemont said. "Do you have it?"

Shaw glanced at the baboon statue. "It's staring at me right now."

"I drove to the shipping yard myself this afternoon just to see how you managed the trick. And found my card where you left it. Amazing."

"When do you want to make the exchange?"

"Are you free this evening? Sebastien Rohner would like to meet you."

"I'm busy tonight."

There was a momentary silence. Shaw had the impression that his answer had lacked the expected deference. When Edgemont spoke again, her tone was fractionally less cheery.

"Tomorrow, then. It will have to be early. Mr. Rohner has a flight at ten o'clock."

"Fine."

"In fact, why don't we meet at Paine Field at nine? Ask for Revol Air."

"I'll be there."

Once they'd ended the call, Shaw rewrapped the baboon in its protective towels. The little god's snout seemed to sneer as Shaw closed the terry-cloth shroud over it.

"Have you heard of Sebastien Rohner?" he asked Wren. She was leaning over the sink in the apartment's master bathroom, applying eyeliner.

"Yes, a little. A businessman and philanthropist. Though all very rich people seem to call themselves philanthropists. He's Swiss. Married to an American, I think. I remember seeing a news story when I was in London about the couple meeting one of the royals."

Shaw nodded. "I saw that article when I was doing my homework on him and his company."

"Droma?"

"Droma. I'm meeting Rohner in the morning to return his lost pet."

Wren swept her hair to one side to place a tiny gold stud in her upper ear. She looked sideways at Shaw as her fingers did the work.

"You know interesting people," she said.

Or they know me, Shaw thought. Rampage Rohner. Shaw had never gotten a celebrity's autograph, but if the signature was on a check for ten grand, there could be a first time for everything.

FIVE

The last time Shaw had seen Paine Field was more than a decade before, during his initial months as an active soldier. His unit had been part of maneuvers out of Lewis-McChord, joint exercises that included the 4th Battalion SOAR, one of the first Spec Ops teams Shaw had seen in action.

Shaw and the rest of the boots were mere seat fillers, learning the pace by watching more experienced teams do the fun work of fast roping. His fireteam had been hustled onto a big twin-rotor Chinook that had touched down and then just as promptly lifted off again. As though the chopper had been playing a game of tag.

Paine had been renovated from the foundation up since then. They'd built a new passenger terminal and introduced commuter routes that had been squeezed out of SeaTac forty miles to the south. Even after the expansion, Paine was only about one-twentieth the size of the larger airport. Shaw was able to park within a hundred feet of the new terminal and stroll inside, crossing the road without having to wait for a break in traffic.

Inside, he reviewed the departures screen. The screen had been designed to mimic an old-fashioned train station's reader board, complete with clicking sounds as each letter or number changed. He didn't see a flight listed for Revol Air. Upon asking, he was informed that Revol was a charter service. The clerk directed him back across the lot.

The charters terminal was sedate, with a communal waiting area flanked by various company desks. Most of the desks were unoccupied. A slim brunette woman in a blue pantsuit and red necktie sat behind the nearest desk, intent on paperwork. Her name tag was shaped like a gyroscope, with her name, C.J., stenciled across the horizontal axis. She looked up at Shaw's knock on the doorframe.

"Good morning," she said. Her eyes touched on Shaw's scars and her widening smile faltered for a fraction of a second. "Do you have a flight today, sir?"

"No. I'm here to meet people from Revol Air."

"Mr. Shaw?" Shaw nodded. "Welcome. I'll take you through."

She stood and draped a lanyard with airport IDs and other pass cards dangling from it around her neck. His gym bag with the baboon statue inside it received a quick examination from the lone TSA agent, who stared at the sneering little visage for a moment before shrugging and handing the bag to Shaw to swaddle the figurine in its towels.

"Is Mr. Rohner some sort of diamond-level flyer?" Shaw said to C.J. once they were on the other side. "Shepherding me seems beyond the usual duties for airline personnel."

"Mr. Rohner owns Revol Air," she said, in a tone that implied a wink. "It's a new subsidiary of Droma International. I just joined myself a few months ago."

Sebastien Rohner seemed to have no shortage of ventures. Despite Edgemont's claim that Rohner wasn't famous, Shaw's online research had found everything from a profile in *Forbes* to a spread in the French edition of *Architectural Digest*, showing off the pied-à-terre that Rohner and his wife had created on the Île Saint-Louis in Paris. Shaw's French pretty much stopped at ordering croissants, but it didn't take fluency to read affluence in every fold of the apartment's silken drapes.

The billionaire's professional background had been easy to piece together from twenty years of sporadic articles in the *Wall Street Journal* and other business periodicals. Born in Geneva and educated in England, Rohner first appeared in the public eye when Droma Solutions began to make some real money through its contracts to provide resources to UK and European stock-trading firms. In the past decade, Droma had expanded its reach into North America and its specialties into property development and industrial sciences.

A personal profile of the man, including the nickname Rampage Rohner, had come to light more recently.

The earliest mention of Rohner's private life was twelve years earlier, when the captain of industry had sponsored and led an expedition to the South Pole. Shaw would have dismissed the trip as a wealthy man's try-hard vacation, more to boast about than to actually achieve. Except that Rohner and his team had made the trip without help from planes or snowmobiles. Two months on skis, over seven hundred miles from the coast to the pole. Rohner had been around forty then. Shaw was at least ten years younger and wasn't certain he could endure that trek.

From there the stories became more frequent—and more dramatic. Mountain climbing, which drove Rohner to conquer at least one tough peak every year or two. BASE jumping into pit caves in Mexico. Wingsuit flights over the Alps.

Along with the exploits came conflicts. A nasty divorce from his first wife, both of them alleging mental abuse. A second marriage almost immediately after. From the single photo Shaw had seen, wife number two looked to be in her late twenties, the same age as Rohner's daughter at the time. There had been public shouting matches with competitors and some partners alike, one of which, in a three-star Michelin restaurant in London, had earned him the first Rampage Rohner headline. Rohner's people had issued a statement immediately after, claiming that Rohner was reacting to his companion's being verbally attacked by a rival, but the name had stuck.

An enthusiast, Linda Edgemont had called Rohner. Shaw admitted the tycoon didn't lack for energy.

C.J. tapped her keycard on an exit door, and they stepped outside. The bright early sun made Shaw squint.

"There," she said over the whine of plane engines and other machinery. She led him toward a small jet parked seventy yards from the charter terminal. The aircraft's white paint gleamed from every rivet but lacked the Revol Air gyroscope emblem. Shaw wondered if the fledgling air service shared the vehicle with other companies. He and C.J. crossed the tarmac to a mobile stairway leading up to the jet's open door.

The interior of the plane was a balance of austerity and luxury. Ten chairs, all the same, each spaced a body's length or more apart along the clean white fuselage walls. The ceiling was similarly white, and tall enough for Shaw to stand without feeling cramped. Recessed cabin lights ran in two gleaming silver rows like crown molding along each edge. The ovoid windows beneath were much larger than those on a commercial jetliner, allowing a flood of sunlight to fill the space. The boldest color inside the plane was the leather of the chairs, a buttery tan.

"Sir?" C.J. said.

One of the chairs near the rear of the plane turned.

Sebastien Rohner stood up from where he'd been working at a table that folded out from the wall. The CEO was an inch or two over six feet tall and very lean. His dark blond hair had turned mostly white, giving the chiseled planes of his head a platinum sheen that went right along with the private jet's decor.

"Mr. Shaw," Rohner said. He didn't come forward, and it was left to Shaw to walk down the length of the plane to meet him. They shook hands. Rohner gestured toward the chair opposite him. "Please."

"I'll see to the flight papers, sir," C.J. said. "One hour until takeoff."

Rohner nodded and she retreated down the stairway. They sat.

Seeing Rohner in person, Shaw had little trouble imagining the man trekking the Andes. Or marrying a socialite twenty-five years his junior. His clear gray eyes were wide set, as if to offer deference to a strong, slightly avian nose. He wore a ribbed fleece jacket over a turtleneck sweater and wool pants. Shaw didn't recognize the emblem on the jacket, assuming it was a European brand, but he knew a thousand-dollar casual ensemble when he saw it.

"I appreciate your meeting me today," said Rohner. "A sliver of available time in a very busy week. I was impressed with your achievement." He glanced at the gym bag, now on the floor by Shaw's chair.

Shaw made no move to hand it over. "Thank you," he said.

"How did you accomplish taking it?"

Rohner's Germanic accent was faint, the voice cultured. Maybe cultivated, Shaw mused. A refined tone that would suit a business leader who had to give frequent speeches.

"My full report is in the bag," he said.

"Tell me in person. I would greatly enjoy hearing your story. It's not every day I have such an opportunity." Rohner spread his hands as if the matter were out of his control.

Shaw recounted his casing of the Droma campus and took Rohner through his choices and actions at each step of besting the system. The summary reminded Shaw of his mission debriefings in the Rangers, as a squad leader or a platoon sergeant. Except that Rohner seemed less inclined to interrupt and challenge Shaw's decision making after the fact than the Army brass had. The Droma founder asked questions to clarify particular techniques and seemed especially intrigued by Shaw's ploy to recon the freight yard by mailing himself a crate.

It had also occurred to Shaw that a formal confession of a crime, delivered to detectives instead of a corporate executive, would cover exactly the same ground. Maybe that was the cause of his unease. It went against Shaw's every instinct to verbalize what would normally be kept secret.

"If you hadn't come prepared to defeat the infrared sensor," Rohner asked when Shaw reached that part, "would you have found another way?"

"Eventually. It would have been possible to remove the statue without entering the cage. I could've cut a hole in the roof and hauled it up."

Rohner nodded. "Still, your having the tools you needed might have been good luck rather than skill."

"Or skill making luck," Shaw answered. "I'll take fortune any way it comes."

"Don't misunderstand me. I believe in chance. I myself am very lucky. And I am also a distracted host, not offering you anything. We have coffee in the galley." Rohner nodded toward the back of the plane.

"Thank you. I'll take a wire transfer. Or cash."

"Linda will be here shortly. She has your payment. There's something else I wish to discuss while we are in private."

"I'm a captive audience."

"I wish to offer you another assignment. Similar to the first, with additional aims."

Shaw raised an eyebrow. "So the warehouse job—an audition?"

"You proved your expertise. If you accept the role, we will pay four times what you earned for the original task. Without your having to wager on success this time."

Sixty grand. Wren might be right, Shaw mused. Maybe this was a new vocation.

"What's the gig?" he said.

"I have recently built a home here in Washington State. A retreat, for both my family and business associates. Along with my home is an art collection that holds considerable sentimental value apart from its tangible worth."

"You want me to test its security?"

"I want you to *be* its security, Mr. Shaw." Rohner leaned forward. "I believe someone will attempt to steal one or more pieces of art from me during the next week. I require you to stop them. Set a thief to catch a thief, yes?"

SIX

Shaw stared. The booming engines of a plane lifting off from the nearby runway made the fuselage of the private jet quiver. "Explain."

Rohner leaned back in his seat, seemingly pleased at how he'd captured Shaw's attention. "This week I will be hosting a number of colleagues. Heads of their own substantial companies. We are cordial, even warm, with one another. But there is always a competitiveness present, too."

"I know a teenage kid. She'd call that being frenemies."

"Accurate, if reductive. I suppose it has always been so with men who must be first in their fields."

"Probably women as well."

Rohner waved a dismissive hand. "My daughter, Sofia, might tell us. But it stands that these men and I, plus a few others in my circle, have something of a contest. We acquire things that the others care for. Two years ago I bought an antique vase at auction simply because I knew that an associate wanted it for his wife. Foolish, perhaps. But I traded that vase later when the same associate mysteriously came into possession of a wristwatch that had belonged to my father, a watch I had thought was secure in a home safe. He had clearly hired a professional."

"Breaking the rules?"

"If there are rules. Pushing those boundaries has become part of our competition, too."

Shaw was fascinated despite himself. Rohner and his ilk, despite running huge corporations, somehow had too much time on their hands. The games rich people play.

"And you think this guy is going to have a burglar break in and steal a painting while you're all enjoying brandy and cigars," he said.

"You misapprehend. Or I haven't fully explained. This is a business event at its heart. These colleagues will be staying at our home for a few days. They will bring key employees. I will have household staff and my personnel, too. It will be an active time, with many people involved while we negotiate details of a new partnership."

"What about hiring me? Is that another flex of the boundaries?"

Rohner inclined his head, not quite a nod. "I view it as a logical progression. A knight to take a pawn."

"And if the pawn is captured? Do you trade this guy for the next wristwatch?"

"No, no. I gain . . . the upper hand, I suppose it would be."

"Bragging rights."

"Suffice it to say that I want you there, protecting my collection. A unique task often requires a unique individual."

"I'll give my first impression for free. It's nuts. You can hire a trainload of bodyguards and off-duty cops. Enough to have two men guarding every piece of art around the clock and a dozen left to guard the guardians."

"Which would look absurd to my guests. This is an important time for Droma, Mr. Shaw. For me as well. I won't embarrass valued clients by having them feel as though they are under suspicion."

"Even if they are."

"Perhaps *especially* if they are." Rohner glanced out the nearest window toward the terminal. "There are other reasons. Some of the pieces in my collection are . . . disputed. Their ownership. Not, I assure you, by the authorities. Everything I own has been acquired through reputable sources."

"But."

"But the provenance of art can be complex. Employees may be bribed by the unscrupulous. Tiny details can be twisted, or even invented, in the pursuit of salacious stories." He shook his patrician head. "The fewer people involved, the better. I have an instinct for such things. This instinct tells me to have a man with your eyes watching for what only you might see."

Or to send the serf to fight the laird's battle for him, Shaw thought.

"Will you accept the challenge?" Rohner said.

Shaw inclined his head to the same angle Rohner had before. "The price is right. When do your guests arrive?"

"Tomorrow afternoon. But you should begin early. That will give you time to examine the gallery and acquaint yourself with the estate."

Estate. Jesus.

"You've obviously thought this through," said Shaw. "What's my cover story?"

Rohner picked up the china cup and cradled it in manicured fingers. "A work in progress. I'd originally thought you might pose as one of the household staff. However . . ."

"I don't really blend," Shaw agreed. "What about security staff?"

"We employ such people already. You'll meet my head of security. Warren Kilbane."

"But you're not relying on him to solve your burglar problem." Shaw didn't put it as a question.

"Warren has been told that you will be evaluating our alarm system. It's not necessary to involve him beyond that."

"How's he feel about that? Your bringing in outside help on his turf."

Rohner sipped from his cup. "The turf is mine. And we were discussing your . . . cover. You have some background in building construction, I understand?"

A complete little dossier they'd compiled, Shaw thought. Then again, Droma was a recruiting company. Deep background checks would be second nature.

"My grandfather was a general contractor. I apprenticed with him."

"In that and in other things," Rohner said. "You'll be our new facilities manager. On site during the event this week. Checking with the guests to see how comfortable they are and whether the estate's new construction requires any modifications. That should permit you to circulate, within reason."

"Where's your home?" Shaw asked, imagining a mansion in Madison Park or Medina. Something with three French Colonial stories and a lawn that could field Olympic archery competitions.

"Briar Bay Island," said Rohner.

"In the San Juans?"

"Yes. Do you know the islands?"

"Some of them."

"Then you're aware there's one bearing your name, too. Shaw. Our island is not nearly so large, barely a mile long."

Shaw blinked. Only a billionaire could downplay owning an entire landmass.

Someone knocked at the plane's entrance.

"Yes?" said Rohner.

C.J. stepped in. "Ms. Sofia and the others are here, sir."

"One minute."

She dutifully retreated. Rohner fixed Shaw with a look.

"This is a private matter, Mr. Shaw. You and I and my chief of staff are the only ones who are aware. I don't wish to worry my family or distract my team from the work to be done."

"And the contract?"

"Will detail your role and your pay, along with granting access to the estate and grounds." Rohner smiled microscopically. "No need for additional housebreaking."

C.J. reemerged and stepped aside to allow a line of people to troop into the plane. The first was a slender blonde woman in her mid-thirties Shaw recognized from his online searches as Sofia Rohner, the CEO's daughter and executive VP of at least one division of the family business. The second was Linda Edgemont. Trailing her was a group of four more executives, all male, all around Sofia's age.

The two women walked the length of the plane. Shaw stood up. The businessmen hovered at the entrance, perhaps awaiting instruction.

Edgemont gestured. "Sofia, this is Van Shaw. Van, Sofia Rohner."

"Mr. Shaw has accepted a position as facilities manager for the Briar Bay property," Rohner broke in from his seat.

Sofia's right hand was holding her briefcase. Shaw shook her left, his fingers automatically gauging the size of the diamond in her wedding ring. She hadn't inherited her father's height, but the platinum hair and pale skin were unmistakable. On her, the Rohner nose looked less hawklike and more regal.

"Welcome to the team, Mr. Shaw," she said. "Will you be joining us this week?" Her accent was English, reminding Shaw of movies he'd seen with public-university students hurrying through castlelike halls and rowing on the Thames. She was dressed more for the office than for comfortable travel, in a slate-gray skirt and matching jacket and heels the color of a heavy fog.

"Yes," said Shaw, "thank you."

"Then we will see you there." She turned to Rohner. "I need to review today's presentation with you during the flight."

Shaw took the hint. He said good-bye to Rohner and glanced at Linda Edgemont, who walked with him back to the front of the aircraft and down the stairs.

The young executives eyed Shaw with curiosity as he passed. Probably trying to classify him. Clearly not competition. But he'd been granted a meeting with the big boss, one-on-one. Shaw's barn coat and jeans could be misleading clues to his social status in casual Seattle. The slim cut of their suits and shorter lengths of sleeve and trouser legs on all four said Savile Row or Milan to Shaw.

"Where are you flying?" Shaw asked Edgemont once they'd reached the bottom of the gangway.

"Just a quick trip to Silicon Valley, to meet with clients while Sebastien is on the West Coast. We'll be back tonight or tomorrow, depending on how things go."

On a Sunday. Shaw supposed Droma executives had long ago abandoned the idea of weekends.

"And I'm sure you'll want this." Edgemont handed Shaw a closed white envelope. His initials, VS, were penned discreetly at the top right corner. The envelope was thick enough that its flap barely reached the opposite side. "Your payment for this past week and papers to sign for your new role. Please bring those to the island."

Already printed and sealed. Shaw had to smile at Rohner's confidence that he'd accept the job, even if he felt unsettled at being predictable.

"My new role," Shaw echoed. "Is there a dress code?"

"For you? If work clothes are most appropriate for what you're doing, that will be fine. I'm sure you'll be invited to dinner with the guests the first night at least. You'll want a coat and tie for that."

"The first night. How long do the meetings run?"

"Plan on three full days. Though I suspect the conference might finish early." She held her finger and thumb half an inch apart, signaling a slim chance. "There's a tendency for business leaders to enjoy the first day and push hard to wrap up on the second, even if it means working into the night. Men of Mr. Rohner's stature often have half an eye on the next objective."

"I'm getting that impression."

"Rangi will provide you with travel details," Edgemont said, indicating a heavyset man wearing a black suit, standing across the tarmac by the door to the charter terminal. "Happy to be working with you."

Shaw said thank you, and the lawyer quickly rejoined the passengers.

As he walked back to the terminal, the figure of Rangi grew almost out of proportion. Shaw had originally thought him shorter than his own height but quickly realized that was an illusion created by Rangi's impressive width. From shoulders to knees, the man was a solid cylinder. Samoan, Shaw guessed, or maybe Maori.

"Van Shaw," he said. They shook hands. Rangi's suit and somber expression lent him the look of a pallbearer. One who could heft the coffin all by his lonesome. Absent the serious mien, his face might have looked boyish with his smooth high cheekbones and deep black hair and eyebrows.

"Rangi Sua," he said. "You're brand-new?"

"Yeah."

"Okay. It's a good company. Good people. Come on."

Shaw followed him down the short hallway back into the terminal lobby.

"How long have you worked for Droma?" Shaw asked.

"I work for the family. But one is the other, most of the time." Rangi took a phone from his pocket as they left the gates, out through the secure exit to the ticketing area. "What's your number?"

Shaw told him, and Rangi tapped buttons with a wide thumb as they walked. Shaw's phone pinged. "There. Got you on a noon hop tomorrow with C.J. Hope you're cool with flying by seaplane."

"C.J. The attendant?" Shaw glanced back in the direction of the Revol Air plane.

"Attendant on the jets. Pilot on the prop planes. I manage all the travel on land or sea, C.J. has the air covered." Rangi held up his phone. "She and I have everything synced so she knows when I'm picking them up and I know right when she's dropping them off. You need a lift to the plane tomorrow?"

"I'll have a ride, thanks. Your team is efficient."

"Have to be. The family and the big players with Droma travel a lot. I got a hand on a steering wheel every day."

"Boats, too?"

"Oh, yeah. You'll see the one they keep locally at the island, a forty-five-foot Regal. I love sailing her. In New York we have another motor yacht. The biggest is in Genoa, but that has its own crew."

"Heck of a life."

Rangi smiled with one corner of his mouth. "You have no idea. Or maybe you will soon. Enjoy the ride."

Shaw saluted and headed off.

From what Rohner had said, Rangi and Edgemont—as well as his own daughter—were unaware of the peculiar competition between the moguls to acquire one another's possessions. The man himself had called it a private matter.

Juvenile, Addy might say. But money forgives a lot of eccentricities. For sixty grand Shaw could handle a little madness.

SEVEN

Cyndra and Shaw had made a handshake deal. He'd helped her complete some extra credit for her American Government class the previous week—a last-minute push to shore up the girl's GPA as she closed out eighth grade—if Cyn would dedicate her first free Sunday morning to stuffing envelopes for Shaw's nascent foundation. Addy lent a hand so they could finish before the bar opened at two o'clock. Wren had brought her laptop and a portable printer, which was spitting out pages of address labels from a list of Washington State social services.

Shaw had dubbed the foundation Crossroads, his nod to a defunct outreach program called New Road that his mother, Moira, had been working for when she'd died. Shaw figured the name suited where most of the kids would find themselves. Making the choice, consciously or not, whether to follow the same path as their incarcerated elders.

Between Addy's long and rich life and Hollis Brant's ability to forge alliances in the strangest places, Shaw sometimes guessed that he was only two or three degrees of separation from every living human on the Pacific Northwest and a majority percentage of the dead ones. Addy had enlisted a friend named Penelope, a former executive recruiter who was, as Penelope put it, "doubly bored" being both retired and under specialized care for a heart condition. Penelope in turn had found former nonprofit executives to advise Shaw.

Now that Crossroads officially existed under state law, the mailers and an email campaign would let other social services know about the foundation so that they could partner to assemble a list of potential clients, which would give them supporting evidence for grants and donations.

Sometimes it made Shaw's head swim. Money had seemed a lot easier to come by Dono's way.

He took a break to go into the main bar and pour one stout, one Hefeweizen, a cup of lemon tea, and one Coke. He brought the drinks back on a tray, with the certified check from Droma International Solutions placed at the center.

"Well," Addy said, "if I have my choice, I'll take the money."

"Let's toast to solvency," said Shaw. "Ten grand of my fee is going to Crossroads. There'll be more after this week." In between the folding and stamping, he had told them all the story of Sebastien Rohner's private plane and the CEO's even more private concerns about an art thief.

"If you catch this guy, can you arrest him?" Cyndra said. "Like citizen's arrest?"

"He probably won't have to," said Addy. "Just identifying the culprit should be enough to stop any crime from happening."

Wren smirked. "You should do that. Point at the person and cry 'Culprit!' for all to hear."

Cyn laughed and mimed standing up to thrust out an accusing finger.

"Rohner doesn't want the cops involved. Too vulgar," said Shaw, taking a long pull on his stout.

"I'm not surprised," Wren said. "Especially if the art was—how did he put it?"

"Disputed."

She made a face. "A lot of the world's art is. England looted Egypt of its treasures. William Randolph Hearst acquired art by the shipload while Europe was desperate after World War One. The Nazis stole half of what was left."

Shaw set down his pint. "I didn't know you felt so strongly about this."

"I was born in a country carved up like a pie between the French and the Spanish. My parents still remember the time before independence. I love France, and my heritage, but my feelings for it are . . . complicated." She looked at Shaw. "Like yours, about your nation's foreign policy."

He grinned. "Don't change the subject."

"I'm serious."

"I know you are. But I can't get into another debate on whether America is a protector or an opportunist. Especially when we can never decide who's arguing which end of it."

"One thing I don't understand," said Addy. "If a thief was hired to steal from the art collection, why would he do it this week? While the island has so many people around?"

"I'd wondered that myself," Shaw said. "Maybe it's part of the game these guys are playing. 'See, I can take your stuff from right under your nose.' The whole contest is an ego trip."

"Or there will be sentries with broadswords and plate armor guarding it later," said Cyndra. "That's what I'd do."

"Also possible. Once the business conference is over, there's no reason for Rohner not to have the island protected by trained croco-diles or any other loony idea that comes into his head. He seems like the type."

"A megalomaniac?" said Addy.

Shaw shrugged. "No more so than most world tycoons. Rohner's an obsessive, I'd bet. The news articles about him show a pattern. Mountain climbing, charter airlines, arctic expeditions. When he gets into something, he goes all out, as fast as he can. Which is damn fast, since money is no object."

"Then he gets bored and goes to the next thing." Cyn snapped her fingers to signal the speed of the change. "My friend Billie is like that."

"Perhaps that's the real draw," Addy mused. "Now he has worthy opponents."

"For an unworthy game," said Shaw.

"You don't like him," Wren said.

"I don't dislike him. He's aloof and he's probably felt superior since he was a fetus, but he's not an idiot. I can be civil around the king's court for a few days."

"For a good cause?" said Addy.

"We need the money."

"Not so much that you should—"Addy glanced at Cyndra. "Should rent your honor, if that's what it feels like."

Wren looked at her with curiosity. When Wren was interested in something, her focus was like a spotlight, Shaw had noted. The amber pinpoints in her chestnut-colored eyes glowed. "What do you mean?"

"Van is class-conscious," Addy said. "Occasionally to his detriment."

Cyndra screwed up her face. "What's class-conscious?"

"She means I tend to piss off rich people," Shaw said.

"Because you try to," said Addy. "You needle them so they'll know you're not impressed."

"And because it's fun to see them squirm."

"You're joking," Wren said, "but do you really hold that much emotion over someone's income?"

Shaw frowned. How had this become a therapy session? "They're big fish."

"You mean good eating?" Cyndra guessed.

He looked at her. Cyn was small-boned, her frame disguising the toughness that came from growing up in a series of L.A. County group homes and foster families. She'd dyed her hair pink to celebrate the end of her middle-school career, and the skin around her hairline had turned a rosy hue from the tint.

"You remember about my granddad?" Shaw said. "Like your dad, Mickey?" A career felon.

The teen nodded gravely.

"Growing up with Dono, I got to think of the rich as targets. Which is another way of saying they were the enemy. They had money, we didn't."

"Prey," said Wren.

"Yeah. Then I grew up and realized that at least half the people and businesses we stole from were just as crooked as we were, but smarter about it. Maybe their families had smuggled diamonds a couple of generations back, or they'd fleeced partners in a real-estate deal, or they just crushed their competitors through bribes and undercutting."

Shaw pointed at Cyndra. "That doesn't mean what Dono and I did was justified. Especially to the few who'd made their money honestly. You get my point?"

"Two wrongs," Cyn said.

"Bingo."

"So your opinion of the wealthy is . . . ?" Wren prompted.

"Big fish eat little fish. That's how they got to be big fish in the first place." Shaw drank his beer. "Complicated, like you said. I try to be polite. But kicking the deserving ones in the shins doesn't cost me anything."

Addy raised her cup of tea. "Here's hoping Sebastien Rohner remains among the unbruised."

EIGHT

Wren drove Shaw to the address provided by Rangi, near the southern tip of Lake Union. The primary location for seaplane flights out of the city. A handful of passenger and sightseeing companies operated off the same collection of docks, with space for private aircraft to tie up during the day.

"Don't forget your bag," Wren said.

"In a minute," said Shaw, leaning across to kiss her.

She'd stayed at Shaw's apartment overnight, a rare occurrence. In the six months they'd been seeing each other, Wren had slept over an equal number of times. Sleeping being a relative term, and not only because of sex. Wren stayed awake much of the time, in Shaw's living room, reading or watching television. She had told Shaw she didn't rest well away from her own bed. Shaw had tried staying at her place twice, and her story checked out. Wren had slept soundly while Shaw had been the one staring at the ceiling, either awkwardly twisted in the sheets on her cramped full-size bed or trying to ignore her housemates arguing or screwing or both. Maybe it was a childhood thing, he thought. Wren had come from a large family. Shaw had barely had anyone around at all.

"You're back on Thursday?" Wren asked when they surfaced for air.

"Best guess. Could be longer or shorter."

"I get back to town and you leave. We should coordinate the next trip."

"Together?" he said.

"Why not? Perhaps if the bed is new to both of us, it'll even out."

He grinned and reached into the backseat of her battered Jeep to grab his duffel. He'd packed underwear and socks for four nights, three changes of clothes, spare boots, and a heavier coat than the gray barn jacket he wore now. The forecast claimed the beautiful June weather would continue all week. Maybe Rohner had paid off the clouds. Shaw preferred to trust his own experience when it came to the mercurial Seattle climate.

The clothes served as padding for his gear. Frequency scanners for wireless alarm signals, portable power tools, a spare tablet computer, and a few other electronics. Rohner had said no burglary would be required, but even a cursory evaluation of the estate's system might require a specialist's touch.

"Ever been to Kyoto?" Wren asked as Shaw shut the passenger door.

"I've never been across the Pacific," he said. "Every place the Army sent us out of Fort Benning was east."

"I'd like to see Japan. With you."

"Is Japanese one of your languages?" Shaw said.

"No."

"Good. We'll both start from square one."

Wren said, "Race you there," and drove off.

Shaw slung the duffel over his shoulder and headed for a long, white two-story building.

C.J. was waiting at the railing. No flight-attendant uniform today. Just a white shirt and blue jeans and running shoes even brighter than the blouse.

"Good morning," she said.

"Hello. Is this a Revol Air flight, too?"

"Kinda. We run a regular shuttle to Vancouver. Droma has a lot of managers and executives working here or there or both. Part of the innovation corridor between our nations."

"And your clients pay for that?"

"The clients pay for the talent," C.J. said, with the same implied wink as she'd had at Paine Field. "The shuttle helps recruit that talent for Droma."

Shaw followed her into the office. The orange *D* logo of Droma was painted on the front window and again in reverse on the window to the rear. The office's interior was simple to the point of being deliberately bland, though the view of the lake made up for it.

"Pilot for one airline, attendant for the other," Shaw said, "and Rangi told me you arrange the executives' commercial flights, too. That's a lot of juggling."

"It was just the pilot work at first," C.J. said, moving behind one of the desks to collect paperwork. "Paid by the job. Then their local travel coordinator quit, and I made an offer to handle everything Rangi doesn't. Worked out. I'll be a pilot for Revol Air, too, once I'm certified for that level."

"Onward and upward," Shaw said.

C.J. smiled. "Exactly, Mr. Shaw."

"Van."

"Van. And which diversification of Mr. Rohner's are you with? Not everyone rates a private flight to Briar Bay."

"I'm also an independent. Facilities manager for the island. If this week goes well, we'll see."

She placed the papers into a satchel. "Help yourself to coffee while I complete the prechecks."

Shaw poured a cup and followed her out to the wide floating dock. The day promised to be perfect for flying, with a light wind and only a few scattered mares' tails of cirrus clouds. Shaw fished his sunglasses out of his pocket. Floatplanes of various vintages bobbed gently on either side of the dock, their pontoons squeaking against the recycled tires that formed an unbroken line of fenders. Like young birds eager to leave the nest.

The Droma plane was second on the right. A sleek white-over-blue single-prop. C.J. unlocked the door, tossed her satchel onto the pilot's seat, and began a preflight check of the plane's exterior. Shaw understood her surprise at his being granted a private hop. The plane had room for eight passengers not counting the pilot and copilot, and enough space at the rear of the cabin to store a full set of luggage for every one of them.

C.J. caught him looking over the plane's fuselage. "You know planes?"

"Some. Last prop plane I was in was a Huron, I think."

"In the military?" Shaw nodded. C.J. patted the plane's wing. "This girl's an Otter. A DHC, from the Great White North."

"How long's our flight?" Shaw asked.

"Just over an hour. Are you in a rush to get there?"

"No."

"Good. We can take a little time and go up Rosario Strait and around. It's a sightseer's dream today, and I've barely seen that part of the islands."

He finished his coffee while C.J. ran through the rest of her checklist. She invited Shaw to take the copilot's chair, indicating a set of headphones hanging from a hook under the dash. He buckled in and adjusted the headset as she started the engine and cast off the last line. The engine heightened in pitch, and the plane eased away from the dock.

C.J. taxied slowly, careful of paddleboarders or other people on the lake. The nose of the plane drew parallel with the row of buoys that marked the runway on this side of the lake. She eased the throttle forward and the Otter surged ahead, the propeller spinning until only an afterimage of lazily rotating sickles was visible. Shaw felt the water under them dragging at the pontoons. Then they were hydroplaning for an instant before the craft lifted away.

She banked left. They passed over the Fremont Bridge and its bumper-to bumper traffic at the start of the workweek.

"Was that your wife dropping you off?" C.J. said through the intercom.

"A friend."

"She's lovely."

"I agree. How often do you fly to the island?"

"It was once every couple of weeks at first. I only started with Droma three months ago. All the island construction and the family moving in happened last year." She waggled a hand. "I guess moving in isn't quite the way to put it. They still live in Seattle when they're in town, most of the time."

"A vacation home for people who don't take vacations," said Shaw.

"Could be. But in the past week, I've flown Mr. Rohner there twice already, along with a bunch of his VPs. And then the household staff with all the food and supplies. That took three trips. Everybody's getting ready for the conference to start."

"What's the big meeting about? Rohner didn't go into details."

"I don't know either. Could be nobody does, except the principals. I'm sure there will be a press release once all the papers are signed. Hey, check that out."

She pointed to the Sound, where a submarine was cruising on the surface, flanked by two smaller navy vessels. The warship making headway toward the straits and the open sea beyond swiftly enough to send a steady plume of waves over her rounded bow.

"Out of the shipyard, I guess," C.J. said. "Look at her go."

"Are you local?"

"Me? No, I'm one of the terrible people moving here and eating up real estate." She smiled. "But I like to get my bearings quickly. Part of the job."

"You must hear a lot, flying the executives around. Any conflicts inside Droma on your radar?"

"Like arguments?"

"Yeah," he said. "I like to know the lay of the land, too. Part of my job is making sure things run smooth. That's tough if coworkers don't get along and then they're stuck on an island together for three days. Anyone have beef with the family?"

"Nothing like that. I do the Vancouver hops occasionally. Younger management, sometimes late in the day after they've had dinner and drinks, you know? Two of them got into a squabble about whether they could ever rise through the ranks. They're American, for one, and for two—" C.J. looked at him. "I don't want you to think I'm talking smack about the boss."

"Smack away. Keeping secrets is in my DNA."

She smiled. "This wasn't really about the Rohners anyway. The junior guys, they think because Sofia Rohner is head of client development and Mr. Rohner's son runs operations in Europe, that there's no place for them. You want my opinion, that's not just counting chickens before they hatch—they're counting the whole farm. These guys haven't even made department head yet."

"But they see Droma as a family joint."

"And that the Rohners being here on the West Coast is just a jumping-off point to Asia. World conquest."

"Even though they just built an estate here?"

"'Three hundred acres of overcompensation.' That's a quote I overheard." She stopped and frowned. "But I can't tell you who from. I don't want my butt kicked back to Jersey."

Shaw had the impression he'd overstepped. For the rest of the flight, he kept his thoughts about the Rohners to himself, speaking up only to remark on the scenery.

And the view was spectacular, he had to admit. C.J. set a course north-northwest, following the elongated reach of Whidbey Island and back to the water again, where Shaw had a close enough look at Deception Pass to see beachcombers strolling at the edge of the state park. Rounding Orcas Island, C.J. had loosened up again, spotting a pod of dolphins half a mile off the coast, splashing as they dove and rolled and feasted on some unseen school of fish below the surface.

Soon she pointed to what looked like a spit of land beyond the masses of bigger islands. "There. That's Briar Bay."

At first Shaw thought she might be joking. Compared to the nearest populated islands, Briar Bay looked barely larger than the submarine they had passed, and about the same shape. Then, as the plane drew nearer, it became clear that the island was much longer than he'd first seen. He tried to estimate its size. Almost a mile from tip to tip, perhaps, and more than half that wide, in a broad crescent with the wider edge to the north.

The land rose rapidly from the waters of the strait, as if to ensure that the tides would not overwhelm it. A heavy forest of hemlock and white pine blanketed the northern side and the center mound of the island. The inner edge of the crescent, to the south, was barren. The forest ended in a shallow cliff. After that only bedrock from the cliff all the way to the water.

The island looked like a hooked blade, Shaw realized, with its thick outer curve to the north and the stark interior shore forming a wicked edge.

"Let's take a pass," C.J. said.

As they neared the island's eastern tip, the first signs of human habitation appeared. First a small field of midnight-black solar panels, then in quick succession a fenced area containing a cell tower and a satellite dish the diameter of a sewer pipe, a tall pole with the American flag fluttering at the top, and a flat twenty-foot square of concrete slab that Shaw guessed might be intended for a helipad. Half a dozen corrugated metal sheds were last in the motley strip.

In front of the sheds, a single floating dock extended ten yards out into the water before making a ninety-degree turn to continue parallel to the shore for thirty more. Enough moorage to fit Hollis's *Francesca* and three more just like it.

The estate itself took up the final sixth of a mile, at what would be the handle of the island's knife shape. Shaw found himself craning his neck, trying to take in every detail.

What he guessed was the main house was farthest from the end. A square of two tall stories, with a veranda encircling the ground floor. Its sides looked north and south. Expansive picture windows allowing every room a view.

The rear of the house was lent privacy and shade by the tall forest, while the front looked out into an elongated courtyard between two lengthy wings that extended toward the tip of the island. All three of the buildings were of the same style. Shaw dubbed it Mammoth Craftsman. Eaves over the windows, columns around the veranda, and cedar siding. Roofs of blue metal shingles merged with the water that would be in the distance almost any direction you looked.

At the very tip of the island, a short stretch from each of the two wings, was Rohner's pièce de résistance.

"What the hell is that?" Shaw said, feeling C.J. grinning next to him.

"The pavilion," she answered.

His first impression was of a diamond exploding from within. Or a monstrous, especially aggressive crystalline sea anemone. The structure was the size of the main house. Larger, if you counted how far its spikes and spires extended from the interior, upward and outward.

It appeared to be made entirely of glass. If there was a right angle anywhere, Shaw didn't see it. Looking through what passed for its ceiling—through the clear facets created by the pointed spires reaching in a dozen directions—he could tell that the inside of the pavilion was one huge room. Someone standing within would look like a doll left in a vacant and kaleidoscopic greenhouse.

"Amazing, huh?" said C.J. "Reminds me of the Louvre, you know?"

Shaw hadn't been to the Paris museum, but he understood what she meant. The classical building with a strikingly divergent glass pyramid in front. Sebastien Rohner's estate wasn't on that scale, but what it lacked in size it made up for in audacity.

"Here we go," C.J. said, and the Otter banked hard right to reverse direction, leveling out as it descended. In the wind shadow of the strait, the waves were calmer. Near to shore barely a chop. C.J. brought the plane down so easily that the pontoons kissed the water for a full two seconds before sinking lower. She let the plane give in to the drag before nudging the throttle to goose it toward the dock.

Someone was waiting for them. A very tall and lean bald man, stooping to gather a coiled line that would secure the plane. The wind lapped at his tan suit coat and pant legs. His shaved head glinted in the afternoon sun.

When the plane drew within reach, the man ducked under the wing and deftly looped the line around a small cleat at the rear of the pontoon. C.J. killed the engine and stepped out onto the pontoon to jump to the dock. Shaw retrieved his duffel from behind the seat and clambered through the door after her.

"I don't guess you two have met in person," C.J. said as she secured the bowline. "Mr. Anders, this is Van Shaw. Van, this is Mr. Rohner's chief of staff. Olen Anders."

"Hello," Shaw said, shaking hands.

The tall man nodded slowly. His long face seemingly stretched by hollow cheeks and a chin as meticulously shaved as his head. To Shaw the nod looked less like a greeting than as if something Anders had long believed had finally been confirmed.

"A pleasure to finally meet you, Mr. Shaw," he said.

NINE

C.J. gathered her flight bag from the cockpit. "I didn't know you were on the island, Mr. Anders."

"A final check before our maiden voyage." Anders glanced briefly in the direction of the pavilion spires, just visible over the rise of the land.

"I need to see to things," C.J. said, indicating the plane. Its engine ticked softly as it cooled in the sea breeze. "Don't let me hold you up."

"I'll show Mr. Shaw to his quarters."

The two men walked up the dock, which bobbed with each slow wave off the strait. Anders's long legs covered the ground rapidly. Six-five, Shaw estimated, without the dress shoes. He was probably Rohner's age, and like his boss he gave the impression of having a younger man's fitness. Maybe Anders joined Rohner on his mountaineering excursions.

A flagstone path led up the incline and past the main house. Anders remained silent as they neared the south wing. The wing's shape was reminiscent of the Salish tribe longhouses Shaw had seen on museum trips as a kid. But like most things on the island, the wing was on an inflated scale. A single straight box with a peaked roof, two stories tall and at least ninety yards in length.

Shaw pointed to the glass spires in the distance. "The pavilion. Is that where your conference will be held this week?"

"Yes. We have meeting rooms and offices in the north wing, along with larger kitchen and dining facilities than in the family house. But for this event Sebastien chose to make full use of our pavilion. The weather this week should oblige."

Shaw nodded. *We have. Our pavilion.* Anders might not bear the Rohner name, but he gave every indication of considering himself part of the inner circle. The man's accent was different, however. More French-sounding than Sebastien Rohner's, less British than daughter Sofia's. Shaw knew that Switzerland had multiple official languages, German and French included.

Maybe Wren could place Anders's region if she ever heard him speak. When Raina Marchand was agitated—or aroused, Shaw thought with a private smile—he had occasionally imagined he could hear her Gallic heritage in her voice.

As they came to the top of the rise, Shaw got a closer look at something he'd only glimpsed from the air. An enclosed passageway between the main house and the south wing. At the far end of the long wing, a similar passage led to the pavilion. And like the pavilion, both corridors were fashioned mostly from glass. Shaw could see through the passageway to a portion of the tree-lined courtyard beyond.

"Those must be handy in rainy weather," he said, nodding to the closer passage.

"Indeed. It's not necessary to go out of doors to reach any building in the estate. Especially important for the staff."

"You must spend a fortune on Windex."

Anders gave the sort of minimal smile that acknowledged a joke had been attempted.

"Our staff quarters are here," he said as they neared an exterior door to the south wing. Shaw heard a faint click before Anders reached to pull the door open.

"Proximity sensor?" he guessed.

"Yes." From the chest pocket of his suit jacket, Anders removed a small black plastic rod. Like a thicker, shorter ballpoint pen, complete with a metal clip to attach the wand to a pocket or onto a lanyard. "The staff carry these wands. Depending on the time of day, the wand allows entry into most of the buildings."

"The main house being the exception."

"Correct. For privacy the family retains the house to themselves. This wand is already encoded for you. Please keep it with you at all times."

Access, Shaw thought, and likely more. It wouldn't be difficult to have the wands track the location of each person anywhere on the island.

They entered a foyer about the same size and decor as an elevator bay in an upscale hotel. A console table with a lapis vase had been placed precisely halfway along its length. Shaw spotted a tiny bit of plastic stuck in the seam of the table leg, likely torn off when the furniture had been unwrapped after shipping. As he followed Anders down a hall into the building, he caught a faint whiff of paint fumes. The sage-green interior latex in the hall had dried, but the coat on some nearby room was still fresh.

"Just under the wire for the grand opening," he said.

"This building is primarily for Droma employees," Anders said, not bothering with the smile this time. "Twenty rooms, though the island should normally require less than half that many staff on hand."

"Where do guests stay?" The accommodations seemed pleasant enough, but nothing that would impress visiting dignitaries.

"In the north wing. Any overflow can be accommodated here."

All the cherrywood doors along the hall had been left open, perhaps to air out the rooms. A discreet brass number marked each door, adding to the hotel feel of the place. Shaw glanced into the rooms as they passed. Each contained a queen-size bed and simple but weighty furniture in the early-twentieth-century Craftsman style. Dark green diamond-patterned carpeting. Bed on the left side, door to the bathroom on the right.

The furnishings in each bedroom, even the single chair and reading lamp, had been set in precisely the same spot. Even the angle of the lamp arm was the same thirty degrees. Seeing one indistinguishable space after another as he walked past made Shaw slightly dizzy.

At the door marked 8, Anders stopped. "Your room. You may leave your bag here. I assume you wish to see the art collection immediately?"

"Why else would you meet me at the plane? Any of the staff could have brought me here."

"Indeed."

Shaw tossed his duffel onto the queen bed and retrieved the Droma employment papers from the pocket of his jacket. He handed the folded sheaf to Anders.

"Let's take in some culture," he said.

Anders nearly winced.

TEN

In the courtyard, rows of ornamental cherry trees ran alongside evenly spaced plots of rosebushes. The trees looked sparse when compared with the towering forest that loomed behind the main house. In another year they might flower and cover the courtyard lawn with white and pink blossoms.

The rosebushes, whether planted wrong or just too early in the season, were barren. Long beds of spiny branches and prickly leaves. Shaw saw a few nascent buds in between the thorns. He guessed that if Sebastien Rohner spared a thought to the landscaping, he would consider the roses a disappointment. The blooms had refused to meet his deadline.

"How long did it take to build all this?" he asked Anders.

"Twenty months. The planning of a similar home and compound had begun over a year earlier, before the island was purchased. Mr. Rohner's wife holidayed in this region when she was younger. That informed the decision to build here."

"Will she be here for the event this week?"

"Mrs. Rohner is in Zurich," Anders said, his face impassive. Shaw inferred that Mrs. Rohner might not often be in the same vicinity as Mr. Rohner.

They cut diagonally across the yard and through doors that allowed them to traverse the glass passageway between the main house and the north wing. A young woman in a robin's-egg blue blouse and navy skirt and carrying an armload of linens crossed their path, coming from the house.

"Good afternoon, Mr. Anders," she said.

"Good afternoon, Greta. The guests will be arriving by two P.M."

"Yes, sir. Miss Sofia told us. Everything will be ready."

Anders nodded, and Greta continued on her way.

Beyond the passage was the lusher northern shore. There was no tended lawn outside the courtyard, only flagstone paths winding around the natural stones and hillocks between the shore and the forest at this end of the island. They had a panoramic view of Boundary Pass and its swells, rolling past the island with the speed of a railroad handcar and the power of a freight train.

Squinting, Shaw could make out a thread of green at the far edge of the horizon. Or maybe it was his imagination.

Anders noted his interest. "Three miles," he said. "Three to South Pender Island in British Columbia, in that direction. Three to Waldron." He pointed east. "And three to Stuart Island." Pointing southwest, parallel to the current.

"The center of the triangle," said Shaw. "We must only be about a mile from the Canadian border, then."

"A mile and a half," Anders corrected.

"If the goal was to impress clients," said Shaw, "this place should do the trick."

Anders began walking in the direction of the main house. "Clients and friends. Mr. Rohner knows many political leaders and heads of other industries. Briar Bay Island was envisioned as a retreat for their use as well."

"Camp David Northwest."

"Just so."

At the side of the great house, partway down the slope to the north shore, was a structure Shaw hadn't spotted from the air. It was built of the same cedar siding as the home and the two wings, but with a flat roof that extended out from its walls rather than the sea-blue shingles of the larger buildings.

"The art gallery," Anders explained.

Another glass passageway sheltered a set of flagstone steps connecting the gallery to the main house farther up the small hill. The gallery itself had no windows. Anders stopped at the lone exterior door, under a shaded eave formed by the broad roof.

He removed one of the access wands from the breast pocket of his suit coat. Anders's was silver rather than the black wand given to Shaw. Anders touched the silver rod to a metal plate above the gallery door. The heavy clunk of a magnetic lock releasing followed.

"Only the family and I have admission," Anders said. "Which is why I wanted you to review the security features today. Tomorrow there will not be time."

Suspended track lights inside the gallery switched on as the men entered, adding to the illumination from three skylights above. The single room was forty feet square and fifteen tall. Whitewashed wooden planks covered the walls in vertical stripes. The floor had been paved in tiles of carmine-colored stone. Each skylight was an opaque white. Shaw guessed the glass had been treated to shield the art from UV radiation.

He had seen only one piece from Rohner's acquisitions, the Egyptian statue of the underworld baboon who devoured the souls of the unworthy. Now he realized that the piece was part of a whole.

The gallery held thirty or more cylindrical pedestals, just like the one at the Droma campus. Each pedestal held its own small statue of stone or ceramic. A handful of additional figures occupied wall cabinets made of white oak. Shaw knew a small amount about art from working with his grandfather—Dono had enjoyed a short run of heisting midcentury modern paintings when those had been in vogue for Seattle's elite—but his experience didn't extend to statuary.

He couldn't get a sense of a unifying theme. There were two pieces that could be Egyptian, like the baboon, one with a jackal's head and one of a bird. The most colorful was a seated Buddha in glazed ceramic. A crude bronze Nordic figure might be the oldest. The most valuable, to his eye, was a dark stone statue of a multiarmed feminine entity, probably East Asian. The figurine's little platform and headdress were set with rubies.

Shaw pointed to Anders's suit pocket and the silver wand. "How many of those are programmed for gallery access?"

"Three, currently. Mine, Sebastien's, and Sofia's."

"And the unprogrammed ones?"

"None of this type on the island." Anders tapped the silver tip of the wand. "I have four spare black wands in a safe, in my room, in case one of the wands for the staff stops working or"—he indicated Shaw—"if a new person joins us."

"How are they programmed?"

"By me, using my computer. Which is also kept in the safe when not on my person."

"What about your head of security? Why doesn't he or she handle that small stuff?"

"The Rohners prefer that I do so."

Shaw raised his eyebrows at the evasion. "Can the black wands be programmed to open these doors?"

"I don't understand your concern. Your focus should be on this room."

"The easiest way into a locked room is to have the key. If I were a thief—"

Anders frowned at that.

"—my first choice would be to obtain or reprogram one of the wands. Much easier to pick Ms. Sofia's pocket than to break in," Shaw concluded.

"I see. The answer is no. The silver wands have hard-coded encryption that allows particular access points, as well as climate control and other features not available in the simpler version."

"Climate? The wands change room temperature?"

"For the family members. If they are alone in an area of the estate, the rooms will adjust to their preferences."

Shaping the world to suit them, Shaw thought.

The soft spot was how well the principals kept track of their silver wands. He could believe that Anders was diligent. Sebastien and Sofia Rohner might be easier targets.

"Tell me about the alarm system," he said.

"Breaking one of the doors or the skylights"—Anders pointed upward—"activates the alarm. Entirely wireless. I receive the signal on my phone and on any of my computers, as do Sebastien and all of our security personnel."

"Police?"

"The closest are in Friday Harbor. County officers. Warren Kilbane, our security head, and his team are best prepared to handle any trouble."

"How many on the team?"

"Is that relevant?"

"It is if we have to watch the gallery around the clock."

"That level of scrutiny won't be required. But there are three security officers on the island this week, counting Warren."

Shaw examined the contact points on the doors and the little transceivers above the door frame on each. He knew the make. American, reliable, working off an encrypted cellular signal exchanged constantly with a central hub.

"Where's the control panel for the system?" he said.

Anders went to one of the oaken cabinets. It swung away from the wall on a hidden hinge. A small white case like a fuse box jutted at chest height. Anders took a key from his pocket and unlocked it. A touchscreen and the black brick of a twelve-volt battery were bolted within.

Shaw tapped the screen. The maker's logo appeared, and then a menu of options for testing and configuring the system. He flipped through the selections. Standard fare. Rohner apparently hadn't customized the setup.

"I saw the solar array on the way in," he said. "Does that supply all the island's power?"

Anders nodded. "There are backup generators and batteries in case of interruption."

"What about juice to the alarms in here?"

"They receive power from the main system but have batteries as well, as you can see." He indicated the twelve-volt. "If either the power or the cellular signal is interrupted for more than five seconds, the alarm is activated."

"Same for the cell tower? Does it have its own batteries?"

"Yes."

Shaw looked at the panel again. Checks and balances. Interrupt the power, the alarm goes off. Interrupt the signal to any one of the contacts, the alarm goes off. You could knock out the cell tower entirely, but even that might not be quick enough.

Pretty good. Not perfect.

"Anything else?" he said. "Pressure plates under the statues? Hidden cameras?"

"The family has chosen not to install cameras on the estate." Off Shaw's doubtful look, Anders added, "This is a home, and a place for honored guests."

Foolhardy, Shaw thought. Putting appearances over millions in irreplaceable art. Maybe it was some sort of flex.

Anders closed the control panel and swung the wall cabinet back into place. He touched the tip of one long finger to the blue-tinted statue in the cabinet. A man with four arms, holding a shell and a discus among other things.

"Sebastien's humor," he said. "A protector god."

"Vishnu," said Shaw.

"Yes." Anders showed a hint of surprise. "Do you need to know anything else?"

"Yeah. I'd like your best guess as to who I'm looking for."

"I would not know."

"You know who's attending the conference. If one of them is planning to lift one of these trinkets, you must have an opinion. Who's the number-one contender?"

"Really."

"Then forget our mystery burglar for a minute. Tell me about them as business associates."

"Mr. Shaw, your questions are immaterial. Sebastien wants assurance that his collection is secure. That will be satisfactory."

Shaw folded his arms. "You don't believe there's going to be a theft."

"I believe your job here is complete."

Anders opened the door to the outside and motioned for Shaw to exit. After a moment he did.

"The Rohners have invited you to dinner this evening," Anders said. "Apart from that event, I expect you to allow the guests their privacy. There is little for you to do. You may stay in your room to write your analysis of the system here. If you wish to be outside, you will remain near the maintenance buildings on the south side of the island. An appropriate place for our presumptive facilities manager."

On the opposite side of the estate from the gallery. Short of marooning him in a dinghy offshore, Shaw couldn't be placed much more out of the way.

"As to Sebastien's concerns about theft," Anders continued, "should you have any suspicions, you will bring those to my attention and my attention alone. Are we clear on the point?"

"Crystal."

Anders stalked away in the direction of the main house. Shaw watched him go before heading down the slope, to where the waves lapped at the rocky shore.

It struck him, as he walked, what the statues in Rohner's collection had in common. Deities. Each one an idol of a major or minor god to their culture. All of them objects of worship.

At one time, maybe millennia past, someone had knelt and prayed to every piece in that gallery.

OLEN ANDERS REACHED HIS ROOM—the only private room in the main house not given to a Rohner family member—and sat at his desk. He looked at the small metronome that had once been his father's.

Anders was not given to mementos. His father, Klaus, had been a piano teacher, and when Klaus died, the device had passed to his second son. Anders had found its ticks soothing as a boy. He'd decided to keep the metronome. Over the years it had become habit to take it with him while traveling. Especially on important trips. He was self-aware enough to know that its mere presence quieted his mind. He freed the metronome's pendulum and slid the weight to the top of the rod. Its slow beat filled the room.

He had allowed the criminal Shaw to agitate him. The man was different from what he had expected. Not a lout, skilled with his hands but dull in reason. Sebastien had told him Shaw was blunt, even rude, but intelligent as well. Anders had assumed that Sebastien was simply giving the thief the benefit of the doubt in his desire to move ahead without delay.

Shaw *was* impertinent. Sebastien had been correct on that as well. Even the scars that marred the man's face so dramatically lent him something of a mocking look. Anders felt certain that his orders that Shaw remain at a distance from the art gallery had fallen on selectively deaf ears.

He and Sebastien wanted Shaw on the island, a memorable presence to be seen by the guests. Shaw's absence later would be similarly noted. That was the sum of the man's purpose. To be noticed and then suddenly gone. Sebastien—and himself, too, Anders admitted—had assumed that Shaw would pass the days on the island as idly as possible. That he would gladly accept an early departure with his payment, hurrying off to squander the money in due speed.

But if Shaw persisted in lurking about the gallery at all hours, trying to prevent a crime that would never come, he might create trouble. Perhaps irrevocably.

Steps must be taken to limit Shaw's movements, sooner than originally intended.

Anders silenced the metronome and reached for his phone.

ELEVEN

Shaw returned to his room to unpack. Nearing the door, he heard the bolt unlock automatically, a trick of the magic wand in his pocket. As an experiment he backed away. After a count of three, the door locked again. Convenient.

Room 8 looked out on the courtyard with its bare rosebushes. He felt exposed, like being in a first-floor motel room next to the parking lot. Shaw switched on the lamps and pulled the curtains.

Anders's obstruction had pissed him off. But more than that, the chief of staff's attitude had been perplexing. Showing Shaw the art collection and then all but threatening to fire him if he took reasonable steps to protect it.

Before he left the room again, Shaw made some subtle adjustments to the clothes in the dresser and the gear inside the duffel. A T-shirt had the top position on the pile. Shaw pinched the left side to create a single shallow divot in the fabric. Then two more divots on the right. In the duffel he overlapped the coils of a light extension cord so that the third loop was slightly higher than the others. He moved two power tools apart exactly the width of his thumb.

Tiny changes, but effective. Even if someone searching his things were careful to replace everything how they found it, at least one crease or loop would be out of place, if only by a few millimeters. As good as a neon sign.

He had decided to walk the island's boundary before the guests arrived. He left the south wing to cross the courtyard and enter its twin. A wide hall running down the center made the north wing simple to navigate. The long building had been divided into three distinct parts. Kitchens at the end nearest the passage to the main house, dining areas at the center—Shaw noted that the walls between areas could be removed, to make a single space large enough for a basketball team to play half-court—and guest suites and conference rooms on both floors at the end. The Rohners had enlivened the wing with art reminiscent of Northwest Coast tribes, including a life-size orca in carved relief, hung as an archway above the doors to the suites.

Shaw walked past an unattended housekeeper's cart in the corridor, then backtracked for a second look. A clipboard hung below the cart's push handle. The top sheet on the clipboard was a checklist of supplies and cleaning steps for each room. Down the left-hand side of the sheet was a list of guest names and their room assignments.

A door opened down the hall. It was one of the household staff in the unofficial uniform of robin's-egg blue, exiting a guest room carrying a stack of magazines and newspapers. Before she could turn in his direction, Shaw snatched the sheet out of the clipboard and escaped down a side hall.

Outside, he walked the length of the estate. The flagstone path followed the natural dips and rises of the land and curved to avoid humps and rocks, closer to a trail than a sidewalk.

He passed the art gallery and the main house. When the path ended, he cut down the steep slope and kept walking. The beach of the north shore was craggy and strewn with mussels and sea kelp. Twice Shaw had to jump over deep fissures. Though the water was low, the power behind each wave signaled that the tide was flowing. Before dark the crevices in the rock would fill again, bringing fresh food for crabs and other creatures.

The beach gave way to dirt and grass as the land rose in height from the water. Here the tide lapped directly against a ten-foot vertical bluff. The forest trees, as if making a stand against the sea, grew as far as the lip. Shaw had to stomp through a low blackberry thicket along the forest's edge to create a path into the evergreens. Fewer brambles and ferns grew beneath the thick forest canopy—less sun, less abundance—and he was able to continue hiking westward without many sidetracks. Insects buzzed and rattled in a constant symphony.

The forest floor was almost like carpet, softened by decomposing leaves and pine needles and dirt that may have never felt human tread.

It took him half an hour to reach the far side of the woods. The western terminus of the island was the tip of the curved knife, the farthest point from Rohner's showpiece pavilion. To Shaw's right he saw the last few trees of the forest. To his left the beginning of the long, barren shore on the island's southern edge.

At the island's tip, the vertical drop to the beach was only five feet high. Shaw jumped down and headed back along the southern shore toward the estate. The height of the bluff increased rapidly until it leveled off at about thirty feet above the beach. A few hardy scrub trees grew from splits in the cliff face, their lean trunks curving upward toward the light.

It was faster going on the bare bedrock. The only hindrance was the wind pushing against him. Within ten minutes of walking, he saw the gray dots of the first maintenance sheds and the toothpick-slim line of the floating dock. The seaplane was gone. C.J. must have flown to pick up the guests.

He passed the solar panels and the flagpole to arrive at the square concrete slab. His guess had been right about its being a helipad, and a work in progress. Eight stainless-steel lights had been placed around the landing pad's border, looking like small cooking pots around a table. The lights weren't bolted to the concrete slab, not yet. They sat loose on the ground, sharing a single power cable, a string of cheerless Christmas lights. The cable snaked off through the grass toward the nearest maintenance shed.

Shaw wondered if the landing lights had been hastily placed, in the event that the Rohners or their guests decided to travel by helicopter at the last minute. Nice to have options.

As he came abreast of the main house, he saw Sofia Rohner walking past one of the grand picture windows. She looked up, and their eyes met. As smoothly as if she'd been expecting his visit, she motioned for him to approach.

She came out onto the veranda at the front of the house and waited by the railing while he walked up the grassy slope. He stopped on the narrow strip of manicured lawn at the side of the house.

"Good evening," said Shaw.

"Mr. Shaw," she said. "I didn't realize you were on the island."

"I came in to get acclimated before the guests arrive. It's quite a place."

"Thank you. We're not the first to live on Briar Bay. There was a settlement here briefly in the nineteenth century, searching for limestone deposits as on the larger islands. Their speculation wasn't rewarded, unfortunately."

"I hope you'll have better luck."

"What has my father asked of you this week?"

"Asked of me?"

"Your duties. As a . . . facilities manager, being so new to the grounds."

On the porch her feet were level with Shaw's head. He wondered if that had been an intentional choice of the architect, elevating the masters of the estate.

"Mostly to see if the guests require anything that isn't already here," he said. "Looking for possible improvements."

"Do those improvements include our art collection? I noticed Olen taking you inside."

Shaw paused. "I have some background in security systems. Part of why Mr. Rohner hired me."

"To evaluate whether the gallery is safe."

"Yes."

"And is it?" Sofia said.

"Your alarm setup is very good."

"But not impregnable."

"No system is. Are you concerned someone might break in?" he said. Perhaps Sofia Rohner knew more about her father's little contest of acquisitions than she'd let on.

"No. I don't imagine we're at risk of burglary. But when it comes to our artwork, I am personally invested."

Shaw looked at her. "You curated the collection."

"Yes."

"Your father didn't mention that."

"I don't imagine he would. The family's achievements are shared victories."

Unless they're his, was the message Shaw took from that. He realized how few of the articles about Droma International had mentioned the company's VP of client development.

"I'll keep watch," said Shaw. "Just in case."

"I appreciate that," Sofia said, perhaps humoring him. "We'll be offering tours of the estate, including the collection. Not that I expect anyone to slip a figurine into their pocket."

"Mr. Anders implied this was an important week. A business deal, along with the first visitors to the island."

"Indeed." She glanced to her left. Shaw followed her look. A broad-shouldered man in a gray pinstripe suit and a black tie was striding down the courtyard in their direction.

"This conference has been a long time in coming," Sofia continued, "and our guests have come a long way. We've had hopes of establishing a partnership within the Chinese market for years. You can understand our desire that they enjoy their stay."

"Everything all right here, Ms. Rohner?" said the man, stopping alongside Shaw on the lawn.

"I'm fine, Warren. Mr. Shaw, this is Warren Kilbane, our head of security."

Kilbane looked Shaw up and down. He was younger than the retired cop or former MP that Shaw had expected the Rohners to have as a security chief. Not much more than Shaw's own thirty years. His sandy brown hair had been recently barbered and his dress shirt was unblemished by creases. Ready for his official corporate photo, though imagining Kilbane smiling was a stretch. He stared at Shaw with a blank expression.

"I imagine you two have much to talk about," Sofia said. A dismissal.

"Nice meeting you," Shaw said to her.

Kilbane fell into step beside him as he walked to the south wing.

"Mr. Anders told you to stick to your room," the security man said quietly.

"Just stretching my legs before the guests arrive."

"From now on you'll clear all movement with me."

"Relax, Warren. I'm not here to take your job. Three days and I'll be a memory."

Kilbane moved in front of him, forcing Shaw to stop. "Your job is what I say it is. Write your report. Stay away from the guests and the family."

Shaw grinned. People giving him orders often struck him as funny. He'd been commanded by professionals, most of whom could eat Kilbane on toast.

"It's Rohner's initials on my hiring papers," he said. "The way I see it, he's the only one who can tell me to shove off."

Kilbane stared back. Shaw revised his earlier opinion. Anders was inexpressive. Kilbane seemed more like a fucking robot.

A big enough robot to take seriously. An inch taller than Shaw and maybe two-twenty. Kilbane's neck came straight down from his ears. Lots of barbell shrugs and weighted neck curls had gone into building those bulky tendons.

"Mr. Rohner might have hired you," Kilbane said, "but it's Anders who signs off on your fee. Be smart. Have dinner tonight, make some polite conversation, and then get lost. The less we see you this week, the better."

He stalked away.

Shaw exhaled. Carrying out his assignment was looking more difficult by the hour. Anders and Kilbane had both taken what seemed to be an instant dislike to him. If he kept up this streak, the Rohners would force him to swim home before nightfall.

TWELVE

The island staff assembled on the floating dock at a quarter to two. Kilbane and the two members of his team joined them. One man and one woman, neither as imposingly muscled as the security chief but not willowy either. Suits aside, the three of them might have been the attackmen on a championship prep-school lacrosse team. They stood at the crook of the angled dock, as if to broadcast that they were not there to tote luggage nor guide the newcomers to their suites.

At three minutes to the hour, Sofia and Anders descended from the main house. They walked past Kilbane's team to stand with the staff.

Shaw, the only person on the island not in the welcome party, watched from the end of the row of maintenance sheds. He'd spent the past hour and a half examining the island's power supply and the cellphone tower to reinforce his cover for any island employees paying attention. Short of confirming that the backup batteries for phone and electricity service were in working order, the time had been a waste. The only event of interest had been a large powerboat pulling up to the dock. The forty-five-foot Regal that Rangi Sua had mentioned. Shaw had seen the big man disembark and tie off the lines before disappearing into the cabin again. No one had gone ashore. Two o'clock had come as a relief. Shaw watched the seaplanes' steady descent. The lead plane was C.J.'s blue-and-white Otter. It touched down with nary a splash. The second aircraft, canary yellow with twin props and a longer fuselage by half than the Otter, followed within half a minute.

Staff members rushed forward to moor the planes to the dock. The passengers began to disembark.

Shaw had used some of his time around the sheds to review the list of guests he'd swiped from the housekeeping cart. In addition to the room numbers, the printed sheet had organized the guests by company. He glanced at the names at the top of the page again.

Chen Li	**Jiangsu Special Manufacturing**
Bao, Nelson	
Zhang, C.	

Flynn, Bill	**Bridgetrust Group**
Lokosh, Karla	
Morton, Avery	

The lower half of the list was filled with Droma International Solutions people, including Kilbane's team.

Shaw assumed that the two bolded names, Chen Li and Bill Flynn, signified that those men were the heads of their respective companies. He hadn't heard of either Bridgetrust Group or Jiangsu Special Manufacturing. A quick online search had told him that the former was a capital-investment company from New York City, while Jiangsu was a multiheaded industry in the Chinese province of the same name, with specialties in chemical and agricultural research.

Sebastien Rohner and Linda Edgemont and two other men climbed from the Otter. Rohner offered a steadying hand to each as they stepped off the float. The first, a stocky Asian man in a suit the color of dark chocolate and matching tie, accepted the help. Chen Li, Shaw guessed. Making the second man Bill Flynn from Bridgetrust Group. Flynn had a lean build and a sharply tailored blue suit that shimmered with a slight iridescence, a red pocket square adding to the flash. His bristled brown hair rustled like grass in the wind. He seemed not to see Rohner, distracted as he was by the view of the island.

The junior execs had been flying in the yellow twin-prop. Shaw made a game of matching the supporting players with the companies by their level of dress. The two Chinese men in suits and ties were a gimme—they would be Jiangsu Manufacturing. He recognized two of the other men from the Revol Air flight, and presumably the other man and a woman in European tailoring went with them. That made four from Droma.

Which left a reedy guy in a brown leather jacket and jeans and a red-haired woman in a short-sleeved yellow blouse and a high-waisted skirt with her coat over her arm. Bridgetrust Group, by elimination, though the guy's leather jacket didn't exactly broadcast NYC investment capital.

C.J. and the other pilot saw to their planes as the staff finished collecting luggage on the dock. The long, loose line of people made its way up the dock toward the flagstone steps with Kilbane and his team on point.

According to Sebastien Rohner, one of his guests couldn't be trusted.

Presumably the potential burglar wouldn't be one of the two CEOs. Those men had stayed with Rohner, who pointed to various aspects of the estate as they steadily ascended the steps.

What if the thief were one of Rohner's own people? Shaw had been thinking of the burglar as someone like him, with a criminal background. Maybe B&E wasn't the plan. A Droma employee might have acquired inside information. Or even one of the silver wands that would allow access to the gallery.

The guests ambled along, taking in the scenery. No way to tell whose eyes might be seeking out cameras or sensors, just as Shaw's had when he'd arrived. The guy with the leather jacket hung back to take out a vape pen and inhale. Checking the sight lines from the house's windows at the same time? The two Chinese men leaned their heads together, talking quietly as they seemed to examine the solar panels and the satellite dish. And Shaw, standing near the sheds.

The red-haired woman in the skirt spotted him as he walked toward the head of the dock. She watched him for an extra beat as if playing the same game, trying to place Shaw's jeans and button-down chamois ensemble in the hierarchy. Too casual for Kilbane's squad. Not casual enough for a groundskeeper.

Sofia Rohner halted at the top of the steps, and the line congregated into a group once more. Close enough now for Shaw to listen in.

"Welcome, everyone," Sofia said. "We're delighted you could join us. I'm sure you'd all like an opportunity to settle in. Our staff will show you to your rooms and give you one of these." She held up one of the black wands. "It'll allow you passage through the buildings. Feel free to walk around the grounds and enjoy this lovely day. We'll all meet in the pavilion at five o'clock for dinner. If you're hungry in the meantime, you'll find refreshments in your rooms. Please make yourselves at home."

She smiled to a perfect degree, warm but not unprofessional. Sebastien Rohner shook hands with each of the visitors before they followed the staff to the north wing. Flynn, the CEO with the boar-bristle haircut, clapped Rohner on his shoulder. Sofia and Linda Edgemont hugged hello. Kilbane and his team trailed the procession.

Shaw watched them go. Burglary often required some physical prowess. One of the Chinese employees, either Zhang or Bao, looked much more athletic than the other. Oversize shoulders on a medium frame. Shaw guessed swimming, or maybe gymnastics. All the Droma people were young and on the slender side. Harder to gauge their fitness. Might be triathletes or might just be skinny. The redhead from Bridgetrust walked on the balls of her feet with easy grace.

Once the people had dispersed, Shaw returned to the maintenance shed for his jacket. He would spend the hours before dinner writing his evaluation of the gallery's alarm system. Maybe someone would actually read it.

He'd just scooped up his coat when two members of the household staff in what Shaw was beginning to think of as Rohner Blue walked from behind the main house down to the dock. Rangi came out to meet them. The three entered the powerboat's cabin and returned carrying what looked like a large black shipping crate.

They lowered the crate carefully to the dock and boarded again to retrieve two smaller boxes to sit beside their bigger brother. Rangi retreated to the cabin once more. The two men hefted the largest crate and began to carry it up the slope toward the house, pausing once to set it down and rest their arms.

Curious, Shaw walked behind the maintenance sheds and up to the forest. A gap in the wall of brambles allowed him to slip into the trees. He wove his way through the undergrowth. In between the stands of pine, he caught flashes of the rear of the house. The forest smelled of sap and new grasses, bursting with spring.

Voices carried over the hiss of wind through the branches. The two men from the household staff, toting their burden behind the house and across to the other side of the island. Shaw followed their slow progress on a parallel track, until the men disappeared down the opposite slope.

Toward the art gallery.

Shaw walked to the edge of the woods to conceal himself behind the trunk of a thick hemlock tree. He saw the tall form of Anders at the bottom of the slope, his shaved head looking like the eraser nub on a mechanical pencil. The two men were out of view, presumably having carried the crate through the exterior door on the far side of the gallery. As Shaw watched, they emerged and quickly retraced their steps behind the house and back across the island. Anders waited, checking something on a tablet computer with a glossy ivory cover.

The two men returned within five minutes, each carrying one of the smaller crates. They took the crates inside the gallery. After a word or two from Anders that Shaw was too far away to hear, both men left in the direction of the north wing. Anders walked up the slope to the main house and went inside.

What had that been about? Shaw wondered. More pieces of art for the family collection? The large crate was much bigger than any of the little statues would have required, even packed for shipping. There'd been something furtive in Anders's attitude. And the unloading of crates, even valuable artwork, seemed like something that a chief of staff would have delegated to the help.

The gallery was the most secure room on the island. Maybe the crates held surprise swag for the guests. A new iPhone under every seat. Portable shiatsu massagers. Shaw faded back into the shelter of the forest and returned to the south beach.

Near the dock his path crossed with C.J.'s. She carried a cardboard file box with both hands. Her Otter seaplane hadn't left with the twin-prop. A runabout speedboat had arrived and moored behind the larger yacht, occupying the space where the yellow plane had been. Busy morning.

"How was the flight?" said Shaw.

"Harried. Mostly because Rangi wasn't in charge of the ground transport to get everyone there on time." She nodded to the big Regal cruiser.

"I saw the boat come in earlier. Do you know what they were off-loading?"

"No. Just that he had to bring some cargo from Seattle overnight. Hey, can I ask you a favor? I'm in a rush to take the plane to Roche Harbor for supplies, and one of the Droma people left this on the other plane." She hefted the box. "Can I ask you to take it to the north lobby? I'll call and let them know."

"Sure." He took the box. It was loaded with papers or books, heavy enough that Shaw leaned back to get the weight over his hips. "You're strong."

"Obstacle-course races." C.J. grinned. "Shakes out the kinks from too much time in the pilot's chair. And speaking of running, I'm off. Thanks." She jogged down the path toward the dock.

On his way to the north wing, Shaw found the four executives from Droma sitting at a table in the courtyard.

"Oh, good," one of them said as Shaw set the file box on the table. The man opened it eagerly. Inside were a dozen identical three-ring binders titled "Resource Opportunities in Industrial Chemicals, Pacific Rim."

"You got this from the lady pilot?"

"C.J."

"Cool." He reached into his pocket to hand Shaw a lacquered blue fountain pen. "This is hers. I borrowed it before the flight and forgot to return it. Can you get it back to her?"

"Must be one of those days for you," said Shaw, looking at the box.

"I guess. So could you?"

Shaw decided that acquiescing would be faster than arguing. He put the pen in his breast pocket next to the black wand. Maybe his report to Rohner would look better if he signed it in India ink. He left the Droma drones to their work and returned to his room to dress for dinner.

THIRTEEN

Shaw arrived at the pavilion at five o'clock sharp. The slate-blue outfit he wore was his only suit, acquired earlier in the year. He'd bought the olive-green tie a month ago, bringing his grand total of neckties to two. Wren had joked that at that pace Shaw would have a full wardrobe in time for retirement.

The crystalline pavilion was even more imposing within. Its spires and vaulted ceiling gave it the feel of a cathedral. Large enough to encompass most of an acre. The steel frame supporting the huge panes of glass had been burnished to a glossy silver, so that it blended with the transparent walls. Even the exit doors had been designed to be unobtrusive. Nothing to distract from the grandeur. Shaw stared at the facets of the roof until the refracted light gave him vertigo.

His impression of the room's size was enhanced by the fact that the broad space was mostly empty. Three round tables had been set at the center. Waist-high troughs filled with ferns and tropical plants near the walls softened the endless angles of the towering space.

He felt a brush of cool air from an unseen vent. The interior of the pavilion wasn't a sweltering greenhouse. Nor was the direct afternoon sunlight glaringly bright.

Linda Edgemont approached to say hello. Shaw indicated the muted sun. "That's a nice feature. Treated panes?"

She smiled. "Better. It works on a principle like privacy glass."

"An electrical current turning the glass clear. Switching it off makes it opaque."

"Yes. But in this case the process is reversed, and the current is what clouds the glass. Also, it can be shaded by gradations, like a dimmer switch on a lamp. An innovation not yet widely available."

And hugely expensive, Shaw guessed. The largest of the pavilion's panes had to be fifteen feet wide.

"I understand you arrived this morning," Edgemont said. "How are you settling in?"

"Early innings yet," said Shaw.

"But you've had a look at the security system. Everything's in order?"

"Orderly is what I'd call it."

"Wonderful. Then you can relax and enjoy your time here."

To encourage mingling, the Rohners had assigned places to the guests. Sebastien Rohner and the two business leaders, the tranquil Chen and the boisterous Flynn, sat at the center table, along with Anders and Sofia Rohner and Linda Edgemont.

The second table was more of a mishmash. Kilbane and the female member of his security team, named Pollan. Two of the Droma people. The athletic-looking Jiangsu exec. And finally Morton from Bridgetrust, still in his leather jacket. Shaw was happy he wouldn't be forced to share a meal with Kilbane. He'd be off his feed before the soup course.

He was seated between the smaller Jiangsu man and the forgetful Droma drone who'd owned the box of three-ring binders. A second Droma exec sat across from Shaw, flanked by Karla Lokosh and the male half of Kilbane's security team. Shaw had caught his name as Castelli when he'd reached across to shake the redheaded woman's hand. She had changed from her skirt into a dark gray jacket and pants, a warmer choice for late in the day.

"Karla," she said, holding out a hand to Shaw. He introduced himself, and they both turned to the slim Jiangsu executive.

"Nelson Bao," he said. "How do you do?"

"Has either of you been to this part of the country before?" said Shaw.

They both shook their heads. "Closest I've been is Utah on vacation," said Karla.

Nelson Bao smiled. "You have me beaten. I've flown over Washington many times but never landed until yesterday." He looked at Shaw. "Are you from here?"

"Seattle," said Shaw, "but I'm brand-new with Droma. My first week and first time on the island. So we all have that in common."

"It's an astonishing place," Karla Lokosh said. "What do you do for Droma?"

"Facilities manager. I'm still figuring out exactly what that means."

She laughed. "It took me a year to get my feet under me at my job."

"What is your role?" Bao asked her.

"I'm vice president for Bridgetrust's business development. So I expect Mr. Chen and I will be talking about ways to get your firm some operating capital this week." She nodded to the Jiangsu leader, who was deep in conversation with Lokosh's boss, Flynn. Flynn was describing something, his hands drawing pictures in the air, as Chen nodded along. The Bridgetrust president had a blunt nose and light blue eyes that were bright with the energetic discussion. Chen had permitted himself a soft smile at Flynn's effusiveness. Shaw guessed smiling might be as demonstrative as Chen got.

No way to know which CEO was a likelier candidate to have a thief in his employ. Maybe Chen was a high roller at Macau casinos. Maybe Flynn was competitive to the point of obsession.

Hell, maybe they'd both brought thieves. Wouldn't that be a party?

The salad was served promptly. Shaw garnered a few morsels of information from his dinner companions in between bites. Chen's company was looking to establish a presence in the United States. Droma would provide resources and get its foot in the door of the lucrative Chinese market for skilled personnel, as Sofia had mentioned to him. Bridgetrust Group, Karla Lokosh's company, might provide capital as well as the necessary American percentage of ownership to gain legal approval and political support.

Nelson Bao was a chemist, and so was Avery Morton, he of the leather jacket, whom Bridgetrust had contracted to review technical specifics for this deal. Exactly what chemical plant or invention

Jiangsu had in mind for its proposed U.S. branch was unclear. Shaw got the gist that was need-to-know information. This week the teams would be talking through options and negotiating terms.

By the time they had finished their entrées, Shaw's head was filled with business-speak like "core competency" and "B2B." The terms might be different from the Army's, but the love of euphemisms and acronyms was the same.

None of them seemed like thieves. Maybe Castelli, who'd sat quiet and slightly sullen during all the business talk. The most he'd volunteered was that he and Pollan, the woman on Kilbane's team, sometimes went fishing. As the plates were being cleared, Castelli excused himself and went to join the other table. From the glances Shaw had taken during dinner, that bunch had been even less bubbly than Castelli.

At the main table, Linda Edgemont and Sofia Rohner laughed together in animated conversation. The most emotion Shaw had seen from the younger woman. But the biggest gestures were from Flynn, who was telling a humorous story that involved shooting a bow and arrow, judging from his pantomime.

Morton took advantage of the empty seat to switch tables, and soon he and Nelson Bao were deep in esoteric talk of molecular chemistry. With a swapping of chairs, Karla Lokosh sat next to Shaw so Bao wouldn't be talking over her.

"What do you do when not on a private island, Mr. Shaw?" she said.

"Van." Shaw had a cover story for his profession but not his personal life. Mentioning the charity he was trying to build was out. It might lead to questions, voiced or not, about why he was interested in helping families of convicted felons. "I volunteer with some veterans' groups. I read. And I exercise to stay sane."

"You look very fit." Karla smiled. "Weights?"

"Or running or MMA. A friend is introducing me to yoga. If it's always new, it's never dull. You?"

"Dance. Ballet as a girl, modern in college. It was going to be my major until I realized Alvin Ailey was never going to call but Merrill Lynch might. I switched to get my M.B.A."

"A native New Yorker?"

"Boston transplant," she said. "I started my career there, and a New York company made me an offer too generous to ignore, so I hid my Sox cap and moved."

He grinned. "Better or worse?"

"I've adjusted. The winters aren't any easier."

"You're seeing the Northwest on its best behavior." Shaw gestured to the expansive windows of the pavilion and the sun accelerating in its fall behind the forest to the west. "The weather that tricks people into moving here. Then comes the sucker punch. Eight months of gray. The mountains don't reappear on the horizon until summer."

She laughed. "But not as much snow. There's that."

"No. Not as much."

The server came to the table to ask the guests which dessert they would prefer, chocolate mousse or lemon tart. Shaw managed to keep from asking for both and opted for coffee instead.

Karla smiled. "I didn't realize you could get plain old coffee in the Northwest. I've been here a day and counted twenty different shops."

"Constant caffeine staves off suicidal impulses during the bleak months."

Sebastien Rohner stood up at his table. The room quieted. The servers stopped in midstride, their arms full of dessert plates.

"Before you all get some well-deserved rest," Rohner said, "I wish to say how much I'm looking forward to our discussions tomorrow." He nodded to Chen and Flynn. "It's not often that we can realize a key moment as it happens. To form a partnership such as ours, mutually beneficial and with such potential for growth, is truly extraordinary. I know there are many decisions yet to be made—and many lawyers yet to sign off on our agreement." That prompted a laugh from the guests, Linda Edgemont most of all. "But I'm confident that Jiangsu Special Manufacturing and Droma International Solutions will be recognized as a new vanguard in international business relations and that

Bridgetrust Group will be first to reap the benefits. We have a brilliant week ahead. At any time when we're not in conference, please enjoy these wonderful surroundings. Take a boat out on the water or a walk along the beach. This is our home, and it was meant to be shared with friends."

Shaw had been smiling wryly to himself ever since Rohner's implication that he and the guests had been working hard, consuming their salmon and risotto.

Despite the coffee, Karla Lokosh was stifling yawns by the time they'd finished their cups. "Sorry. I'm still on New York time."

Nelson Bao looked at his watch and then at Zhang, who was staring at him from the far table. "And we were meant to call home this evening. It was very nice meeting you."

Shaw said good night to Bao and Karla and the rest. The pavilion had three exits leading directly outside. Shaw picked the one to the south. The sun had dropped behind the hump of the island, and the steady wind had begun to whisk away any remaining heat the landmass had absorbed during the day.

Split logs embedded in the grassy slope formed a set of stairs to the beach. The knee-high lights lining the paths didn't extend to the slope, perhaps to avoid spoiling the view for anyone gazing out at the horizon. The stairs descended into murky dusk. Past their end a slow regular splash of waves against the shore called.

He had abstained from wine during dinner, but the rich meal was enough to leave him feeling slowed and heavy. The soft life, he brooded. It hadn't been so long ago that he'd been on active duty. Running all day, literally and figuratively, sometimes on only a couple thousand ravenously devoured calories. The main course alone had been that much tonight. Maybe feeling like you were losing a step was just another part of the transition to becoming a civilian.

Not that his time outside the Army had been calm. Shaw had found himself in enough trouble during the past two years to fill half a dozen deployments, and without an entire platoon backing him up.

No. That wasn't totally honest. He'd gone looking for danger at least as much as it had come to him. Partly to keep from losing that step. Mostly to have some purpose. He wasn't a soldier anymore. It had taken time to figure out what he wanted to do; helping kids the way his mother Moira had. If he could get the charity off the ground.

He wasn't a thief anymore either. Not for himself. Would he steal to fund the charity, if legitimate jobs like Droma petered out? He'd evaded that question whenever Addy Proctor probed his intentions. Worried that Shaw might be constructing a noble cause to allow dishonorable pursuits, perhaps unconsciously. He wasn't sure of the answer.

A decision for another day. There was work to be done.

He returned to his room to change and to wait. With only a week until the summer solstice, sunset came late. Full dark even later. It was nearly eleven o'clock by the time Shaw slipped out of the staff quarters.

He took the black wand from his pocket and buried it under a small rock. No need to broadcast his movements tonight any farther than he had to.

FOURTEEN

Shaw had picked the spot earlier. A deep, narrow split in the slope of the north shore, out of the range of the estate's lights. The grass grew tall in the split. He could lie almost prone and remain unseen by anyone more than twenty feet away. Looking through the reeds and flowering strands, he'd spot anyone approaching the gallery from the estate.

The gap in the slope was as comfortable as he could expect. Under the breeze, the sugary scents of pollen and decaying salal berries filled his nostrils. He would be covered in grass stems and seeds when he got up. Couldn't be helped.

If Rohner wasn't imagining the threat, what was the thief's plan? A missing piece of statuary wouldn't go unnoticed for two days until the guests left. No sane person would try to spirit it away in their luggage.

A boat could easily beach on the shore under cover of darkness to pick up the statue. Maybe to pick up the thief, too. But leaving the island would be the same as admitting guilt, for both the thief and whichever of the executives had brought them. Shaw supposed that one of the unwritten rules of their strange game was to get away clean and for the missing piece not to be noticed until it was too late.

He couldn't guard the gallery around the clock. A burglar would have to at least case the place, and there were only six or seven hours of darkness to allow any thief a close examination of the collection's defenses. He'd grab sleep while the execs were in conference tomorrow if he needed it.

Shaw continued watching. It was a skill he'd been practicing as long as he could remember.

First with his grandfather. Absent a babysitter, Dono would bring young Van along while casing possible scores. The two would sit in Dono's work truck or in a vacant apartment or house. When Van asked what they were looking for, his grandfather would have him assist by writing down the times of people coming and going. He would later quiz Van on what he remembered about them. Their clothes, their attitudes. As Van became more confident, Dono took full advantage of the presumed innocence of a child, sending him through neighborhoods on his bicycle or chasing a Frisbee onto private grounds, to report back on the security features he'd seen.

The Rangers had trained his patience to another level. On one mission, before he'd made sergeant, Shaw and his fireteam had been in Khost Province near the Pakistan border to recon a river crossing. Intel suspected that an insurgent convoy would cross the river on the ramshackle bridge of stone and repurposed steel beams. The where was vague enough. The when was even less certain. The platoon had hiked from the LZ at night and concealed themselves at key vantage points along the road and the river. Shaw's team wallowed in muddy wetlands a quarter mile upstream.

One day had passed, then another, while the platoon barely stirred. Still the intel reports insisted that the convoy was imminent. Finally, after six days of almost complete silence, not daring to move during daylight hours, they'd received word that the convoy had chosen another route. The fireteam stood upright for the first time in nearly a week that night. Their five-mile hike to the extraction point was such a relief it had felt like a vacation.

So Shaw waited in the island grass. Almost philosophical. He couldn't control whether the thief decided to hit the gallery tonight or at all. For now, until he had another trail to follow, this was what he could do.

Midnight came and went. The main house a black temple behind the squat block of the gallery.

The thief might not show. Shaw weighed the idea of breaking in himself, if only to see what the black crates contained.

He removed a device about the size of an old-style pager from his pocket and switched it on. The strip of display screen on the device glowed yellow-green as numbers blurred too fast for the eye to follow. Broadband frequencies. Within five seconds the device had locked on to a wireless signal. The signal sent by the alarm's control panel to the transceivers on the doors and skylights.

Jamming a cellular alarm signal was no trick with the right equipment. But jamming was also prone to error. Shaw's method was better. His device would mimic the nearest transceiver, catching the signal from the control panel and sending it back again. Shaw could then open a door or a skylight without interrupting the expected exchange.

A chink in the gallery's armor, assuming there wasn't a backup system that Anders hadn't mentioned. Shaw wouldn't put it past the enigmatic chief of staff.

He switched the device off and tucked it away. Messing with the gallery and its safeguards tonight could only lead to trouble and maybe scare off the burglar before Shaw had a chance to catch them in the act.

Shaw frowned and stretched. Perhaps there was no thief. Anders seemed to subscribe to that theory, even if he wouldn't voice it. Was Rampage Rohner more than eccentric? Maybe the magnate was delusional and his family and inner circle were doing their best to shield him from the consequences.

The lights in the passageway to the main house came on. Shaw sank back into the grass.

Olen Anders descended the steps from the house to enter the gallery. Shaw saw its roofline brighten as the interior lights came on, shining through the skylights.

The chief of staff was a night owl. Checking on whatever was in the crates, Shaw surmised.

Within five minutes two figures appeared on the flagstone path between the house and the south wing. Shaw could make out their shapes and hear their footsteps, but it wasn't until they descended the path to the exterior door of the gallery and its overhead light that he could identify them.

Nelson Bao and Avery Morton. The two chemists. The door opened, and Shaw saw the long arm of Anders ushering them to enter.

He waited another half hour. The three men remained inside. Whatever reason they might have for their midnight visit, it was taking a while.

A thief wasn't going to make a run at the statues with the gallery occupied. Shaw's stakeout was a bust, at least until Anders and the chemists left. Better to relax while he could and circle back.

He slipped away from his hiding place and down the north shore. From his high-rise apartment, Shaw had an enviable view of downtown Seattle and the bay, but even on the clearest of nights he could see at best a scattering of pinpoints in the sky. Here on the island, the stars made an infinite mural overhead. A hint of what it must have been like for fishermen and sailors in centuries past, before human innovation began to blot out the heavens.

As he walked, he picked at the grass and bits of bur stuck to his barn jacket. His fingers brushed across C.J.'s fountain pen in his pocket. The pilot was probably already asleep in the staff quarters. He might not catch her tomorrow if the plane left early. He decided to walk down to the seaplane. If it was open, he could leave the pen in the cockpit.

Someone had switched off the dock lamps. The only illumination came from flat solar LEDs screwed into the planks every ten feet, equidistant between the mooring cleats. Shaw walked the L shape of the dock to the seaplane. The pilot's door was unlocked. He set C.J.'s pen on the seat where she'd be sure to find it.

He'd closed the seaplane door when footsteps on the wooden planks of the dock made him turn.

Kilbane. With Castelli and Pollan just behind.

Kilbane was showing some expression for once. The hint of a smile. Shaw didn't care for it at all.

FIFTEEN

Kilbane pointed to the twenty-foot runabout, the little brother to the larger Regal cruiser.

"Get in," he said.

Shaw looked at them. "Early for a fishing trip."

The three enforcers spread out, blocking the width of the dock.

"You're relieved of duty, Shaw," said Kilbane. "We'll take you to the mainland and drop you off. Your things will be sent to you."

"Bullshit."

"You'll get your money. But you're leaving the island. Now."

"I'm done when Rohner says so. Until then piss off."

"Get in the boat."

Shaw didn't move.

"Fine," said Kilbane. He removed something from his belt and flicked his wrist. A steel alloy tactical baton snapped to full length. Castelli took out his own baton, and Pollan, the female member of their team, unholstered an evil-looking Taser pistol. The underlings held the weapons loosely at their sides. Waiting for orders. Or letting Kilbane have a literal first crack.

Shaw took half a second to review his options. The list wasn't long. Jump in the water and swim away, in which case Kilbane and the rest would be there when he came ashore, wet and cold and tired. Rush past them up the dock or try to board the cruiser behind him and get whipped over the head by a baton or zapped into oblivion before he made it three steps. They were ready for him to rabbit. They'd been ready since before Shaw arrived. They had the air of people happy to see a wait of uncertain length come to an end.

Or he could fight. They were ready for that, too. Two of them at least as large as Shaw, and Pollan was no twig either. She had the same excited expression as Kilbane. Even discounting her stun gun, those tactical batons could break a skull or an arm as readily as a hammer against a chopstick.

Surrendering and boarding the boat could be suicide. There were a lot of miles and a lot of water between Briar Bay and the mainland. All too easy to get lost forever.

"You were warned," Kilbane said. His tiny smile still fixed in place, as if the internal program that controlled his face had become stuck in a loop. "You can comply and still be able to walk and talk when we put you ashore, or you can spend a month in the hospital after we dump what's left of you on Neptune Beach. But you're leaving here tonight. For good."

The three took slow steps forward. Shaw drifted back, along the length of the moored cruiser. No one was in a hurry. Shaw would run out of dock soon enough.

"It's late," Kilbane said. "Let's get to it."

Shaw saw Rangi before they did. Emerging from behind the cabin of the cruiser, one foot on the cowling, launching himself into the four-foot drop to the dock. Castelli, closer to the boat, caught the motion in the corner of his eye as Rangi jumped. Too late.

It was a study in inelastic collision. Three hundred fifty pounds of momentum against two hundred pounds standing static. And unprepared. Rangi hit Castelli square on his right side. A huge huff of impact as Castelli flew like he'd been fired from a cannon, across and off the remaining six feet of dock. He hit the water with an ungainly splash.

Pollan had sprung away from the surprise attack like a startled cat. She looked at Rangi and raised the Taser.

Shaw took one big step forward and drove his elbow into the side of Pollan's head. He'd never fought a woman before; he reflexively pulled the blow. A little. Pollan grunted and collapsed as though her strings had been cut. The stun gun skittered across the planks and into the water, chasing Castelli.

Kilbane tensed, ready to lash his baton at the first person who came near.

"This isn't your fight, Sua," he said to Rangi while still watching Shaw. Rangi, for his part, had half an eye on Castelli, who coughed and sputtered in the water. The security thug probably wouldn't drown, but it wasn't a sure thing. Rangi had knocked the wind out of his lungs even before Castelli had swallowed half the strait.

"Can't let you cripple the man," Rangi said. "You want to fight now, go ahead."

Shaw and Kilbane looked at each other. The odds had shifted dramatically in the space of five seconds. Shaw smiled.

"Here's my counteroffer," he said to Kilbane. "I'm going to kick your ass. You can use your fists, in which case I might leave you able to report to work tomorrow. Or"—he pointed to the baton—"you can keep the stick, but then it's open season. I'll take it away from you and use it myself. A month in the hospital, you said. That sounds fair."

Kilbane looked at him, then glanced at Pollan, who was beginning to stir. "I don't need them. Or this."

Shaw whistled softly. "Prove it."

Kilbane spun the baton in his hand and jabbed its tip into the wooden planks, collapsing the baton's length back into the handle. He pocketed the weapon. He walked to an open area of the dock, away from his fallen partner and from Rangi, to remove his suit jacket. The preparations seemed to restore his confidence.

He stepped forward with his hands up, crouching, bobbing slightly. His balance good and his shoulders loose.

Shaw recognized game. Kilbane feinted and threw a heavy right hand. Shaw slipped and moved to the side. Kilbane kicked at Shaw's knee, and Shaw pivoted, the security man's foot missing him by an inch. Kilbane was faster than he looked. Shaw moved one way and then the other, never pausing in front of the larger man. The dock was long enough for him to dodge all night. Kilbane knew it, too. Shaw flicked a jab that Kilbane slipped. He moved, feinted. It would be too easy to break his hands on Kilbane's hard skull.

"Come on, you shit," Kilbane said, breath huffing out of his nose. "Fight."

He came swinging. A battering ram, little finesse but enough power to flatten Shaw against the side of the boat if he caught him. Shaw slapped Kilbane hard across the cheek with his left palm and spun away from the knee that had been aimed to rupture his kidney.

Kilbane was fast. Shaw was lightning. He ducked a huge, infuriated haymaker to coil low and explode out, sinking a savage hook into Kilbane's exposed ribs. The blow made a thud like a sandbag being dropped.

Nothing hurts quite like a shot to the liver. The pain is delayed for a moment, then comes on like a crosstown express, paralytic and sickening. In those two seconds, Kilbane turned, and Shaw hit him twice more, one flickering right to raise Kilbane's head and a harder left to the soft side of the throat. Kilbane fell to his hands and knees. Then he slowly curled into fetal position, maybe an involuntary response to the agony in his vitals.

"He's gonna die," Rangi said, with the same tone as if reporting the time.

"Not today," said Shaw.

Kilbane lunged up onto his knees. Fists balled as if still in the fight. A herculean effort that Shaw applauded by backhanding him across the temple. This time the security chief stayed down.

"Motherfuck." Rangi frowned.

As if on cue, Castelli shambled up the dock. Looking like an oversize rat that had become trapped in a washer on spin cycle.

"How 'bout you?" Shaw said to him. "I'm up for the hat trick tonight."

Castelli stopped and raised his hands exhaustedly. "Hey, man. I didn't want this."

"Sure." Shaw picked up Kilbane's suit jacket and pocketed the tactical baton.

"What now?" Castelli said. Pollan was sitting up. Maybe not certain where she was just yet.

"Now you go away. And stay away. Tonight was sparring for fun. Next time I'll hurt you and make it permanent. Understand?"

"Yeah."

"Say it."

"I'll stay away."

Shaw looked at Kilbane. The man's shirt had come untucked, and two buttons had torn off. A damp patch darkened his trousers on the left thigh. Involuntary voiding of the bladder.

Undignified. The kind of humiliation that could break a man's spirit. Or make him insane with rage.

"Convince your boss," Shaw said to Castelli, tossing him Kilbane's suit coat.

Rangi motioned for Shaw to climb aboard the cruiser. Shaw followed the big man into the cabin.

The boat was nicely if indifferently appointed. This was not a home like Hollis Brant's, with books and mementos and half-finished projects lying about. The cruiser was like a themed room at a bed-and-breakfast—Nautical Getaway. A rack in the minuscule galley held a row of coffee mugs in a shade of teal that precisely matched the carpet. The frame around a mirror had little anchors painted on it.

Outside, Castelli was helping Pollan to her feet. Rangi closed the cabin door.

"You make a lot of trouble," he said.

"That wasn't my doing."

"You coulda gone along with them and called Mr. Rohner later. Instead you forced Kilbane to nut up in front of his people. Way I see it, that's on you."

"But you chose to step in anyway."

Rangi grimaced. He wore canvas sweatpants and a green T-shirt that had words in what Shaw guessed were Samoan, over a bright yellow sun. His feet were bare. Shaw could have used either the pants or the T-shirt as a blanket.

"Those staff quarters aren't Plaza suites," Shaw said. "More elbow room here on the boat?"

Rangi nodded. "And privacy."

"So why didn't you let Kilbane and the terror twins smash my bones to oatmeal?"

"Because Mr. Rohner wouldn't like it. Or me asleep next door and letting it happen. I'm supposed to help keep the peace."

"So's Kilbane. And Anders. This family has more protection than most monarchies."

"Kilbane." Rangi said it in the same way someone might say *cockroach*. "He creeps around Greta."

"I saw Greta this morning, while Anders was giving me the tour. You and she going together?"

Rangi's morose expression brightened a lumen or two. "Yeah. I'd crush Kilbane's head myself, but . . ." He shrugged.

"So when he came after me tonight, you hoped I would knock him down a peg. Without creating a problem for whatever HR department you all share at Droma."

"Might be."

"And if I lost . . . no harm, no foul."

"I didn't think you'd lose. Not without the others backing him up. Kilbane's a mean shit and he spends a lot of time working the iron, but you got that look I seen on other guys in the Army. Spec Ops, yeah?"

"Yeah. Rangers. What was home for you?" Shaw asked.

"7th Transportation Group. Me and half my high-school class in Pago Pago enlisted at the same time. About the only jobs around, you know?"

"That's what got me to sign, too. Three hots and a cot. Ten years later I couldn't remember what it was like to be a civilian. Shit, I'm still figuring that part out."

"I did six," Rangi said. "They taught me to drive trucks and boats and everything else. It made sense to keep driving once I was out. People like a chauffeur with some size. Makes them feel high-status."

"And now you're here."

"It's a good gig. Don't fuck it up for me, man."

Shaw nodded. "I wouldn't. Even if I didn't owe you for the assist.

Thanks." He glanced around the cabin. "You brought the boat in this morning, right?"

"The *Vóllmond*."

"How's that?"

"*Vóllmond*. That's her name. 'Full Moon,' in German."

"Got it. Do you know what was in the black crates you brought to the island?"

"Kitchen equipment," Rangi said. "Mr. Anders had them ordered for this week."

"Where'd you pick them up?"

"A freight company delivered them to the marina. What this about?"

"My job. I'm the facilities manager. Crates are in the facility."

Rangi glowered. "You already see what curiosity got you, dude. Now go and let me crash."

Shaw walked out of the cabin and stepped down to the dock. Against the far lights of the estate, three figures made their way up the hill from the shore, their shadows trailing far behind. Castelli and Pollan and Kilbane. Moving slow and careful, like children walking with bare feet on sharp gravel.

"You were just sparring, huh?" Rangi said.

Shaw smiled grimly. "I spread the bullshit a little thick. Might give them second thoughts about trying again."

"It might." Rangi shook his head. "Were me, I wouldn't go to sleep till the door was locked, you know? Locked and barricaded and one hand on my baseball bat."

SIXTEEN

Despite Rangi's fears, the rest of Shaw's night passed without further havoc. He returned to the gallery to find it still occupied. Anders and the chemists, hard at work on whatever had prompted their late-night meeting. It would be dawn in another three hours. Shaw determined to get what rest he could before the day began and retreated to his room.

He woke before the alarm rang. The room was stale and overheated, though the morning sun had barely touched the curtains. He splashed cold water on his face and drank a few mouthfuls before spending half an hour doing body-weight exercises with no pause between sets. After years of Ranger PT and countless recreation hours in fighting gyms, not to mention Wren teaching him yoga poses that were at least twice as hard as they looked, Shaw had a repertoire of drills large enough to keep him moving until the next century. By the time he finished a set of handstand push-ups with his heels against the wallpaper and its repeating design of tangled grapevines, sweat was dripping from his hair onto the bath towel he'd laid down.

Part of his energy came from anger, he knew. At android Kilbane and at condescending Anders. And at himself, for taking such a freaky job. It was time to corner Sebastien Rohner for a direct conversation. To hell with whether he roused the rich man from his sleep.

He showered and shaved. Hair didn't grow from the scarred tissue on his face. After a decade he could shave around the pattern of the furrows without needing a mirror, retracing the old wound every day.

Outside, the courtyard was bright with promise in the new day. Even the barren rosebushes seemed lush from the dew glistening on their thorns. Shaw walked to the main house and up onto the wide veranda to ring the bell.

"Mr. Shaw?" Sofia Rohner, leaning to look around the north corner of the house.

"Good morning," he said. "I'd like to see Mr. Rohner before the conference gets started today."

"About your altercation with Warren Kilbane last evening, I assume."

Shaw blinked. "Word gets around fast."

"Rangi sent me a message last night. I happened to be awake and phoned him back. Are you injured?"

"No."

"Good. I'm very relieved to hear it." She motioned for Shaw to join her. He walked past picture windows and half a dozen porch chairs made of varnished teak to the side of the house.

The veranda looked down on the art gallery and the beach beyond. Sofia was ready for the day's meetings, dressed in a pale pink business suit with her ice-blond hair in a bun. She carried a tablet computer. Shaw noted that the tablet had the same sleek ivory cover as the one he'd seen Anders holding when the crates were being loaded into the gallery.

Sofia nodded to him. "After discussing with Rangi what had happened, I went to see Warren to get his side of the story. I was not satisfied with his answers. He overstepped his instructions from Olen by a considerable degree. I'm terribly upset."

She didn't look upset, but maybe that was European reserve.

"What exactly were Anders's instructions to Kilbane?" Shaw said.

"As I understand it, simply to make certain that the guests were undisturbed. That any concerns you had should be brought to him. Warren told me that you were out of your room last night. All night, was the way he put it."

"Sounds like the only person that disturbed was Warren."

"My thoughts exactly. I told him that he and his team would have to leave the island for the duration of the conference. Clearly we can't have you all in close quarters, and you shouldn't be punished for their poor judgment. Please accept my apologies."

"So they're leaving?"

"I expect they already have. Rangi arranged for them to take the small boat."

"Decisive," said Shaw. "What was Anders's reaction?"

"I didn't bother to wake Olen. I'm confident he'll be as appalled as I am. We'll have a formal review of Warren's actions once time allows. He did seem suitably chastened."

Shaw almost replied that he had done the chastening himself but held his tongue.

"Is it true that you remained out of your room all night?" Sofia asked.

"I'm used to late hours." He nodded to the gallery. "Were you checking on your collection just now?"

"No. In fact, I can't get the door to unlock."

"Using one of the silver wands?"

"Nor with this." She held up the tablet. "Administrative software for the estate. Climate and security and the rest. This *should* open any door."

"I saw Anders with one of those yesterday. Or is that the same one?"

Sofia touched a fingertip to the pad. "This is my own copy. I prefer direct control."

And now that control was denied. Shaw realized he wasn't the only one looking for answers.

"I think you and I need to show our cards," he said. "Can we talk inside?"

She looked at him quizzically. "Certainly."

Sofia led him back to the main entrance. They stepped inside, into a stone-walled foyer with an alcove for coats and boots. A marble center table held a vase with a bouquet of fresh flowers nearly the size of one of the rosebushes in the courtyard.

On their right was a large sitting room with a tan leather couch and chairs arranged around a fireplace. Like the exterior of the house, the decor inside was a classic Craftsman style, blown out of proportion. The fireplace was large enough to roast a full-grown sheep. Air swirled in the room, perhaps automated climate adjustments cued by Sofia's wand. She set her tablet on a table with a chessboard made of inlaid wood. A screen on the wall, barely thicker than a matchbox, softly lightened into the image of a Chagall painting with angels seated around a table. Such high resolution that one could almost see the brushstrokes.

She motioned to the chair opposite. "Please sit."

Shaw did. "Your father hired me because he suspects that a thief will attempt to steal one or more pieces from your collection this week. I've been hired to prevent that."

Sofia stared at him. "A thief?"

"He says that this is part of some ongoing challenge between him and Chen and Flynn and some other masters of the universe. That they have a game of stealing one another's valuables, or desired items, before the other can acquire them."

"That's . . . I've never heard anything about this."

"He says that one of them stole or arranged to have stolen a wristwatch that had belonged to your grandfather."

She thought for a moment. "You don't believe him."

"Doesn't matter. He hired me to keep the gallery safe without mortifying the honored guests, so that's what I'm doing."

"And Olen?"

"I don't think Anders buys it either. He says the art's safe enough without my help."

"And he ordered you to stay away."

Shaw shrugged. "Your father outranks Anders. Unless he tells me to go, I'm staying."

"At least you have tenacity. Why didn't you tell me this from the start?"

"One of Mr. Rohner's requirements was secrecy. Just him and Anders."

She frowned. "You should have known he didn't mean me."

"He was very specific about not telling you."

Sofia sat with that for a moment, her face clouded. "Yet here you are," she said.

"Because I'm not getting the whole story. That, if you'll pardon my language, pisses me off. Yesterday Anders had three crates loaded off the *Vollmond* into your gallery. He and Avery Morton and Nelson Bao met there after midnight. They were inside for a few hours. And later Kilbane tried to escort me off the island, with prejudice."

"Crates?"

"I'm guessing stevedore work is usually beneath Anders's attention. Any idea what he would have in those crates? And why he would prevent any intrusion?" Shaw pointed to her tablet on the chessboard table. "He seems to have locked you out, too."

"An error, no doubt. You said Mr. Bao and Mr. Morton? The scientists?"

"Right."

She drummed her fingers on the leather armrest. "I believe I know what's going on, Mr. Shaw. And while Olen may be overreacting, I understand his desire for security. He and the scientists are preparing for one of our discussions with Jiangsu and Bridgetrust, most likely to be held tomorrow."

"A business meeting?" Shaw didn't bother to hide his disbelief.

"A specific one, yes."

"So what's in the crates?"

"I'm afraid I can't be forthcoming about that, Mr. Shaw. This is highly proprietary information. Hence why Olen is keeping the necessary materials in the gallery."

"Great."

"This may explain my father's . . . subterfuge with the story about the potential art thief. He wanted your expert eye watching the gallery without revealing exactly why."

"If he'd wanted that, he could have just hired me to stand outside holding a halberd like a palace guard. No deception required. What are the odds that someone might be after your company secrets?"

Sofia leaned back. "You think we may be at risk of that?"

"Ask your dad."

"I intend to. In the meantime, if there's even a chance . . . We find ourselves without a security detail. I realize you have no obligation after what happened last night, but if you'd continue in the same capacity, we'd all appreciate it."

Shaw wondered if Anders would share that appreciation. "I'll earn my pay."

"Thank you."

Shaw rose and walked to the door. He turned back.

"Why were you checking on the art collection so early this morning?" he said.

"Warren told me he believed you had been . . . skulking, was how he put it, around the main house last night. From what you said, he wasn't entirely wrong about that."

"You thought I might have paid your statues a visit."

"They are very valuable. To me at least."

And I'm a known criminal, thought Shaw. At least he knew where he stood in the Rohners' estimations.

SEVENTEEN

The corporate leaders and their teams assembled in the pavilion at ten o'clock in the morning. They'd had breakfast in the main dining area of the north wing, with ample time after for espresso drinks served by a professional barista. The center of the huge pavilion had been restaged since the banquet the night before, with rectangular tables, a projector and screen, a rolling whiteboard, and other sundries.

Maybe that's what had been in the damn crates, Shaw thought sourly. A decade's supply of highlighter pens and Post-it notes.

Olen Anders looked up from his seat and saw Shaw standing on the flagstone path outside the pavilion. The chief of staff's expression went rigid. Shaw waited, but Anders made no sign of wishing to speak with him. Too busy with the day's negotiations to address a tiny matter like Shaw's brawl with the company bullies.

Sebastien and Sofia Rohner seemed solely focused on their work as well. If Sofia had confronted her father about the art gallery earlier in the morning, they had apparently set the topic aside for now.

Shaw's phone rang. Cyndra.

"Hey," he said. "How's the first week of summer?"

"Good. I'm playing Elder Scrolls."

"Who's the farthest today?" Shaw and Cyn kept track of new and far-flung international players in her online games, marking them on a map. Cyn hadn't quite convinced Addy that this was the same as studying geography, but at least they didn't argue about it.

"There's a girl from Belgium. We have that one already."

"Yeah. Where's Addy?"

"At Holliday."

Holliday House, the care home where Addy's friend Penelope was receiving treatment. Cyndra had been on her own for at least a couple of nights each week as Addy took a shift.

"What's the island like?" asked Cyndra. Shaw could tell she was continuing to play the game as she talked.

"It's a supervillain lair without the sharks."

Cyn chuckled. "Are you going to blow it up? You really should."

"Not in my job description. But I'll try to bring you back a death ray."

"Cool."

"You all right?" he said. It wasn't like the teenager to call out of the blue. Not to call Shaw anyway. She spent hours each day online, receiving a constant flow of information from what seemed like six dozen friends.

"Uh-huh."

"You lonely? Stanley's a good dog, but he never gets my jokes."

"I guess."

"Give me another day here and I'll be back. I can hang around the house more while Addy's away. We'll marathon the horror movies she doesn't know you rent."

"'Kay. Love you," Cyndra said, the final bits of her attention slipping back to the multiplayer world.

"Back at you."

With everyone except for the household staff ensconced in the pavilion, it was easy for Shaw to keep an eye on the art gallery. The day was cool. The salt air smelled good. He raised the collar of his jacket and watched the boats on the strait, some of them a mile off. The wind was high, and the sailboats, heeling with their spinnakers as full as balloons, gave the illusion of matching the speed of the power cruisers. Shaw wondered if Hollis would be out on the water today. Weather like this was catnip to the cheerful smuggler.

He hadn't seen Hollis as frequently the past few months. Shaw had been busy with Crossroads, and Hollis had been spending a lot of time with Paula Claybeck. They were an odd pair, the effusive Ulsterman and the stoic patrician doctor. Hollis seemed happier than Shaw had ever seen him. That was something. He knew that Hollis had been married once, very young. It hadn't taken, and the breakup had been part of Hollis's reason for relocating an ocean and a continent away.

After the teams had eaten lunch, there seemed to be a time designated for all the participants to stretch their legs. The glass passageways made it easy for Shaw to track their movements on the north side of the estate from a distance. Like watching mice scuttling through the plastic tubes of a habitat. Once the meeting restarted, Shaw returned to his surreptitious patrol, circling by the gallery every half hour. The afternoon passed without apparent resolution to the business deal. At least no one popped champagne corks. The meeting broke just after five o'clock, and the teams scattered, some back to their guest suites and some to the shore. Sebastien and Sofia Rohner and Olen Anders returned to the house.

Staff began to prepare the dining area for the evening meal. Shaw's stomach growled. He'd cadged quick meals from the kitchen during the day when time had allowed, mostly cold cuts and cheeses he could eat while walking the grounds. He avoided looking at the dinner roast steaming on its silver tray as he crossed the patio outside.

An hour later, Shaw spotted Karla Lokosh cutting across a passage to the courtyard. She wore a shiny green long-sleeved workout shirt and running shoes and shorts that gave him a chance to admire her dancer's legs. Her hair was tied into a ponytail and her face flushed pink all the way to her ears from the run. Shaw waved in greeting, and she changed direction to jog up to him.

"Hey," she said, "where have you been all day?"

"Stocking the forest with pheasant and stag," said Shaw.

"I look forward to the grouse hunt later. Are you joining us for dinner?"

He shook his head. "Duty calls."

"Then maybe we'll have a drink after. The Rohners are showing a movie in the dining hall at eight."

"I'll swing through if I can."

"Good. And I'm late—again. See you then."

Shaw went to his room to rinse off and change clothes. Warmer gear for the windy night. Black carpenter pants and a turtleneck with a fleece vest and light jacket. He put on his black hiking boots and stuffed a watch cap into his pocket on the way out the door.

Dinner service was on to the entrées by the time he returned to the north wing to scarf some food. He went to the kitchen and made small sandwiches of rolls and roast and wrapped them in a linen napkin to take with him. The staff eyed him oddly, as they had since he'd first come to the island, but no one asked questions.

Though the sun was still above the horizon, a crescent moon was out, mimicking the shape of Briar Bay. Give him a monstrous pen and he could have drawn a map of the island on the lunar surface.

He chose a different spot from which to watch the gallery, in the first stand of trees past the main house. The placement didn't have a direct line of sight on the gallery's outside entrance, but he could see the beach leading to that door, and he would be hidden from view himself. If a cautious thief had spotted him on the shore last night, maybe Shaw's absence tonight would coax the burglar into action.

Dusk came quickly, with full dark dragging its feet. Whatever movie the Rohners were showing would be nearly over. Some prestige drama, Shaw guessed. A new release still on its first run, playing in theaters, with an expert projectionist to run each reel. The family wouldn't miss a chance to show off their influence by acquiring a personal copy.

Between the looming forest and the back of the great house, the rest of the estate was hidden from his view. The strait looked empty and black. Any boats still on the water were too far out for Shaw to see their running lights.

Rohner's island really was an astounding place. Shaw wished the trip were under different circumstances. He'd have liked to bring Wren here, if only to show her the stars and the moon.

Just before one o'clock in the morning, he saw a man with a flashlight walking up the estate path toward the gallery and the main house. Short, cautious steps on the flagstones. As the man neared, moonlight shone off the leather of his jacket.

Avery Morton, the chemist from Bridgetrust Group. Walking directly to the gallery. Shaw couldn't see him open the exterior door, but in another moment the familiar glow of the gallery's track lights switching on appeared from the skylights atop the roof. How had Morton gotten inside? Had he borrowed Anders's access wand? Or had Anders programmed Morton's to allow the man free rein?

After fifteen minutes the skylights dimmed again. Morton reappeared, walking back the way he'd come. He was carrying something now, a small container that he held cradled with two hands like a football as he navigated the path.

The container was much too small to hold one of the statues. Shaw slipped out of the forest to follow Morton. Maybe he could get a look at what the chemist was carrying.

He kept close to the slope above the shore, moving between clumps of rock. Morton seemed oblivious, intent on keeping his footing on the flagstones. Shaw followed the chemist past the north wing to the darkened pavilion.

Not completely dark, Shaw saw as he knelt in the shadows beyond the flagstone path. Bill Flynn, the Bridgetrust head, sat with Sebastien Rohner and Linda Edgemont at a table close to the main entrance. Morton entered through one of the pavilion's outer doors to join them. Standing lamps had been set by the table. The small bright pool within the huge glass house was like a single flaw catching the light within a diamond.

Morton removed bottles from the container. Flasks and small jars, tapered and sealed at the tops and filled with liquids. He sat and began speaking with the two CEOs and the attorney. Unlike his almost glum demeanor at dinner the previous day, now Morton seemed jazzed. Big gestures and urgent scribbling on papers in front of him.

The group talked for half an hour. Rohner seemed to call an end by standing up. Morton replaced the flasks into the container while Flynn gathered the papers that Morton had been making notes on.

They left through the main entrance to the pavilion and headed for the north wing. Flynn and Morton and Linda Edgemont presumably to their guest quarters and Rohner on to the main house.

Shaw recalled Linda Edgemont's comment about the business leads pushing to finish their conference early. Meeting at one-thirty in the morning seemed to stretch the concept. And if they had been talking chemistry, where was Bao, the other scientist? Or Chen, for that matter.

Shaw retreated to the shore and headed for the gallery again. He stepped nimbly over the splits in the rock and the small permanent pools waiting for the advancing tide to refresh them. Moonlight tinted the phosphorescent curl of each wave.

Then he saw the hand.

It extended up from the rock, as if the shore had somehow formed around it. Pale fingers stretching skyward. Reminiscent of every zombie-movie poster Shaw had ever seen, a clutching claw dragging its way out of the grave.

EIGHTEEN

Shaw stared for an instant. A wave splashed over and around the hand and then retreated, leaving the pale fingers dripping.

He moved toward the ghastly scene. A deep crevice in the rock revealed itself, like a sliver of night in the island. Each step allowed Shaw to see another inch of the arm attached to the white hand. The sleeve of a dark jacket had fallen nearly to the arm's elbow.

In another few strides, he was next to the fissure, looking down at the rest of the body within.

Nelson Bao. Unquestionably dead. He lay on his right side, with his head toward the water and a few inches lower than his legs and feet. An awkward position defined by the shape of the rock beneath him. Bao's left knee rested on a cluster of barnacles. The serrated edges of the tiny shells had torn the fabric of his trousers. His left arm had become wedged in one of the crevice's stony wrinkles, holding it aloft. Without the beckoning hand, Shaw might have stepped over him and not even noticed.

Bao's head didn't look normal, even under the circumstances. Shaw knelt for a closer examination. The crown of the chemist's skull was misshapen. Staved in. His left profile as pale as his hand. Lips parted and teeth showing. The eye halfway open.

As Shaw watched, a surge flooded the crevice, washing over the body. Bao's clothes flapped, and his hair swirled momentarily. Even the body moved, buoyed by the water. Then the wave retreated, and everything settled back into place. Only the trapped arm remained perfectly still.

Shaw took a deep breath. Bao had lost a lot of blood. His crushed head almost certainly the cause. A powerful enough blow to create a large divot in the man's skull. The waves had washed the body clean and would continue to do so.

Perhaps Bao had been walking and distractedly missed seeing the crevice and fallen headlong into the gap, his skull striking the side of the fissure. But then the wound should be on the forehead, or the temple if Bao had reflexively turned away from the coming impact.

And the tide was going out, not in. Bao would have been farther up the shore if he'd been walking, assuming the chemist hadn't been wading hip-deep at the time. Shaw looked inland. Hard to imagine Bao tripping and falling so violently on the flatter part of the beach. Had he been running for some reason and taken a spill?

High tide had been around midnight. Both Morton and Shaw had passed close to this spot on the shore an hour later, as Shaw followed the Bridgetrust man to the pavilion. Assuming Bao had died here, it must have been afterward. Maybe only by a few minutes. An ebbing tide couldn't have come high up the beach and carried his body outward.

Assume that Bao had suffered the injury to his head farther up the beach, out of the water. For what happened after that, Shaw could think of only two possibilities. Bao had crawled or staggered into the water and died. Or someone had dragged him in, maybe with the hope that the tide would carry the body out into the strait. Either way Bao had become lodged in the crevice by the surging waves, and here he was.

Shaw stood but did not move away. He didn't want to chance stepping on or kicking anything loose from where it might lie.

People didn't generally carry around blunt objects. They took advantage of what was there.

He walked slowly in a wide circle, scanning the ground. He left his flashlight in his pocket. No reason to attract attention until he was ready. When his first circle came up empty, he walked a larger one, without much expectation. If there had been a weapon, a rock or a driftwood log, it could have been taken away or thrown a distance, on land or into the water. It wasn't close in any event.

Shaw reached for his phone to call Anders. Then changed his mind.

He returned to where Bao lay. Another surge of tide forced the body into a false dance. When it subsided, Shaw knelt and leaned down to run his hands over Bao's clothing. The corpse felt no different from the cold, wet fabric draping it. Warmth had long since left the body. Any texture of its flesh was lost in the icy drops numbing Shaw's fingers.

A squarish lump filled the pocket of Bao's suit jacket, pinned under his weight. An obliging wave came in, lifting the body a fraction. Shaw dipped his hands into the chill froth to get hold of the jacket's lapels and heaved, pulling the body from the crevice. Bao's trapped arm came loose and flopped coldly onto Shaw's face. Grimacing, he set the arm down gently. The least he could do, after Bao had signaled for help from beyond the grave.

From the dead man's jacket, Shaw removed a wallet and a passport folder. Bao's black wand was clipped to his shirt pocket. His smartphone had been shattered by the fall. It didn't respond when Shaw tried turning it on.

The wallet clip held American bills—flimsy after their saltwater soak—and a Chase Bank debit card along with a Washington State driver's license. That was a surprise. Bao had said he'd never been to the state before, and here was his license with an address in the Central District of Seattle.

Shaw replaced the wallet and unzipped the passport holder. The deep red cover of the People's Republic of China. He flipped it open. The photo was undoubtedly the chemist, staring placidly back. The name given, in English lettering below the Chinese characters, was Yuen Si-Lung. Born in Guangdong Province. The issue date for the passport was two years prior.

Not necessarily odd, Shaw thought. Loads of people from other nations had Westernized names to go with their birth names, and the link between the two wasn't always obvious. Maybe Yuen had been his father's last name and Bao his mother's, and Nelson/Si-Lung had chosen that when he'd moved to the States.

But combined with Bao's white lie about his Seattle address, Shaw wondered how deep the man's secrecy went.

He rezipped the passport folder—wiping his fingerprints from it—and set it back in Bao's pocket with the wallet. Another tidal surge filled the crevice. The water lapped over the edges and onto the corpse. Bao stared up with sightless eyes. He looked slightly accusatory at being left in this undignified state.

"Sorry," Shaw said to the dead man, and reached for his phone to call Anders.

NINETEEN

"You found the body?" said the county deputy.

"Yes. Nelson Bao."

"Did you touch him at all?"

"I called to him," said Shaw. "When he was unresponsive, I pulled him out of the split in the rocks to check for breathing and a pulse. That's when I saw his head wound and how pale he was."

They sat across from each other in a small conference room in the north wing. The sun hadn't breached the horizon, though the world was rapidly brightening outside the window.

It had taken about ninety minutes from the time Anders had called 911 for San Juan law enforcement to cross the fifteen miles of water from the county seat in Friday Harbor. They had responded in force, four deputies and the sheriff himself in two patrol boats. Another hour had passed while the new visitors goggled at Rohner's estate, inspected where Bao lay on the beach, and collected the guests, finally landing on the north wing as the best place to conduct interviews.

Once they learned that Shaw had been first on the scene, he was separated and asked to wait in the meeting room. An officer hovered in the hall, making sure he stayed put. From what Shaw could discern by the movements between rooms and people passing the open door, the sheriff was talking to Rohner and his family in the main house. C.J. walked by with Bill Flynn, the Bridgetrust leader. She gave Shaw a faltering wave hello.

After another half hour, the deputy had entered the room and begun to question him. Thirtyish, fit, in a black polo shirt with the seven-pointed star of the county embroidered on the left chest and G. PARRY and DEPUTY stacked on the right. Looking like a man eager to catch somebody at something.

"And you recognized Nelson Bao," Parry asked.

Shaw nodded. "We were at the same table at dinner."

"What'd you two talk about? At dinner?"

"Almost nothing. Hobbies. He said he liked playing backgammon, in tournaments."

"Had you and Mr. Bao met before dinner?" he said.

"No."

"Why were you on the beach tonight?"

"I was taking a walk."

"Kinda late for a stroll."

"I'm used to night hours," said Shaw.

"What's your job?"

"Before this I worked at a bar in Seattle. Two-thirty in the morning is quitting time."

"So what do you do here?"

"Mr. Rohner hired me as the facilities manager on Sunday. I arrived Monday afternoon."

Deputy Parry made a face. "Tough first week."

"Yeah."

"Where'd you walk to? Were you going out or coming back?"

"Coming back. I walked from the south wing around the southern tip and back, all along the shore, or as close to it as I could."

"That's a long hike."

"It's a small island."

"So you were on the beach and you came across Mr. Bao. What'd you do then?"

"I pulled him out and checked for signs of life, like I said. Not finding any, I called Olen Anders, and he came down and saw the body for himself."

"Either of you try CPR?" the deputy asked.

"No. His head was badly damaged, and he'd lost a lot of blood."

"But you couldn't be sure."

"I've seen dead people before. He was dead."

Parry stared at him for a moment. "What happened then?"

"Anders called Mr. Rohner and 911."

"Rohner first?"

"He's the boss."

Parry hummed. "Okay. Stay here. The sheriff might want to talk to you." The deputy stood and went to the door before turning back. "Can I ask you something unrelated? How'd you get that?" He flicked a finger toward Shaw's face.

"Afghanistan."

"Huh. My brother got glassed in a bar fight, long time ago. Looks kind of the same. I just wondered."

Shaw nodded. Parry left and closed the door behind him.

He hadn't told the deputy everything about Anders. How the tall man had come from the direction of the main house at almost a lope, as if anticipating the trouble he would find. Anders had shone a flashlight on the body, staring with an intense expression, and then, as Shaw had done, he began to pat Bao down. Shaw had kept silent about his own search of the body.

Anders had removed the items from Bao's pockets, then shone his light over the beach, foot by foot, careful not to miss whatever he sought by rushing.

"I already looked for whatever brained him," Shaw had said, "if that's why you're searching."

Anders had turned his light onto Shaw. "Did you find anything else?"

"No."

The tall man had regarded Shaw for a long moment.

"This was an accident," he said.

When Shaw didn't reply, Anders had returned to scanning the beach. Whatever he was seeking was small enough that the tall man took pains not to miss finding it in the cracks and hollows of the rocky shore. It couldn't be one of the statues. Any of those pieces would have stuck out like a flag on a football field.

"We should check the gallery," Shaw had said.

"Why?" Anders continued to search the crags.

"Because we're only a hundred yards from there. Because maybe Bao interrupted the thief. Morton was inside the gallery earlier. Bao might have been, too."

"You were told to stay away," said Anders.

"Who gave Morton access?"

"If I were you, Mr. Shaw," Anders had said, not glancing up, "I would not ask nor invite questions. Not with your criminal history."

Shaw said nothing.

"I'll call Sebastien," the chief of staff had said finally. "Damn it all. This was so long in the making."

He stalked off toward the estate. Shaw had stayed behind with Bao.

While waiting in the conference room for the sheriff, Shaw continued to mull over Anders's strange actions. Bao's death might have been a mishap. Anders clearly preferred Shaw to believe that. But if it had been homicide, odds seemed very good it had something to do with whatever was going on in the gallery and the proprietary secrets Rohner and the rest seemed so anxious to keep under wraps. Maybe they'd been worth killing for.

The door opened. A man with oval glasses and a black triangle of mustache stepped in. His green baseball cap and windbreaker were both emblazoned with the county star.

"Mr. Shaw? I'm Sheriff Dayle. Come with me, please."

Shaw rose and followed Dayle into the hall, through the doors and passageway leading from the conference center into the pavilion. Most of the island's guests and staff had gathered there. Nearly all wore clothes that looked like they'd been put on in a hurry. Karla Lokosh, in a tracksuit and with her red hair tamed into a simple braid, gave Shaw a quick nod.

"Folks," said the sheriff. "Thank you for being patient while we took your statements."

"What happened to Nelson?" said Morton. Shaw noticed that neither Chen Li nor Zhang, Bao's coworkers, was present.

"Was he really killed?" said Linda Edgemont. Shaw suspected she might win the prize for the most haggard of any of the rudely awakened guests. Not so much for her clothes or her makeup, which was fresh. She looked stricken.

"It's too early for conclusions," Dayle replied, "but for the moment we're looking at this as an accident. We have asked Mr. Rohner, and he's agreed, to clear the island of any nonessential personnel. That means guests and all staff, except for two or three people. Some of my deputies will remain here until we're sure everything is secure. Mr. Rohner has said he'll make their boat available to take people to Friday Harbor or down to Seattle in an hour or so."

"What about the plane?" said one of the Droma people.

"You'll have to ask him about that. Right now he's tending to his family over in the big house." Dayle pointed a thumb in that direction. "He'll be here shortly to talk to you. Until then please stay close and stay inside the buildings. You can go to your rooms to pack your things, but nowhere else."

The sheriff's tone didn't invite debate, and the small crowd turned their attention to each other. A few took out their phones to begin making arrangements for flights or hotels or, in the case of the household staff, just to return home earlier than expected.

Karla Lokosh crossed to where Shaw stood, near one of the long troughs of greenery and flowers.

"You all right?" he said.

"Stunned," she said. "It's . . . surreal. And awful. Are you staying on the island?"

"I don't know yet. The cops might want to talk to me some more. I was the one who found Bao."

"I heard. We're all sharing every new trickle of information about what happened, real or imagined. You okay?"

"Better than him."

Karla grimaced, and Shaw said, "Sorry. Old habit, making a joke of things."

"Gallows humor, I'm down. It just caught me by surprise. I'll be on one of the planes to Friday Harbor, I think. If you're heading in the same direction, let me know." She handed Shaw her business card, embossed in red and black. "Maybe we can have breakfast."

"Flynn won't have you and Morton working?"

"Whenever a client turns up dead, I'm off the clock," she said with a sorrowful look. "How's that for dark comedy?"

"You win. I'll find out if I'm leaving with the rest of you."

Shaw headed down the passage toward the staff quarters. One hour until the boat would leave. Packing his bag would take two minutes, tops. He could think of an excellent way to use the other fifty-eight.

TWENTY

The morning sun was low and the western side of the estate still dark with shade. Shaw moved fast to take advantage. He threw a few items into his light ruck and left the south wing to jog around the main house to the forest, keeping out of sight of the shore and the county patrol boats at the dock.

He took the same path through the forest that he'd used when following the men loading the black crates into the gallery. After a quick check to be sure the porches and windows of the house were clear, he ran to scale the glass passageway over the steps and climb to the gallery roof.

At the first skylight, he took the transceiver from his pocket and switched it on. While it locked on to the alarm's signal, he removed a climbing rope from his pack and looped it around a stubby vent tube nearby. When the device's light glowed green, indicating it was successfully imitating the skylight by swapping authentication codes with the alarm box, he popped the external latch on the skylight.

He propped the hatch open, tossed the coil of climbing rope down, and wormed his way inside, feetfirst. The entire sequence from the moment he'd first touched the gallery roof had taken less than ninety seconds.

Shaw had pre-tied knots along the rope to aid in climbing. Still, it took all his strength to grip the slim line with his legs with one hand and reach to close the skylight lid behind him with the other. He lowered himself hand over hand into the gallery.

The scene below his dangling feet was a surprise. The gallery had been rearranged. His rope had fallen amid half a dozen pedestals, crowded together. Each was covered with a white dust sheet. All the artwork had been moved into this end of the gallery, including the wall cabinets, with a narrow path in between the shrouded statuary to the passageway door. Shaw descended, taking care not to swing and knock one of the figurines off its base.

Two long tables had been set in the cleared space on the opposite side of the gallery. Shaw stepped around the crop of pedestals and the stack of disassembled black shipping crates for a closer look.

One table held a collection of chemical jars and flasks, some full and others empty and waiting in their racks. Morton had taken a few of the same flasks to his midnight meeting in the pavilion with Rohner and Flynn and Edgemont.

A complex-looking machine dominated the second table. The central component was a box that looked like a cross between a small photocopier and an electronic safe, complete with keypad and readout screen. The small name at the top read WYVERN GPC-IR. Shaw popped the front panel, which swung open on a hinge. The inside of the machine gave him no help in figuring out its purpose. Just a shallow space at the front, with flexible tubes feeding into long steel vials.

On one side of the big box was a stand holding two large bottles, sealed with red caps and plastic tubes instead of screw tops. A blue-white liquid filled one of the bottles; the other was empty. A computer monitor, also connected to the machine, was the final object on the table.

At least he knew now why the two chemists had been in the gallery overnight. Setting up this machine. Whatever Rohner's secret deal might be, it apparently relied on this equipment.

Drugs? Unlikely. Cooking meth or opioids required more space, more ventilation, and produced a lot more toxic trash than the single plastic thirty-gallon can next to the second table could hold. The Wyvern machine was likely manufactured for use in a university or a corporate lab. Even if Shaw could buy the crazy notion that mountain-climbing business mogul Sebastien Rohner might be starting his own cartel, this was an inexplicable place to put his kitchen.

What knowledge Shaw had of chemistry was limited to his demolition training in the Army and certain handy applications of acids. The names and symbols on the bottles and equipment were arcane.

Time was short. The boat would be leaving in ten minutes. He took his phone and used it to quickly snap pictures of everything in the lab.

The dust sheets draped over the pedestals made the collected art look like a crowd of shy ghosts. From deities to specters in one short day.

Climbing back out through the skylight was a chore, but the surprise of finding Rohner's secret laboratory had given him a shot of adrenaline. He heaved himself onto the roof, retrieved the rope and closed the skylight, then made a hasty retreat down to the ground.

Moments later an air horn blared from the dock, its shriek echoing off the island and startling birds from the trees. Shaw hurried to his room to grab his duffel and run for the boat.

TWENTY-ONE

Olen Anders nodded along to what Sheriff Dayle was saying, silently willing the man to talk faster. Most of the policeman's points were painfully obvious. Make sure Anders stayed available in case additional questions proved necessary. Make sure the officers had the names and numbers of all guests and of anyone who might have been aware that Mr. Bao was on the island this week. Make sure to call if any of the staff found anything or remembered anything. Make sure, make sure.

The only certainty Anders was concerned with was that Chen Li might be boarding one of the floatplanes back to Seattle at that very moment. Anders needed to have a conversation—*make sure* that Sebastien had a conversation—with Chen before he left. After might be too late.

Anders shook the sheriff's hand, complimented him on how adroitly he and his deputies had handled this terrible situation, and strode to the dock as swiftly as his long legs could carry him.

He needn't have worried. Chen sat on one of the benches along the stone path outside the south wing, intended for island guests to pause and watch the sunrise if they happened to be up that early. Chen's man Zhang stood a yard off his superior's right shoulder. Nearer than Anders thought necessary; Zhang's attitude practically announced *bodyguard*.

Then Anders remembered that Bao was dead. Naturally Chen and Zhang would both be on edge, no matter how little of it showed on Chen's composed face.

"Mr. Chen," Anders said as he drew near, slowing his pace a bit so as not to worry Zhang. "We should talk about what happened."

"Yes," said Chen. "I've already called for them."

Anders followed Chen's glance. Sebastien Rohner and Bill Flynn were coming from the main house, Flynn talking in his usual impassioned manner, hands gesticulating.

"It's really in our best interest," Flynn concluded before catching the mood and going silent.

"Thank you for coming," Chen said.

Rohner stepped forward. "I should be thanking you. I'm very sorry for what happened to Nelson Bao. He seemed like a good man."

Sebastien had barely met Bao, Anders thought. But what else did one say in such circumstances?

Chen indicated the dock and the conveyances tied to it. Most of the people on the island were already preparing to leave, the household staff aboard the motor cruiser and the planes waiting to receive the guests.

"Time is limited," Chen said. "I suggest we speak plainly. Nelson will not mind."

"The sheriff seems to be leaning toward a finding of misadventure," said Rohner.

Flynn crossed his arms. "What do *you* believe?"

Rohner looked at each of the men before responding. Anders was familiar with the tactic, which didn't mean that it was ineffective. Sebastien was expert at making each person in any gathering feel engaged and included.

"I believe two things are possible," the Droma CEO said. "One is that Nelson slipped and struck his head. I feel strongly that will be the sheriff's conclusion. As soon as the police allow us all back on the island, we can resume our business." Rohner inclined his head in sympathy. "The other possibility is that Nelson was attacked. However unlikely that is, we should consider it. If so, then he was assaulted for some reason, and the most logical assumption is that he was carrying something his attacker wanted."

Rohner turned to Chen. "Was Nelson holding anything for you? For us? Perhaps he noted some details of our deal on his computer or phone . . ."

"My concern is identifying Nelson's assailant," Chen replied.

"I've been thinking about that as well," said Rohner, as if Chen had not ignored his question. "To state the obvious, all of us have a substantial interest. We still have validation tests to run, but we all share the confidence that those tests will be successful. None of us here has anything to gain from delaying our deal."

Chen nodded.

"This would point to an outsider," Rohner continued. "Someone seeking to steal one of our components or inhibit our progress. I don't have to remind you of the potential value of our collaboration."

"And how would that person know what to steal?" Flynn said. "How would they know about any of this?"

"Inside information," Anders said. "It would have to be."

"Yes," said Rohner. "Information provided by someone aware of our tests here this week and how much the resulting solution could be worth. But not one of us."

He looked at the three other men in the circle. None of them volunteered anything beyond frowns.

It was Zhang, of all people, who broke the silence. "The caretaker. Shaw. He is not a caretaker."

They looked at him. Chen didn't turn around but inclined his head slightly to one side. An invitation for his man to continue.

"He is too . . ." Zhang reached for the words in English. "He watches too much."

"Observant," Chen said.

"Yes. He is military, or government. A high percentage of training."

Chen hummed agreement. Zhang seemed to take that as a sign that he'd said enough.

"Shaw did strike me as capable," said Anders.

"A tough-looking SOB," Flynn said. "No question. You're the one who brought him on, Sebastien."

"He was recommended," Rohner clarified. "But let's not run ahead of ourselves. Shaw was the one who found Nelson Bao. Though he also called Anders to the scene. Would he do that if he were Bao's attacker?"

Flynn shrugged. "Maybe Shaw thought someone spotted him on the beach. He had to cover his tracks." He pointed to Chen. "He kills your guy for what he's carrying, hides it somewhere, and pretends to find the body. Which leads me back to the first question. Is anything missing?"

They all looked at Chen. After a moment he nodded.

"Shit," Flynn said.

"You're certain?" Rohner had gone stone-faced.

"A portion of the chemical sample," said Chen.

"Not the whole thing, then? Is there enough left to test?"

"Perhaps."

Flynn paced. Not so close as to distress Zhang, who Anders noted might be spoiling for some flavor of conflict. "What kind of answer is 'perhaps'? If we can test it, let's move forward."

"We cannot," Chen said without changing the even tone of his voice, "until I have a new chemist."

That stopped Flynn abruptly. "We've got Morton."

"No."

"You can trust his skill. I only hire the best."

"I require independent verification," said Chen. "Someone I will engage."

Flynn fumed. Rohner stepped in before the impulsive Bridgetrust man said anything else. "How long will that take, Mr. Chen?"

"I will be in touch when I know. Gentlemen."

Chen rose. Zhang fell into step next to him as they walked toward the dock.

The Bridgetrust CEO waited until the two were out of earshot.

"Our Mr. Chen is playing games," he said.

Rohner was still looking after Chen and Zhang. "His employee is dead. He's cautious."

A moment passed before the other man turned to Rohner. His heated emotion gone, as if his face and spirit had been wiped clean by a damp cloth. Even the blue eyes had dimmed to a flat steel.

Anders stared. It was a surprising transformation, even knowing that Bill Flynn was merely a mask that the man had donned for Chen's benefit.

When he spoke, even the voice was hollow. Stripped down to icy syllables.

"A few billion on the table, you'd think Chen could see his way past one chemist," he said. "Call me the moment you hear from him."

When Rohner and Anders didn't reply, he marched away in the direction of the estate.

When he was gone, Sebastien Rohner turned to his chief of staff.

"If Shaw truly is to blame for Nelson Bao, then we have a larger issue to contend with."

Anders's lips tightened. "I should never have sent Kilbane to oust Shaw from the island."

"No."

"A miscalculation," Anders said. "I thought that with Shaw's intractability, having him leave sooner than planned would be better. We could still have blamed him for the theft once the solution went missing."

"And now a key element truly is lost. And Shaw may have it. I don't enjoy the irony, Olen."

"No. Of course not," Anders said.

"If Shaw took the sample from Bao, he can only be a pawn. We hired him barely a day before coming here."

"I agree. Someone must have made Shaw aware of the chemical's value—or simply paid him to betray us."

Rohner glanced in the direction of the man who had just left. The one whom Chen Li and the rest of the guests knew as Bill Flynn.

"It has to be Hargreaves," he said. "We know how he operates. Infiltration. Duplicity."

Anders considered that. Sebastien was at least partially right, of course. James Hargreaves was not to be trusted. Anders had no difficulty imagining the man resorting to violence if it suited his aims.

But the timing was wrong. If Hargreaves had been behind the theft, maybe with Shaw as his catspaw, then surely he would have waited to steal the chemical sample until the tests had proved its worth. Else he might be left with nothing.

The same reason that he and Sebastien had chosen to wait. There was little point in purloining the solution from the gallery—and making enemies—before they were certain of the rewards.

"It *may* be Hargreaves behind the theft," Anders said. "Though I don't believe even he would risk upsetting the deal this close to victory." He cleared his throat. "There is one other person within Droma familiar with Shaw. And our history with the chemical."

Rohner's brow creased. "Linda?"

"She knows all of the particulars. She could easily have contacted Shaw before he arrived here, and come to a mutual agreement."

"No. I won't entertain the idea."

"It's doubtful, I agree. I'm merely weighing the possibility. We'll investigate. Lay our fears to rest."

The sputter and roar of a seaplane engine came from the dock. Anders had taken the initiative to call the pilot of the larger yellow aircraft, who had lifted off from Seattle shortly after the police arrived. It would return to the city with most of the guests, while C.J. would fly the remainder to Friday Harbor. The staff would have to make the brief trip aboard the *Vollmond*.

Rohner looked at the stream of people leaving.

"We need this to happen, Olen," he said. "To keep all that we've built, we need this."

It was rare that Sebastien allowed a chink to show in his armor of confidence. Anders treated his friend's openness with the care it deserved.

"I know," said Anders. "We'll see it through."

TWENTY-TWO

Shaw left the choice of restaurants in Friday Harbor to Karla. She chose a pub on Front Street called the Cask & Schooner. A window table was open, with a view of the marina from where they'd walked. On a Thursday morning, the traffic on and off the ferry to the mainland was light. They watched a slow thread of cars and foot passengers making their way through the roundabout in front of the pub.

"We've been awake so long it feels like lunchtime," Karla said. "Reason enough for a Bloody Mary."

Shaw ordered a stout, and when Karla noticed him eyeing the shepherd's pie, she added a turkey burger to go with her drink. Since the sheriff's announcement at the pavilion, she had changed from her tracksuit into a black blouse with epaulets and a gray skirt with black flats. Her hair was out of its ponytail and slightly windswept, even though she'd taken C.J.'s plane to Friday Harbor rather than the boat like Shaw. Shaw had changed clothes aboard the *Vollmond* after noticing dirt on his pants and shirt from crawling on the north wing's roof. Rangi, at the helm, was the one to point him to a stateroom. The boat's head had been constantly occupied, with fifteen people sharing space on the cruiser.

"Do you still have a job?" Karla asked.

"Doubtful. I don't think the island will have another meeting for a while."

"And not many facilities to manage until they do. Sorry."

"It was a temporary deal," he said. "I took it on a lark as much as anything else. Are you going back to New York?"

"Not right away. Since we're already in Seattle, Bill Flynn wants to see if we can meet with potential clients. The personal touch."

"Do you like your work?"

"Aspects of it." She waved a hand at the marina and the tiny hump of Brown Island beyond, which formed a sort of natural breakwater for the harbor. "The travel occasionally takes me to nice places. Not so often that I'm forced to live out of a suitcase. I've done those jobs, and they get old fast. Plus, there's the challenge. Every client has different problems, and they're pretty intense about solving them fast."

"Like what? Cash-flow issues?"

"Yes. Or their investment equity, which has been a roller coaster for everyone the past few years." The server brought their drinks. Karla sampled a taste of hers, then stopped. "Wait. We should toast. To Nelson."

Shaw tapped his pint glass against hers. "Did you see Chen or Zhang afterward?"

"Only in passing. I think the Rohners invited them to the house while the police sort everything out. Which might take a while. The sheriff doesn't really believe it was an accident."

"No?"

"No," Karla said, frowning. "For one, a whole team of people with tackle boxes arrived in a police boat. You didn't see them?"

Shaw hadn't. He'd been inside the gallery, adding to the list of crimes committed on the island that day.

"Well, it looked to me like more people than you'd need to examine the scene of a tragic fall," Karla continued. "And when they collected our wands, they tagged them all with our names and asked everyone again where they were around one o'clock in the morning. They're looking for a mismatch between the stories and whatever the wands say. You know those things probably track movement in and out of the buildings, too."

Shaw's own wand would show a whole lot of hours spent in the same strange spot, just outside the south wing where he'd buried it each night before watching the gallery. That could become a problem if the police started digging.

"Sounds about right," he said.

"Not the sort of thing police do when they think it's a mishap."

Karla nodded. "That whole island was just plain strange. Half vacation home, half fortress. Neither fish nor fowl. I don't suppose Sebastien Rohner is some sort of doomsday prepper?"

Shaw laughed. "Only for financial catastrophes, I'd bet."

"Well, it won't be my first choice of vacation spots. Speaking of which, I was thinking after our client meetings are concluded I might take a couple of days off to sightsee. If there's anything worth seeing." Karla stirred her drink, the salt on the rim catching the red swirl and absorbing it to become pink granules.

Shaw stalled by taking a sip of stout. Wren had made it clear that she and Shaw weren't exclusive. The fact that he *wasn't* seeing anyone else seemed to make her uneasy, like he might be just waiting around for Wren to finally commit to the relationship. This was new territory.

"If you'd like a guide," he said finally, "I suddenly find my days open."

"Yes. I'd like that very much." Karla smiled. Dazzlingly enough that the server seemed to pause in the action of setting down their salads to bask in the glow.

WITH THE LAST OF THE police leaving the island, Anders turned to business. The calamity with Nelson Bao had put him well behind. He kept a small office in the north wing of the estate for his personal use. He decided to begin with the morning's voice mails on his mobile phone.

That was when he saw the alarm notification.

The estate system had multiple levels of alerts. The top level was of course for any activation of the alarm itself, or an outage that might leave the house or gallery vulnerable. Lower levels of notification were informational, such as logging the time whenever one of the Rohners or Anders himself entered the gallery or whenever doors opened and closed.

Doors or skylights.

Anders preferred to see everything—it was his painstaking nature—but he had set these lesser notifications to silent. His phone

had made no sound when the skylight was opened earlier that morning at 06:04. And the little banner of text had quickly become submerged in the constant river of other messages.

He stood up and fairly raced down the hall, his urgency nearly
carrying him out of the wing before logic prevailed and he slowed his
pace. Whatever was done was done. And he would need assistance.

He found staff members working in the kitchen, two of the handful remaining on the island. "I require a ladder," he said to the senior of
the two. "Twenty feet at least. Have one brought to the gallery at the
side of the house."

Anders left the man to it. He walked through the glass corridor to
the house and upstairs to his bedroom. He retrieved his tablet computer from the safe. The computer had logged the same intrusion,
the skylight opening just after six in the morning. But no alarm had
sounded, even though it should have.

He went outside, where two of the groundskeepers were propping
the ladder against the side of the gallery.

"What needs fixing, Mr. Anders?" The groundskeeper had donned
his tool belt and had one foot ready on the first rung. Anders impatiently waved him aside and began to climb. The two younger men
hurried to hold the ladder at its base while he ascended.

On the roof he used the tablet to deactivate the gallery's alarms
and unfastened the latch of the skylight. The natural accumulation of
dirt and tar grit on the roof around the bubble-shaped window had
been disturbed. Upon opening the hatch, Anders found scuff marks
on the white aluminum frame. He knelt for a closer look. A black fiber
had caught along the frame's edge.

A rope, Anders judged. Dropped into the gallery, whereupon Shaw
had climbed down.

There was no question in Anders's mind that it had been Shaw.
The criminal had means and opportunity. It was his motive that concerned Anders now.

Bao had been dead hours before dawn. The sample taken from his body. What purpose could Shaw have had in breaking into the gallery at six o'clock that morning? Had he stolen some of the art?

Anders climbed down the ladder and told the men to remove it. He waited until they were gone before entering the gallery.

All the statues were in place, still draped in muslin. Every component of the laboratory as well. It didn't appear that any of the solvent or other materials Morton had prepared had been taken either.

Perhaps Shaw's reason was simply to see what he could see. Curiosity and cats, Anders pondered.

Shaw's discovery of the laboratory was unexpected. But it might be a clue. Shaw had told Anders that he hadn't found anything near Bao's body. If he'd been lying—if he did have the chemical—then it was possible that Shaw had broken into the gallery in an attempt to discover what it was he held, and its value.

Anders smiled. Sebastien's original plan had been to have the distinctively scarred thief seen by all the guests, and an ample amount of his time spent near the gallery. Shaw would then be paid and quietly sent away. A diversion, to allow Anders to take the final steps to secure Droma's future and make certain that neither Chen nor the treacherous Hargreaves could cheat them out of what was rightfully theirs.

Now, if Shaw truly did hold the missing sample, Sebastien and Anders could still appeal to his mercenary nature. Money had proved an effective enticement for Shaw before; it would do so again. Sebastien could offer a better price than anyone else.

Triumph snatched from the closing jaws of disaster. And once Shaw took that bait, Anders would make sure the man was sent far out of their way. There could be no more risk of interference.

TWENTY-THREE

Shaw walked Karla to the ferry terminal, where she would meet Flynn and Morton. She shook his hand in farewell, holding it for just a moment longer than a business handshake.

He reversed course down Front Street to the marina. Hollis had sailed from Seattle to give Shaw a lift. The *Francesca* was already moored in a guest slip just past the fuel pier. Shaw could see the barrel-chested figure of Hollis Brant sitting on the foredeck, leaning back against one of the railing stanchions as he worked on something with his hands.

"Always liked gingers," Hollis said as Shaw drew near. "They've got spirit."

Shaw looked back the way he'd come. No way Hollis could have spotted Karla with him from this distance.

"Carnac the Magnificent knows all." Hollis set down the bilge pump he'd been repairing on a towel and picked up a paper cup. "Plus, I went for coffee and saw you and the girl sitting in the restaurant."

"Who the hell is Carnac the Magnificent?"

"Johnny Carson. Before your time. You want to untie that line there, we'll get going."

Shaw looked at the dismantled pump. "If you're sure we won't sink."

"What's certain in this life?" Hollis wrapped the pieces of the pump in the towel and stuck the bundle into his open toolbox. He closed the latch and began walking crablike along the narrow side deck toward the stern. "You're in a fine mood."

"The new job went south fast. I found a dead man on the beach last night."

Hollis's toolbox banged against the side of the cabin as he turned around. "That's southerly all right. For that poor soul most of all. Jesus Mary."

"It's not over. The betting line is that he was murdered."

After Shaw had cast off, he joined Hollis on the flybridge above the cabin. Over the steady thrum of the twin diesels, he recounted his time on Briar Bay Island. Hollis grunted with satisfaction at hearing of the scuffle with Kilbane and puzzled along with Shaw at the strange assembly of executives and their lieutenants at dinner.

It wasn't until they were almost two miles out from the harbor, far enough to change course and make a beeline for the open water south of the islands, that Shaw got to finding Bao's sodden corpse trapped in the rocky shore. When Shaw told Hollis the part about breaking into the gallery and finding the hastily assembled laboratory, the older man sat down heavily in the helm chair.

"You have the strangest days, Van," he said.

"The nights aren't proving much better. I'm not even positive *why* Rohner hired me. If it wasn't to protect his art collection, was it because he suspected that a thief was after whatever they had in the lab? There was nothing there that looked worth the trouble. And if his whole story about crazy tycoons filching one another's valuables was bullshit, why walk me through the gallery? Was Bao a thief himself? Or just an innocent who took a walk at the wrong damned time?"

"Easy. It'll sort itself out."

Shaw inhaled deeply, willing the salt air to clear his head as well as his lungs. "I don't like being a witness. It gets me on cops' radar."

Hollis shuddered. "Give me peace. But you can't be a serious suspect. You said the man was positively exsanguinated by the time you found him."

Shaw ticked off the points on his fingers. "I'm not rich like the Rohners. I'm not a corporate exec like the guests, or even an employee. And I've got a record. Who would you look hard at if you were Sheriff Dayle?"

"But why would you kill the poor fellow?"

"They can invent why. Maybe I tried to mug Bao. Or he hit on me and I'm a gay basher. None of it may ultimately stick, but if they rule it a homicide, it's me they'll grill for the next few weeks."

"Time to call your lawyer."

Shaw agreed. He'd already left Ganz a message. Though hiding behind Ganz's legal shield wasn't his first order of business. He had some hard questions for the diminutive attorney about Sebastien Rohner and his own mouthpiece, Linda Edgemont.

The day had turned out bright and clear, with a whisper of heat on the wind coming from the stern. The mercury would be peaking in the city by the time they arrived in five or six hours. Hollis had the *Francesca* cruising easily at fifteen knots, her bow high enough to pierce the horizon. Running with the current for the moment. Shaw took a deep breath and sat down, trying to relax.

"Exsanguinated, huh?" he said to Hollis. "Hooking up with Doc Claybeck is improving your vocab."

"Seeing. I'm seeing the lady."

"Right. My mistake. Is she well?"

"Better than. She's a fine woman."

"Good."

"And you? Still with Raina?" Hollis said, showing off that he remembered how to pronounce Wren's given name properly, *Rain-ya*.

"Yes. When she's in town."

"How much does she travel?"

"It's not so much the time." Shaw shifted in his seat. "She sees other people. Has since the start. And she plans to keep on seeing them."

"And you don't like that."

"I'm figuring it out. I like that she's up front about what she wants. Or what she needs, maybe. I don't have to try to decipher anything with her." He shrugged. "I've never been . . . *polyamorous* before. Not sure I want to be, even if Wren is."

"Sounds as confusing as your situation back at the island."

"Yeah." Shaw grinned. "But a lot more pleasant. Like you said, a fine woman."

"And the redhead?"

"Karla. I just met her."

"You don't even have to say hello to like the look of someone. And she *is* a looker, if you'll pardon my uninvited opinion."

"She also lives in New York."

"So? Maybe that's a boon. Knowing where you both stand. If the girl is going home soon, why not enjoy the time while it lasts? Always been my motto."

Shaw laughed. "You could be right about that."

"I've been told I'm smarter than I look."

"Speaking of smart." Shaw took out the phone he'd used at the gallery. "I need a chemist."

Hollis regarded him quizzically. "Not in the Brits' meaning, I'm guessing. Unless you're readying for a first night with Miss Karla."

Shaw showed Hollis the photographs, swiping with his thumb that held the phone so his other hand could keep a loose grip on the safety rail as the *Francesca* steadily rose and fell. "I need somebody who can tell me what this machine is and translate the labels on these bottles. There aren't many ingredients here. Whatever that lab was created to do, it's something very specific. Maybe a onetime deal."

"Then the room transforms back to a museum." Hollis shook his head. "The rich are certainly odd."

"Addy knows a lot of university types," said Shaw, talking half to himself. "We'll track down somebody with the right education. What's in the lab might give me a clue to what's really going on."

"Drugs," Hollis said. "It has to be, doesn't it? All this secrecy and paranoia. You said Bao was a scientist. They've developed some superopioid that'll make the nation's epidemic ten times worse."

"It's not meth. I could tell that much."

"Well, nothing to do about it until we reach home. Take the helm and I'll find us some food and libations."

Hollis disappeared down the ladder. Shaw sat in the captain's chair. Driving the boat on open water was mostly a matter of not hitting anything, and there was no other vessel within half a mile. Shaw nudged the wheel with his knee whenever the *Francesca* strayed a few degrees.

Superdrugs. Damn. That would be just the arsenic icing on the cyanide cake that was this whole week.

TWENTY-FOUR

The *Francesca* reached her home berth in early afternoon. Shaw had closed his eyes for a couple of hours in Hollis's guest stateroom during the passage, but sleep had floated out of reach. With the promise of a dinner with Hollis and Paula Claybeck soon, he excused himself and caught a rideshare to his apartment.

He made coffee in the French press that had been a gift from Addy and took the carafe to the balcony. He was growing to like living in the heart of the city. Most things he needed to buy were available with a short hike and a willingness to lug groceries home on his back. It probably helped that the howls of sirens and bellows of the drunks and the crazies arguing at three in the morning were thirty stories distant. In his old studio off Broadway, he could have joined their debates by leaning out the window. He pulled the leather wingback chair to the slim balcony and opened the sliding door to prop his feet on the lowest rail.

Nelson Bao was a problem. Not just the puzzle of the man's death, though that was troubling enough. The image of Bao's body, waterlogged and bloodless, persisted in Shaw's mind. His fish-white skin. The hiss of the tide as it had dripped from the sodden clothes. Shaw could set aside the memory for a few short minutes if he were focused on something—breaking into the gallery or talking to Karla, who was the right kind of distraction—but in every quiet moment in the hours since, the dead chemist had been there.

His phone rang. Ephraim Ganz.

"Ephraim," he said. "I'm back from Rohner's island."

"Oh, I'm aware. I got an earful from Linda yesterday, and today she called to fill up the other one. You assaulted some of Rohner's employees? Are you shitting me?"

"Guess you had to be there."

"Then you stick around—maybe looking to make a bad thing worse—and some guest turns up dead with you standing over him. I've never seen someone screw themselves over so fast. And I've known some real headaches. One guy spat a glob of phlegm fifteen feet onto the judge just before His Honor pronounced sentence. You should wish you were that moron."

"And now you've lost your chance to nail your schoolyard crush."

"Fuck you."

Shaw gritted his teeth. "Ephraim. You got me into this shitshow. I don't know what's going on with Rohner and his plans for world domination, but sure as hell this job wasn't what Linda Edgemont sold me. Or you."

He could hear Ganz's infuriated breathing over the line.

"Tell me," Ganz said finally.

"Are you on retainer with Droma? 'Cause if you are, this is one whopper of a conflict of interest."

"Not yet I'm not. And after vouching for you, I won't wait for their call. I just want to know what happened."

"You and me both." Shaw laid out the series of events, including his decision not to tell the cops about Rohner's suspected thief.

"Well, you adhered to your promise of secrecy. At least Rohner can't sue you for that."

"So. Edgemont."

"What about her?" said Ganz.

"Whatever Rohner's secret chemistry set is intended for, she's in on it. She was at a midnight meeting of most of the principals."

"You said yourself it didn't look like drugs. Maybe it's some trade secret and Rohner made up the bullroar about the art thief because he didn't want to tell you that part."

"I thought about that. Anders's dog-and-pony show at the gallery might have been to keep me from asking questions about the deal. Anything in Linda E.'s background I should know about?"

"You mean anything criminal. No."

"Ethics violations?"

"You're fishing. Linda was ambitious. She wanted a major income and all the perks. Those traits aren't exactly rare in our profession. Linda left the firm where I met her to become a corporate trial gunslinger. She did okay, but between you and me she never cracked the ceiling on where she expected to be. When Rohner made her an offer six or seven years ago, she went with him. Less pay, but steady. Fewer hours. Lots of attorneys do the same when they . . . mature."

"You didn't."

"I like running my own ship. And who you calling mature? My advice is be glad to be done with it. You made some money from checking their security at the Droma office. You got a couple days' free room and board. If Rohner never pays you for the island, what have you really lost?"

"Sleep."

"Yeah, well. Not to make light of a man's death, but . . . you've seen worse, haven't you?"

Shaw couldn't say anything to that.

HE DROVE TO PICK UP Wren at the house she shared with three other people in West Seattle. Her roommate and business partner, Lettie, lay on a swayback sofa on the porch, texting madly. She pointed Shaw toward the backyard with her nose. He walked straight through the house and out the warped screen door to the yard. Wren was seated on a miniature stool, tending to one of the dozens of container plants arranged in haphazard rows in the small gravel plot.

"Oregano?" Shaw guessed, looking at the leafy mass.

"Basil." She used shears to snip two inches off the center stem of one of the stalks and put the leaves into a toy bucket by her feet. "Doing so well. Another month and I'll have to repot it."

"You still have spare pots?" Shaw made a show of looking around. "I figured the city was tapped after this. We'll be forced onto the black market for terra-cotta."

She smiled and handed him the bucket. It was filled with leaves and sprigs of lavender from one of the troughs along the fence. The whole yard smelled of the lavender vying with a dozen other scents for which could bloom fastest in the new June sun. Shaw was inhaling as Wren rose smoothly into his arms for a long, deep kiss.

"Would you put that in the kitchen for me?" she said. "I'll wash up."

Shaw carried the foliage inside. The kitchen had a window to the yard. Wren rinsed her hands from the stream of a light hose coiled at the end of the row. She dashed the water from her fingers and walked to the storage bin to put away the shears.

He liked watching Wren move. They had met when she was working as a trainer for Cyndra's junior-league roller-derby team. In the months since, he'd seen her sprint and swim and throw a baseball, all with the same agility. Shaw worked out to keep fit and to burn off stress. His time in the Rangers had accustomed him to pushing himself until he dropped and then getting up and continuing. But for Wren Marchand, exercise was fun, an innate human joy like that of a child who's just mastered how to run and jump.

"Hey," she said as she wrestled the crooked screen door out of its frame. "I missed you."

"Me, too. And I'm starved. Italy or Korea?"

"For dinner? Korea."

They drove to the northern tip of West Seattle and Marination Ma Kai. The warmth of the day was hanging on tight. They took their plates of pork katsu and fish with house-made pickles to one of the picnic tables on the restaurant's patio. A water taxi from downtown named the *Doc Maynard* arrived at the nearby dock. Shaw and Wren ate their meals while watching commuters disembark and a fresh group of passengers board the hundred-foot ferry.

"You're quiet tonight," Wren said.

"Thinking. There's something I need to talk to you about, and I'm trying to figure how to start."

She rested her chin on her hand. "Start at the end and work backward. Hit me with the final statement."

"Okay. I've met someone I'd like to date, and I want to know doing that won't screw up what we have."

"That's two statements." Wren's mouth twisted in a polite smirk. "This is someone new?"

"Yeah. Her name's Karla. She'll be in Seattle for a few days."

"It's cool with me if you see other people. As long as you're safe about it."

He nodded. "You've said that."

"But you're not sure if you can believe me."

"I know you're telling the truth. I also know that if we didn't talk about this ahead of time, I'd still feel like I was betraying a trust somehow. And that I'd be setting us up for a fall. Those might be contradictory emotions."

She nodded. They sat for a moment. Wren reached across to take Shaw's hand.

"You've never asked me to stop being with Rebecca or Terry," she said. "Though sometimes I feel like you want to ask and you stop yourself."

"It crossed my mind a couple times. Rejected the idea."

"Why?"

He shrugged. "It was the price of admission. You were straight with me about how much they meant to you. That took guts."

"Do you wish I would stop seeing them without you having to ask?"

Shaw thought about that. The sun had dipped low enough that its beams reflected off the distant downtown skyline, turning the skyscrapers into brief candles, alight and then dimmed within minutes.

"No," he said. "Maybe at the start, but not anymore. They make you happy. I've had relationships break up because I wasn't around enough, or because the times I was physically present I was actually somewhere else in my head half the time."

She rubbed the ball of her thumb on the back of his hand. "I was engaged to be married once, have I told you that?"

"No."

"When I was twenty-two. It wasn't for long. When we split up, when I stopped forcing myself into knots, it was such a relief. Not having to be everything that someone needs in a partner, every day."

"I guess I don't mind that. Or trying to be that. But right now I'm good with being part of what you need."

"Me, too," she said. "Very."

"And I don't want to go out with Karla as some sort of half-assed attempt to balance the scales either."

"That's good. That wouldn't be fair to her. There aren't any scales, you know."

"I get that. It's not a contest."

"If you like Karla, you should see her. I'll still be here."

"Okay."

"Just as long as you keep looking at me like you do."

"How's that?"

"Like you're still ravenous. Can we stay at your place tonight?"

"Can. Should. Will," he said.

TWENTY-FIVE

Linda Edgemont looked at the clock on the mantel for the third time in as many minutes. A quarter to eleven at night. It felt both later and earlier.

She'd been awake since before dawn, when the deputy in his black shirt and baseball cap had thumped on the door of her suite at Briar Bay. One knock among many, as other policemen roused the rest of the guests. She recalled stumbling to the suite's door and barely following what the deputy had said to her. Not that he'd revealed much. It wasn't until she'd joined the others in the pavilion that she learned that Nelson Bao, the younger, smaller Chinese man, had died.

Not just died. *Found dead.* Very different, that phrasing.

Those two words had repeated in her mind many times throughout the long day. After an abrupt trip home she'd been delivered to her house by midmorning. She had tried to work and given up after her fourth attempt at reading the same paragraph. The notion of sitting and watching television was absurd. Offensive. As though she would be disrespecting the dead man somehow.

Which was crazy. She hadn't known Nelson Bao. She'd had relatives, even close friends, die over the years. Their passing had left her less troubled than the death of the Chinese man whom she'd met only a day before.

She knew why it bothered her so. There was a third word that threatened to reverberate in her brain, along with the other two.

Culpable.

The wine had helped some. Or at least buoyed her resolve. It was time to do what she'd been building up to—and dreading—for weeks.

She went to the kitchen and opened the bottommost drawer by

the refrigerator. Hidden beneath the muffin tins and baking supplies was a simple flip phone.

The phone only had one number programmed into its memory, with a Maryland area code and no name assigned to it. The person at the other end wasn't in Maryland, but that phone had been purchased there originally, just as hers had. Twins, like the set of walkie-talkies she and her brother had played with when they were children.

Linda pressed Call and listened to the phone at the other end ring. "Yes?"

Ed's answering startled her. She'd expected voice mail at this hour, two in the morning on the East Coast.

They didn't use names. That had been one of Ed's first instructions, when he'd handed her the phone. But she knew his voice. It was husky and a little Noo Yawk, which Linda had once found charming.

"I need to speak with you," she said.

"Here we are."

"Have you . . . do you know what happened last night?"

"Oh, yeah," said Ed. "I've been on the phone all day, handling the fallout."

"So it's done, then? The deal's canceled?"

"What? No, of course not. It's just a setback."

"A setback," she said.

There was a long silence. Ed gave in first.

"It was an accident," he said. "That's all."

Linda's head ached. She took another moment to select the right words, cautious not to blurt out something best left unsaid, like a name or an amount. Or an accusation that had nothing but her suspicions fueling it.

"It's not being treated like an accident anymore," she said. "Officially."

"Is that direct information?"

"Yes."

"Okay. That doesn't mean they're right. They have to make sure ev-

ery theory is checked off. Procedure. You know how these things roll."
He sounded as though he were persuading himself.

"I think we should stop. That I should stop."

"There's no need. Nothing has changed."

"I have. Or I need to." Linda rubbed her temple. "It's overdue."

He hummed doubtfully. "Are you negotiating? At this late date—"

"No. It's not about getting more. I don't even want what I already
have."

It was Ed's turn to take a pause. Maybe she'd said too much.

"If you need to stop, of course that's what we'll do." He coughed
lightly. "You sound worried . . . There's no reason to be concerned. I
promise you. It's just a tragedy at a terrible time for all of us. You'll see."

"Very well."

"Let's talk tomorrow. Whatever you need, we'll make that happen."

"Yes. Thank you."

Linda hung up. She closed her eyes and inhaled slowly. It felt like
the first deep breath she'd taken in weeks. Funny how stress caught
up to you. Dealing with pressure for ages and ages, thinking you were
just fine, and then all at once you were crushed in a vise of your own
making.

Ed's reassurances had helped. Of course Nelson Bao's death was
only an accident. With awful timing.

Having taken the first step, Linda felt prepared to take the worst
one. Confessing to Sofia what she'd done.

That was a conversation so fraught that the mere idea of it had
plagued Linda's dreams. She continually invented reasons it shouldn't
happen. For a time she'd even thought she might be able to live with
the situation, as terrible as it was. But no longer. Linda supposed that
was the tiny blessing that had been born from this horrible week.

Sofia would be wounded. Furious. Learning the truth might be
catastrophic to their friendship and likely Linda's career as well. But
without that confession, she couldn't face Sofia again.

Linda put the phone back in the drawer and decided that she was ready to try sleeping. Tomorrow she would reach out to Sofia. Privately, away from the office and its many inquisitive eyes.

IN THE LIGHTLESS DEN OF his Brooklyn apartment, Ed Chiarra sat and stared at the phone as its tiny screen dimmed. Its ringing had woken his wife. She was used to him receiving calls at all hours, but the ringtone of the phone assigned to Linda Edgemont was different from his regular work phone. She'd glared at him while he got out of bed in his boxers, as he'd said "Yes" into the phone and then shut up until he'd found his sweats and left their bedroom. He knew she was angry at her sleep being disturbed and probably convincing herself right now that he was having an affair.

Which was almost insulting. If he'd wanted to spread it around, shouldn't his wife of thirteen years think he'd be smarter about it than that? Keeping a cheap little burner phone in his suit jacket's pocket like some plumber from Poughkeepsie?

That domestic concern wasn't even close to being important right now. He knew that. He was just bitching to himself. Putting off what had to come next.

He went to his desk. His regular work phone was there, plugged into the charger. He called the number that was first in his contacts. James Hargreaves.

"Sir? Sorry to disturb you," Ed said.

"I was awake," said Hargreaves, with the voice that always reminded Chiarra of frozen tundra. Flat and well below zero.

"I just received a call from our Seattle asset. They're very upset. They would like to withdraw."

"Did they give a reason?"

"Not directly. But the events of the past day were . . . emotional."

"Hold."

There was a change in the pitch of the open line. Ed listened to the almost-silence for three full minutes. Staying calm. He knew what Hargreaves was doing. Listening to a voice record of the conversation

Chiarra had just had with Linda Edgemont. Every call to a company phone—temporary burners definitely included—was recorded, regardless of whether the party at the other end was aware. Standard procedure for Paragon Consulting.

"All right," Hargreaves said when he returned. "Maintain contact."

"If our asset leaves—"

"Then they leave. We always viewed them as a temporary resource."

"Okay. Sure."

"Make it clear that their silence is still required. Keep all transaction records close at hand. We may have to apply some pressure to be certain."

"Yessir. I will."

Hargreaves closed the call.

Chiarra rolled his neck to loosen the muscles. He hadn't realized he'd been so clenched. He'd thought—he didn't know exactly *what* he'd thought would happen.

There were whispers about Hargreaves around their company. The head man kept himself at a remove. Never lunching with personnel, taking most meetings by videoconference long before and after Zoom was standard procedure for everyone in the world. He even floated in and out of the office at unpredictable hours. When Chiarra had first joined the firm, he figured that distance was some air-of-mystery affectation Hargreaves cultivated to keep things professional. But before long he'd realized that, no, the man really was apart from everyone else. By nature or by training. No one seemed to know for sure where Hargreaves had worked before he'd started Paragon.

Most of what they did was bread-and-butter: a little surveillance, some forensic accounting. For Chiarra's part it was largely the same work he'd have been doing at any white-shoe firm, legal reviews of contracts and advising clients on their options. It was the other ten percent that was exciting, when he got to play a part in one of the company's cover stories. The normal mood around Paragon was casual, even fun.

Then, on an otherwise average afternoon, some hard-faced operative like Emmet Tucker would turn up unannounced, walk into Hargreaves's corner office, and shut the door. Everyone on the floor would become very subdued. Rumor had it that guys like Tucker only appeared when a job was going sideways. The office would wait, hushed, to see what mood prevailed. *Scorched earth*, he'd heard one of the senior staff call it once.

Maybe that's why he was so tense, Chiarra thought. Why his knees felt rubbery as he stood. This job, running Linda Edgemont, had been a step up for him. Her withdrawal could be viewed as his failure.

Chiarra shook his head. That wouldn't happen. He'd brought Linda in, and Paragon had gleaned great intel from her. Surely that was one in the win column.

Still, when he went into the office tomorrow, maybe he should gather a few records of his own. Some insurance. He could collect what he needed without leaving an online trail. Print a few pages and keep them close.

He nodded, feeling more at ease. Couldn't hurt to be ready to scorch some earth himself, in case it looked like Hargreaves might be sending Tucker to knock on his door some dark night.

TWENTY-SIX

At ten o'clock the next morning, Shaw arrived to pick up Addy and Cyndra. Addy's tidy yellow house sat a few doors down from where Shaw had grown up. The Shaw family home was gone now, replaced by a much more modern and far less interesting house on the same lot at the top of the block. Shaw had noticed that he didn't tend to look in the house's direction, preferring to pretend that the old place was still there, looming over the surroundings like a dented helmet on a polished suit of armor.

He drove the big black Ford pickup truck he'd acquired from the former owner of the high-rise. The truck wasn't as fun to drive as the Barracuda, but it was easier for Addy to climb in and out of.

Cyndra fell asleep in the backseat on their way to the university.

"Up all night gaming?" Shaw asked Addy, with a nod to the snoring teen.

"Gaming, talking on the phone, watching TV. All at once. So much energy she has on summer vacation, so little during the school year."

Shaw smiled. "What were *your* summer vacations like?"

"Toil and trouble, mostly. I had a job at a concession stand at Playland as a teenager. That was an amusement park near San Francisco. The place was on its last legs by then. Half the rides didn't work, and the big coasters had been torn down years before. I didn't care. I loved it. Much better than being at home, fighting with my sisters. You?"

"Felonies. With school out, Dono had me as a full-time accomplice."

"Of course."

They parked, roused Cyndra with some effort, and strolled onto the Washington campus. Addy had come with Shaw to make introductions. Cyndra stayed glued to her phone while walking.

"Eyes up, dear," Addy said, in a way that told Shaw she said the phrase multiple times each day. Cyn navigated the flock of similarly distracted undergraduates crossing their path and managed to halt before running into Shaw's back.

He'd stopped in front of the big fountain. The water soared in a twenty-foot-high central plume as half a dozen smaller jets arced outward from their larger brother. None of them spraying far enough to douse the students who sat around the rim. It was the Thursday of finals week, Addy had told him, the very end of the school year. Shaw could feel the energy. Half exhausted panic, half hysterical elation.

Shaw had been on the Washington campus a few times. Most memorably when he was near Cyndra's age, with Dono. At this same time of year, he recalled, with the spring quarter finished and before the smaller summer classes began. A job on consignment. They had removed some equipment from the storage area of the physics building in the dead of night, just a few hundred yards away from where they stood now. Shaw didn't recall what the equipment had been, only that it was heavy and still in multiple crates after being delivered a couple days prior to their visit. They had brought handcarts to pull the crates directly out the door and along the pedestrian paths to the other side of the building and into the back of a truck parked on 15th Avenue. The day before, Dono had instructed Shaw in the use of a miter saw to cut the two-by-fours that they used for a ramp into the truck bed. Shaw, as strong as he'd been at fourteen, had still needed Dono's help to pull the loaded handcart up the ramp.

"That's Bagley Hall," Addy said, pointing to a blunt building that looked to Shaw like the high school from every movie set in the 1950s. Redbrick, arched stone entrances, a flat aspect with each window divided into nine equal panes. "Professor Mills's class should be letting out. Cyndra, have a look around. You might go here someday."

"Ugh," said Cyndra. "I just got *out* of school. Let me *vacation*."

Shaw grinned. This was a running debate, a close second to wrangling Cyn's fashion choices. She had celebrated the end of her middle-school career by dyeing her hair pink and cutting the sleeves and hood off her gym sweatshirt, which she wore inside out so as not to show the now-outgrown school logo. She added cargo shorts and a pair of Doc Martens that Shaw had bought for her birthday. Addy had sighed resignedly when she saw the ensemble but let it go as they were already running late.

"I'm not saying you'll enroll tomorrow," Addy pressed, "but look at the opportunity. Educational *and* social. There's nothing to equal your college years. Everyone should have that."

"Van didn't."

"I was in the Army," Shaw said. "A different kind of schooling."

"But you didn't do college. You turned out fine."

"'Fine' might be stretching it." Shaw looked around at the rush of students hurrying between classes. Most of them didn't seem much older than Cyndra. But then he'd probably been just as wide-eyed and gawky when he'd enlisted.

"I signed up because I didn't see a better path," he said to Cyn, "and it worked out. But I was lucky. Usually." He tapped the left side of his face. "If I'd had the chance, maybe I would have gone to college instead. Here's one thing the Army taught me: Don't reject an option before you've looked hard at it. Otherwise you'll always wonder if you could have done better. You know what I'm saying?"

Cyn nodded. Addy mouthed *Thank you* over her shoulder.

"Here's the professor," she said out loud.

Shaw turned to see a tall black woman in a light blue car coat and cat-eye glasses headed toward them at a pace halfway between walking and jogging.

"Ms. Proctor," the woman said, her voice causing a passing coed to jump. "How wonderful to see you."

"Professor Mills, hello," Addy said, extending a hand. The women were similar builds, Shaw noted. What Hollis might call sturdy, meaning it as a compliment. But Mills was nearly Shaw's height, a full foot over Addy's. Like nesting dolls from the same set. And she was younger than he'd associated with the word "professor." Midthirties, max. The edge of a purplish tattoo showed above the neckline of her cotton shirt.

Mills scoffed. "Call me Jemma, please. What do you have for me here?"

Shaw realized she meant him. "Van. Hey. I've got some pictures . . ."

"Follow me. This is the one hour I have before a meeting, and I'm going to spend it in my favorite spot, with shade and a smoke, except I gave that second part up."

She strode on. Cyndra giggled as they all hurried after the professor, along a path bordering a green lawn that extended for a quarter mile. On a clearer day, Shaw knew, you might see Mount Rainier. Today the overcast sky made the professor's desire for shade moot.

Mills seemed to quickly realize the difference in leg lengths and made a circle to slow her pace and walk next to Addy.

"Habit, moving so fast," she said. "Sorry. It was Van, right? Addy here was my aunt's favorite deejay. So much so that she wrote a letter to the radio station when they moved her time slot."

"Your aunt was about the only one who noticed," Addy said, "but I appreciated it."

"You were on the radio?" Cyndra said, staring. "When was that?"

"For about fifteen minutes back when tube tops were terrorizing the nation," Addy answered. "But I wrote to thank Jemma's Aunt Bess, and we became friends."

Mills pointed to a row of benches and they sat, Shaw and Addy on either side of Mills and Cyndra happy to sprawl on her own and disappear back into the online ether.

Shaw brought up the pictures he'd taken of the laboratory and handed the phone to Mills.

"This machine," he said. "Wyvern GPC-IR. I did enough online homework to learn that GPC stands for 'gel permeation chromatography' and I know the machine has something to do with analyzing molecules. Beyond that I need your help."

Mills began speaking even as her fingers zoomed in on the image. "Good brand, the Wyvern. Yeah, this all looks like standard stuff. How much do you know about chemistry?"

"I stopped at making baking-soda-and-vinegar volcanoes in second grade."

"Okay. What GPC does is take a complex molecule—a polymer, usually—and break it down into its components so you can analyze it better. With me?"

"Yes."

"Say you've got a sample of a polymer made of many other molecules. Like nylon, to use one example. That nylon polymer will be suspended in a liquid. A machine like the Wyvern uses one or more solvents—see this bottle here?—and infrared detection to separate the different molecules based on their size in the solution and their molecular weight and other factors. What you end up with is a comparison of the different molecules that make up the nylon and data about them."

"So the GPC machine tells you what the polymer is made of?"

Mills waggled her hand. "Not exactly. It can't tell you for certain that a component of the nylon is caprolactam, for example. But if you're a chemist and you know that molecule's weight and hydrodynamic size and you already expect to find it in nylon, then it's easy to make the logical jump. GPC isn't a push-button process, but it's more advanced than the analyzers I used in grad school just a few years ago."

"What if you already knew what the polymer was made of?" asked Addy.

"Then you're testing for purity, or quality. Making sure your sample matches the expected form of the polymer."

Mills pointed to one of the photos Shaw had taken of the flasks of chemicals. "That's a polystyrene. Used to calibrate the machine. From the look of it, I'd guess the Wyvern analyzer is right out of the box and somebody just set it up for the first time."

That followed, Shaw thought. Morton had looked as excited as a kid with a new toy.

"How long does all that take?" he asked. "The setup and the testing of a sample?"

"Setting up a new machine takes at least a few hours. Looks like that job has been completed for the Wyvern, or close to it. Testing time can vary, but with a new-generation system like this I'd say only an hour or so."

"And there's nothing unusual about this in manufacturing?" he said.

"Not at all. Any company making or developing new chemicals might be running tests like this every day, maybe around the clock if they're really busy. Quality testing is often done overnight so the next-day shift has the results. One of my internships was in a QC lab." She looked again at the photo. "Where'd you find all this? That doesn't look like a chem department."

"An art gallery," Shaw said, half his mind on Chen Li and Jiangsu Manufacturing. Jiangsu was looking to establish itself in America. Did Chen's company have some innovation in polymers that would pave the way?

"It may not be art to most people, but it's beautiful to me," said Mills. "If your friends ever want to loan that Wyvern to the U-Dub, I'll buy them a big lunch. My students would love to take it for a spin."

"You never know," said Addy. "Van has the strangest way of acquiring things."

Shaw thanked Mills for her time, and she invited him to be in touch if he had further questions.

On the way home, Cyndra sat in the front seat of the truck. It was Addy's turn to nod off in the back. She'd been keeping odd hours the past week, spending half her nights at Holliday House on First Hill looking after her friend Penelope. Cyn, being on summer vacation, had been left at home to happily raid the pantry for herself.

"Do you still steal things?" Cyndra said to Shaw out of the blue.

"Are you thinking about what Addy said? My acquiring stuff?"

"Uh-huh."

"I gave burglary up a long time ago. But." Shaw waved a hand. "Life gets a little gray. I can tell you I don't take anything from honest people. From anybody at all, if I can help it."

"But you do crimes."

He looked at her, as much as he could while the truck was doing thirty miles an hour down Montlake.

"I sometimes break the law. Not for my own profit anymore. And usually when I don't see another choice. I know that's not a great answer, and I sometimes wish it were different. But it's the truth. I promised I'd always tell you the truth. As much of it as I can."

Cyn turned to look out the window. She was so small that Shaw occasionally forgot she was almost fifteen.

"You worrying on something?" he said.

She didn't answer.

After another mile he nodded. "Tell me when you're ready. I'll be here."

The rest of the ride passed in silence.

TWENTY-SEVEN

Shaw's phone buzzed just as he stepped into his apartment.

"Hi. Did I catch you at the right time?" Karla Lokosh. She had a good voice. Light but full of mirth.

"I was just about to defuse this nuclear device. But sure."

"Well, if you're still in one piece after cutting the red wire, would you like to have dinner tonight? The longest week in history will finally be over, and I have to be anywhere that's not a conference room."

"Dinner with me would qualify as anywhere."

"Thank God. I was seriously considering going to a Czech double-feature if you were busy. I doubt they have Mike and Ikes at the concession stand."

"Not nearly serious enough," Shaw agreed. "Probably goose liver pâté instead. Seven o'clock?"

"I'm at the Crowne Plaza. By the freeway."

"Right." His line beeped. "That's another call. See you tonight."

"You're in demand. I like that."

Shaw hit the button to End and Accept.

"Mr. Shaw, this is Brady from Ephraim Ganz's office. I have a Mr. Rohner on the other line, whose people have been very insistent about reaching you. Mr. Ganz won't give out this number without your approval, but . . ."

"Put him through. Thanks."

"Thank *you*, sir." Brady sounded as though he couldn't push the buttons fast enough.

While he waited, Shaw picked up the temporary phone he'd used for the job with Droma. The only number Rohner's people had for him. It had been turned off and sitting on the kitchen counter since he'd come home from the island.

The phone's log listed thirteen missed calls during the past day. Something like desperation there, he thought.

"Hello?" a female voice said.

"This is Shaw."

"One moment please. I'll have Mr. Rohner for you."

Shaw smirked. The emperor wasn't so desperate that he would stoop to dialing the phone himself.

"Mr. Shaw?"

"Yeah."

"Good. Glad we reached you. Beyond the obvious tragedy with Mr. Bao, I've become aware that your time at the island was a poor experience."

"Your chief of security tried to use my head for T-ball practice."

"Warren Kilbane has been suspended from his position, pending a review. I learned the true facts of what occurred from my daughter, and from Rangi Sua. I'd like to extend my apologies."

"A dozen calls since yesterday. That's a lot of remorse."

"There is something else we need to discuss. In person. Are you available now?"

A request rather than a summons. Rohner really did want to talk.

"I can be," Shaw said. "Where?"

"Do you know the Showbox Theater?"

"Yes." The Showbox was downtown on 1st Ave, less than a mile away.

"I'm there now."

"Fifteen minutes."

Shaw hung up and walked back out the door.

Rohner hadn't paid Shaw for his time on Briar Bay Island. But if that was all the Droma CEO wanted, he'd have told Linda Edgemont to cut Shaw a check. Maybe Rohner was going to level with him about the laboratory. Miracles do happen.

THE SHOWBOX HAD BEEN OPERATING in one form or another for over a century. In its long life, it had been a thriving ballroom and a jazz club and a furniture store and had also sat empty and unloved during the fallow years. Shaw's high-school friends Davey and Trace had once convinced him to sneak into the theater through the fire exit. Davey had been so desperate to see the metalcore band headlining the show that he'd tried to bribe the bouncers with Shaw's cash when they'd inevitably been caught. More recently Shaw and his ex, Luce, had gone to a midnight concert of Ingrid Michaelson, one of Luce's favorite performers. He'd bought tickets that time.

Shaw knocked on the locked entrance. A moment later Rangi opened it, filling the doorway from frame to frame.

"Hey," said Shaw. "What time does Nirvana go on?"

Rangi sighed, low and slow, as he moved aside to let Shaw enter.

"Rohner said you filled him in on Kilbane," Shaw said. "Thanks."

"My job. If I lie to the boss to save Kilbane's ass, my priorities are out of whack."

Rangi led him into the club, which seemed much larger when not packed shoulder to shoulder with concertgoers. Sebastien Rohner stood at the far side of the room, near the larger of the hall's two bars. Another man wearing a homburg hat and a brown plaid suit was behind the counter. In place of drinks, a file with a stack of papers thick enough to be the phone book of a major suburb lay on the bar between them.

"Mr. Shaw," Rohner said. He excused himself to his companion, who turned his attention to making notes in the file. Rohner motioned to a small table by one of the theater's unique flower-shaped pillars. "Please."

Rohner wore a tan suit with blue cuff buttons and a tie with tiny diamonds in the same color. His white-blond hair looked sleek, as if he'd just come from a health spa's steam room. He set a slim blue folder on the table.

Shaw sat across from him. He glanced at the man with the hat, who was sorting the papers with the dexterity of a Vegas dealer. "Your bookie?"

"An estate agent. I'm considering purchasing this venue."

"I didn't know Droma was in show business."

"We're not. But corporate events are an increasing part of Droma's expansion, as well as our clients' needs. Being able to offer a thousand-seat venue in downtown Seattle would be a prime motivator."

Shaw looked around at the hall. The architecture had changed since then, but he could have pointed to the spot where the bouncer had cracked up laughing at Davey's clumsy attempt at greasing his palm. Stage lights illuminated the dark blue backdrop. By the wings at stage left, he and Luce had ducked into the shadows to tease each other while Michaelson had played on.

"From concerts to product launches," he said.

"All things change. Often for the better." Rohner slid the blue vinyl folder across the table. The cover was emblazoned with the familiar orange *D*.

"What's this?"

"A two-year contract. I'd like you to fill the position vacated by Warren Kilbane. Head of site security for Droma."

Shaw's brow furrowed, and he flipped the folder open. The papers inside had been affixed to the folder with a metal clip piercing two holes punched at the top of each sheet. EMPLOYMENT AGREEMENT was the header of the first page. The legalese below it started by defining the parties of "Employer" as Droma Solutions International and "Employee" as Donovan Shaw. He hadn't seen his name on a form like this since his Army discharge papers.

The annual base salary was listed at two hundred thousand dollars. Plus a signing bonus of fifty grand, payable on his first day.

Rohner had noticed where Shaw's eyes were looking. "You would also be eligible for a specific profit-sharing bonus, related to our coming agreement with Jiangsu Manufacturing. If that deal is signed by end of month."

Shaw read a sentence near the middle of the page. "'Salary for the full term of contract guaranteed unless terminated for cause.' Like Kilbane."

"We had hired Warren on a reference which, at the time, we should have seen as a risk. I believe you are more stable. You handled the situation with poor Mr. Bao extremely well. Olen said he was impressed with your coolness and your discretion, under the circumstances. That's why I believe it's fair to include you as a key contributor to the Jiangsu deal."

"Do you always do your own hiring?"

"When there are amends to be made, I do."

After the momentary astonishment at the numbers, Shaw felt like he was getting his bearings. The job was a kind of payoff for keeping quiet. About the supposed art thief and what little Sofia Rohner had told him about the pending deal.

And maybe more. Did Rohner suspect that Shaw had discovered their laboratory? He'd been in a rush. It was possible he hadn't fully covered his tracks.

He turned to the last pages, which constituted a second document.

"The nondisclosure agreement." Rohner removed a gold pen from his pocket and set it on the table. "You'll often be in the room as we discuss details of client agreements or knowledge proprietary to Droma."

"It's backdated to last week."

"So that your starting date and salary will take effect immediately. If things go as well as I expect, there is the option of making the role permanent."

The NDA looked comprehensive. Shaw scanned a dense paragraph that forbade discussion of any aspects of Droma, the Rohner family, and all related ventures and subsidiaries in perpetuity. There was more, but he had the gist. Unless express and specific permission were granted in writing by company executives or a court order required it, Shaw would hold the company's secrets.

The salary had been a large carrot. The agreement was obviously the stick, in three pages of single-spaced type.

"I'm surprised," Shaw said, leaning back. "Or stunned. I thought you and Anders suspected me of being involved in Nelson Bao's death. Linda Edgemont called Ephraim Ganz and chewed his ass for recommending me in the first place."

"Sheriff Dayle has been good enough to keep me apprised of progress. I observed that at low tide later that afternoon his investigators were examining a loose stone on the shore, below where Mr. Bao was found. I inquired with the sheriff, and he confirmed that the case is being treated as a homicide now."

"A stone. The murder weapon?"

"He was not that forthcoming."

Salt water would have removed most of any blood and hair and whatever else of Nelson Bao had violently transferred to the stone. But "most" was not "all." Forensic labs could find damn near any trace when they knew what they were looking for.

"Given their discovery," Rohner continued, "Sheriff Dayle asked if there was anything untoward on the island during the week, and of course I informed him of Warren Kilbane's attack on you. I believe they are interviewing Warren and his team today."

Shaw continued to scan the contract, though his thoughts were elsewhere. The theory fit, to a point. Kilbane had been humiliated and dismissed. It wasn't hard to imagine the man returning to the island to make trouble. But Shaw would be the logical target for his rage, or maybe Rohner himself. How Bao had wound up dead was anybody's guess.

Rohner pointed to the pages. "Travel will be frequent. At times you will be on call around the clock. With your military background, I don't imagine that's an issue for you."

"No."

"I will need you to start immediately. We have a client in Hungary opening a new facility. I've told them that Droma will make certain their resources are safe."

Shaw looked up from a paragraph about the NDA applying to all physical properties owned by Droma and its subsidiaries and ventures in perpetuity.

"Hungary?" he said.

"Budapest. You would leave tomorrow and be on site Monday."

"It's strange timing."

"If the compensation isn't to your liking—"

He shook his head. "Whatever the opposite of sticker shock is, I've got that."

"What can I do to encourage you?" Rohner said.

Shaw closed the folder. "Let me sleep on it."

Rohner's lips tightened for an instant before relaxing into a wan smile. "Yes. You should, with a decision this size." He reached across and drew back the contract. "This will be ready for you in the morning. Contact Linda. She'll arrange for an immediate transfer of funds to your account upon signature. Assuming we have reached an arrangement by noon, we'll have you on a flight immediately." The smile broadened a fraction. "First class, naturally."

"Thanks. It's a generous offer."

"We are a generous company for valued employees. And again, I apologize that our relationship started with such turbulence. We will make that up to you. The storm before the calm."

Rohner extended a hand, and Shaw took it.

As he left the theater, Shaw nodded to Rangi, leaning against a wall like a bulwark. The big man looked back with an odd expression. Shaw was halfway down the block before he placed it.

Mournful. That was how Rangi had looked. As though he were the bearer of terrible news, the kind no one wanted to share.

TWENTY-EIGHT

Shaw didn't return to his apartment. He walked past the building, bought an egg-and-cheese sandwich at Biscuit Bitch a couple of blocks down, and ate it while watching dogs fervently chase one another in the little fenced off-leash park on Bell.

Nelson Bao's death was a homicide, according to the cops. Shaw had known that, in his gut, even while leaving himself open to the possibility of something less sinister. The chemist's bludgeoning implied something spur-of-the-moment, maybe desperate. Grab the first stone of any size and swing it. Maybe death hadn't been the intention. Manslaughter. Self-defense, even.

Kilbane may have a screw loose, but it was tough to imagine the security chief as the killer.

Tougher the more he considered it. Kilbane and Pollan and Castelli had left in the Droma runabout, Sofia had said. Before dawn. Had they gone to another island, waited the entire day and evening before coming back to . . . what? Carry out their threat of putting Shaw in traction?

And how would they have come ashore? Someone would have seen the boat if it had returned to the dock. Beaching the craft on that jagged north shore at night would have been a challenge. They would have been drenched, wading in through the waves.

No. Too many unlikely factors to fit Kilbane as the obvious suspect. Shaw felt certain that if Bao had been murdered, his killer had been someone already on the island.

Love or money or fury. Those were the big three motivations. Leave love out of it. Try wrath. Had Bao seen something or said something that had provoked an argument? From what little time Shaw had spent with the man, he'd seemed as mild as they came. A company man. If Bao had a worry, he'd have taken it to Chen, or Zhang.

So: money. Bao's death might have delayed the deal between Jiangsu and Droma, for a few days at least. Drastic as hell, if that had been the intent.

He had seen Bao's driver's license. The chemist's address was an apartment building in the Central District. After a moment's thought, Shaw brought forth the mental picture of the license in his hand. Cherry Street. Unit 204.

He tossed the last bite of his sandwich over the fence to a Labrador who caught it on the fly. The dog barked a thank-you as Shaw jogged back to the garage at his place.

He drove to the CD and parked two streets away from Bao's. The building was new construction, a three-story apartment block painted seafoam green with white-framed bay windows. Another dab of gentrification in a neighborhood changing fast. Bao's building lay at the intersection of a T. Directly across the road was the back of a much older, squatter apartment building and a deserted-looking two-bay garage that had probably been an unlicensed body shop before it closed. Shaw gave it less than a year before someone razed the abandoned shop to build town homes. On the other side of the cross street was a fellowship hall for AA meetings and other community events. Its small lot was empty save for one car.

The apartment block was a good target. Too upscale for college students, too new to have many retirees. Most of the residents were probably at their day jobs right now. And the surrounding buildings were golden. Few neighbors who might take notice of a stranger poking around.

Slim bars blocked the windows on the first story. The neighborhood wasn't and would probably never be so renovated as to not require bars. He climbed the stoop to the entrance. The intercom to ring residents was a digital model. He looked up Bao and typed in the call number. The screen said CALLING—though there was no sound. After a moment the screen went back to the list of names. No answer. No camera inside the foyer either.

He used his pick gun on the entrance and was walking up the

stairs within half a minute. The air in the second-floor hallway was stale. His weight didn't cause the floor to squeak; an advantage of new construction. The building's designers had created shallow niches in the wall between each apartment door and a green plastic spider plant in a clay pot adorned each niche. He examined the door to Unit 204 without haste or much worry. Almost no apartments at this price level would have alarms preinstalled for the residents. Too much hassle with resetting codes for every new tenant and people accidentally activating them day and night. And no tenants would have put in an alarm for a place they would leave when the lease was up.

There was always the chance of DIY security. Nanny cams and similar off-the-shelf measures were cheap and easy. But Bao was dead. He wouldn't be checking the feed from a Wi-Fi camera. Shaw put on his gloves, entered the apartment, and searched the obvious places for an alarm panel. Clear.

It didn't take more than a glance to peg the one-bedroom apartment as a bachelor's. A tidy bachelor, but still. There was a casualness to the place. Magazines and ashtrays and sundry items on every surface. The furniture crooked. A rumpled blanket and pillow tossed to the side of the couch. Shaw could smell the cigarette fumes that had permeated the fabrics.

He gave the apartment a rapid search. The drawers and coat closet and larger closet in the bedroom held a surprising amount of clothes and shoes; Bao seemed to have outfits for every occasion.

In the drawer of the coffee table, he found a manila envelope. Inside were pay stubs and a W2 form for the past calendar year from a company called Avizda. The latest pay stub was from February. The name on all the papers was Yuen Si-Lung. Bao's Chinese name. Avizda was in Dallas. Shaw put the envelope back where he found it.

Most of the magazines were in Chinese, the lone exception being an issue of *Car and Driver*. The seven-foot couch and a fifty-five-inch TCL with Roku for streaming made it clear where Nelson had spent most of his hours while at home.

The food in the kitchen was basic bachelor chow in both English

and Asian packaging. Soups and large frozen meals and noodles, anything that could be heated and eaten inside of ten minutes. Shaw felt a
little sympathy; Bao's apartment seemed like more a place to keep his
clothes and television than somewhere he called home.

In the bedroom Shaw found a power strip plugged into the wall
outlet and filled with various chargers waiting for phone and laptop
and tablet. The tablet turned up in the nightstand drawer, flanked by
folded washcloths and a plastic bottle of silicone lube. Shaw tapped
the tablet screen with a knuckle. The device was locked, but the wallpaper image behind the password prompt was that of an Asian woman
lying on a bed, the sheet arranged to enhance rather than conceal her
attributes.

At least Bao had some secrets, Shaw thought, predictable as they
were. It would have been weirder *not* to find porn in a single man's
apartment.

That thought made Shaw stop. A single man.

He went back to the closet. Lots of clothes. Not all the same size.
A few of the dress shirts would have billowed on the slight Nelson
Bao. Two of the pairs of shoes were size ten and the rest size eight and
a half.

A partner? The image of the woman on the tablet implied Bao was
straight, or maybe bisexual. Another man's clothes in his closet hinted
at something different.

Shaw looked at the bed. It had been made. The sheets were a fraction straighter on the left than on the right. One nightstand. One
lamp. He pulled the top layers back to look at the fitted sheet underneath. The right side had many more wrinkles and creases than the
left, and the mattress sagged slightly.

Bao slept alone on the queen bed, at least most of the time, Shaw
concluded. Not definitive, but interesting. Why would an occasional
lover keep so many clothes here?

Not *that* many clothes. No more than might fit in a suitcase.

Shaw went to the coat closet in the front room. Two large roller
suitcases had been stacked beneath the hanging jackets. Different

brands. He looked again at the blanket and pillow on the overlong couch.

Not a lover. A guest. Somebody from out of town, crashing here.

Shaw had a pretty good idea who. The other half of Chen Li's team. The larger clothes and shoes in the closet would fit the athletic Zhang just fine.

He turned his attention to possible hiding places, starting with the living room. The closet doors were hollow-core, like in most rental apartments, but their laminated wood edges were glued tight, straight off the factory line. He shone his penlight into each air vent. Pressed every cushion on the couch and checked the seams for anything sewn within. The apartment had no baseboards or crown molding that might conceal a hidey-hole. The curtain rods were solid.

Shaw wound up back at the door, frowning at the impassive room. It would be easier if he knew what he was looking for.

The kitchen was next. He looked behind and within the oven and the refrigerator. When he went to check the range hood above Bao's little-used stove, he placed the Phillips-head screwdriver tip into the first corner screw. The mesh vent screen lifted at the slight pressure.

He withdrew in surprise, and the screen clanged softly back down. He pushed on the screen with a finger. It lifted again, tilting up into the chimney of the hood on an unseen hinge, like an upside-down trapdoor.

Shaw reached up and inside. Just past the open screen, his gloved hand encountered something familiar and unmistakable.

The grip of a gun.

He withdrew and shone his penlight up into the hood's chimney. A rigid Kydex holster had been duct-taped to the metal interior of the square pipe, the butt of the gun protruding from it. The gun was pointing straight up, held in place by the tension of its holster. On the opposite side of the chimney, a small parcel of black fabric had been similarly taped in place.

Shaw reached up again and drew the gun out by pinching it near the rear sight. He examined it, taking as much care as he could not to smudge any prints on its grip or barrel. Etched on the slide was the model: QSZ-92. Chinese manufacture. He'd never seen one before. Its magazine was full of nine-millimeter rounds, the chamber empty. Unfired since its last cleaning. The oil smelled like something bought in a hardware store, not the more industrial scent of a protectant straight from the maker. A few light scratches on the slide and at the tip of the barrel suggested that the pistol had seen some use.

A personal weapon, then. A gun that had been fired many times, at least on a range.

Shaw replaced the pistol in its suspended holster and pantomimed standing in front of the stove and reaching up to the gun, his right side angled toward the stove, since the holster had been set for someone right-handed. He punched upward, and the range hood's screen popped open and the gun was there. With practice, drawing the weapon would take barely a second.

He looked toward the front door. For someone standing where Shaw was now, the refrigerator and the stomach-high counters made good cover. Of all the places in the apartment, it was the best choice for defense.

Question was, defense from whom? Maybe it didn't matter. Zhang seemed the type to be prepared for the worst-case scenario.

Shaw reached up into the vent to unpeel the tape and remove the small black parcel. It was a bag, its fabric wrapped snugly around the contents. He emptied the bag onto the kitchen counter.

A Chinese passport, with the familiar red folder, plus a Hong Kong Special Administrative Region passport in royal blue. An extra magazine for the pistol, also loaded. And a stubby clear vial with a white cap, about the size of his little finger, like a travel jar for eye cream or other cosmetic.

Shaw looked at the vial first. The liquid inside the glass cylinder was thick and brownish. Fluid, but just barely. The consistency of molasses. Just enough of it to fill the bottom third of the little vial.

A slim ribbon of white label with a green stripe had been affixed to the vial. Printed in tiny font on the label was a bar code and a string of characters. 146/22.3b/115214012021/JBF. The twelve sequential numbers could be a time and a date from the past January. Beyond that the label was a riddle to him.

He unscrewed the vial. The liquid's astringent scent made Shaw draw back his head quickly. Definitely not eye cream, if you wanted to keep that eye.

The Chinese passport was for Zhang Chao. The name on the Hong Kong regional passport was Liu Fan. Both had a photo of Zhang, taken at different times. Same slightly angry expression in each. Both documents looked authentic, with biometric data chips. Paper-clipped to the inside back cover of each passport was a laminated resident ID card, much like a driver's license, each with its own photo and matching the name and region of its passport.

Four different pictures of Zhang. None of them telling him the whole truth.

The gun, the different IDs, what looked to be a cover story with Jiangsu. All of that painted a pretty clear picture of a spy, or at least some kind of Chinese government operative.

Shaw put the items back into the bag, wrapping the fabric around the bundle and refastening it with the tape inside the chimney.

He'd been inside the apartment for thirty-five minutes. Too long for an occupied residence. But the range hood might not be Zhang's only stash. He decided on a quick check of the bedroom.

Within twenty seconds, he regretted his choice. He had just knelt to check the baseboards in the closet when footsteps clomped in the hall just outside the front door.

Shaw lunged for the window and stopped himself just as abruptly. The door was already opening. If he took the few seconds to open the window and knock out the screen to jump, the sound would attract immediate attention. He would be seen running away. He dropped down on the far side of the bed.

Caught like a junkie sneak thief, he thought furiously. Overconfident. He should have disabled the door lock to buy himself time. The stuck lock might have been chalked up to malfunction.

The door shut. He heard the steps on the faux-hardwood floor. Dress shoes, not sneakers. Likely a man, from the weight. It must be Zhang, coming home.

Shaw inhaled and let the breath out slowly. The man was back from his day at work, whatever that work was. He would use the bathroom, or turn on the oversize television, and Shaw would have the moment he needed to slip out the window.

Then he heard a hollow clang of metal hitting metal. He'd made the same sound himself just minutes before, when he'd opened the vent on the range hood above the stove.

Zhang was retrieving his gun.

Did he know Shaw was here?

Shaw didn't fancy trusting in the angry-faced operative's mercy if Zhang walked into the bedroom and found him hiding behind the box spring. Nothing to do but run for it. With one eye on the doorway, he reached up and unlatched the window and slid it sideways, as silently as he could. He was about to shove the screen out and jump when he heard the front door open, and close, and its dead bolt click home.

Had Zhang left? Was it a trick? Shaw listened. No sound from the outer rooms. He risked moving to the bedroom door and peering out, ready to run and dive full force out the second-story window if the spy started shooting.

The apartment was empty. He gave it a count of five before looking out the living-room window, down to the street.

Chen Li was on the sidewalk in front of the building, in a wool overcoat and cloth cap, walking in his deliberate fashion to a silver Infiniti sedan parked at the curb. As Shaw watched, Chen got into the sedan and drove away.

It had been Chen he'd heard, not Zhang. And the senior man had gone straight to Zhang's hiding place.

Shaw returned to the range hood. The parcel with the passports and the vial of chemical was gone, and so was the gun.

Cleaning house. Moving Zhang's items to a more secure location, or perhaps leaving town entirely.

Of the things Zhang had hidden, the vial with its chemical was the most intriguing. The Jiangsu men had thought it worth stashing. And the laboratory on the island had been set up to analyze chemicals. Not a huge leap to guess that the chemical might be crucial to the business deal. Perhaps it was the motivation for all Rohner's secrecy. Maybe even valuable enough to kill for.

Shaw left the dead man's apartment and made sure to lock up behind himself.

TWENTY-NINE

He was due to pick up Karla Lokosh in an hour at the Crowne Plaza, a business hotel just off the interstate. A choice that implied Bill Flynn didn't make his Bridgetrust team travel on the cheap, but he wasn't going to spring for the Fairmont Olympic either.

He showered and thought about what to wear. Shaw had forced himself to acquire some clothes other than jeans and work shirts during the past few months. Dating Wren had been part of that decision. She dressed well whenever they went out, which he perceived as her way of showing a kind of respect, for the occasion as well as for him. He'd wanted to meet her halfway.

The night was warm. He picked a plaid shirt in muted red, gray trousers, and a dark blue lightweight jacket. Addy had proclaimed it a Harrington jacket, which he'd had to look up. Shaw didn't think he looked much like James Dean in it, but it fit across his shoulders, and that was good enough. Shaw had never liked dress shoes. He was accustomed to hiking boots or running shoes, anything that he could move in. Hard soles on dress shoes slipped, and rubber ones looked like a cop's footwear. He compromised by finding chukka boots with crepe rubber soles and working conditioner into the leather for a week until the boots were as flexible as fabric.

He drove to the Crowne Plaza and found a spot at the curb. As he walked toward the hotel, a text chimed on his phone.

I'm in the lobby. K.

The Plaza lobby was a two-level atrium. On the upper level, bar tables made a line along the railing overlooking the entrance. Karla was seated alone on the left side, typing into her phone.

As Shaw came off the elevator, a waiter removed two half-empty wineglasses from her table. She looked up from signing the bill and smiled.

"That was fast," she said.

"I'm early. I figured I'd have time to hang around and make the concierge nervous."

"I just finished meeting with Morton." She waved with her free hand, *What can you do?* "He's brilliant at his job, but it's like pulling teeth with chopsticks to get him to tell you something. And when he does . . ." She shook her head.

"He's a jackass?"

"A condescending jackass. And clients feel it, too. Once we're home from this job, I'll recommend we toss him out with his used vape cartridges."

"You speak your mind."

"Yes I do. And I trust you. Even if you had a reason to throw a wrench into this deal with Droma, I don't think you would."

"Not if they've been straight with me."

Karla looked at him quizzically. "You say that like they haven't. Is there something I should know?"

"Yes, but it's a longer story. Shop talk over dinner?"

"Great. Wine on an empty stomach isn't my usual habit."

She stood up. She wore an emerald-green cowl neck blouse with a skirt that was short enough to show off graceful knees and an inch of thigh as a bonus. Like Shaw, Karla had chosen footwear for comfortable walking, some sort of combination shoe and sandal. The low heels put the top of her red curls near Shaw's chin.

"We can find good food almost anywhere," he said. "You're the sightseer. What sights would you like to see?"

The corner of her mouth turned up. "Take me somewhere touristy. The cheesier the better. What's that place where they throw fish?"

"The Market. But the fish will be grounded by now. Salmon are morning fliers." He jabbed a thumb in the direction of downtown. "We could walk the waterfront, plenty of souvenir shot glasses and

snow globes made with Mount St. Helens ash down there. Or the
Space Needle."

"Yes. Perfect."

They walked out of the hotel and down to the car. Karla tilted her
head at the sight of the Barracuda, with its gleaming paint the color of
an old penny and its black vinyl top.

"A muscle car," she said.

"Happenstance," said Shaw. "I needed a vehicle. The owner's heir
was letting this go."

"Handy when Smokey's on your tail, I'll bet."

He grinned and opened the passenger door for her. "Yeehah."

They parked the car in a lot across from the blobby red façade of
MoPOP, the museum for pop culture. By the undulating bronze walls
at its north end, Karla stopped at the statue of Chris Cornell. Shaw
pointed out the monorail speeding toward them on its elevated track.
It hissed past, a dragon on urgent business.

The Needle stood almost directly behind the museum. Karla inhaled as she leaned back to take in the sight.

"It's . . . delicate," she said. "Amazing."

Shaw looked at the spire. He'd seen it half the days of his life, it
seemed. Often from an angle just like this one, when he would mess
around Seattle Center as a kid. Just another part of the landscape. A
big tree in the backyard.

The summer-evening crowd around the Needle was thick with
families, the kids tired and complaining after a day of activity and the
parents anxious to be on the observation deck in time to see the sunset. Shaw and Karla opted out of the line and bought tickets for two
hours later. They walked three blocks south to Denny Way and a Thai
restaurant Shaw knew.

"Sebastien Rohner offered me a job," Shaw said once they'd ordered and poured tea.

"Really? I thought . . ." Karla mimed breaking a twig.

"That was my impression, too. That Droma wouldn't trust me to
change the soap in the company bathrooms. But Rohner said he liked

how I handled the trouble with Nelson Bao. A two-year contract as their new security chief and an apology from the man himself rolled into one."

"That's wonderful. So you and I will be working together."

"Nope. If I take the job, I'll be on a plane tomorrow for Budapest."

"What's in Budapest?"

"Goulash? Rohner was a little vague. Site security for a new client was as far as he would go until I sign the papers."

"Ah, those lovely NDAs." Karla blew on her tiny cup of tea.

"Have you heard whether their deal with Jiangsu is going to continue?" said Shaw, thinking of Chen Li making off with Zhang's passports and the little vial of chemical.

"We hope so. It's up to Mr. Chen. He has to come to the table and prove viability."

"Viability to do what?"

"To create a product with a decent ROI. Return on investment. Within three to five years, ideally. Chen's company is expanding now because they say they have a breakthrough, or at least a good shot at one, theoretically. Nelson Bao was brought in to talk through the details on Chen's innovation. Morton's here to explain it to us laypeople."

That would explain the laboratory, if they'd intended to demonstrate some part of the chemical reaction or whatever that Chen had invented. And it would certainly explain the secrecy.

"I'm guessing you can't tell me what this innovation is," Shaw said.

"I can't. It's proprietary information for Bridgetrust Group. But even with that, I hardly know anything beyond a cursory description. The conference at the island didn't get too far."

"So what happens now? Chen brings another chemical engineer from Hong Kong to replace Nelson?"

Karla's eyes widened. "If we're being detached about it, yes."

"Sorry if that sounded cold. If I'm going to be Droma's new security chief, my first concern is for the safety of the next guy in line."

"I thought Nelson died by accident."

"Rohner says that theory isn't holding up. The cops are looking at Warren Kilbane now."

"Oh, my God. Why would he have killed Nelson? He'd barely met him."

The food came. They both let the plates sit.

"I didn't have a clue before," Shaw said. "But from what you've told me, now I'm wondering how much Kilbane knew about the pending deal with Chen. If he was going to get canned from Droma, maybe he came back to the island looking for information on Chen's break-through. A formula, a design spec, anything that might help him sell the innovation to another manufacturer."

"And Kilbane found Nelson Bao. Could he have forced Nelson to tell him the details? Or . . ."

"What?"

Karla looked at him, her hazel eyes doubtful. "If Bill knew I was talking about this, I'd be as finished as Morton . . ." She sighed. "Chen's team brought a sample of . . . of a chemical they'd created to the is-land. Morton and Bao weren't only there to talk about the process— they had planned to do some actual tests. Preliminary assessments, but enough to build some confidence that Jiangsu Manufacturing had the goods."

Shaw thought of the vial of chemical at Bao's. Had that vial been the sample? Or just one of multiple batches? Chen might have brought a gallon of the stuff from his manufacturing plant.

"Could Bao have been carrying some of the chemical on him?" he said.

"I don't know. Once Nelson was found, Mr. Chen and that tough guy Zhang just clammed up. I'm not even sure they talked with the Rohners. I *know* Chen didn't tell Bill what was going on. Only that they would be in touch soon. My boss is chewing his nails off. He wants answers, and Sebastien doesn't have any to give. I'm talking too much."

She looked at the restaurant. No one was seated near them, and the staff was well out of earshot, which Karla likely knew, but her glance seemed more from nerves than any real concern.

"Whoever has that chemical sample—if it was taken—is holding something that could ruin the deal if it's not returned," she said.

"It's that critical?"

"A career maker. No, a company maker."

"Can't Chen just whip up more of it?"

"Sure. But if the sample falls into other hands, like a rival manufacturer, then they might reverse-engineer the formula. It becomes a race to see who can perfect the product and provide the details to apply for a patent. A company has to provide rafts of testing data, which can take months or years. They must prove its marketability or utility, too. A big corporation could put a lot of resources behind that race."

Shaw understood. Secrecy was paramount until Chen got his backers and made enough progress to outpace any competition. Rohner's job offer and the gag order that went with it were making more sense. Maybe the hasty travel plans, too.

"If Kilbane did steal the chemical," Karla said, "the smart thing to do would be to offer it back. He could conceivably get more money by selling it to a rival company, but it's a bird in the hand. Chen would pay very well just to keep it safe."

She looked at her bowl of red curry. "I guess we should eat. Though I've lost some of my appetite."

"Let's change the subject. Tell me about growing up in Boston."

They talked through the meal. Shaw learned Karla was thirty-two and had been divorced six years from a guy who sold commercial real estate. She and her husband had both had enough doubts about the marriage to put off having children. She made use of her background in dance by teaching classes for kids and teens at a local studio. Shaw told her some of the more socially acceptable parts of his history, including adjusting to civilian life after the Army. They agreed that good things came out of those unexpected swerves in life, but at the time they were a bitch and a half.

"Are you seeing anyone?" he asked.

The left corner of her mouth turned up again. Shaw was growing to like that expression of hers. It hinted at sly humor.

"For once I'm not the first to ask," she said. "Nothing serious. You?"

"One thing serious. But not exclusive, and it's not going to be."

"Huh. Is that her choice or yours?"

"Started as hers. I think we've come around to both of us. The relationship works."

Karla nodded. "Well, that's the prize. It's hard enough just creating something functional. I've tried." She toasted that sentiment with tea.

Shaw neglected his food to watch her as they talked. When Karla told a story, she committed. Her mouth was wide. She had a habit of tucking the locks of her red hair behind her right ear when she said something even mildly risqué. He was so wrapped up in their conversation they nearly overshot their ticket time. The sun had set by the time they left the restaurant. Karla took Shaw's arm while they walked quickly back to the Needle and gripped it tight as the elevator whisked them skyward to the observation deck.

They stood at the rail on the western side for a time, just looking. A few last paint strokes of silver hovered over the Olympic Mountains. The rest of the sky had become a precarious balance of blues: midnight for the clouds, navy to match Lake Union to the east, and sapphire for the open horizon ahead. The truce was short-lived. Even as they watched, the blues bled into a more uniform charcoal gray, like a blackboard wiped with a sponge at the end of the day's lessons.

Karla tugged Shaw downstairs to the showpiece of the renovated landmark, a revolving glass floor with a view of five hundred vertical feet to the pavement. They looked down past their shoes at the gilded glow of the streetlights and the brighter ant-farm paths of traffic, until the inexorable movement of the floor, shifting a single degree every ten seconds, gave them vertigo.

"That's not fair, Van. You promised me a tourist trap." Karla looked out at the horizon. "This is beautiful. How often do you come here?"

"This is it. First time."

"How is that possible? You grew up here."

"How many people in Cairo never visit the pyramids? You're here, you see it every day, going up to the top seems redundant."

"Huh. Well, I got you to try something new." She grinned. "And I'm buying the drinks to celebrate, since you bought the tickets. C'mon."

They discussed possible bars while waiting for the elevator. Shaw asked what Karla liked to drink, and the revelation that they both leaned toward whiskeys, neat, led them to talking about favorite bars in their pasts.

Karla was also doing a more direct kind of leaning, pressing softly against Shaw's arm. The crowd for the elevator wasn't so tight as to demand such close contact. Her hair smelled faintly of cloves and a flower he couldn't place. A rose, maybe, like on the island. He found himself inhaling slowly.

"We could just buy a bottle . . ." he said.

"And take it back to my room." Karla raised a skeptical eyebrow, but the twist at the side of her mouth was back. "Is that what you had in mind?"

"That's in my mind. Yeah."

Karla tilted her head up to whisper in his ear. "Okay. But I pick the poison."

KARLA'S ROOM WAS ON THE fifteenth floor, with a view of the interstate winding its way out of downtown. She kept most of the lights off so they could enjoy the diffused orange radiance of the city coming in through the window. They drank, and talked, and then without more discussion set their glasses down at the same time and began to kiss.

She undressed with a kind of urgency. Shaw helped with her skirt, sliding it down and off her elegant legs as she leaned forward and caressed the muscles of his back with her fingers. When he stood up, she kept her arms around his neck, and it was the easiest thing in the world to lift her and carry her to the bed.

Naked, their paces met and matched. They drew their hands over each other, finding the places that evoked low, trembling reactions and circling back to them a little faster each time. Karla moved sinuously, without apparent effort. Gliding with his movements. Shaw wondered briefly whether her fluid harmonization was a by-product of her dance training, before what she was doing to him made any coherent thought impossible.

HE WOKE MUCH LATER. The tangerine glow from outside had dimmed as wind swept the overcast sky. No clouds to catch and hold the light. He stared at the black wedge of night for a time. Karla lay beside him, breathing the easy rhythm of deep sleep, the bedsheet pulled so far up her body that only her feet and a tangle of red locks showed.

Shaw rose and went to the bathroom. He closed the door before flipping the broad switch and squinted in the aggressive brilliance of the mirror bulbs. The water was cold out of the tap. He splashed his face and shoulders. An assortment of folded towels had been left by the housekeepers on a rack above the toilet. He took one and dried himself, looking idly at the collection of makeup and other sundries that covered the narrow shelf below the mirror. Karla invested in higher-end cosmetics.

Her travel kit hung from the back of the bathroom door, atop the hotel robe. A plastic card was tucked into one of the mesh pockets; Shaw recognized the edge of the purple-and-blue logo of a national chain of gyms, whose selling point was being open around the clock in every location. No photo on the back, just a magnetic strip and a bar code and a name at the bottom in block letters. The name wasn't Lokosh. He drew it out to look. HAIDEN, K.

Haiden. Karla had been married. The card looked new. Maybe she used her maiden name for her professional life and her married name for personal stuff, or vice versa. Seemed complicated, but then Shaw didn't have to worry about privacy and safety in the same way that a woman did.

He set it back in the travel kit and returned to the bed. A couple more hours of rest, and he would leave his car where it was and walk up the hill to see how Addy was doing with her friend Penelope.

Karla rolled to nestle against his back. She murmured and was asleep again. He felt her slow exhalations on his spine, the condensation of her breath warming and then chilling the vertebrae there.

THIRTY

Shaw emerged from the hotel onto Seneca Street. The sky atop First Hill was a lusterless gray, the clouds backlit but not yet given definition by the dawn. Addy would be at Holliday House. Less than half a mile's walk, and Addy was usually up before the sun.

He'd meant to start even earlier. But Karla had been the first to wake and had roused Shaw in a way that, if he were King of the World, he might choose to start every day. The situation had escalated. By the time they parted, overheated and gasping, the red digital numbers on the hotel clock had ticked past 5:30. They had showered and shared a cup of coffee from the in-room brewer. She'd asked him to let her know what he decided about the job with Droma.

Chalk it up to Karla's considerable charms; Shaw had hardly thought about Rohner's offer since early last night. He might be on a plane to Hungary within hours. Fifty grand richer, plus benefits, if he was prepared to become a corporate employee for the first time in his life. Addy might offer some advice on that.

He made a straight path across the empty intersection into Freeway Park. Following the diagonal slash of green space in the heart of the city would take him over the interstate and deposit him near Terry Avenue and the care home.

He hadn't been through the park since before he'd left Seattle for the Army. The city had cleaned it up some. When he was a kid, Dono had warned him about walking through the park at night, which of course had just encouraged Van and Davey Tolan and other friends to go there whenever they could. At least four of them were required, their unvoiced rule for safety in numbers. If the fountains were turned on, they would wade in the pools until someone told them to get the hell out. They'd climb the striated concrete blocks like monkeys to sit on the top ledge and watch the traffic on the overpass or, later, to look at girls walking the paths. Somewhere around age fifteen, they'd lost interest in just looking and began to hang out in other parts of the city. The park had been forgotten.

Seeing the park now, Shaw appreciated the contrast of the trees and lawns with the Brutalist boxes above the fountains. The concrete slabs would have been ugly anywhere else, rain-streaked and spotted with lichen. The enveloping green and the water below made the blocks seem like misplaced bits of some ancient Incan temple. As he walked past, he caught the glitter of dozens of coins beneath the still, shallow water. Offerings to the rain god. Or maybe for sun, since that was the rarer deity.

Running footsteps, coming from behind. More than one set. Too fast and too purposeful to be casual joggers.

Shaw didn't hesitate, just sprinted forward. Instinct told him that turning to look would be enough for his pursuers to close the distance. He heard a curse from one of them as he launched himself forward.

He had started from a walk. They had already been in full flight. Their steps neared even as he accelerated. Almost at his heels now. A relay baton could have been passed between outstretched hands.

Shaw was fast for his size. Sprinting had come easy to him as a kid, and he could still burn up a track. One of the men grunted, maybe reaching to grab a handful of Shaw's jacket and missing. They rounded the turn at the end of the park. Up the long stone staircase, his pursuers one step behind, then two. He was winning. The interstate was below them now and the top of the stairs within a few steps. A fast dash to 8th Ave and he would be home free.

The tackle came from his right. Shaw saw the man coming, saw the triumphant eyes above the surgical mask, and he juked to dodge the hit. A heavy arm caught him for an instant around the waist, and it was over. One of his pursuers slammed full tilt into his back, and the other hit him low on the thigh, and they all crashed to the concrete paving.

Shaw threw a fist into the mask to his left. Something crunched behind the fabric. His legs were pinned beneath the weight of one of the others. A third man grabbed his right arm, trying to twist it over his head. Shaw flailed wildly, getting enough space to reach out, feel the man's mask with his fingers. He jabbed his thumb into the eye socket. The man yelled, and for an instant the pressure lightened. Then one of them fell, knees hard into Shaw's chest. His head banged off the pavement. He couldn't breathe.

"Stick him, goddamn it," said the largest of them, the one pinning his legs.

Shaw saw the syringe, and the needle. He tried to get his arm free to grab it, block it, anything.

"Hey!" A shout, not far off. A whistle blew, high and piercing.

The slim one holding the hypodermic turned toward the sound. Shaw thrashed with all his strength. The man toppled off his chest. Another blast from the whistle speared through the park.

"Fuck. Deal with that," the big one gasped, crawling to reach for Shaw's arm with dark hands as his partner let go.

He missed. Shaw had a hand free. He lashed out at the closest of them, the same face he'd punched a moment before. Blood sprayed from behind the man's mask, and he fell back, tangling with the smaller man who held the syringe. Shaw kicked hard and hit the large one in the shoulder, hearing a hiss of pain.

His legs were free. He rolled and got to his feet and ran.

Too slow. He had no wind. They would catch him in seconds. To stay in the park was suicide. He lunged left, toward the short concrete wall edging the grounds. If there was an embankment beyond, he could jump down, get to the streets and have a chance of losing them in the streets—

No. They were still over the interstate. A thirty-foot vertical drop onto the northbound lanes.

Below and to his left, a mound of dirt had been heaped on a square abutment between the freeway and a curving on-ramp. Maybe intended for some construction project within the park supports beneath them. Twenty feet down to the steep pile.

No time to debate. They were coming. He sprinted two yards to his left and vaulted the wall. A grasping hand brushed his jacket, an instant too late.

Shaw plummeted.

He hit the soft earth feetfirst and crumpled into a ball from the impact even as he rolled to his right, his momentum carrying him down the mound like a wheel. Dirt filled his mouth and eyes.

Too fast to stop. He was going to tumble off. Fall into the six-foot gap between the dirt mound and the elevated lanes, to break his back or worse far below. As his legs came underneath him, Shaw pushed off desperately, trying to launch himself over the span.

He struck the road on his side, rolling onto the interstate. Pitted concrete scraped the fabric from his elbow and the skin from his hands. He felt a rush of hot wind on his face as a car flew past at sixty miles an hour. A furious bull bellowed. Shaw scrambled to one knee, dazed. The colossal grille of an eighteen-wheeler bore down on him. He flung himself aside, catching a shuddery glimpse of the driver's terrified face and the wheels turning. The truck boomed past, its wake whipping Shaw's shirt and jacket as if he'd been slapped. Its rear tires missed his leg by the width of a bootlace.

More horns howled. But Shaw was on his feet now, teetering on the faded white stripe between lanes like a man walking a tightrope. The oncoming traffic blared and screeched its terror. He dodged a minivan and stumbled across the remaining lanes. His knee twinged with every step. He ignored it. His attackers might still be in pursuit, circling on foot or in a car.

He reached the shoulder on the far side, touched the wall of the underpass with raw palms, and pushed off to keep going. North. A hundred yards up the freeway, Hubbell Place curved to run alongside the northbound lanes. City streets, and a dozen ways to disappear. Shaw focused on putting one foot in front of the other, faster and faster as the morning sun broke through the pall of clouds. Racing for daylight.

THIRTY-ONE

My Lord," Addy said. "What happened to you?"

The adrenaline rush of having escaped had worn off by the time Shaw reached Holliday House and snuck around back to tap on the TV-room window. His fingers left daubs of wet dirt on the glass, matching the smears he made on the stucco wall as he leaned exhaustedly against it. Addy had pulled back the curtain and, after a moment's understandable gawking, motioned to the back door. She'd made him take off his muddied jacket and boots before coming inside. His pants were equally filthy and torn in two places from his tumble into speeding traffic.

Addy led him to what appeared to be a game room for the residents. The floor was linoleum, easy to wipe up the clots Shaw left. He tried to get his teeth to stop chattering.

"Don't suppose you have an extra hoodie or something," he said.

"There's a lost and found. It might have a discard. You had a bad night, I take it."

"The night was first-rate. It's the morning that's been rough." He sat down on the floor to rest his back against a Barcalounger. Donated, like almost all the care home's furniture. Its covering felt like steel wool. Or maybe that was his skin. His legs ached as though each muscle had been struck with an aluminum bat. His knee protested at being straightened.

"I need to check on Penelope," said Addy. "Make us some tea or something." She waved a distracted hand at the kitchenette opposite the TV room.

Shaw stayed where he was. Preoccupied by thoughts of what had happened at the park.

Three men had attacked him. More than that, they'd tried to

dope him. Or worse. The memory of the hypodermic made Shaw's jaw clench. At least it stopped his teeth rattling.

If he hadn't known better, the assailants would be an easy match with Kilbane and Castelli and Pollan. Those three had plenty of motivation to make a run at him.

Except that the Droma security squad was uniformly tall and white. Even the woman on Kilbane's team, Pollan, had a honed V shape from long hours in the weight room.

The men in the park had been unalike, from one another as well as from Kilbane's people. Shaw remembered the dark hands and forehead above the mask of the largest attacker, the man who seemed to be their leader. The one whose nose he'd likely broken was broad and short, with a powerful bulldog physique. The last man, the one with the syringe, had been wiry.

A different crew. New enemies.

That didn't necessarily absolve Kilbane. He might have hired thugs to take Shaw out. What had been their plan? To give Shaw a hot shot of heroin and antifreeze and watch him spasm his way into death? Maybe the dope was to knock him out for a while, get him someplace where Kilbane could take his sweet time breaking every bone.

Then Shaw thought of Karla. The crew must have known he was at the hotel with her, to have been waiting for him outside.

Had they tailed the Barracuda from his apartment? That would require them to know where Shaw lived. A big hurdle. The apartment's lease had been signed over to Shaw, but it wasn't where he received his mail, nor was it his address of record for banking and credit cards. Leaving aside friends like Wren and Addy, the only people aware of Shaw's real address were the management company, the lawyer who'd handled the lease, and a lieutenant he knew in the SPD.

No. He hadn't been followed. They must have latched on to him after he'd arrived at the Crowne Plaza.

Maybe they'd been watching Karla. Spotted Shaw on the date

with her and waited through the night. Once they saw him leave the lobby and walk away on foot, they took the opportunity. Dropped two of the team off to run into the park after him while the other man circled to close the net from the other side.

Possible. But if it were true, it meant Karla was under surveillance. Who'd have a whole team assigned to watch one financial analyst?

Which left the simplest explanation. Karla had told them Shaw would be there. Perhaps even signaled them the moment he left her room.

Shaw didn't like that theory. Or didn't want to like it. But he made himself examine it as coolly as he could.

Karla had told him Chen Li had brought a chemical sample to the island for testing. And that everyone was asking what had happened to it after Nelson Bao was killed. Shaw rubbed his sore shoulder. It was a workable supposition that the sample was what the three men had been after. Did they think he had taken it off Bao's body? Had Karla been setting him up from the start?

Odds were ten to one that Karla was exactly what she seemed to be. A bean counter, trying to put together an important deal.

So how did they know where you were? the cold, furious part of him whispered.

He shook his head. The whole tangle with Chen and Zhang had him seeing spies everywhere. Too many theories, not enough hard facts. He needed a closer look at Karla Lokosh, or Haiden.

Not that you could get much closer to her than you've been already.

Damn it. He liked Karla. Both her company and the sex, which had been extraordinary.

That could be how she works. Getting close. Gaining your trust.

Shaw got to his feet and went to make the tea. The voice wouldn't shut up.

Did she make sure you left a little later than you'd planned this morning? Giving the hit team time to get into position?

She'd told him about the chemical sample, even though it was proprietary information. Risking her job.

Sure. That's what con artists do. They show how much confidence they have in you. Wasn't it she who suggested whoever had the missing sample could sell it back for serious cash? That might have been an offer for the man who could recognize it.

Shaw's fingers tore the lid from the box of Darjeeling. He made himself take a breath and shoved the thoughts away hard.

Maybe she really does *like you,* the cold voice said as it retreated.

And just maybe you can use that.

JAMES HARGREAVES HAD BEEN EXPECTING the call from Tucker by half past six. Even with a margin of a quarter hour, the men were late. When his phone finally rang at eight minutes after seven, he had already accepted that the news would be poor and was assessing the likeliest contingencies.

"Shaw escaped," said Tucker. The man knew better than to equivocate. "We converged in the park outside the girl's hotel. A civilian interrupted. We chased her off before she could bring the police, but Shaw broke loose. He fell down to an embankment and onto the freeway."

"Injured?"

"Not significantly. He's a fighter."

"So are you, supposedly. All three of you."

"Yes, sir," Tucker said.

"Outnumbered and taken by surprise, and he still eluded you and Vic and Louis put together. Perhaps I should be employing Shaw instead."

Tucker didn't say anything. Hargreaves imagined the furrows deepening in the man's grim black face. His lead field operative was not demonstrative, but Hargreaves knew how much of Tucker's self-worth was tied to successful execution of his job. And, correspondingly, how much harder he would work to make good on a mistake.

"Right," said Hargreaves. "Call this a lesson learned. It reinforces our original assessment of the man, that he's resourceful. Likely in business for himself."

"What about the woman?"

"Plan B becomes Plan A. We hired her for a reason." Hargreaves smiled to himself. "Let's see what Karla can do."

THIRTY-TWO

Shaw said a brief hello to Penelope when she woke in her room at Holliday House, initially groggy from the sleep and her medications.

"How's the foundation? Crossroads?" Penelope managed to say after a sip of water. Her elfin frame was bundled in blankets, with only her thin face and a fall of light brown hair streaked with gray above the folds. But her eyes were bright and clear after a night's rest.

"The therapists you found are great," said Shaw. "We're in the money-gathering stage now."

"That stage never ends. You let me know if there's something I can do. I should be going home from here within the week."

Addy prepped a few things for the daytime staff and kissed Penelope on the cheek before they left. Shaw drove Addy home in her battered Subaru.

"Did Penelope mean she was going home because she's on the mend or because there's nothing more they can do for her?" he asked as they waited at a stoplight.

Addy sighed. "The former, happy to say. But it's all fits and starts. We don't expect the girl has much more than a year, even with the best prognosis." Addy frequently referred to her friends as girls, even though, like Penelope, most had seen their seventieth birthday pass some time ago.

"It's amazing that she wants to work."

"Well, of course she does. Nothing keeps the spirit up like feeling wanted. Useful."

Cyndra was asleep on the living-room sofa when they arrived, the massive white bulk of Stanley lying on the floor next to her like an ice floe. He raised his head and his tail thumped heavily on the rug, but he stayed put.

"Kept you up all night, did she?" Addy said, sitting on her ottoman to scratch Stanley's taco-size ears. "Poor boy."

Shaw tapped Cyndra's shoulder until the girl sat up, blinking. He found some running pants on the shelf reserved for his things in the linen closet, changed out of his ragged trousers and threw them in the trash, went to the kitchen to make coffee, and returned to the living room to find Cyn still in the same position, staring blankly at the curtains. He sat on the floor by Stanley and stretched his legs, trying to get some blood moving. He could tell that his knee wasn't seriously hurt, but it would be a few days before he'd feel up to throwing any roundhouse kicks. Cyndra stood up with the blanket and disappeared into her room without a word.

Addy glanced at him. "So were you going to tell me what happened this morning?"

"I'm not sure myself. I was attacked. I got away."

"That's all?"

"The abridged version, yeah." Addy could handle hearing about the violence, but Shaw had decided he was too wiped to argue with her about involving the cops. "I got offered a job."

"While you were being assaulted?"

"Before that. It's good pay—very good pay—and all the perks. It would also mean a lot of travel. Starting immediately. Today."

"On a Sunday. They must really want you. This is legitimate work?"

"Yes. Or technically legit. The offer might be a kind of payoff. The company's trying to make some sort of big merger. I know a lot about it. As an employee I'd be beholden to keep my mouth shut, at least until the deal was finalized."

"Protecting a company's secrets is pretty normal fare. What's the catch?"

"Somebody died while I was on the island. And a corporate secret might have been stolen. It's all very warped, and I know I'm not getting the whole truth."

"Yet with all that you're undecided."

"Crossroads could use the money. So could we, for that matter."

Addy waved a hand. "The house is paid for. The child has food. We're fine."

"Maybe it's me." Shaw smiled. "I'd have to grow up."

"Ask them for more time to think about it. Maybe their reaction will tell you something."

He nodded. "They wanted an answer before noon. I'll do it now."

His call went to Linda Edgemont's voice mail. Shaw explained that he needed another day to weigh the offer and to set his things in order to be out of town, and that he appreciated the consideration. The business-speak didn't feel natural, coming out of his mouth. He hung up unsure if he'd sounded like he was mocking them. Maybe he had been, unconsciously.

Addy readied herself for bed while Shaw used the living-room computer to search for mentions of Karla Lokosh. She had a LinkedIn listing, noting her time at Bridgetrust and previously at a company called Atwater Marketing. Both were finance jobs. She'd been promoted twice during her five years with Bridgetrust.

She had social-media accounts, too, none of which showed many posts beyond intermittent individual photos of her on skiing trips to Colorado and Utah and some snapshots of restaurant meals. That wasn't odd in itself. He imagined that investment firms were conservative by nature. Posting selfies during wild nights out or leaving photos from past relationships wouldn't do Karla's career any good.

He tried searching for Karla Haiden. There were other women on the eastern side of the nation with that name; none of the top results was the redhead he knew. He refined the search by trying "finance" without success, and then "dance." Karla had said she taught classes; she might be listed on the faculty of some studio.

One result on the second page caught his eye, from Berklee College. In Boston. He clicked on it.

It was an archived photograph from the school's performance season of twelve years before. A troupe of fifteen or sixteen dancers, caught in motion. Radiating out from center stage, leaning back with an angle and length that would be impossible for the average human.

The show was called *Lonesome Heart: Beats*. Each of the dancers wore black long-sleeved leotards and capri dance pants in metallic gold and black stripes. All their hair had been pulled back and ruthlessly tamed into buns.

The performers' names were listed along with the director and key technical crew in a tightly spaced paragraph below the picture. Shaw found hers squeezed into the lines below: *Karla Haiden, 3rd year.*

The picture was sharp but taken from a distance. He examined the photo again, trying to discern the faces of the dancers who were white and female. Their figures were too much alike, given the naturally lithe people who would pursue dancing into adulthood and the years of hard training that had refined their bodies in similar ways.

He found her on stage left. Leaning back like the others, right arm thrown high and balanced on her left leg. Her hair had been a darker red then. She was turned partly away from the camera. But it was her. Shaw was sure. He could almost smell the clove scent of her hair.

It didn't tell him any more than he'd already guessed. She had been born Karla Haiden, changed her name to her husband's, most likely, and kept it after the divorce.

And if her online presence was as carefully trimmed as a topiary animal, so what? There were good and rational reasons for a woman to have little to no online presence. Privacy. Security. Professionalism.

None of that eased his mind.

At any other time, he'd have let the lack of information go. But after Karla's subtle nudge about the value of the missing chemical sample and the attack on him this morning, Shaw's antennae were quivering.

Addy returned to the living room to say good night, or good morning.

"I'd like you to do me a favor," he said.

"From your tone I can tell I may not enjoy it."

"It's easy. But it's also a little . . . creepy. You told me once that some of the jobs Penelope had filled were government posts with security clearances. Deep background checks and things like that."

"Yes."

"I want a profile on someone. They might have changed names one or more times. They might even have covered their tracks to make a search hard for the average person."

"What's her name?"

"How'd you know it's a woman?"

"You said it was creepy. You wouldn't think twice about this for a man."

"The name I know her by is Karla Lokosh. It used to be Karla Haiden." He spelled the names for Addy. "She went to Berklee College in Boston. She supposedly works for an investment firm called Bridgetrust Group. That's the sum total of the verifiable facts."

"Do you know her personally?"

"How'd you guess?"

"I'd take more credit, but you are an open book."

"If this isn't something you want to do—"

Addy scoffed. "Part of the reason you're easy for me to read is that I know you well. You're not asking me to help you stalk the woman. There must be some impetus beyond your sex drive. Is she in trouble?"

"More like she *is* trouble. The short version is that she may have a connection to the men who made a run at me this morning. Or maybe not. I need to know."

"Whether she can be trusted. I see. Sounds urgent. I'll tell Penny later today."

"Thanks, Addy."

"All part of the service." She headed off to the bedroom. In another moment Shaw heard her pulling the blackout curtains closed. He'd hung those when Addy had started subbing the night shift at Holliday House.

He went to the kitchen and fried some sausages and rolled them in buttered toast. Stanley had been paying attention since the meat had touched the cold pan. The dog found the strength to get up from the rug and lumber out to join him on the front porch. Shaw sat in one of the Adirondack chairs and ate the food with a liter bottle of water. He tossed bits of an extra sausage to Stanley. When they were done, he set the plate down for the dog to lick and resumed stretching his back and legs. His shoulder ached where the guy built like a fireplug had twisted it. He figured the bastard's nose was in worse shape. That was a satisfying thought.

As he stretched his quads, his subconscious nudged him about something.

Nelson Bao had worked at the company called Avizda until at least February, according to his pay stubs. The date stamp on the chemical sample Shaw had found in Bao's apartment had been from January. Could the sample be from Avizda instead of Jiangsu Manufacturing?

He returned to the computer to look up Avizda. It wasn't difficult to find. The company looked to be a close competitor of DuPont and other industrial conglomerates. Based in Dallas, as Shaw had seen on Bao's pay stubs.

It was a leap to guess that the sample might be from the Dallas company. Chen and Zhang could have brought it from China. Hell, the label on it might mean nothing. The vial could have been reused a dozen times since the label had been printed. But all the secrecy and what Karla had told him about Chen's purported innovation made Shaw wonder if there was another wrinkle to the corporate deal.

He texted Professor Mills, asking her to call when convenient. The phone rang within a minute.

"Hello, Professor," he said. "Thanks."

"No problem, I was just starting the day."

"I have a question. Or a guess. You know the company Avizda?"

"Everybody does in my world," said Mills.

"Do you know if they've had any thefts of their research in the last few months?"

She made a sound of surprise. "Nothing they've shared publicly. That would be industry news. Why?"

"It's conjecture. But I came across a chemical sample like we were talking about." He described the vial and label and contents to her. "It was in the hands of a former Avizda employee. I wondered if it might be stolen. And why."

"It does sound like something out of a QC lab. A five-milliliter vial, probably one of a batch of other samples that would be tested during the same shift. The first number, 146, would be the lab's room number, the rest being the batch number and the date and the initials of the chemist who created the sample."

"All the . . . activity around the sample makes me think it could be worth a lot. Worth stealing, maybe straight from Avizda's Room 146."

Mills paused for a moment. "You said the vial was only about a third full. That's a tiny sample on its own. Could be they've already done their testing and used up most of the vial."

Shaw considered it. Could Morton and Bao have completed their work on the island before Bao had died?

"I know some employees at Avizda," the professor said. "And even more people who have friends and relatives there. You'd be surprised how interwoven the scientific-research community can be. People gossip. I'll ask around and see if anyone knows whether they've had trouble."

"Thanks. Again. This might be nothing."

"Or it could be industrial espionage. I'm intrigued by all the mystery."

She hung up.

Espionage. The word made Shaw think of Zhang's hidden passports and Bao's multiple names.

Bao's—and Karla's.

"Karla," said Cyn, coming around the hall corner. Maybe reading Shaw's thoughts.

"Yeah?" he said.

"Who is she?"

Shaw looked at her. "Big ears you have."

"I wasn't *listening*. It's a small house. Who is she?"

"A friend."

"A girlfriend?"

"We could go round and round like this all morning, Cyn. What do you want to know?"

"Why are you going out with her?"

"Same reason you have a dozen video calls going every day with your friends. I like her. I want to spend time with her."

"You don't even trust her."

"Different question. Maybe a different answer."

"Well, it sucks," Cyndra said. Her feet planted as if straining to grow roots.

"Which part?"

"It's a shitty thing to do to Wren."

Shaw leaned back and folded his arms. "That's between me and Wren, kid."

"You owe her more."

"And neither of us owes you an explanation. Not if you're gonna plant a flag on the moral high ground before you know what the hell you're talking about."

Cyn turned and walked into her room and slammed the door.

Shaw let out a breath. Stanley stared at him from his place on the rug.

"That sure could've fucking well gone better," he murmured to the dog.

Stanley, maybe reluctant to take sides, laid his huge head on his front paws and sighed heavily.

THIRTY-THREE

Back in his apartment that afternoon, Shaw took a shower, turning the water on to full cold after he'd soaped up. He forced himself to stay under the frigid spray until his knotted muscles gave up and relaxed. He slept until evening and made a patchwork meal out of leftover pasta, roast beef, and half a head of questionable lettuce that he chopped into a salad. After he'd finished the food, he took out the contract from Sebastien Rohner to look it over again. He owed Droma International an answer.

His phone rang before he'd gotten past the first paragraph of legalese.

"Van? This is Penelope Walker."

"Hello. How are you feeling?"

"Better. I've found some information for you."

"That was fast."

"It was nice to work a bit. I felt strong this afternoon. Addy said this woman might be some kind of con artist, is that right?"

"I'm not sure what she is."

"I once saw Addy tell off a U.S. senator to his face. If she doesn't care for someone . . ." Penelope whistled softly. "You didn't give me much to go on, but fortunately the name Karla Haiden was uncommon enough. I've got a few pages of preliminary background notes here. Do you want the full rundown?"

Shaw didn't want to exhaust the woman, even if she was feeling stronger. "Give me the high points."

"All right," Penelope said. Shaw heard her shift in her seat, winding up for the pitch. "Karla Ann Haiden, born Salem, Mass. Attended Bishop Fenwick High School. Graduated Berklee College with a bachelor of fine arts—"

"I'll rephrase. What surprised you?"

"Got it. Well, first thing, Karla Haiden was a police officer for six years."

Shaw sat up straight in his chair. "Say more."

"Massachusetts State Police. Stationed in Brighton for a while and then in Andover. Received a citation for bravery in helping citizens escape an armed shooter and another for community service. She left the force as a corporal. She got married to a man named Stephen Reid, and they divorced three years after, while she was still on the force. Earned an M.B.A. from Boston College during those years, too."

"Busy woman."

"Then she moved to New York City and obtained a private-investigation license."

"This gets better and better," said Shaw.

"In New York she worked for two years and a few odd months for a small PI firm called A&A Investigations. They're in the West Village. Then the public record of employment ends. That was about three years ago."

"Ends?"

"Yes. I imagine she has tax records from somewhere, though I wouldn't have access to those. But there's no public trace."

Shaw thought about that for a moment. "I didn't find much on Karla Haiden online. Not even a marriage record. It was like she had vanished after college. And now again, after A&A Investigations."

"In my experience, candidates with law-enforcement or government-agency backgrounds learn early not to post much online. And to remove anything that might identify them. No pictures, especially if their job might involve undercover work."

"There's nothing to indicate where she's employed now?"

"Her PI license is still valid. She's kept that up."

"And yet Karla Lokosh exists as an employee of Bridgetrust."

"Such as it is," said Penelope. "Bridgetrust Group exists, too, as a New York corporation established eight years ago. They have all the required public filings. There are some news stories of client deals on online business blogs, cut and pasted from press releases. Nothing in any of the major periodicals. And even their clients are unknown factors. Their nominal president, William Flynn, has a few professional data points but nothing substantial behind them. I can't even ascertain where he went to school."

"Is it a front?"

"I wouldn't go that far, but if Bridgetrust is really a capital-investment firm, they don't do much to promote themselves. Which is odd in itself. That line of work is all about trumpeting your victories, real or imagined."

Karla Haiden did have an M.B.A. Was she putting that to use after a short career as a PI? Or was Bridgetrust something else?

Penelope broke in. "Do you want me to e-mail you everything I've found? It's dry reading, but maybe there's something else in all this that will be useful to you."

"Yes."

There was a pause on the line. "Can I give my opinion? As a woman who's seen more job histories than blades of grass?"

"Please."

"I'd remind any hiring manager of the obvious points here. Within a decade Ms. Haiden has had at least two major shifts in career, police and PI, and maybe a third if you count the M.B.A. and Bridgetrust. Plus the short marriage and changing cities. This isn't just a person looking to find a job, this is someone looking to find herself. She's willing to wipe her slate clean to do it. I'd caution anyone against investing too much in a flight risk."

"Personally or professionally."

"Exactly."

Shaw remembered what Cyndra had said. *You don't even trust her.*

"You okay?" Penelope said.

"Yeah. Thanks. This was great work."

"Funny how doing a good job uncovering secrets rarely makes anyone happy. Bye."

Shaw got up and poured himself three fingers of bourbon. The sun was low. The western light streamed in boldly through the glass door to the balcony. He sat on the chair in front of the TV but didn't turn it on.

Karla had been a cop, then a PI, then . . . something else. Whatever job she had now, Shaw felt sure it wasn't within spitting distance of financial services. Even if she'd put on a good front.

An *expert* front, he corrected. It wasn't just that Karla could talk mergers and acquisitions like a Wharton grad. Shaw had been attuned to spotting cops from childhood. He hadn't seen one hint—a leading question, an overly focused gaze—that Karla had once been law.

The woman was a damned chameleon. Impressive. He'd have been even more admiring if his embarrassment at being fooled weren't so complete.

No legit private cop would have slept with him, he thought ruefully. Whatever she was now, Karla hadn't felt obliged to follow any professional ethics. Whoever she worked for might be similarly unbound.

He picked up the phone again.

"Hey," he said when Karla answered. "It's Van."

"Hello, you," she said, laughing. "Glad you called."

"Good day?"

"Slept in and woke up happy, and except for trying out the hotel's gym I haven't gone farther than the bathtub. How are you? Wait. You're still in town?"

"I am. I asked for the day to consider Rohner's offer."

"And the day's almost done. Are you leaning one way or the other?"

"I've been too busy thinking about what happens if that chemical sample really is missing. If someone stole it from the island. Would it really torpedo the deal with Jiangsu Manufacturing?"

"Bill Flynn thinks it will. Mr. Chen contacted my boss and the Rohners today to say he expected a new chemist from China in about a week. Bill suspects that Chen's plant is manufacturing more of the chemical but that Chen might also be stalling while he decides whether to continue."

"And maybe to see if someone comes forward with an offer."

Karla paused. "You mean the thief?"

"Yeah. Kilbane or someone else. I've been thinking about what you said, about the smart play being to sell the stolen sample back to Chen. Or Rohner."

"Sure. To sell to anyone else, the thief would have to know exactly what the chemical was and how it worked."

"He'd also have to be very careful. It would be natural for anyone to assume the guy who took the sample was the same person who killed Nelson Bao. Even if he were innocent of Bao's death he might wind up hanging himself if the Rohners decided not to play ball."

"That's right," said Karla.

Shaw waited.

"I suppose the right person to approach about buying the sample back would be the one who needs the deal to happen," she said. "The one who'd lose the most if the thief went to jail and the sample was lost."

"Rohner's already a billionaire. Chen can make more of his chemical."

"Yes," she said. "I see. You think Kilbane might offer the sample to us. Bridgetrust."

"I might. If I were the thief."

Shaw waited again.

"It would be safe," Karla said at last. "I'm sure Bill would make any exchange safe for everyone. He's . . . experienced."

"We'll see," said Shaw. He laughed, low and soft. "If Kilbane's really clever, he'd come to you instead of Flynn."

"How's that?" Karla returned his laughter. It sounded a little uncertain.

"You're smarter than Flynn. And a lot better company."

"I am," she said. "But you know me better than most."

"Not as well as I'd like. If I'm not on a plane to Hungary tomorrow and you're not busy putting this deal together . . ."

"Yes." Karla hummed happily. "I'd like to see you again, too."

"Great. I'll call you when I know more."

Shaw hung up.

He'd set the bait about as well as he could manage. Somewhere beyond his perception, he felt sure that something was circling. Something large and hungry, with very sharp teeth.

SHAW CHANNEL-SURFED UNTIL HE FOUND a Mariners game, already in its fifth inning against Tampa Bay. The M's were up by two. He left the picture on with the sound muted while he cleaned the apartment. His thoughts on Karla Haiden. And the crew that had attacked him in the park. Where were they now?

The ball game ended, and a postgame show filled the next hour, telling viewers what they'd just seen and what they should think about it. Shaw didn't need the sound turned up to follow the line of chatter.

Something made his own Spidey-sense tingle. He turned and looked at the front door. Movement, in the hall outside. Not his neighbors from down the hall. Too quiet.

Shaw walked to the bedroom and flipped up the screen on his laptop. An application window brightened to life. The app had a wireless connection to a camera roughly the size of a suit button, which Shaw had placed as a security measure on the side of the illuminated stairwell exit sign in the hallway. Every week he swapped the camera for another with a fresh battery. Its feed was high resolution and full color.

A crystal-clear picture of the cops waiting just outside his door.

THIRTY-FOUR

Bad: A pair of uniformed Seattle officers stood about twenty-five feet from the camera and only ten from Shaw's apartment door.

Worse: The cops hadn't knocked yet. Which meant they were there to make sure he didn't leave while they waited for someone of higher authority, probably a detective. Detectives usually made house calls when they had a search warrant or were sure of an arrest, or both.

Shaw rewound to see the camera's feed from the last two minutes. The image of the cops reversed, walking backward to the elevator. Rollie from the Empyrea's front desk joined them. Shaw let the video play at normal speed. They'd brought Rollie for his card to allow them access to the floor and maybe to keep him from calling Shaw and warning him. The image of Rollie pointed a finger down the hallway in the direction of 3105 and vanished back into the elevator as rapidly as a prairie dog into its burrow.

Shaw looked at the balcony. He could escape. The residents just below him were summering in Europe. Shaw had learned that from Rollie, who tended to talk too much. It would be simple enough to tie a climbing rope to the balcony rail and scramble down one story. A very quick exit, and he'd try not to think about the equally rapid thirty-story fall if he screwed up the safety line.

No. If the cops were here to bring him in for questioning on Nelson Bao and maybe toss his place, better to let them and get it done.

He glanced at the feed from the camera once more. Two men in civilian clothes exited the elevator and joined the uniformed cops.

Shaw knew one of them. He wondered if it was too late to consider the mountaineering option again.

Before leaving his laptop, he activated a different application. The app would wipe the computer clean of all data, all images, all apps not hard-coded into the original device. The next-best thing to tossing it off the balcony.

When the insistent knock came, he was already at the door.

"Kanellis," he said, opening the door.

The detective grunted. "No surprise at all. Maybe you knew we'd be coming. Got a guilty conscience?"

"It was the smell of body spray wafting up the elevator shaft ahead of you." He held out a hand. Kanellis tapped his palm with a folded sheet of paper. Shaw took it.

"Step aside," Kanellis said. Shaw did. The detectives walked into the apartment. The uniforms stayed outside the door, bottling the exit route.

Kanellis dressed like a young liberal-arts professor—textured brown wool sport coat, slim-fit plaid shirt, knit tie. His badge hung on a woven leather lanyard around his neck. His black five-day stubble had been painstakingly shaped under his cheekbones and in the sparse patches on both sides below his bottom lip.

"Place has the wow factor," Kanellis said, looking around the living room with its odd assortment of furniture. "What is it you do for money again?"

Shaw sat in the leather wingback chair. Short of the new bed, the wingback was the only piece that looked elegant enough to belong with the high-rise apartment. Shaw had bought the chair on an expensive whim because it resembled his grandfather's favorite chair when Shaw had been a kid.

"This is Cole," Kanellis said as if Shaw had answered his question. His partner nodded to Shaw. Cole's suit was gray, off the rack, and fit him like a tarp draped over a wooden post fence.

Cole and one of the uniforms got to work searching the place. Shaw wasn't concerned that they would find any contraband. He didn't keep burglary gear or weapons in the apartment.

What *did* worry him was that Kanellis was SPD. Nelson Bao's death was San Juan County jurisdiction, or State if it had escalated somehow because Bao was a foreign visitor. Why were the Seattle cops involved?

He unfolded the warrant. After the boilerplate paragraph describing the various whereases and wherefores about probable cause, the page got to the painful particulars:

There is in the **City of Seattle, KING County, Washington,** a suspected place and premises described and located as follows:

A firearm of .22 or similar caliber and/or ammunition, clips, or related accessories. Materials which may apply to the construction of a firearm suppressor, including but not limited to solvent traps, aluminum or steel cones or cups, drills, machining jigs, steel wool, oil, grease, or gel.

The suspected place is in control of each of the following person or persons:

Donovan SHAW—White Male

At said places you shall search for and, if same be found, seize and bring before me the property described in the affidavit, as follows:

Documentation of personal communications. This documentation may be both written and digitally stored. Therefore, this evidence could be located on any and all computers or devices that can store digital information, which includes hard drives, external hard drives, zip drives, CDs, DVDs, thumb drives, iPods, memory cards, and cellular telephones.

The warrant concluded with another standard paragraph about executing without delay and was signed by a district-court judge.

A .22 and a suppressor. That meant a professional, or somebody working hard to look like one. Easy to obtain. With the right hardware attached and subsonic rounds, the weapon would be about as loud as a twig breaking.

"Who got shot?" said Shaw.

Kanellis waved a hand while he was going through the kitchen cupboards, like, *We'll get to that.*

"Heard your exgirlfriend got married," the detective said. "That must sting."

Kanellis had met Luce a couple of times. His eyes had rarely roamed north of her chin on both occasions.

"I heard you made a play for her after we split," Shaw said, loud enough for the others to hear. "And that she told you to go piss up a rope."

"Stand up," Kanellis said. Shaw did. Kanellis reached down to take the leather cushion from the chair and handed it to one of the officers. "Open that."

The policeman unfolded a knife and split the seam along one side, corner to corner, to pull out the layers of foam padding. Shaw watched, without expression. He didn't want to give Kanellis any satisfaction.

"You going to tell me what's going on?" Shaw said.

"Tell me how you spent this afternoon."

"What happened this afternoon?"

"C'mon. Where were you?"

"Here."

"You know a Linda Edgemont?"

Shaw hesitated. "Yeah."

"How?"

"She hired me on behalf of her employer for a security job." He pointed to the coffee table. "Contract's right there."

Kanellis walked over and picked up the manila envelope. "Security. You. That's brushing elbows with funny." He slid the papers out and reviewed them. "How'd the job go?"

Shaw waited.

"She's dead. Edgemont." Kanellis said it offhandedly, though his eyes were on Shaw. "Homicide."

"This afternoon?"

"Anybody here with you then?"

"No."

"Too bad. I'll take that." He motioned to the phone on the kitchen counter. Shaw stayed where he was. Kanellis walked over and picked it up. "Anybody you want to call, you can do it after we book you. I remember that lawyer of yours. That slick mother will get all the details when the time is right."

Ganz.

"Let me have the phone a minute," he said to Kanellis.

"Not a chance."

"You can listen in. Hell, you can video me. Linda Edgemont was a friend of Ganz's. He shouldn't hear about her death from the news. Or from you."

Kanellis's mouth twisted. "Don't mess with me, Shaw."

"Not about this."

The detective glowered for another moment.

"Stay inside. In case you get a notion to step off the balcony and cheat the hangman."

He handed Shaw the phone. Shaw looked up Ganz's home number and let it ring as Kanellis watched. From the bedroom he heard the thumps and bangs of Cole and the uniformed officer, turning his place upside down and giving it one hell of a shake.

THIRTY-FIVE

Kanellis and Cole handcuffed Shaw and put him in the back of the police cruiser. The uniformed officers drove him one mile south to SPD headquarters while the detectives finished searching his apartment. The cop driving used a remote control strapped to the visor to open the heavy steel door to the HQ garage. It rattled upward, they slid into its maw, and the building swallowed them.

Shaw didn't resent the handcuffs. Regulation. Kanellis had at least waited until they were at the car before putting them on, rather than parading Shaw like a perp past Rollie and anyone who happened to be on the street.

The uniforms removed the cuffs and left him in an interview room, alone with his thoughts.

Ganz had been shaken by Linda Edgemont's death. He'd been silent for half a minute after Shaw had broken the news on the phone. Thirty seconds of quiet on an open line felt long enough under normal circumstances. With someone as energetic as Ganz, it was like a chasm.

"How?" Ganz had finally said.

"Homicide is all they'll tell me."

"You're with the cops now?"

Shaw knew that Ganz was already filling in the blanks. Linda was dead. Cops are talking to Shaw. Ergo: suspect.

"I'm going to need you," Shaw had said.

"No." The answer came immediately.

"They're going to hold me downtown."

"I can't."

"I haven't seen Linda since Briar Bay Island." Kanellis's ears had pricked up at that.

"It doesn't matter." Ganz's voice tapped eggshell cracks between the words. "Any defense worth shit means digging into every part of the vict—" His voice broke, which he covered with a cough. "You don't know. The things I have to learn about people. No."

"Ephraim—"

"I'll find you someone. Someone good. Just . . . leave me out."

Kanellis held out his hand. Shaw put the phone in it.

"Uh-oh," Kanellis had said. "I smell a bridge burning."

Shaw had caught the same scent. Now, sitting in the interview room, he might be looking at a long stretch of time ahead to mull over where he'd gone wrong.

Someone had killed Linda Edgemont. Or had her killed. To what purpose? The lawyer had been a minor player in the pending deal. Her death wouldn't seem to delay or accelerate anything, from what Shaw could see. Even Bao, the apparently replaceable chemist, had been more crucial.

His situation was going to get worse. Whatever suspicions the Seattle cops held for him in Edgemont's death, those would be redoubled once they learned about his proximity to Nelson Bao's murder. And when San Juan County heard about his arrest for Edgemont, Shaw might replace Kilbane as their lead suspect. Screwed coming and going.

He had to get out in front of the problem. Which meant doing something that bucked up against every instinct he had and every lesson his grandfather had taught him.

Shaw stood up and pounded on the door. They let him wait two minutes before a uniformed officer showed.

"I want to talk to Lieutenant John Guerin," Shaw said.

"Sit down," the cop said. "Somebody will be with you soon."

"Guerin. Or nobody. Make sure Kanellis hears that."

The cop glowered but closed the door again. Shaw sat back down. Talking to the cops. Jesus.

His grandfather Dono had been cremated. Shaw himself had taken the ashes out on the Sound with Hollis and scattered the gray remains across a mile of water, on a day when only the two of them were drunk enough and stubborn enough to put up with the rolling swells and a rain that fell like needles on their faces.

Dono had never been buried. Yet somehow, Shaw knew, the old man was rolling over in his grave right now.

"A LABORATORY?" GUERIN SAID.

"Beakers and vials and the whole damn thing."

"Hidden in the art gallery." Guerin sat across from Shaw in the interview room's other chair. Kanellis had brought a third from down the hall. It was Kanellis's case. Shaw talking to Guerin wouldn't change that. "And how'd you manage to see the lab if their security is so state-of-the-art?"

"Somebody left a door propped open. Maybe to let the sea air in."

"Right." Guerin folded his hands. "Tell me what you saw."

Shaw described everything he recalled about the lab, including the names of the chemicals. He didn't mention his primer in chemistry from Professor Mills, pretending to have dredged up his sudden expertise in GPC testing via the Internet. Neither of the policemen took notes. Writing notes drew focus off the subject, and if the subject was talking, nothing should change. The video camera on the wall would capture Shaw's every expression and syllable.

"Good memory," Kanellis said, not bothering to disguise his doubt.

Guerin adjusted his glasses. He'd bought new frames since Shaw had last seen him, in roughly the same dark honey color as the chemical he'd seen in Bao's apartment. "So what do you think Sebastien Rohner is doing with this lab? Drugs? Making bombs?"

"No. The chemicals in the lab are used in analyzing polymers."

"So they're nothing illegal."

"Not that I know of."

"Then what's the point?" said Kanellis. "If Rohner wants to play Dr. Frankenstein on his private island, what does that have to do with the dead guy from China?"

"Maybe nothing," Shaw said. "But when I left the island, I thought Rohner was pissed at me."

Kanellis snorted. "That tracks."

"Then suddenly he offers me a job that pays enough to knock me sideways and wants to hustle me onto the next plane out of the country. He says it's to make amends, but the job also requires me to sign a secrecy agreement. One of the Bridgetrust people told me in confidence that Chen's team was bringing a new chemical sample to the island for testing. Some moneymaking innovation. If that chemical went missing after Bao's death and Rohner and the rest think I took it . . ."

"His job offer to you might be a tax-deductible way to mask buying stolen goods," finished Guerin. "Why wouldn't he just ask you flat out if you have the stuff and how much you want to return it?"

"I don't know," admitted Shaw. "Maybe because if I'm not the guy who stole the chemical, Rohner doesn't want me getting curious about it. Or maybe he can't let on that it's missing until he's sure I have it."

"And Linda Edgemont?" said Guerin.

"I've been thinking about her since Kanellis redecorated my place. Edgemont found me through Ganz. She brought me into Rohner's orbit."

The lieutenant tapped the table with a fingertip. "And if you turned out to be disloyal and stole the chemical sample, that reflects badly on her. Is that it?"

"More than that. Maybe I knew to steal the sample because Edgemont told me how valuable it was."

"That's a lot of leaps to get to that conclusion. Rohner's worth more than the building we're sitting in. That kind of guy doesn't have his employees whacked. He fires them, gives them a lousy reference. Maybe files a lawsuit if he's really miffed." Guerin folded his hands. "What's the point of his killing her now? Rohner already offered to pay you. Did you turn him down?"

"I haven't given him an answer. But the deadline's already passed. I was supposed to give Linda Edgemont an answer last night."

"There's some irony for you," said Kanellis. "Can't take the job 'cause you're on the hook for killing your recruiter."

"Ever been to her place?" Guerin said.

"No."

"Never went by her house once? Found her door left open for the sea air, like with the lab? Because that would be a more believable story."

"We know you were there," Kanellis said. "Just tell us."

"That's all I got. Anything else can wait for the lawyer."

Kanellis exchanged a glance with Guerin. Guerin shrugged minutely, as if to say, *Go ahead.*

"You were seen, smart guy," Kanellis said.

Shaw stared.

"Yup. Your messed-up face is hard to miss. An eyewitness description from a neighbor and a call to Rohner's guy Olen Anders was all it took to find out you were involved and place you at the scene." Kanellis crossed his arms, mimicking Shaw. "Better come clean now, if you want our help."

The kind of help they would offer would only dig his hole deeper. Shaw closed his mouth and kept it shut until they went away, Guerin shaking his head, like he'd known that talking to Shaw could only be a dead end.

A positive ID. At a crime scene he couldn't possibly have been near. That lawyer buddy of Ganz's had better hurry, before another corpse materialized with Shaw's fingerprints all over it.

THIRTY-SIX

Kanellis had Shaw booked while Cole arranged to move him to the county jail on the next block. Shaw asked to make his phone call—wanting to let Wren know where he was—but Kanellis claimed the call he'd made to Ganz at the apartment counted. He'd have to wait until the lawyer showed.

There was no skybridge over the city streets connecting SPD head-quarters to the jail, as there was between the jail and the courthouse. Transferring Shaw one block involved his being cuffed again, taken to what he guessed was Cole's personal vehicle—a Pontiac with its leather seats cracked and shedding sprinkles of foam—and driven from the HQ garage through four fast turns, right-right-right-left, directly into the sally port of the jail.

The detectives handed Shaw off to a pair of corrections officers who searched him again before taking him up the elevator to the third level. Through the barred gates of the secure access corridor was a two-story cellblock with bright white walls and amber doors. The walkway on the second floor had been enclosed with metal mesh to keep prisoners from jumping or throwing things over the rail. Shaw had the impulse to run his finger along the mesh, letting it flap like a playing card in the spokes of a bicycle wheel. He knew that the urge was purely defiant. To do something, however paltry, other than what they told him to do.

It was long after lights-out. The cell had bunks for two detainees, but Shaw was alone. From far down the hall, he could hear other inmates hollering in conversation between their own cells, talking shit about an MMA fighter Shaw had never heard of. He guessed this was the block used for prisoners awaiting further interrogation or arraignment.

SPD could hold him here for three days before filing charges. Lon-ger if they could convince a judge that the evidence was strong. So far their case against him looked to be hardening into tungsten. It was early Saturday morning. Ganz's lawyer might not show until the workweek.

Shaw felt clammy after the stifling rides in the cop cars and the unventilated interview room. He took off his shirt and washed his face and armpits with tepid water from the sink. Did slow push-ups until his arms trembled with the strain. Then he washed again, letting the water drip from him, and lay down on the lower bunk, the gray jail blanket still folded into a tight spool under his laceless boots.

Kanellis and Guerin could be lying about the eyewitness, of course. Trying to spook Shaw into confessing. But Guerin, at least, would give Shaw more credit than to think he might panic like that.

No. They'd been too certain. Kanellis too gleeful. Their witness was real.

It had to be a frame job. Maybe by the same team that had tried to grab him in Freeway Park. Edgemont had been killed and some neighbor bribed or maybe coerced to ID Shaw, bringing the cops to his door. Had she been murdered solely to serve that purpose? Or had the team been after something? If the goons thought Linda Edgemont had pointed Shaw toward stealing the chemical sample, maybe they suspected he'd handed it off to her.

It made a rough logical sense. They'd tried for Shaw, failed, and gone to Edgemont next. But why kill her?

From down the cellblock, the sports talk had devolved into yelling. Meaningless threats between men who could no more reach one another than they could squeeze through the four-inch vertical slit of window in their cell.

He had to get out of jail. Quickly. Nelson Bao's death had started some sort of chain reaction between the players in the deal. Instinct told him that if Linda Edgemont's murder had been intended to turn the screws on him, that pressure was only going to increase until something snapped.

Or until Shaw was firmly out of the way, serving twenty-five to life.

THIRTY-SEVEN

When a guard opened his cell door at noon, Shaw assumed it was to lead him down to lunch on the second level of the jail. Instead he was told his lawyer had arrived.

On a Sunday. Ganz had come through.

They walked past other inmates sitting and talking in the communal area on the first floor of the block. Two men played checkers with pieces of felt. None of them paid Shaw much mind. Detainment was a high-traffic area of the jail, new faces coming and going at all hours.

Each block had a meeting room reserved for attorney visits. The closet-size room allowed for two plastic chairs, a table bolted to the wall, and two people if they weren't opposed to sitting close enough to smell each other's breath. Shaw turned sideways to let the guard shut the door.

The lawyer extended a hand from his seat, apparently choosing dignity over wrestling his chair away from the table to give himself room to stand. "Ed Chiarra." They shook. Chiarra was slight of build but had a thick head of brown wavy hair that added at least an inch and a half to his height. His suit was conservative navy blue, his tie muted red. As the lawyer withdrew his arm, Shaw saw he wore silver cuff links shaped like bull's-eyes.

"Ganz said he knew someone good," Shaw said. "Thanks for taking me on."

"I don't have a lot of time," Chiarra said. "What did the police tell you about the case against you?" He had a slight New York–New Jersey accent. Maybe Chiarra was an East Coast transplant like Ganz.

Shaw recounted what Lieutenant Guerin and Kanellis had said about the eyewitness placing him at Edgemont's. Chiarra frowned at Shaw's having volunteered the fact of his employment with Droma and Linda Edgemont, and the lines in his face deepened further when Shaw mentioned Nelson Bao.

"You shouldn't have spoken at all," said Chiarra. "Just waited for me."

Shaw nodded. He knew the rules as well as the lawyer, had followed them his whole life. All the more reason that he felt like a fool now, having gambled by telling Guerin about the island and the laboratory.

"What do you know?" Shaw said.

Chiarra consulted his notes. "Linda Edgemont was working at the Droma International office in High Bridge until about two P.M. yesterday—Droma's the same corporation that hired you?"

Shaw said it was.

"A company car drove her to her house in Hillman City. The driver waited at the curb until she got into the house okay. About twenty minutes after that, a neighbor out for a jog waved down a passing Seattle police car and told the officer she'd seen a white man"—Chiarra looked at Shaw—"with dark hair and large scars on his face leaving the side gate of Linda Edgemont's house. The officer investigated and found Linda Edgemont dead by the sliding door at the back of the house. The door was open. They figure she stepped outside and was shot."

"Why would she open the door to a guy standing in her backyard? Even in the middle of the afternoon?"

"The theory will be that she knew her assailant. She knew you."

"Except it wasn't me."

Chiarra nodded noncommittally. "Right now let's deal with what we have. The search warrant for your place listed a .22-caliber pistol and materials to silence it. You own either of those? Anywhere?"

Shaw said no. "Why a suppressor? What did they find at the scene?"

"Shells to match that caliber on the patio and trace metal shavings on the victim's clothes. Tests are still being run, but my guess is that the metal's type and the oils on it are enough to be substantive."

Chiarra tapped his attaché with a knuckle. "Most of their evidence for now hinges on the witness, or it will once they put your picture in front of her. We have to assume she'll ID you, even if human memory can be shaky under stress. We can punch holes in her recollections later. Where were you from roughly noon to four o'clock yesterday afternoon?"

"At home."

"Alone? Call anybody?"

"Not during those hours. I was asleep. Around six o'clock I spoke to a woman named Penelope Walker on the phone. Just after that I spoke to Karla Lokosh, who's one of the Bridgetrust Group people from the island."

"What's your relationship with them?" Chiarra was making notes.

"Penelope's a retired recruiter helping with a charity foundation I'm involved with. Karla I met this past week, like I said."

"And?"

"And we went out Thursday night."

"Okay. No contact with Linda Edgemont on Friday?"

"I left her a voice mail early in the morning asking for more time to consider a job offer from Droma."

"So you had a vested interest in her well-being. That's good. Tell me about Nelson Bao."

Shaw recounted finding Bao on the beach and what Rohner had told him about San Juan County treating the case as a homicide.

"Warren Kilbane's on the hot seat for Bao," Shaw concluded.

Chiarra shook his head. "They're done with Kilbane. They pulled him and"—he glanced at his notes—"and a Debra Pollan and Anthony Castelli late Thursday afternoon and kept them overnight. Bao was killed late on Tuesday, is that right?"

Shaw nodded.

Chiarra hummed unhappily as he read. "They have alibis. They all took a state ferry to Anacortes on Tuesday morning, picked up a car from a lot there, and drove south. Pollan ate dinner at her hotel. Castelli went out with a woman that night. Kilbane was in two different sports bars as late as nine o'clock on Tuesday. All verified, or close enough, the way the sheriff sees it. They weren't near the island, so they aren't suspects for Bao."

"You move fast," Shaw said. "When did you talk to San Juan County?"

"Bao and Edgemont. Neither situation is much on its own," Chiarra continued, "but add them together and you can expect a rough road ahead. The DA may argue to deny bail based on your past record. SPD will definitely be granted the warrants and court orders to look through anything they ask. We can fight it, but it would help a lot if you can offer something."

"I don't have a better alibi."

"If you can trade any evidence, I mean."

"Like what?"

"Something concrete. Did you take anything from Nelson Bao? From the lab on the island?"

Shaw looked at the lawyer for a long moment. Chiarra gazed back. His left eyelid twitched.

"Ganz didn't send you," said Shaw. "Did he?"

Chiarra pressed a hand flat on the table, as if slowly squashing a bug.

"This can all go away if you cooperate."

"Who's paying your hourly rate? Rohner?"

"That's beside the point. You need help. We're your only way out of this shithole, so get on board. Did you take anything from Nelson Bao?"

"Talk plain."

"The sample. Do you have the polymer sample?"

Shaw leaned in.

"Let's say I do," he said. "What happens next?"

"You tell me where it is. Once we have it in hand, we can all move forward. I'm sure the eyewitness will have a memory jog."

Shaw stared at Chiarra, his dark eyes blank. His grandfather had had the same eyes. Nearly black. Like a shark's, when he chose to keep any hint of humanity from showing.

The lawyer shifted and cleared his throat.

"Their case is all about placing you at the scene," he continued uneasily. "We can prove that you weren't there just as easily. I'm certain other witnesses can be found."

"Sure."

"You can be out of here by the end of the week. Just tell me where the polymer is."

"No. Spring me first."

"Impossible. It will take a few days to obtain other witnesses and for the police to corroborate their stories. It can't be done overnight." The lawyer tapped the pages with a manicured fingernail. "This is urgent. If you wait, if you stall, there won't be any deal we can make. You have to trust us."

"No."

"Then we're at an impasse." Chiarra's jaw clenched. "Don't be an idiot. I can't work miracles with the police timeline."

"Then you'll have to find divine help elsewhere. Without me on the outside, there's no way for you to get the sample. Even if I told you where it was."

"A safe-deposit box? A secure drop?"

Shaw waited. It was a twisted kind of fun, watching the attorney's gears grind and click into place. Finding out how far Chiarra was willing to go on behalf of his unnamed employer.

"How do I know you're not lying about having it?" he said.

"It's in a clear five-milliliter glass vial with a white cap. It's viscous, like motor oil for a stock car. And the color is somewhere between honey and molasses. Not that I recommend tasting the goop. It smells as harsh as chlorine."

Chiarra drummed his fingers on the metal table. "Good. Great. How much do you have?"

Shaw went back to waiting.

"We can get you out," Chiarra said finally. "I think. I'll have to confirm that. But a . . . a direct approach might leave you in a bad position with the police."

"But you'll do it."

"Yes." Chiarra exhaled, as if struck by the enormity of what he was saying. "If we can."

"Without casualties. That's nonnegotiable." Shaw pointed. "Anybody gets hurt and I'll hand the cops everything. Including your precious sample."

"That would be a mistake. You need us."

"We need each other. I want the witness to recant, and I want a hundred grand. Once I have the money, I'll get your chemical for you."

"If we paid you more, in advance, would you be willing to tell me where it is right now?"

Shaw's grin was ferocious.

"Better get moving, Counselor." He reached behind him to thump twice on the door. "And watch your back. You know what happened to the last lawyer who got deep in this shit."

Chiarra blanched. The guard opened the door, and Shaw left.

THIRTY-EIGHT

Shaw sat in the cellblock's communal room late that afternoon, lost in thought—the only activity available to him other than talking to the meth head at the next table, who already seemed engrossed in multiple conversations inside his brain.

Kilbane hadn't killed Nelson Bao. And if Shaw had needed more confirmation that the Droma security chief wasn't behind the attack on him at the park, all three members of his team had spent Thursday night as guests of San Juan County.

Rohner could afford plenty of bent lawyers like Chiarra. But the attorney's willingness to consider extralegal options put him in a category more like the covert Chen and Zhang, or like Shaw himself. People whose primary concern for the law was how to get around it. Shaw's bet was that Chiarra had been sent by whatever unknown firm employed Karla Haiden.

The same guard that had taken Shaw from his cell in the morning appeared at his shoulder.

"You got a video call," the guard said. He led Shaw down another corridor to a larger room that might have been for classes or support-group meetings. Stacked columns of the ubiquitous plastic chairs covered one wall. At the opposite end of the room were four thick posts, each with two metal stations shaped like old slot machines, with phone receivers instead of pulling levers.

The guard pointed him to the chair in front of Station 6. "Fifteen minutes."

Shaw sat and saw Wren on the screen. Behind her was a plant-festooned shelf he recognized as being on the wall of her bedroom. He picked up the receiver.

"Hey," he said. "How'd you find me?"

"Great to see you, too." Wren laughed weakly.

"Sorry. Yes. Your face is the best thing I've seen since . . . since the last time I saw it. But how—"

"Your lawyer Mr. Ganz knew to call Addy. Addy called me. I found out about this service and downloaded the app on my phone. I think Mr. Ganz might've pulled a string or two to let me call direct."

"Do me a favor. Call Ganz and let him know that I've found temporary representation. And that if it doesn't work out, I might take him up on his offer later."

"Van, what's going on?"

"These calls are recorded. I can't talk details, but I can promise you I haven't killed anyone. I think the initial evidence caused the cops to look in the wrong direction."

"And in the meantime you're stuck there." She shook her head. "You sound so calm about it. As though being accused of . . . as though jail was a regular thing that everyone has to deal with. Like renewing your car tabs."

"My perspective might be a little skewed. You know my family."

She nodded and looked away. Her light brown eyes shining, a bright varnish on the chestnut wood.

"I'm angry," she said. "For you, if you can't be. Furious enough for the both of us."

Shaw smiled. "I can be calm and angry at the same time. One of my best tricks."

"Don't try to cheer me up. I'm enjoying my fury."

"Tell me news of the outside world, then. Did you spend all weekend weeding the Snohomish garden?"

Wren accepted Shaw's change of subject and spun him a story about Lettie both wanting to protect the honeybees that had discovered the garden and fighting the urge to slap frantically and flee to the car whenever one came near her. She'd fallen asleep on the car ride home, which Wren concluded was only natural, since Lettie had run the equivalent of a 10K that afternoon, twenty steps at a time.

"The counter on this app says we only have a minute left," Wren said.

"Tell Addy I'm all right. If Cyndra doesn't know . . ." He hesitated. "Leave it to Addy's judgment whether to tell her where I am. She and I had an argument just before all this went down. We didn't leave off in a good place."

"What were you quarreling about?"

"You. Sort off. Cyn heard me mention Karla to Addy. She figures I'm cheating on you."

"Oh. Crap."

"That was my thought as well."

"I'll . . . I'll talk to her. Try to explain," Wren said. "If that's all right."

"You couldn't do any worse than I did."

"I'm sure it will be okay. Not just Cyn, but everything. Is it . . . difficult in there?"

"No. It's jail, not supermax. Boredom is the main enemy."

"Tough guy." She touched the screen, briefly concealing her face. "I miss you. Strange to say since we just saw each other . . ."

"But it's different," he agreed, "because we can't."

"Soon."

She ended the call.

The guard led Shaw back to his cell. The communal room was empty; playtime had ended while he'd been talking to Wren. He sat on his bunk.

How soon until Chiarra could make his arrangements? They would need an opportunity. No one would be storming the gates of the King County Correctional Facility. That meant getting Shaw moved to another location. The most vulnerable point would be while he was in transit. How could the lawyer manage that? Claim that Shaw required a hospital visit? Special care of some kind?

Waiting for the jailbreak was beginning to feel like his time in the Rangers. You never knew when the call would come. You just had to be ready to move—and move damned fast.

THIRTY-NINE

Sofia Rohner stood beside the oil portrait of her grandparents, pretending to admire it while the housekeeper Bettina brought the tea and set it on the hearth. Sofia thanked her and said no, she wouldn't require a fire this evening. She waited until Bettina had shut the door before she dared to sit. Fearful that even such a small measure of relaxation might start her to weeping.

It had been her worst day in memory. First the Seattle police had called as she'd crossed the apartment threshold, bags in hand, before she'd even hugged little Iva hello. Informing her of Linda's death. Linda's murder. The detective had peppered her with questions about Linda's recent activities and work life in painful detail. But her own requests to him had been largely evaded.

Sofia had then spent three hours, off and on, consulting with her lawyer. Rianne's expertise was civil cases, but she had connections in official circles as well as social ones. Through her sources Rianne was able to glean that Van Shaw had been arrested on suspicion of Linda's homicide. She had explained to Sofia that an arrest required the police to have at least a modicum of substantive evidence. Shaw's guilt may not be certain, but it was likely.

That revelation had prompted more demands from Sofia and more rounds of inquiry for Rianne. While waiting for the outcome, Sofia had reached out to Linda's daughter, Callie, who was in her second year at Barnard and had been the first person the police had contacted. The girl was so distraught that Sofia couldn't bear to hang up until she was sure friends were on hand to provide Callie comfort. Then there had to be a conversation with Linda's exhusband, with whom Linda had remained on good terms. He would be catching the next flight to New York to see Callie; Sofia had offered him the use of a car for the duration. Finally Michael, her husband, had called from London, and Sofia had shared what seemed like a decade's worth of news from the two days since they had last spoken.

She wished that Michael were here now. He wouldn't say much. He rarely had to, to make her feel better.

By the time she had eliminated everything she could think to do, it was late afternoon. Her mind was no quieter than when the detective had first told her Linda was gone.

It was absurd. Within a brief span of days, two people she knew were dead by someone's hand. Sofia couldn't speak for Nelson Bao's life, but she was sure that no one could possibly feel such animosity toward Linda as to harm her. Violence was . . . an *alien* thing in Linda Edgemont's world.

Shaw. Sofia felt equally certain that brutality was not new to Shaw. Even setting aside the conspicuous facial scars, you could read savagery in the man. Yet Sofia had liked Shaw initially. In his rough way, he'd seemed candid.

Now she felt hatred for him. Hate and confusion in equal measure, because no matter what bits of inside information Rianne had been able to glean, no one had admitted a guess as to *why* Shaw might have killed Linda.

Sofia stood. Delicate cup in hand, she went to her desk. She would see if Callie or one of Sofia's mutual friends with Linda had reached out online. If that came up empty, she would work. She sat down and sipped the tea as her laptop came to life.

She had a message.

From Linda.

For a long moment, Sofia simply stared. The message had been sent on a social network that she rarely used, had hardly remembered that she'd installed. Three years ago Linda had sent her a birthday greeting e-card that had required the extension be installed on her laptop. Sofia recalled feeling peevish about having to do so. Another surrender to online data acquisition, just to see some animated flowers. But to be civil, she had clicked her approval and promptly forgotten about it.

Now the notification appeared in a lavender box at the corner of her screen. The start of the message, like a tease. **Linda E:** *Hello Sofia, I'm so sorry . . .*

The date and time were at the bottom of the little pastel window, in a tiny font. The message had been sent on Thursday. Linda had died on Friday.

Sofia clicked on the box. The window expanded to fill the screen.

Hello Sofia,

I'm so sorry your beautiful estate had to bear witness to such a tragedy. It's unthinkable.

Given how terrible this week must be for you, perhaps the time is wrong for a request. But I need to speak with you when you return, as soon as we can manage. Would you be able to make an hour for me early Monday? We could meet at your home if convenient.

In any event, please reply here, and please don't send an e-mail or book time on our office network. It's important that our conversation remain private. My apologies for the unusual circumstances; I will explain all when we see each other again.

Thank you so much. I pray this strife is quickly resolved and laid to rest.

Love,
Linda

Sofia read the message a second time. Unusual circumstances indeed. In the years they'd known each other, as their office amity had evolved into personal friendship, Sofia could scarcely recall a time Linda had *not* used the Droma system to communicate with her. Nor she with Linda. Even at the worst of moments—when she'd called Linda after losing her first baby four years ago, before Iva had been born—she'd used her company-provided mobile. Now Linda wanted her to keep their meeting discreet.

No. Now Linda was dead. Her wishes for privacy—maybe the need for privacy—rendered insignificant.

Sofia thought about that, looking at the message in its lavender-bordered window.

Only a handful of people would have visibility to Linda's work calendar, including meetings she'd designated as private. Sofia's father, of course. His administrative assistant. And Olen Anders, as chief of staff, and his assistant. It was also reasonable to assume that each would be able to access Linda's Droma voice mail. Recorded messages might be transcribed or forwarded by staff at the executive's request.

Why would Linda want to keep their conversation hidden from Father's eyes? Or Olen's?

Linda had sent the message the day after she'd returned from Briar Bay. Said their meeting was urgent. A possible connection there. Sofia had seen her briefly as Linda had been boarding the flight home. The distress on her friend's face had been obvious from twenty meters' distance. Clearly that anguish had continued into the next day.

Nelson Bao's death had affected them all. But why Linda in particular? Had she interacted with Nelson more than Sofia had known?

Sofia opened her own calendar. She could search back through meetings by categories or teams. Or by specific external partners. For transparency that last parameter was available to all senior executives at Droma. Sofia herself had insisted on having those search capabilities implemented by their IT department. As an aid to her oversight of client development, she wanted a record of all partner interactions.

She searched first for Jiangsu Special Manufacturing, seeing a handful of calls and meetings where Linda had been invited. Her father had dealt with most of the direct conversations with Chen Li. Nelson Bao was not among the meeting participants.

Sofia then tried searching for Bridgetrust. Those results made her stop and run the query again, just to make sure she hadn't entered something wrong. Linda had attended a few preliminary meetings with the New York investment company during the past month, as many of them had in the lead-up to the conference on the island.

Along with one other meeting. One that Linda had created herself. An hour's conversation, all the way back in February. Weeks before Sofia's father, Sebastien, had ostensibly brought Bridgetrust to the table for the first time to discuss a partnership.

Had the February meeting been an initial inquiry from Bridgetrust? If so, Linda Edgemont, Sebastien's counsel, would not have been a logical starting point.

There was no conference call or video-chat link listed for the meeting, Sofia noticed. Linda had either met them in person—though no conference room on the High Bridge campus had been booked either—or she had telephoned Bridgetrust directly.

Edwin Chiarra. That was the name Linda had specified in her notes. Sofia didn't recognize it. Nor were there any other meetings with Bridgetrust or with Mr. Chiarra after that point, until the team negotiations.

Sofia would ask her father. Perhaps he knew who Edwin Chiarra was.

Or, she countered, perhaps she would scrutinize Linda's activities a little more before raising the question.

The tea had gone cold. Sofia hardly noticed, sipping minute amounts as she read the message once again.

Linda had been adamant about secrecy. It might be in her own best interest to honor her friend's final wishes.

FORTY

The next day, twenty minutes before four o'clock in the afternoon, a guard tossed Shaw a pair of white shoelaces and told him to gather his stuff. He was moving. The guard didn't elaborate; volunteering more information would imply Shaw had any kind of say in the matter. Many of the Ranger instructors had taken the same tack, usually adding abuse as punctuation.

A pair of correctional officers flanked him to the elevator and through two checkpoints to the sally port where he'd first arrived. They waited inside of the final steel door, watching through the bulletproof glass of its window until a police cruiser arrived and the rolling gate had closed behind it. A uniformed officer was driving the cruiser. Kanellis was in the passenger seat.

"Have a good stay?" the detective said as the officer cuffed Shaw. "It's not over yet. You've got a round-trip ticket back here. Or maybe someone will decide to ship your ass directly to Monroe so you can kill time in gen pop."

Unless it had been as part of a police-academy tour, Shaw guessed that Kanellis had never been inside a prison. Neither had Shaw. He was happy to remain ignorant.

"Back here after what?" Shaw said.

Kanellis drummed his hands on the cruiser's roof. "San Juan County wants to talk to you. One of their detectives came in this morning to meet with you and your lawyer. Where'd you dig up that guy? He's boring the shit out of Cole right now at West."

West Precinct. On Virginia Street, barely a mile away. Whatever was going to happen, it would happen in the heart of downtown, right at the peak of the afternoon.

They loaded Shaw into the back of the cop car and drove up 4th

Ave. Weekday traffic crawled. The cruiser gained a block and a half at most with every synchronized change of the lights on the northbound street. Shaw scanned the sidewalks, looking for anyone paying attention to their progress. Whoever Chiarra had sent wouldn't wait until the police car arrived at West, where any number of cops might be on the street outside.

It might not happen at all. The lawyer might have oversold his mysterious employer's abilities or readiness to commit major felonies.

Shaw recollected as much as he could about the roads between the two stations. Decided where he would choose, if he were running the op. Perhaps after the turn onto Virginia. There was a large Westin Hotel a block along. People coming and going. Escape up Westlake, which would flow better than most thoroughfares during the middle of the day. Maybe switch cars near Denny.

"Guerin won't be there," Kanellis said, interrupting Shaw's thoughts. "In case you were counting on the lieutenant putting in a good word with San Juan. Not that it would matter. Since they decided the Chinese guy was murdered, they've been dying to get you in an interview room."

They were coming up on Westlake Center mall. The cruiser stopped in line for the light to cross Pine. Next to them office workers filled the tables in the small plaza across from the mall's entrance. The spindly trees lining the plaza had been wrapped with yellow-white Christmas lights, a touch of yule on a bright summer day.

A car alarm sounded from far up on the next block. Two blaring notes, howling every second at a volume that would make pedestrians wince and walk quickly in any other direction.

A second alarm joined the first. Then a third. A bicyclist flew down 4th coming the wrong way on the one-way street, pedaling like he was being chased by Dobermans. He skidded to a stop beside the cruiser.

"Hey, man." He pointed and bent his stubbled and sunglassed face over the handlebars. "Lady got hit by a car up there. It's bad, dude."

"Shit," Kanellis said. The driver flashed the lights and tapped the siren to slowly force the cars in front of him out into the broad intersection with its red and gray bricks arranged in zigzag patterns. Kanellis got out and ran to stop the cross traffic on Pine to give them room.

Shaw looked hard at the cyclist as the man stood on the pedals, already pulling away. Was he lying? Had Chiarra's team sacrificed someone for a distraction?

The driver stopped the cruiser on a diagonal in the center of the intersection. Its lights whirled, reflecting off the store windows and the vehicles surrounding them. Ahead, the block between Pine and Olive Way was a snarl of trapped cars and buses. They could go no farther.

A sharp crack and a flash of light from beyond the traffic jam caused both Shaw and the cop in the driver's seat to rear back in surprise. A woman standing at the crosswalk screamed in fright, her cry almost lost in the combined shrieks of the car alarms, echoing off the buildings as if redoubling their panic. Smoke rose in a thick white plume from the next block.

Shaw had seen that light and heard that sound before. A flashbang. And the smoke was almost certainly pouring from another grenade someone had popped at the same time.

The cop in the driver's seat jumped out, locked the doors, and ran after Kanellis, who was sprinting ahead toward the supposed destruction.

A loud whack on the left rear door made Shaw whip his head around. For an instant he saw nothing. Then the cyclist stood up from where he'd been kneeling by the wheel. The man had dropped his helmet, revealing a sweaty mop of curls. His stubbled face was now concealed by a gaiter mask.

The door opened. The cyclist reached in to click Shaw's seat belt open. Shaw didn't have to be told. He wormed his way sideways and out of the car.

"Hold still," said the cyclist from behind him. Shaw looked at the cruiser door. A hole about the diameter of a tennis ball had been cut in the sheet metal. A stiff wire still hung from where it had snagged on something inside the hole. Crude but fast. Punch the hole, reach in with a hook, pop the inner lock mechanism. A technique that took some practice, Shaw knew.

"Hey," somebody called from behind them. A horn honked from the tangle of cars.

A tug on Shaw's cuffs, a snap, and his hands were free, each wrist with a steel bracelet.

"Come on," the cyclist said, dropping his bolt cutters and jogging away at an almost casual pace. Shaw took off after him. The cyclist kept his left hand in a carry pouch slung under his jersey as he ran.

A muscular black man dressed in running gear launched himself off the opposite curb as they turned onto Pine. For an instant Shaw thought he was a citizen, seeing the escape, playing hero. As good as dead. He looked to the cyclist, ready to grab the man if he went for his gun.

But the newcomer slowed and angled to run just behind Shaw and the cyclist. He had an unzipped pouch of his own slung across his broad chest. Shaw prayed no one would be idiot enough to try to stop them.

Two of his attackers from the park, he knew now. The lean guy who'd held the hypodermic and their large leader. The third, the squat bulldog, wouldn't be far.

Maybe waiting in a vehicle. Shaw looked for one idling at the curb in the empty lanes off the blocked intersection. Behind them the car alarms continued their jarring symphony, with a rising accompaniment of angry horns from drivers trapped in the jam.

The cyclist turned and headed directly for the street entrance to Westlake Station. A light-rail terminal that ran beneath the entire block.

Shaw hesitated. Going underground was about the worst choice they could make, short of trying to run all the way to the waterfront and swim to freedom. The big man in the running gear shoved Shaw in the same direction. "Move." He flashed the grip of his pistol inside the pouch.

A fight could quickly become a slaughter, and not only for Shaw. The sidewalks were crowded with pedestrians stopped in midstride by the unexpected chaos at the mall. Shaw followed the cyclist, his burly minder close behind.

Their group slowed to a rapid walk, down the first escalator and through the department-store concourse to a second. Heading deeper underground.

Shaw's minder kept the rear, watching for any pursuit. Anyone near the cruiser and not distracted by the noise a block away would have noticed them escaping. What had other bystanders seen amid the confusion? A group of men jogging unhurriedly. If any of them had noticed that one of the runners was dressed oddly in street clothes, that was Seattle for you.

A cop would have paid more attention. If they'd been clocked heading belowground, a call would already be going out. Downtown, the police could scramble a dozen cars and twice as many patrol cops to the scene in minutes. They might already be closing the station's entrances.

Westlake Station had once served as a thruway for downtown buses. Now it was solely the dominion of light-rail trains. Shaw tried to imagine what the crew's plan was. Boarding a train would be the equivalent of throwing up their hands and surrendering. The cops would stop the train before it neared the next station, holding them as securely as rats in a glass cage while a SWAT team converged. Did the cyclist know of some utility entrance to the station, one the police might not think to block?

His minder shoved him on the shoulder again. Taking out his stress. Shaw's pace hadn't flagged, even as the group neared the bottom of the final staircase to the lower level.

The cyclist was talking into a radio. He stopped, and Shaw and the larger man halted after him, clumped together like tourists who had lost their bearings.

Westlake Station was so large it gave you the impression of being outside on an overcast day, rather than sixty feet below street level.

Over five hundred feet of broad, unbroken platform between the tunnels at either end. Because the city stations and tunnels had also served buses until recently, the train tracks were recessed for miles in either direction to create a smooth, flat surface. The platform level of Westlake looked little different from a wide road where highway workers had forgotten to paint lanes between the curbs. A sparse line of commuters waited on the platforms on either side. All of them unaware of the bedlam on the street twenty yards above their heads.

Shaw saw an eastbound train coming into the opposite platform. Good cover. He could sprint across, make for the exit leading up to . . .

"Be smart," the leader said softly. His clippered hair had receded sharply on either side, leaving a blunt wedge of salt-and-pepper over a deeply furrowed brow. He pressed against Shaw's side. "I got a target pistol and I'm a good shot. You run, I'll put a round through your kidney. Might not kill you but you'll wish it had. Hear me?"

The growl of an engine echoed through the station. A silver Chrysler SUV roared out the mouth of the eastern tunnel, doing fifty miles an hour. Its high beams made Shaw squint. Commuters surged to the back, shying like frightened goats from a charging bull.

The Chrysler swerved close to the platform curb. Before it came to a full stop, the leader shoved Shaw after the cyclist, who reached to yank open the back door. "In."

Shaw went. The leader piled in behind him, forcing Shaw into the middle of the bench seat. The driver hit the gas, and the leader turned to pull the door shut. Shaw had an instant urge to push the man out, sending him tumbling headlong onto the platform. But the cyclist had his own gun out and stuck it in Shaw's ribs.

"Easy, asshole," the cyclist said, baring his teeth. "None of us will cry if you don't make it. Especially Vic."

He nodded to the driver, who was rigidly focused on threading the needle as the western tracks split into two tunnels. Their SUV plunged into the right-hand tube. Darkness enfolded them. The dashboard lights flipped on automatically.

Vic's face looked odd, even from Shaw's limited vantage in the backseat. When the driver glanced right to check the mirror, the man's swollen profile became obvious. Violet streaks ringed his eye and had settled into a puffed blackish mass at the lowest point. A busted nose, and maybe his cheekbone as well.

Good, Shaw thought. I'm not the only one still feeling that fight.

He stared through the windshield. Nothing to see but the curved concrete walls of the tunnel and the silver stripes of the rail tracks on the subterranean road, showing the way. Within thirty seconds the bright circle of the next downtown station appeared around the bend.

Vic kept his foot on the gas. The SUV flew through the station's passenger area. Shaw had a snapshot glimpse of one young woman, no more than ten feet from his window, her eyes and mouth wide and hands reflexively thrown up to ward off the snarling beast. Then the world diminished to concrete and dark once more.

He tried to remember how many stations on the line were underground. At least one more, under Pioneer Square, and then maybe Chinatown. One of the commuters would have called the cops. Units would be converging where the tunnel finally rose to the surface.

Except there was no cellular signal underground. Unless a transit cop had spotted them and managed to radio ahead, the SUV might have a clear path, or at least a far enough head start to evade any roadblock.

They roared through the Pioneer Square station doing sixty. Shaw's brawny minder shuffled sideways in his seat to unzip his running jacket. Underneath he wore a bandolier lined with half a dozen black and green canisters. Extra grenades. Dark curls of chest hair showed through his sweat-soaked T-shirt.

The Chinatown station was aboveground but enclosed. The concrete tunnel became two rows of steel fence. Vic didn't pause except to don sunglasses against the abrupt glare.

The cyclist clambered into the backseat of the SUV to look out the rear window. He spoke into a radio. "Heading for the drop."

"You're clear," a woman's voice replied.

Karla? The comm static made it impossible to tell from just two words.

There would be a barrier at the exit, Shaw recalled. A retractable metal blockade that kept crazy or drunken drivers from entering the transit route at the far end and driving headlong into an oncoming train.

Unless Vic stopped—and he wasn't even slowing—they would smash into the barrier any second. Did their crew not know about it? Shaw braced for an impact.

It never came. The baseball stadium loomed to their right. Vic touched the brakes as the road neared Royal Brougham Way.

"Tucker," he said without taking his eyes from the road. "Which way?"

"The ballpark," the leader answered. "We'll switch cars in the first lot."

Vic nodded, intent on the coming turn. Shaw saw the transit gatehouse, where a guard would stand and control the retractable barrier. The little shed was empty. Jesus, had they killed someone just to bust him out? Tucker and the cyclist both craned their necks in the same direction, perhaps wondering the same thing. Vic swung the Chrysler sharp right. Everyone leaned against the sudden lurch.

Shaw shoved Tucker hard against the window as he hooked a finger in the ring tab of one of the smoke grenades in the man's bandolier and yanked. The ring came loose with a sharp pop. Shaw threw an elbow backward into the face of the lunging cyclist and dove for the shotgun seat.

A modern smoke grenade can produce a hundred thousand cubic feet of opaque vapor in well under a minute. Purple clouds erupted from the little canister to fill the interior of the SUV almost instantly. Tucker's big hands grabbed at Shaw, missed as the vehicle came too fast off the turn and fishtailed wildly. Shaw was thrown against the passenger door. The cyclist cursed in the fog. Tucker retched.

Blind in the thick fumes, Shaw smashed the heel of his hand in the direction of Vic's head. He felt the driver's Oakleys snap in two. Vic slumped, his already damaged nose jetting warm blood onto Shaw's arm. The wheel spun. The Chrysler hit the curb straight on with a shuddering bang that was immediately drowned in a second crash as they struck something less surmountable. Shaw's shoulder bounced off the dash, and he fell onto his ass on the passenger floor, folded almost in two.

He scrambled to reach the door handle, found it, and shoved the door open with his foot. Huge billows of violet smoke rolled with him onto the sidewalk. He stumbled through the mist toward what he hoped was the street, caring less about direction than distance. He heard another door on the SUV thump open behind him.

Across Royal Brougham was a Metro depot, a fenced lot with dozens of county buses parked in tight rows. Shaw ran for the chainlink. Traffic was light on the SODO streets, but already two cars had stopped to goggle at the SUV engulfed in purple fog. Cops wouldn't be far off.

Shaw glanced back. The Chrysler had struck a streetlamp, crushing the grille and one headlight. Tucker stumbled out of the purple murk. He'd managed to toss the smoking grenade away.

Lines of barbed wire topped the eight-foot fence to the bus lot. Shaw ran down the avenue to a spot where one of the fence posts was crumpled inward at knee level. Some driver had backed into the post from the sidewalk, buckling the chain-link toward the street. Shaw grabbed the top to haul himself up and under the first line of wire. Barbs tore his shirt as he hooked a leg over the top and wormed his way sideways and over.

His left side caught fire. He fell to the pavement, more from surprise than distress. Had he punctured his skin on the barbed wire? He pushed himself up and rushed for the line of buses.

This time he heard the crack of the gunshot. He was nearly to the first of the indigo-and-gold buses, running for the six-foot gap between its rear bumper and the flat front of the next in line. Moving well, though he knew something was wrong. His ribs burned.

Would they follow? A dozen witnesses on the city street might not stop them, not if they were desperate.

He ducked between the buses and kept going, winding through

the maze of closely parked behemoths. The smoke and gunfire would bring first responders. Tucker's crew would have to catch him fast or give up the chase.

Someone in the next row of the transit lot laughed. Shaw changed directions, seeking a new path. If he made it out of the lot, could he get far enough away? Would they be watching the exits? Did they know he was wounded?

Warm wetness saturated the left side of his shirt. His vision had begun to blur around the edges. Shock. Nothing he hadn't felt before. He kept going.

One of the buses had been left open. He deliberated for half a second before climbing inside. Blood dripped to the steps behind him like a trail of rubies. He found the button to close the bus's front door and sat heavily on the floor between the rows of seats, out of sight of the windows.

A fire engine's horn blared from the direction of the waterfront. Maybe drawn by the smoke. No cop sirens yet.

Shaw looked down at his left side. Blood loss, yes, but not enough to be life-threatening if he could stanch it. Giving a pint at one of the mandatory drives at Fort Benning would drain more.

He unbuttoned his shirt and peeled it away. Half-congealed blood snapped like weak chewing gum between the fabric and his body. He craned his neck to look. A three-inch gash had torn away skin and sub-cutaneous tissue along the second rib from the bottom. Blood seeped from the center of the laceration. The edges were already clotting.

One of Tucker's target rounds, he guessed. Aimed for his kidney as promised and not missing the rapidly moving bull's-eye by much. Jesus.

The shakes would pass. A few moments of rest were all he needed to get his bearings.

And then what? He had no wallet or phone. His apartment at the Empyrea was only a couple of miles away, but even if he'd had his keys or his lockpicks, SPD might be pounding on that door right now. The Barracuda was parked in the residents' garage and registered in his name. No good.

There was another option. Shaw kept his Ford truck in a garage not far from Bully Betty's on the hill. The pickup was still under the name of the man who'd once owned the apartment, which was itself a false identity. Safe enough transport. If Shaw could reach it.

He crawled to the driver's seat again to find the first-aid kit. The kit and an extra boon. A Metro worker had left a jacket stuffed between the seat and the window. Safety gear, in Day-Glo yellow and gray. Shaw took it and the aluminum box to the rear of the bus.

His side flamed angrily as he removed his shirt. A sticky blackish patch saturated the fabric from the armpit to the lower hem. With gauze pads and tape from the kits, he bandaged his ribs as firmly as he could, then folded the shirt to tape it over the bandage. Putting the safety jacket on was another chore, but at least he didn't look like one of the undead. It hung low enough to cover the blood-soaked belt line of his jeans.

A protective mask was tucked into the kit as well, a leftover from the pandemic days. He put it on.

It was still early afternoon. Shaw didn't have his watch—another thing that remained in the hands of King County Corrections—but it couldn't be much more than half an hour since Kanellis had escorted him out of the jail. It felt more like thirty hours than thirty minutes.

A siren whooped once from a block away. He couldn't stay hidden here for much longer. Shaw left the bus and carefully made his way through the rows of buses toward the far side of the depot. The stadium station was there. A train would be the fastest way out of the area, and he could walk right on. Provided that Tucker and Vic and the curly-haired cyclist hadn't figured that out for themselves. If they were waiting, Shaw would have to hope the cops got to him first.

The depot's exit looked clear. The station was next door, mere yards away, its platform empty save for a handful of commuters at the end of their workday. Shaw waited behind the last row of buses until he saw a train coming north. He hurried across the tracks ahead of it. The train stopped. He boarded.

He backed himself into a corner of the train car to watch the platform. None of Tucker's crew rushed to beat the closing doors. No cops boarded to begin a sweep through the cars.

Shaw slumped into a seat. The train would take him back the way he'd just come, plus one stop farther, to Broadway. From there he could walk to the garage and the truck, if his legs held out. The recorded voice cheerily announced the next station, as if all were right with the world.

His side burned. Not as hotly as his thoughts.

He was positive the cyclist had been talking to a woman. Even if he wasn't a hundred percent that the voice had belonged Karla Haiden, it would be willful ignorance to assume the duplicitous former PI wasn't the leading nominee.

And despite his pain and exhaustion, Shaw felt elated. He knew why. The same rush that he'd always felt after a mission with his platoon or after a score with Dono.

The enemy had taken their best shot at him and missed. He was alive. And free.

Despite his exhilaration, the smile that creased Shaw's drawn face was less from pleasure than an animal baring of teeth.

FORTY-ONE

Dono had constructed hidden compartments in his old cars. Simple holes above the ceiling fabric or cut into the wheel wells. Shaw had been improving on the concept in recent months by experimenting with electronic relays. He parked the truck and remained in the driver's seat—keeping weight on a pressure plate within—and pressed the rear defrost, child lock, and cruise control in that order. With a hum of small hydraulics, the backseat slid forward three inches on its rails.

The compartment was so new that Shaw hadn't had occasion to load it with anything save for a burner phone and two bundles of cash, twenties and fifties. He took them all before leaving the truck and walking to the large storage facility off Union in Capitol Hill. His walk was slightly crooked, a combined result of the pain in his side and his knee, which had begun to twinge again. One more thing he owed Tucker and the boys.

On the way he turned on the phone and sent a text message to Hollis: GO GET AN ICE CREAM. He powered the phone down again.

His fifteen-by-ten storage unit was at the far end of the hall. He lifted the rolling door cautiously to keep from stretching any muscles on his left side. The throb from his wound felt like it might be visible, like the wildly beating heart of a lovestruck cartoon character.

Once inside he found an empty gallon bucket and walked to the water fountain by the elevators to fill it. He returned to switch on the ceiling fluorescents and shut the door. Hanging the lights had been his first task after renting the space. Better illumination than the original sixty-watt bulbs for detail work with locks and electronics. His second chore had been building basic shelves of pine wood. The shelves had steadily filled with duffel bags containing various tools of his trade, from spare computers to cobalt drill bits.

What he needed now was the duffel containing his trauma kit, assembled from smaller first-aid packages and some additional purchases. Shaw dragged the kit from its shelf and sat on a stool to open it. Sample packets of Percocet were in one of the kit's inside pouches. He tore open a packet with his teeth and washed the pill down with a handful of water from the bucket.

He took off the Metro jacket and the folded and gory shirt taped to his torso. The gash reopened when he peeled the gauze away, fresh beads of blood welling up in the clotted line.

Ugly but minor. The laceration would heal within a week if he kept it protected and didn't move too much.

Of course, moving was exactly what he would have to do. Far and fast.

The bullet graze was too wide and too shallow to permit Derma-bonding or stitches. Or at least the kind of stitches he could apply himself. He'd end up making the problem worse if the sutures tore. Cleaning and covering the gash would have to do.

He removed what he needed from the kit and set each item within reach. More gauze pads plus tubes of lidocaine and antibiotic ointments along with a large roll of athletic tape.

It had been ten minutes since he'd sent the text. Long enough for Hollis to have taken a quick walk, if he were home. Shaw turned on the burner and dialed a number before putting the phone on speaker.

"Little Coney," a female voice said. Young-sounding, maybe a teenager on her summer job, selling soft-serve and sandwiches to the boaters at the big marina.

"Hey," said Shaw. "I'm looking for a friend of mine who might be there. Older guy, looks kind of like a nice redheaded gorilla."

The girl gave a snorting chuckle. "Um. Nobody's bought anything for a few minutes. Hang on." Shaw waited. "Ooh, I think I see him. He's coming from the docks."

"That's him. Could you put him on when he gets there?"

"Um. We're not supposta."

"It's kind of urgent. I've broken down, and he's going to help." If the kid assumed Shaw meant a busted car, that wasn't technically lying to her. "And he's a good tipper."

"Okay. Just for a minute."

"Thank you."

Shaw dipped a clean cotton rag into the bucket of water and began to wash the blood and cloth fibers from his left side. He had most of the skin around the wound clean when Hollis's voice came on.

"It's me," said Shaw.

"Who else?"

Shaw held the rag against his side with his elbow and opened the tube of antibiotic. "I need to keep this short. Do you have a spare phone?"

"Several."

"Post the number on the bulletin board." The Web page for marina residents to share notices of lost belongings or special events. Not open to the public and a site Shaw knew that Hollis could get to immediately without needing further help. Hollis Brant was at least as ingenious as Shaw when it came to building things with his hands, but the finer points of current technology often eluded the smuggler. "Once I call, you can erase the post."

"Right," said Hollis. "You okay? You sound . . . strained."

Shaw had been spreading antibiotic over the wound, which continued to seep. Red dewdrops that swelled until their weight allowed them to dribble onto the congealed edge of the gash. Maybe he should have started with the analgesic salve. The Percocet was taking its time kicking in.

"I'm fine. Give the counter kid a few bucks. I'll talk to you in fifteen." He hung up.

With the wound as clean as he could make it, he taped a stack of three gauze pads over the red furrow and reinforced the tape with additional strips, making an X over his ribs.

He was desperately thirsty, he realized. The water in the bucket was bloody from his cleaning job. He found a bag with spare dark-colored clothes, there in case he needed to change on the fly for night work. With some care he worked his left arm into the sleeve of a black turtleneck and put it on. Too warm for the season, but at least he wouldn't attract flies. He dumped the bloody shirt and the yellow safety jacket in the trash on his way back to the water fountain.

It might be a long time before he could return to the storage unit. He deliberated over what to take. No more than could fit in one medium-size rucksack, in case he had to hoof it. A spare set of lock-pick tools and other basics were obvious. As was his available cash, a larger stack than in the truck, ten thousand dollars in used fifties. He added a laptop and extra burner phones.

Shaw looked hard at the more sophisticated gear and chose half a dozen items designed to tackle alarm systems of office buildings or high-end apartments. Big-city jobs. If something more specialized became a necessity, he would see what he could construct on the go.

He packed more first-aid items and some clothing. From a pocket in the clothing bag, he took a small plastic zipper case containing chewable fifty-milligram tablets of Vyvanse. If he had to drive for a couple of days without stopping, the amphetamine derivative would make it possible.

Finally he turned to the duffels with his guns, each firearm individually wrapped in cloth. A long bag held a Benelli shotgun and a fine Merkel .30-06 that had once been Dono's. He rejected those immediately. Too big for travel. The handguns required more thought. Would he be getting on a plane at some point? If so, any pistol would have to be tossed.

Shaw had been raised to think of all guns that way. As disposable as the bandage on his side, something to be used once and then discarded quickly. Dono had matured out of his violent youth by the time Van came into the picture, but the habits had remained and the old thief passed them along to his grandson.

On deployments with the Rangers, Shaw had cleaned and checked his weapons nearly every day, sometimes more than once. His life and the lives of his brothers had relied on the arms' operating flawlessly. Even so, he'd never considered his M4 or Beretta sidearm to be prized possessions. Nor had he become part of gun culture like many of his friends in veterans' groups. A gun was a tool. Shaw owned only so many as need demanded.

And this was a time of need. Twice he'd almost been victim to Tucker and Vic and the curly-headed cyclist. He couldn't let them be third-time lucky, even if it meant the risk of adding a firearms charge to his rapidly accumulating list of felonies. He chose a scuffed but serviceable SIG P226 with a fifteen-round magazine he'd bought under the table from a former SEAL and a pocket Glock 26 in case he required something more concealable than the burly SIG.

Both guns took nine-millimeter ammunition. Shaw packed a box of fifty rounds into the ruck along with the handguns. If he couldn't survive whatever situation found him with fifty shots, more ammo was unlikely to make a difference.

On his way out of the storage facility, Shaw stopped at the front desk. The guy running the shop selling moving boxes and strapping tape was engrossed in watching a video on his phone. Over the guy's shoulder, Shaw saw the monitor of the office computer cycling through screen-saver images of tropical vacation spots.

"Hey, man," said Shaw. "My phone crapped out on me, and I need to get a buddy's number online. Okay if we look that up?" He pointed to the screen, which was showing what looked like a cottage replica of the Taj Mahal in the Maldives.

The guy nodded idly without turning his eyes from the video. "G'head."

Shaw typed in the URL and logged onto the marina's website. Hollis—or *FrancescaQ*, his boat name and dock letter—had been the most recent post. Shaw memorized the phone number in the post and dialed it as he walked back to his truck.

"Where are you?" Hollis asked immediately.

"In the city. Not for long."

"The last I knew, your good lady Wren told me you were counting the hours while the police decided whether to press charges. I take it that went well, if you're walking free?"

"Not exactly." Shaw plugged in an earpiece so he could talk to Hollis as he drove. By the time he'd reached the part about popping the smoke grenade in Tucker's face, Shaw was parked south of the Industrial District in front of his final stop in Seattle, and Hollis was sputtering.

"I'm looking at the news right now," Hollis said. "One of the local cable channels. There's been nothing about gunshots or other violence near the stadiums."

"Their team was probably gone before the cops showed." Shaw reassured Hollis that he was fine before mentioning the graze on his side. "I'm headed out of town now."

"That sounds like the best of some terrible options. Sweet Jesus, Van. How . . . is there anything I can do?"

"Better that you don't do anything. You're a known associate of mine. I guarantee the cops will be keeping tabs on you during the next few days to see if I turn up. Maybe more than just cops. I don't know how far the reach of these people goes. If they're funded by Sebastien Rohner, they might not have an upper limit to their budget. Assume lots of eyes, lots of ears. This should be the last conversation we have while you're aboard your boat."

"I understand. What should I tell your ladies, Wren and the old broad I love so much?"

"Let Addy and Wren know I'll be in touch as soon as I can. Probably online—that's safer than phones. Thanks. And I'm sorry."

"Won't be the first time the police have followed me around for their amusement." Hollis sighed. "There's a border trip, a meet with some acquaintances I'll have to postpone. But perhaps this is a sign."

"Keep low."

Shaw put on sunglasses and a baseball cap before checking the street once more. He entered the small business, a twenty-four-hour private-mailbox service. The ID wasn't invulnerable to the wave of gentrification that had swamped the city, but there were still factories and fulfillment centers working odd hours. The mailbox business catered to workers, documented and otherwise, who might need a consistent address for their mail if not their homes. Shaw leased one of the smallest boxes, which served as a kind of safe-deposit. Its key was hidden back at his apartment, but the lack hardly slowed him down.

Inside the box was an envelope, and inside the envelope was a driver's license and a Chase Bank debit card and a low-limit Visa under the name Steven Blake Ingram. The license showed Shaw's face.

All three cards were authentic. It was Ingram that was a phony. The man had existed for barely a year. Over time Shaw would have slowly created a history for the identity, enough that the name might have school records and tax history and a birth certificate. As it was, Ingram was as thin as the cards themselves. Any scratching below the surface would reveal the paper man for what he was.

Beggars and choosers, thought Shaw. It would have to do.

He left the mailbox and drove to the on-ramp for I-90. The interstate was the longest freeway in the country, a wavering line all the way to Boston. If things went to plan—for once this week—Shaw would stay on 90 until Ohio, then keep due east to New York.

He was a fugitive. His head rocked a little at that. But there was a limit to what the cops could and would do to find him. They wouldn't throw up roadblocks or have troopers patrolling every road leading out of the state. Not for a suspect who hadn't been formally charged yet, much less convicted. If he slept in the cab of the truck and avoided showing his distinctive face to cameras at gas stations, he would stay off their radar.

It was his other pursuers that concerned him. He'd barely escaped Tucker's crew, twice. Who knew what the team had planned for him if the jailbreak had gone their way? Torturing him for Chen's chemical—the sample he'd lied about having—might be only the start.

He had to assume they knew his history. They might guess that he had prepared for a time when he'd have to run.

His level of risk depended on who Tucker and his crew were ultimately working for. He felt sure that they were part of whatever shadowy enterprise lay behind the Bridgetrust front. Tucker's crew, and Chiarra, and Bill Flynn, and Karla as well.

If they were independent operators, their resources would be limited. But if Sebastien Rohner was putting his money and influence behind them, their reach might extend far beyond any border Shaw could cross.

His single slim advantage was that his enemies couldn't know he had learned Karla's real name and her background. That could be a lead in finding whoever was pulling her strings. She and Flynn had gone to huge trouble to hide behind Bridgetrust. Uncovering why might give Shaw some leverage against them. Or at least something he could take to Guerin.

But to find it, he'd have to risk going onto their home turf. That decision had come to him almost without conscious thought on the drive from Capitol Hill. He was in for a long trip.

Drive until nightfall, Shaw decided. By then he'd be east of the mountains and the Columbia River. He could find a place somewhere around Moses Lake to park the truck out of sight and sleep. Save the go-pills for an emergency.

From there it would take three full days of driving, assuming some miles on the back roads if he needed to skirt the largest cites. And taking what time he could to rest and heal. He would have to be as sharp as a razor when he hit New York City.

FORTY-TWO

Sebastien Rohner summoned Anders to his office suite in Droma's main building in High Bridge. Anders's own office was situated at the near corner. He strode down the hall, the agreeable aroma of the morning's first batch of coffee from the executive kitchen permeating the floor. The campus was new and Droma the first company to lease space, before construction was complete. That had allowed them some say in the final floor plans. Droma's executive accommodations were larger by half than in any other building on the campus.

Sofia was there. Standing directly in front of her father's desk, as Sebastien sat behind it, his chin high. Anders inferred a disagreement simply from their positions. Sofia turned, her frown confirming his guess.

"Did you know?" she said to Anders. "About Van Shaw's escape?"

Anders shut the door. The office was soundproofed, a preventive measure he and Sebastien took with all their private workspaces.

"I learned of it only this morning," he said.

Rohner held up a hand. "I was telling Sofia that the sheriff's office called last night to make sure we were aware. In case Shaw should attempt to . . . approach any member of the family." He turned to his daughter. "I'd planned on telling you in person this morning."

"They suspect he killed Linda," said Sofia. "What are we doing about that?"

Anders responded for Rohner. "I've asked Warren Kilbane to resume his duties. I realize we'd intended to suspend Warren pending a review. But given his familiarity with our procedures and his clearance—not to mention that he may be a target for Shaw himself—having him with us is a wiser direction."

"I meant do we believe the police are correct?"

Rohner blinked. "I have no cause to think they are wrong. That's sufficient."

"Not for me. Not with the oddities in your behavior of late." Sofia glanced at Anders.

"Perhaps I should excuse myself," he said.

"No," she said. "You're part of this. First the family collection was moved to the island despite my misgivings. You said you had wanted to offer tours. Then I discover your plan was to use the gallery for the chemical tests with Jiangsu Manufacturing, which you might well have told me from the start."

"I did plan to have guests view the gallery, and I'm sorry you were left out of the decision about the lab," said Rohner. "It was a late choice. So long as we took measures to protect the art, I didn't think you'd mind."

"Protection seemed to be your top concern. You left me in the dark about Shaw's role as well."

"We wanted his expert evaluation of our alarm system. It hardly mattered for him whether the gallery held art or chemicals, did it?"

"It matters if those chemicals were why Nelson Bao was killed."

"Shaw again," said Anders. "The man has a violent past."

Sofia looked at him. "Is that what made him an attractive candidate?"

Anders forced a smile. This was really going too far. Too close.

"We made an error, hiring Shaw," he said. "Please let's not compound it by quarreling. If he's innocent, I'm sure the police will reach that conclusion."

"Our focus should be on closing the agreement with Chen Li." Rohner leaned back in his chair and pressed his hand to the desk, his habitual gesture to punctuate the closing of a topic.

Sofia appeared unmoved. "I'm aware of how important this deal is, how important new markets are. To Droma's future as well as to you personally. I know how hard you've worked to make us successful." Her expression softened. "I just want to be sure you're not sacrificing too much of yourself."

"We'll be fine, my dear," Rohner said. "This will all be over soon. Now, what can we do for Linda's family?"

"I've spoken with her parents, and her daughter. They're planning the funeral for Saturday, pending . . . whether Linda will be released in time. We should cover the expense."

"Of course. Just let my assistant know. She can coordinate everything for them."

"And Jiangsu," said Sofia. "If it can't be concluded promptly, I want to discuss alternatives. We can restructure. Even form different partnerships. At least two of our competitors would leap at a chance to lease our top-level staff—"

Anders nearly coughed. "A merger?" he said. "That's . . . far too premature, Sofia."

"I'm not saying it's first on my list," she replied. "But it's viable."

"We can consider all options," Rohner said, in a tone that invited no further input. "Privately."

Sofia hesitated.

"Good," she said finally. "I'll make time for us next week."

She shut the door behind her, saving Anders the trouble.

"She seems convinced of Shaw's innocence," said Rohner, "and that our hiring him had ulterior motives. She as much as said so."

"She couldn't know we'd intended to take the polymer. And any suspicions Sofia may have hardly matter now. We're past that point. We can only hope to recover the sample and complete the deal as originally planned."

"Yes."

Anders crossed to sit in one of the club chairs in front of the desk, taking the moment to compose his thoughts. Sofia's plea to her father had been couched in concern for his well-being—genuine concern, certainly—but she had hinted at other worries.

"Sofia may have also guessed that Chen did not invent the sample," he said.

"What if she has? She won't press the point so long as we finish quickly and without further misfortune." Rohner frowned. "And still no word from Chen."

"I'll try again today." As he had every day for the past five. "But if Sofia *should* begin asking questions beyond these walls, that could be disastrous. Chen is clearly wary. Hargreaves . . . well, we can imagine how Hargreaves might react if he thought Sofia posed a risk to the deal."

Rohner stood and walked to the window. Perhaps to cover his unease. "We'll have Rangi stay close to Sofia. Armed. We'll tell her it's a protective measure while Shaw is at large."

"A fine idea. And if she goes to the police?"

"She said herself how important this is. Sofia would never . . . jeopardize Droma."

Anders laced his fingers. Unconvinced. But Sebastien was right about the clearest path. They must finish what they'd started. Before the investigations of Bao's and Linda's murders turned to official inquiries about links between Droma and Avizda Industrial, where Bao had worked most recently.

Anders felt a familiar knot in his stomach at the thought. Conspiracy was an ugly concept. He'd thought so from the start.

Just a few more days, and then he could breathe. This whole blighted affair would be a memory.

FORTY-THREE

Shaw reached the outskirts of Staten Island before midnight on Thursday and continued across, over the Verrazzano Bridge into Brooklyn. He didn't know the territory. But the drive since sunrise had provided plenty of time to map his route and to plan.

There were three used-car dealers and one scrap-iron yard within half a mile of one another in the Gravesend neighborhood and on the northern side of Coney Island. Shaw cruised past each of them during the next hour. Taking his time to get a good look. All the vehicles in the scrap yard had been stripped down to the chassis. Two of the car dealers had installed reasonable security.

The third dealership was pudding.

Just an eight-foot fence with a spool of razor wire on its top and a pair of cameras, one pointed at the gate and one at the lot. No camera behind the repair bays and office. The dealer was guarding against somebody stealing a car or some of its engine parts, so why monitor anything but the inventory?

Shaw had bought a thick blanket in Montana three days prior to have something over him while sleeping in the truck at night. He parked in an alley behind the fence at the back of the dealership and climbed from the bed of the truck onto its roof to toss the blanket over the concertina wire. Stepping on the top pipe, he jumped down behind the buildings.

His side thumped back at the impact. Not so much that he thought the scab under the bandages had torn, but enough to make him wince. He'd laid off painkillers during the long days of driving. The endless ribbon of road had been dizzying enough.

He walked around the repair bays, judged the angle of the camera pointed at the two dozen vehicles packed like sardines into the narrow front lot, and low-crawled to the cars on his elbows and knees. The lot was stained with years of oil and gas drippings. By the time he reached the first row, so was his hooded sweatshirt. Worming his way to the back of the pack, he removed the front license plates from two cars with Empire State plates. He tucked the metal rectangles into his shirt to crawl out of the front lot and return to the truck.

The risk that the missing plates would be noticed deep in the dealership's logjam of cars was low. But Shaw wanted one more level of remove. He drove to a big-box retail store and found a scattering of cars on the outskirts of the huge parking lot. Common for employees working late or just people leaving their junkers overnight. He found a rustbucket Chevy that looked as if it hadn't moved in a month, with the same blue-on-white New York plates and up-to-date tabs. It took him less than three minutes to swap the set of the dealership plates for the Chevy's, and to put the Chevy's plates on his truck.

Overkill, maybe. But owners were more likely to notice that their license plates were missing than to realize that the plate miraculously had different numbers today. Shaw had already taken a calculated risk by driving all the way from Washington with the truck's original plates. The truck was clean. There had been no reason for Shaw to gamble by cruising the interstate with plates stolen from Omaha or Indianapolis.

There was another risk he'd have to take: checking in to a motel. Tomorrow would require being among people. After spending most of three days and two nights in the confines of the truck, Shaw knew he reeked of drive-thru food and old sweat. He rolled down the windows to air himself out on the short trip to Red Hook.

The motel he'd chosen looked like a brick of spoiled tofu. Three stories of white tinged with brown. But its accommodations included an enclosed garage that took up most of the ground level. The truck would be out of sight of the street.

Shaw parked in a back corner by the stairwell, changed shirts, and took his rucksack with him to the lobby. Steven Blake Ingram rented a second-floor room for two nights.

The room looked out onto a narrow side street and the green front of a Thai-foods importer. The lip of the window was fifteen feet off the ground. A long drop, but manageable if he had to make a hasty exit. He knotted bedsheets into a makeshift rope and tied the end to the bed frame. He secured the door by wedging the ironing board from the closet at an angle between the handle and the lower edge of the heavy plywood television cabinet. Almost as good as an old-style police lock. An intruder would need a sledgehammer to batter his way inside.

The only unpacking Shaw did was to set his gun on the carpeted floor between the bed and the wall.

He gave the room one last check. His eyes were gritty and his side ached. He knew he should wash the healing bullet graze and change the bandage. Instead he sat down on the bed and managed to take off his boots before he fell asleep, the room lights still blazing.

HARGREAVES'S TEAM BEGAN TO ARRIVE at the Pioneer Square bar just before 11:00 P.M. He had chosen the bar for its back table where they could talk with the noise of the crowd covering their conversation.

Tucker was first through the door. The waitress in a J&M T-shirt passed. Hargreaves gave her forty dollars and told her to bring a pitcher of High Life and four glasses and to keep the change. The order was on the table before Louis and Vic showed. They poured and took cursory sips. The beer was the cost of the table, not for enjoying.

"Louis," Hargreaves prompted.

The curly-haired man nodded. "Shaw's staying off his accounts. There's been no activity on bank or credit cards since before he was in jail. No purchases before that time that might signal he was getting ready to travel either. Cash withdrawals are less than a hundred bucks each transaction for the past two months. If he's got money, it's somewhere else."

"Vic."

Vic sniffed, as much as he could manage. His nose looked like an eggplant left to wilt on the vine. "Last known address is a house on the east side of the city, but another family's been living there for at least a year. I went by the marina to see the known associate . . ."

"Brant," Tucker filled in.

"Yeah. Lives on a big powerboat. Easy for me to hang in the parking lot and watch with field glasses—the place is busy with the sun and summer people. The guy's just fixing stuff on his boat all day. He sits up on deck and eats his meals. He hasn't gone out and bought a lot of groceries or other things that might mean he has a guest. Looks alone. More than that. He looks like he's trying to *show* he's alone, y'know?"

Hargreaves nodded. "These are professional criminals. Brant would have heard that Shaw broke out of jail. He might assume he's under police surveillance in case Shaw shows up. What else?"

"Shaw's got no social media at all. Phone records are scattered," said Tucker. "We only found records to one account in his name so far. Most of his calls are to a woman living near the house Vic checked."

"Girlfriend?"

Tucker shook his head. "Old woman. Former neighbor, so I'd guess Shaw looks after her some."

Hargreaves filed that fact away. A possible pressure point there, if there was a way to make Shaw aware that they could get to the woman.

"And?" he said.

The three men exchanged glances, each apparently hoping the others had something more to offer.

"Here's what I see," said Hargreaves, his affectless voice low enough that the other men had to lean in to catch every word. "He's slipped away from you twice. That's more than simple chance. You've underestimated him. When I offered additional support to break him out of police transport—only two officers there, I'll remind you—you declined. Now he's in the wind. Given his family history and his training, it's a fair assumption that he may be all the way gone, drinking better beer than this shit somewhere in Mexico."

"If he comes to sell the chemical . . ." Louis began.

"I'm no longer convinced Shaw has the sample," Hargreaves said. "If he did, he'd be looking to cash in by now. His first move out of jail would have been to contact Rohner. Or Karla."

"You sure he hasn't?" said Tucker.

"I know he hasn't. Because Rohner doesn't make a move without Anders, and we've got Anders on lock. Also because Rohner's been too busy running around with his ass on fire. His daughter suspects the deal was dirty from the start. He's begging Chen to come back to the bargaining table. Chen keeps stonewalling, saying it's taking longer to get a new chemist. As though his bosses couldn't have a planeload of party loyalists with Ph.D.s here within twelve hours."

"What about Karla? She didn't hear anything?" said Vic.

Hargreaves looked at him. "Let me worry about Karla."

Vic's eyes turned to the table.

Tucker frowned. "But Shaw knew what the sample looked like. He described it to Chiarra. He must have seen it at least."

"Yes. That's the only fact that makes me hesitate. It's possible that Shaw spotted Bao or Chen with the sample on the island. He's a thief. Maybe he poked around in their rooms. He might not have known what the sample was at the time, just that they were protective of it. When Karla told Shaw about the chemical and dropped the hint to sell it back, he put two and two together."

"And used that to trick us into busting him out," finished Tucker. "He's got balls."

"So who does have the junk if Shaw doesn't?" said Louis.

Hargreaves smiled without humor. "It's possible that the chemical was never missing in the first place. That the honorable Mr. Chen is stringing us along, seeing if Bao's killer surfaces. Or if his partners wind up eating each other." He shook his head. "Time is on Chen's side. And ours. We have what Chen and Rohner require. The final piece of their precious polymer."

He waved away the approaching waitress.

"Keep up surveillance. We'll stay on Shaw through the weekend. If there's no change by Monday, then I'll have to find a way to move things forward with Chen myself."

Easier said, Hargreaves thought. He would have to have a very convincing story to keep Chen from bolting once the Chinese agent learned who he really was. But he was confident that Chen's objective would win out over his caution.

He finished his glass. Out of the corner of his eye, he saw Louis glance at Tucker. They were the smarter ones. They would be curious about how far they would have to go to shut this operation down and prevent any comebacks.

"Talk to you tomorrow," he said. Vic and Louis absented themselves immediately. Tucker hung back, just for a moment, and then nodded abruptly and left with similar haste.

Hargreaves knew that Tucker and the others had been talking among themselves about Bao and about the lawyer, Linda Edgemont. Making their own guesses as to what had happened to each. Hargreaves stayed informed of his team's communications, professional and private.

They all doubted that Shaw had been behind the killings. They were correct about that, if nothing else.

Smart, Hargreaves thought again. Smart not to ask the question to which you didn't really want to know the answer.

FORTY-FOUR

Ms. Abrams?" Shaw said, rapping on the open door of A&A Investigations.

The woman behind one of two desks at the far end of the elongated office examined Shaw over the top of her computer monitor. "Mr. Shaw."

"Right. Thanks for seeing me."

It was Friday morning, early enough that Shaw could smell the stale air accumulated during the night in the hallway outside the PI office. Inside, an air conditioner in the window was turned up high, laboring to produce a breeze.

"Lorraine Abrams. How do you do." She swept her hand over the surface of her desk, holding a pair of bifocals with the other hand over her nose. "Pardon, I've dropped a screw out of my glasses. The irony being that I need the damn things to see to— There it is."

Abrams stood up, the errant bit of metal pinched between her fingers. She was above average height with broad shoulders, like someone who had rowed crew in college and never quit. Shaw guessed Abrams was in her midfifties. Her short-sleeved black blouse and gray slacks were crisp enough to have come straight from a dry-cleaning bag.

She motioned to a chair in front of her desk. "My husband stepped out for coffee. You may have passed him on the sidewalk."

Shaw reviewed the one-room office as he walked its length. Landscape watercolors on the left side, the Abramses' framed certifications and photographs on the right. NYPD promotions, distinguished-service awards, medals of valor. State of New York private-investigator licenses. All lined up neat as a pin, Lorraine's on the top row and Ronald's on the bottom. All identical save for the dates and the fact that Lorraine had made detective first grade while Ronald's career had apparently stopped at second. The photographs showed them at various points in their careers in uniform and in suits, shaking hands in classic photo-op fashion with various cops of high rank whom Shaw did not recognize, and at least one former NYC mayor whom he did.

Tread lightly, he concluded. These people know people, even if the most recent photograph looked to be a decade old.

"Impressive careers," said Shaw.

"Up to a point." They shook hands and sat. Abrams set the screw and the disassembled reading glasses on the padded surface of her desk, as if they were surgical instruments on a tray. "Working for ourselves has been better. You said on the phone you were conducting a background check?"

"An unofficial one, yes."

"Who is it that you're checking on?"

"Karla Haiden. More broadly, whoever she works for now."

Lorraine Abrams did not move. Her expression did not change in any way Shaw could perceive with his eyes. But the natural intensity of the woman became a little more rigid.

"Why are you asking?" she said.

"I have a short answer and a longer one. Which do you want?"

"Both. Start with the short."

"I need to know if I can trust Karla. I need to know if the company she's working for now is dirty. Those might be different answers."

"Why come to us?"

They were interrupted by Ronald Abrams coming in through the door, two coffees and a bag from Hudson Bagel in his hand. He was about the same height as his wife, but heavier in every limb and especially around the middle. The dark blue of his golf shirt and trousers matched an NYPD uniform closely enough that Shaw wondered if the choice was intentional. He stood up to shake Ronald's hand.

"Mr. Shaw is inquiring about Karla Haiden, Ronald," said Lorraine.

"I see," Ronald said, in a tone that implied he did not. He went behind his desk to move his chair over to Lorraine's side. Their desks were alike in equipment, each with a monitor and laptop dock and computer mouse that might all have been purchased at the same time. Both desks had framed photographs, presumably of family, though the angles didn't allow Shaw to see them.

The similarities ended there. Lorraine's workspace held no papers, only a closed notebook set to one side of the keyboard, its pen tucked into the spiral binding. Ronald had a baker's dozen different writing utensils held in a Mets mug that looked like a stubby castle tower among the ramparts of paper and binders. Any surface space not given to the computer was covered with something, if only a Post-it.

"Is this about a job reference?" he asked, once both were seated in front of Shaw.

"I'm trying to get a grasp on the history," said Shaw. "From what I know, Karla was a police officer in Boston for six years. Then she moved to New York and joined your firm. She earned her PI license, and after that she left to work for someone else. That was about three years ago. Do I have the timeline right?"

"Those are the basic events," Ronald said. "Not the full story."

"Before we get to that," said Lorraine, "let's cover why you're asking. And who you work for."

"Myself."

"Doing?"

"Most recently I was hired to consult on security systems by the founder and president of a multinational business. That's what it said on the contract. The real job was more like a watchdog. It didn't last long. Before that I worked in a bar, and before that I was in the Army for ten years."

Lorraine nodded as if Shaw had confirmed a guess of hers. "And Karla?"

"That's where this gets tricky. Karla and the company she's supposedly with, a capital-investment firm called Bridgetrust Group, are involved in a business deal with the corporation that hired me. Karla was introduced to me with a false name. I learned Karla had been a cop and a PI. Maybe she still is. Bridgetrust might be a paper front. Or it might be cover for a legit firm who's investigating the corporation that hired me or one of the other players."

Ronald raised an eyebrow. "And you want to, what, protect your former employer?"

"I'm protecting myself. There are three players, besides me. Bridgetrust, the people who hired me, and representatives from another international company. They all met last week, at a conference that was supposed to last three days. That meeting was cut short when one of the participants was killed. A proprietary item crucial to their deal went missing."

"What is it?" Lorraine said.

"A chemical sample. Not narcotics, I know that much. It might be completely legal, or it might have been lifted from another chemical manufacturer. Industrial theft. But I have to assume the sample is unique if someone wants it so badly. Twice since the conference, I've been attacked. Both times an attempt was made to abduct me. I think those men believe I have the missing sample, and they aim to make me give it up."

The couple exchanged a glance. A long way from convinced.

"Why would they think you have it?" asked Ronald.

"My best guess is that I was hired for exactly that purpose. As a fall guy. The job was weird from the start. I couldn't figure out why they would insist on hiring me when they could have had more secure coverage from any rent-a-cop outfit. Now I suspect the plan from the start was to steal the chemical and set me up as the obvious suspect, at least long enough to sell it or copy it or whatever they had in mind."

"Why would you be an obvious suspect?"

"My late grandfather was a career burglar." Shaw spread his hands. "I'm not in the same line. But I know my way around security systems and how someone might get past them. I was told that was the skill they wanted when they hired me."

"You've got a record?" Ronald said.

"Arrest record. No charges, no convictions. I want to keep it that way."

"You said Karla gave you a fake name," said Lorraine.

"A false surname." Shaw took out his wallet and removed the business card with the name Karla Lokosh. He handed it to Lorraine. She picked up the working part of her reading glasses to examine it while Ronald looked over his wife's shoulder. "If her first name hadn't been the same, I wouldn't have found her at all."

"How'd you manage that?" said Ronald.

"I've been motivated," Shaw said. "From things she mentioned, I found her college in Boston and her real name, and that let me track down her job history. And you."

Ronald let out a grunt. Shaw wasn't sure if that meant the PI was impressed or just taken by surprise.

"You know," said Ronald, easing back in his chair, "we could pick up the phone right now and call Karla and tell her you're here."

"Yeah."

"That might screw things over for you pretty well."

"Especially if she's connected to the guys hunting me." Shaw shifted in his seat. The night's sleep had revived his body, but the wound on his ribs felt as though someone had scored it with sandpaper.

"For argument's sake, let's assume we buy your story," Lorraine said. "What is it you want to know about Karla?"

"Your gut reactions, along with some facts. Why you hired her. What motivated her to become a PI. Why she left and especially who she works for now. Anything you think might be useful."

"Is your interest more in Karla or in her employer?" she said.

"My interest is in my own safety. Like I said. If Karla can help me out of this jam, I'll be first in line to apologize for prying into her life."

"But you slept with her," said Lorraine. "Right?"

Shaw was increasingly glad he hadn't tried to bluff his way past the detectives.

"I did," he said. "Or maybe she slept with me."

"Is this a revenge thing? She jilted you?"

Shaw's amused laugh seemed to surprise them. "Nobody's heart is broken. The conference happened last week. Karla and I had breakfast the day after, and we went out that Thursday night. We talked about the conference and its sudden end. She dropped hints that if anyone had the missing chemical sample, they would be smart to sell it back. When I left her hotel the next morning, that was the first time I was attacked."

"You saying she had sex with you to set you up?" Ronald asked.

"Maybe not. Maybe she was just on a date and saw an opportunity to mix business and pleasure. If I had stolen the item, I might be more inclined to work with her than anyone else."

"Since you two had done the deed."

"Or because selling the stuff through her would be safer than the alternative. The hit team coming after me the next morning could have been coincidence. A different group, watching Karla's movements and finding me instead."

"Is Shaw your real name?" said Lorraine.

"Yes. Donovan is my full first name."

The detectives looked at one another again. Communicating the way lifelong partners could.

"We're gonna need to talk this over," Ronald said. "Go grab a coffee, come back in half an hour, okay?"

Shaw nodded and stood. Lorraine looked at him curiously.

"What's wrong with your side?" she said, pointing with her pen.

Shaw pulled up his shirt, revealing the bandage over his rib. "Their second try at me. Shooting to wound while I ran like hell."

"Let's see it," said Ronald.

Shaw peeled the bandage away, pleased to note that the scab hadn't reopened during his morning commute from Brooklyn.

Lorraine hissed through her teeth at the sight of the healing gash. "That should be stitched."

"I've been on the move."

Ronald picked up the Karla Lokosh card from the desk and handed it back to Shaw. "Gotta tell you, if this is manure, you brought a whole field's worth."

Shaw left the Abramses to their deliberations.

He didn't go for coffee. One block down Perry Street from the redbrick building with the A&A office was a similar four-story edifice, this one covered in scaffolding and painted plywood as it underwent renovations. Whatever crew had been working on the reno either wasn't working on Friday or hadn't arrived yet. Shaw stood three steps up the enclosed stoop and watched the street.

If they decided in his favor, great. On the flip side, they might call Karla or even Flynn to warn them. In that case Shaw would have to change tack. Getting out of New York clean was the priority.

The Abramses also had the option of doing nothing, simply refusing to answer his questions and sending him on his way. He figured that was the least likely outcome. The former cops and married PIs didn't seem the type to be passive. They would pick a side and throw their weight behind it.

They would be running his name through their online sources right now. Looking for biography, credit scores, rap sheet. He doubted that whatever BOLO the Seattle police had broadcast would have reached past the Washington border. That was a gamble he'd have to take. Lorraine and Ronald Abrams had been cops, probably still thought like cops. If they found out he was a fugitive from custody, Shaw had little doubt they'd call it in.

The Abramses had chosen a sedate, mostly residential part of the Village. What few businesses there were had grouped around the intersections, and their awnings and stonework meshed well with the environs. No neon, no big SALE signs in the windows. A nervous potential client of A&A Investigations could feel comforted by the dignified surroundings.

Shaw felt reassured as well. A quiet street made it easy for him to note any new arrivals. He watched each car as it passed the Abramses' building, looking for groups of men, or a car that made more than one pass, or anything that might be an unmarked. After fifteen minutes he walked away from the intersection, around the block, to watch the building from the cross street. None of the cars parked in the handful of available spaces had people sitting in them. No one hanging around the street and possibly watching the A&A office through its second-floor windows.

He'd learned as much as he was going to. If the two private eyes had given him up, the NYPD was smart enough not to show themselves. They might close the net once he was back inside. Another roll of the dice.

He knew what Dono would have said. That Shaw was stupid for getting himself into this situation but a true fool if he compounded it by trusting anyone to help. His grandfather had never been one to rely on the kindness of strangers. Or anyone else.

The primary entrance to the Abramses' building provided access to the shop on the first floor, which sold linens and posh housewares, and to the staircase to the second-story offices and apartments on the two floors above that. Shaw had seen earlier that the hallway on the second floor had a back entry. Assuming it connected to another stairwell, those stairs would descend to meet a steel utility door he'd spotted on the cross street.

Exit Only. Shaw let himself in with his lockpicks and walked up the back stairs to the second floor. He checked the hallway. It was empty.

He rapped on the door of A&A Investigations, and Ronald shouted for Shaw to come in. The couple were still seated in the same places as before. Ronald had eaten the bagel.

"What's the verdict?" Shaw said.

"We'll give you some history," said Lorraine, "and our intuitions. I'm not sure if those will answer your chief question about whether to trust Karla."

Shaw nodded.

"Lorraine and I met Karla when she was still with Boston," Ronald said. "A cop conference, maybe the last one before we left the force, right, Lorrie? She made an impression on us. Smart and very focused. And she wasn't much more than a rookie then."

Lorraine continued. "She stayed in touch. Karla was—and still is,

I assume—good at that aspect of her career, the networking. Building relationships." Lorraine paused, and Shaw guessed she might be making a reference to Shaw's own encounter with Karla. "She wasn't happy with BPD. Police promotions and lateral transfers to gain experience happen slowly if they happen at all. Especially for women. It's not a growth field, not with budget cuts happening almost every year. She asked how we liked working for ourselves."

"We were having a bit of a boom," Ronald said. "Picking up clients on referral from friends at the Sixth Precinct. A lot of cold larceny cases and insurance work. We told Karla that if she really wanted a change, we'd bring her on part-time and she could earn her license."

"Was she good at it?" said Shaw.

"Very. She didn't mind the tedious parts of the job, and there are plenty of those. She had a particular skill for questioning people without them being aware, melding with business types and earning their confidence. She didn't give off a cop vibe."

"I've noticed."

"We couldn't give her a regular salary," Lorraine said. "Our client list comes and goes like the tide. So with our recommendations, Karla picked up side jobs from other investigation firms. Including the one she left us for. Paragon Consulting, here in New York.

"I advised Karla against Paragon." Lorraine's mouth tightened. "We'd heard rumors about their methods. And about James Hargreaves, their CEO."

"Rumors of what?" said Shaw.

"Sometimes clients ask you to do things you can't do," Ronald said, "like tapping a phone or stealing mail. All that shit you see PIs do on television. Paragon's nominally an intelligence firm, but what they really are, are fixers. You didn't hear that from us."

"Paragon was linked to a high-profile divorce case," said Lorraine. "The wife said men had approached her friends, intimidating them from providing evidence. It wasn't proven that these men were working for Hargreaves, but word got around anyway."

Ronald nodded. "And there were other bad smells. A fellow PI had a client who wanted him to steal computers holding key data from a competitor. He turned it down. Later on he learned that the client had signed with Paragon. Again, we don't know if Paragon was willing to go that far."

"But you think so."

"Yep. We've met Hargreaves briefly. He's very slick. The product of some covert federal job, NSA or CIA or some group that doesn't even have an abbreviation. Some of the guys he hires are from the same mold. Ex-spooks and ex-military. No offense."

"None here. Is Hargreaves a lean guy, six-one, pale blue eyes, dark brown hair like stiff bristles on a brush?" said Shaw.

"That's him."

"He went by the alias Bill Flynn at the conference. He and Karla and a chemist named Morton were all pretending to work for Bridgetrust. Why would Karla leave you to work for him?"

"Paragon is a bigger operation. Bigger clients, by far. Bigger money. And Karla, well . . ." Ronald looked to his wife for help.

"Karla is very smart and very dogged," said Lorraine. "She grew up poor and wanting to break loose from that. Perhaps enough that she would be open to bending her integrity."

Shaw was no stranger to tangled ethics. "How far?"

Ronald shrugged. "She was pretty straight with us. She might argue for planting a tracker on someone, for example, but she'd accept that it wasn't possible. Grudgingly."

"With Paragon the leash may be off. Or nonexistent," said Lorraine. "That was one of the reasons I advised Karla against working for them. It's easy to lose your compass in an environment like that."

"Bad influences," Ronald agreed.

"But I can't imagine Karla being part of what you say happened to you," Lorraine said. "She loathes violence. That was part of her reason for leaving the police. Seeing the human cost of cruelty and rage every day and unable to do much about it."

"I get wanting to take action," said Shaw, "and being willing to ignore rules that stand in the way."

"She's a decent woman," Ronald said, "but even decent people have to fight sometimes to stay that way. I'm not sure Karla's gonna win that fight. My opinion, but there it is."

"Hiring Karla was about bench strength for Hargreaves, I think," Lorraine continued. "A young woman can go undercover where men can't."

"Any of this what you needed?" Ronald asked.

Shaw nodded. "For Paragon, yeah. I think Hargreaves smells a big payday. He sounds like the type to break whatever laws he has to. Plus, he has the connections to assemble a team of goons like the crew that's been after me."

"And Karla?" said Lorraine.

Shaw mimed flipping a coin.

"Guess I'll find out soon enough," he said. "Maybe she's just as trapped as I am."

"Good luck," Ronald said.

Shaw thanked them and got up to leave, only to turn back at the door.

"How'd you guess that Karla slept with me?" he said.

Lorraine looked at him. "She and I talked plenty during her time with us. I know Karla's type. Tall, dark, and prone to trouble." She pointed at Shaw. "If she's truly in deep water, don't become the millstone around her neck."

FORTY-FIVE

It was still early enough that the heat hadn't gotten a firm grip on the day. Shaw decided to walk uptown. The terrain was perfect for shaking the last kinks out of his legs from three days of driving. Flat and usually a simple two-part equation to get wherever you were going: X long blocks east or west, Y short blocks north or south.

He had been to New York a few times, always as a tourist on leave from the Army. Never for longer than three or four days. He'd rarely had more than that much leave away from Fort Benning in Georgia, and a soldier's salary didn't go far in Manhattan. He liked the energy of the city, could see the appeal of not needing a car and being able to discover almost anything made or sold or experienced in the world within a few square miles, from Argentine tangos to Zairian stew.

But after the first couple of visits, he knew he could never live in the heart of it. The relentlessly rushed pace of the place made him edgy. He'd found himself checking his surroundings more than was rational, even for a Spec Ops guy just off deployment. Hurrying toward an objective was one thing. Hurrying because everyone around you was hurrying was something close to herd mentality. Maybe the vibe was different in the other boroughs.

The offices of Paragon Consulting were in midtown on East Forty-fifth Street, not far off Madison Avenue. Those were the coordinates at street level, at any rate. The company's public listing hadn't specified the floor. A plaque outside the sleek tower read THE JANSSON BUILDING in uncompromising raised steel letters. Its flat mirror-finish exterior stretched from the discount men's clothier and the luxe steak house on its ground floor to the roof twenty stories above. Looking up, all Shaw could see was a bluish reflection of the older, more ornamented buildings on his side of the street.

He bought a coffee from an organic shop three doors down and drank it while watching a steady stream of people walking through the lobby. It was closing in on noon, and the numbers of people going in and coming out of the building were about even.

After an hour he estimated he'd seen four hundred people walk through the Jansson doors. Ninety percent of them wore business attire. Delivery people came out between fifteen and twenty minutes of entering. Shaw surmised deliveries were allowed to take the elevators up to their target floors rather than leaving items at the front desk. That might be a weak point.

The lobby was simple but attractive, with a short colonnade of ridged marble columns leading to the reception desk. Two guards stood behind the desk, one signing in visitors and taking their photos with a webcam to print passes, the other working the phone. Employees flashed their company IDs to the guards, who nodded and smiled slightly in recognition. Then each employee swiped a card at an interior glass door to access the elevator lobby.

Shaw watched as a delivery boy approached, carrying two stacked cardboard trays of coffee and more complicated mixtures. Guard One began making him a pass while Guard Two called up to make sure the kid was expected.

Tight, Shaw thought. Not impossible. He could figure a way to mimic a call from inside the building, ring the guards and tell them to expect a package delivery, then stroll in five minutes later. But they would notice if he didn't return promptly. Tricking his way inside like that and hiding until nightfall was out.

He walked the street, checking out the IDs draped around the necks of people exiting the building. He could steal one of those and hope the guards didn't look hard at the name or the photo, or that the employee didn't backtrack to see if he'd dropped his card. Too many variables.

Shaw would need time inside the Paragon offices. As much as he could get. He wasn't certain what he was looking for.

Seeking another way in, he walked around the block. The Jansson

Building abutted its stone neighbor without even an alley between them. Shaw supposed he could get into the older building next door, but then what? Punch a hole through its walls?

There was no exposed area of the Jansson Building other than the side facing the street. Bluffing his way past the guards was dicey. Scaling the building would be ridiculous.

There had to be a service entrance somewhere. Large enough to receive items like furniture—a building this size must have tenants moving or redecorating their offices constantly—and to remove a small mountain of trash every day. He looked for a utility door or a freight elevator that might open upward out of the sidewalk and didn't find either.

Staring at the building any longer wouldn't help. Shaw went to find food. Three days of drive-thru fare had him craving anything not served in a paper wrapper.

Grand Central was a few blocks south. He had strolled through the terminal on previous visits. Once he'd spent half an hour shooting the shit with a pair of Army National Guardsmen on deterrent duty in full ACUs and carrying carbines. Both of them happy to be away from regular training at Fort Hamilton. Shaw himself enjoyed the station's soaring architecture and the rush of commuters who probably never looked at it, just as he never gave a glance to the Space Needle at home.

Thinking of the Needle made him think of Karla. Did she have an office in the Jansson Building along with the rest of Paragon's New York branch? Would the name on its door say Haiden or Lokosh?

At a bistro across from the station, tucked under the Park Avenue viaduct, Shaw sat and watched the crowds flowing down Forty-second while he ate a lunch of hard-poached eggs benedict with extra toast and drank many cups of black coffee.

Around the third cup, a notion struck him. When you want to know something, just ask.

He paid the check and retraced his steps across Madison and over to Fifth. Patrons at the main branch of the public library lounged on the steps. Tourists waited for their turn to take photos with the lion

statues. Shaw found a corner sheltered from the traffic noise and made
a call.

"Jansson Building, front desk." Shaw wondered whether it was
Guard Two, still working the phones.

"Hey, how are ya?" he said. "I'm with Fields Lighting Design.
We got an installation comin' up for one of your companies there—
Par-gon Consulting, it says?"

"Paragon. Sure."

"Got it. We'll be delivering the materials early next week, and I
wanted to confirm the address and see where we should load in."

"Okay, yeah. This place is a little strange," said the guard. "When
it was built, only half of the structure next to it was torn down, for
some reason only God and the Zoning Commission know. So now
both buildings share a basement and maintenance floor. You'll have
to take the ramp in the building one door over, number 28. The door
looks like it's connected to the shoe shop on the corner—forget that.
Ring the buzzer and the guy inside will point you toward the freight
elevator for Jansson."

"Is there a staircase? This stuff is a pain. We got an extension arm
for one of the pieces, an aluminum tube that's close to ten feet. Sometimes we don't take the big lamps like this on the elevators, too much
risk of something getting scratched, you know?"

"Sure, the maintenance guy can let you into the stairs if that's better. You can take those right to the top."

"The top? Tell me I'm not schlepping this stuff up fifty floors."

The guard laughed. "Eight. Paragon's on eight."

Perfect, thought Shaw.

"Eight I can do," he said. "Thanks a million. We should be coming
by on Monday."

A service entrance that went straight up to Paragon's floor. Ideal,
if he could reach it. He walked through the blocks until he passed
the Jansson Building. The loading entrance the guard had mentioned
really *did* look like it was a back door to the shoe emporium. Peering

through the slatted and scratched windows of the door, Shaw saw that the ramp descended belowground in a curve to the right.

Next to the door, a push button labeled DELIVERIES was shielded from the elements with a hinged plastic lid. Shaw wondered whether the maintenance guy would be around on Saturday. The weekend would be the right time to make his move.

A sign in the window of a Walgreens gave him another idea. He had the store's printing department take two passport photos of himself, which they slipped into a paper envelope to dry. He stopped at the discount clothiers on the ground floor of the Jansson Building and bought a full outfit, blue suit and white shirt and a plum-colored tie plus socks and shoes. The pants were half an inch short, and the jacket pulled tight over his shoulders. None of that mattered.

Three blocks down Forty-fifth he found an art-supply store. He bought some stiff poster board in two colors and some marking pens. Once outside, he tore a page-size piece of each board free and threw the rest away.

Arts and crafts, he thought. Today the art. Tomorrow morning he'd see if he was crafty enough to beat Paragon's defenses.

FORTY-SIX

By 7:00 A.M. on Saturday, Shaw had shaved, showered, dressed in his new business suit, and left the truck in a midtown garage four blocks from the Jansson Building. Most of his gear was stored in the truck's hidden compartment. Win or lose with Paragon, he would be leaving New York immediately.

The few items he carried were tucked into a black messenger bag, slung over his shoulder. Without knowing exactly what security Paragon had installed in its eighth-floor office, he'd had to prepare for the likeliest options.

Thanks to the helpful guard, he knew that the ramp next door to the Jansson would take him down to the basement level. He picked the exterior lock on the rolling door, pulled it up high enough to duck under, and closed it again. The door made a racket as it shuddered on its rails. Shaw pressed on.

Saturday seemed to have left the basement empty. He walked past an industrial-size laundry room and a series of cages holding everything from rolling chairs to boxed computer monitors, held in limbo until granted passage upstairs.

Shaw wouldn't wait for that blessing. He found the service elevator the guard had mentioned and the stairwell door beside it. An office dork wandering around lost would take the elevator. In his motel room the night before, Shaw had cut and glued the poster board and one of his passport photos into an approximation of the IDs he'd seen on the Jansson Building workers the day before. It wouldn't fool anyone closer than fifteen feet away, not with its lettering in felt-tipped marker. But on a security camera, it should pass for the real deal. He slung the ID around his neck on a lanyard before pressing the button to summon the elevator.

All six surfaces of the elevator car were shielded with stamped sheet metal, each silvery wall marked by a thousand scratches and dings from years of haphazard freight. While the materials were different, the box reminded Shaw uncomfortably of his jail cell in King County. He tried not to think about the odds that he might soon be comparing East Coast cells to West.

The doors slid wide to reveal a broad hall on the eighth floor. Shaw could see the main entryway and its bank of elevators at the far end. Between the elevators and where he stood were four sets of double doors in etched Plexiglas, two per side. Four entrances, four companies, he guessed, each one occupying a full corner of the floor.

Paragon was at the southwest corner. A waiting area and reception desk lay just beyond the double doors. To either side of the desk's backdrop, he could see the wider office beyond. The entry was equipped with key-card access, which he'd expected, and a fingerprint reader, which he had not.

The black bubble of a ceiling camera had been set this side of the elevators. Keeping his face turned away from it, Shaw thumped on the Paragon office door. No answer. Either no one was working the weekend or all their resources were in Seattle right now. Focused on finding him.

Two minutes, he guessed, before someone noticed him on camera, loitering in the floor lobby. No time for finesse. He would have to rely on brute force, electronically speaking.

Standing between the camera and the door, he unfastened the plastic plate covering the reader with a power screwdriver. Letting the plate swing loose on its bottom screw, he pulled a modified smartphone and an adapter cord from his bag and plugged the phone into the key-card reader.

The software on the phone mimicked the firmware of half a dozen leading RFID key-card programming manufacturers, telling the reader that it was erasing all codes, including the door's master code, for a fresh start. It left the reader stuck in that bypassed mode with the door unlocked until a technician came to reprogram it.

That dealt with the first hurdle. His approach to the fingerprint reader would have to be even less elegant, but Shaw was past caring if he left a trail the width of Fifth Avenue. Speed was the key.

He had no program with him to disable the biometric machine. Reasoning that the two systems worked on a failsafe—if the fingerprint reader became disabled, the key-card system would take over all access for the door—the fastest way through the door was to take down the fingerprint reader, hard.

Shaw plugged what looked like a homemade flash drive into the reader's USB port. A lithium battery inside the drive promptly discharged hundreds of volts into the fingerprint reader. The screen flicked and popped as the electrical load fried its internal electronics. Shaw caught a tiny whiff of burned diodes as he pocketed the now-dead drive.

The door opened with a tug.

He made a quick circuit of the Paragon offices. No interior cameras on the ceiling. A dozen or so workspaces on the open floor for junior staff, with most of the square footage allocated to offices. Interior enclosures for some, window offices for upper management. He found James Hargreaves's office in the corner and Edwin Chiarra's five doors down from that. He smiled grimly. His first concrete evidence that Paragon was behind the team who'd broken him out of custody and the goon squad who'd done it.

On the south wall he found a smaller window office whose nameplate read KARLA HAIDEN.

Shaw hesitated. Then he turned around and went back to Hargreaves's office. Starting at the top.

TWO THOUSAND EIGHT HUNDRED MILES away in Seattle, in a twelfth-floor suite at the Mayflower Park Hotel, James Hargreaves woke to the ping of his cell phone. The tone was unique to a single purpose. He knew immediately what it meant and was alert within seconds.

Hargreaves attributed much of his success in private intelligence to his reluctance to take people at their word. He preferred to verify facts, whenever possible, for himself. Whether that meant reviewing private call and text records of his clients or the Internet search histories of his employees, information was always useful. It wasn't about knowing whom to trust. Trust was just guesswork. It was about gauging the odds that someone might lie about facts large or small and recognizing their behavior when they inevitably told you something that was untrue.

So when his former CIO, a competent but rigid ex-FBI tech jockey whom Hargreaves had kept away from the more clandestine operations, had told Hargreaves that the new fingerprint scanner would keep the office secure, Hargreaves had nodded and made a mental note to take some steps of his own. One was to install motion-sensitive cameras in the light fixture just above his office door and in the corridor just outside. The cameras sat dormant until his door opened, at which point they would begin broadcasting the images over the Jansson Building's reliable Wi-Fi to Hargreaves's cell phone.

Picking up his phone, he expected to see his administrative assistant, Lacey, scrawling a note on his desk pad. The girl had keys to his office. On occasion she would catch up on invoices and expense reports on Saturdays, leaving the papers for his signature. He appreciated her diligence. Enough to discount the fact that Lacey occasionally ordered more expensive brands of office supplies than the products that filled the desks and printers of his staff. He knew she must be returning the premium items and pocketing the difference, hardly more than a hundred dollars a month. So insignificant a profit that Hargreaves had pondered whether she did it simply as a form of rebellion, to feel as though she had some power.

He allowed her that. For now. Lacey had an acceptable face and a better than decent body. Some marks could be tempted by tits and ass, leaving them vulnerable to extortion themselves if they succumbed to their lusts. There might come a time when holding the threat of an embezzlement charge over Lacey would prove valuable.

The office looked empty. For a moment Hargreaves wondered whether the cameras were malfunctioning.

Then the image of Van Shaw appeared, moving from the far right into the center of the room.

Hargreaves was on his feet in an instant. Impossible. Shaw was in Seattle, or at least holed up in some flyspeck apartment or cabin somewhere in the state, praying the cops weren't about to break down the door.

And yet there he was. Hargreaves watched as Shaw—in a suit and tie, no less—went through his desk and files, the locks offering no more resistance than soft cheese. How had the son of a whore found out who they were?

Hargreaves would deal with that question later. The more immediate problem required action.

He used his laptop to call Tucker's number over Skype. He didn't want to take his eyes off Shaw, who was searching the rest of his office, perhaps looking in vain for a safe.

"Yessir?" Tucker, half asleep. Maybe feeling the night before.

"Shaw is inside the New York office. Right now. Who do we have in the city?"

"Shit," Tucker said. Hargreaves heard the man grunt as he sat up. "Our team's all here."

"Not our people. Freelancers. Is Gannon close?"

"No. Jersey City." There was a pause. Hargreaves knew that Tucker was running through a mental directory. The black man's contacts were extensive and varied. It was one of the primary reasons Hargreaves continued to employ Tucker, even after a titanic misstep like Shaw's escape.

He watched the image of Shaw leave his office. Going down the hall to try his luck elsewhere. Hargreaves swiped the screen, and the image changed to the second camera, showing him a wider sweep of the office floor. Shaw was far in the background, moving down the row. To Karla's office. Of course.

"Riley. And Taskine," said Tucker. "They're both uptown."

Hargreaves grunted. Excessive, perhaps. But effective.

"If you want to go that hard," Tucker added.

Hargreaves dismissed that. Tucker had compunctions. The man would kill—*had* killed, on Hargreaves's orders. But Riley and Taskine enjoyed playing with their food. That made even hard men like Tucker pause, and they had no time for hesitation now.

"Get them," Hargreaves said. "Usual rate, plus a bonus if they take Shaw today without any noise. I want this done."

"You know how they work. We need to set a hard limit."

Hargreaves considered that question while Tucker was busy texting both operatives.

"No bystanders engaged, no attention from the police," he said. "So long as Shaw can still piece thoughts together and talk clearly enough to tell us what we want to know, I'll be satisfied. Beyond that they have free rein."

"Chiarra said Shaw hinted at stashing the stuff in a safe-deposit box somewhere," Tucker said. "You sure we don't need him ambulatory?"

"A ploy to keep us from breaking his bones. If he has the chemical, Shaw would want to reach it any time of the day or night. Would *you* limit yourself to bank hours?"

Tucker coughed. "I wouldn't. Hey, Riley responded. I'm sending him the address and Shaw's picture."

"Warn them," Hargreaves said. "Shaw's dangerous, and he's slippery. Share your story of how he wandered away on your watch. Make sure they hear it loud and clear."

"Yeah. Okay." Tucker was back to sounding hungover.

"Give them my number. They'll report directly to me on this one."

Hargreaves waited for that last twist of the knife to be felt and then hung up.

HARGREAVES'S OFFICE HAD BEEN A BUST. No safe or lockbox, not even a computer Shaw might rip the hard drive from to hack later. The case information and contracts in the filing cabinets beneath the desk had looked like normal business records for a private intel firm. A lot of background checks and overviews of various companies, either clients or targets. None of the files mentioned Droma or Jiangsu Manufacturing. Hargreaves's desk drawer had held ornate fountain pens and a little Ruger LCP in a leather holster. Less showy but also less likely to jam than the writing implements.

Shaw searched Karla Haiden's office as carefully as he had Hargreaves's. The process took a little longer despite the smaller square footage, as Karla had made her workspace a homier environment, including paintings of seascapes on the walls and plants in the corners and on the shelves.

There were two framed photographs as well, one a candid shot of a man in his fifties who had Karla's shade of hazel eyes and one a more posed portrait showing a couple around the same age. The woman in the couple was unquestionably Karla's mother. Same lean height, same shape of face, and still plenty of auburn strands in her graying hair. Remarried, Shaw supposed.

He checked the drawers, finding only paperwork and office supplies and a few beauty essentials. No gun for the former policewoman. And no safe behind the seascapes or anything buried in the soil of the plants. If a hint of her perfume lingered in the enclosed space, that was probably Shaw's imagination.

Shaw moved on, to Ed Chiarra's office. Like Karla, Chiarra had given some thought to decorating his corporate cage. If Shaw hadn't already known that the lawyer was a New Yorker, the preponderance of Giants football swag on the shelves would have broadcast it. A ten-foot red-and-blue scarf made a knitted banner atop the bookcase behind his desk.

Chiarra had an extra file cabinet taking up one corner, a beefier model than the cabinets in the other two offices. Steel instead of wood construction, with locks that required a barrel key. The drawers under the desk had the same reinforcement. It took Shaw an extra fifteen seconds before the top drawer clicked open. After that he had the feel of the lock's model, and the rest came easy.

He went through each in turn. Client contracts, almost exclusively, under the desk. Whatever Chiarra's failings as a lawyer and a human might be, disorganization was not one of them. The man went in for color coding, with client contracts in blue folders and vendor contracts in red. Shaw didn't find any files in either shade labeled DROMA, or ROHNER. He took the time to glance at the pages within a couple of random folders just to make sure the labels weren't concealing something more interesting.

The top two drawers of the cabinet held employee records in gold folders. Shaw grabbed the first name he recognized in the second drawer—TUCKER, EMMET C.—and pulled the file. Beyond the basic facts like hire date and Social Security, the file had photocopies of Tucker's passport and driver's license—the operative's deep brown face looking purposeful in both—and his résumé at the time of hiring. The big man had been 101st Airborne, back before Shaw had enlisted, ending as a staff sergeant. Shaw had finished as an E-7, sergeant first class.

I outranked your ass, Shaw thought. His private joke paled a little when he saw Tucker's salary record on the second page. Being a gunsel for a shifty intelligence firm paid a lot better than bouncing at a Capitol Hill bar.

Shaw used his phone to photograph Tucker's file and went looking for others. Karla Haiden. Chiarra himself. URBANIAK, VICTOR. Vic of the twice-broken nose. With Tucker, that was two members of Paragon's kidnap team. Shaw started back at the A's to hunt through the photos on the copied licenses and passports, looking for the third man, the cyclist.

He made quick progress. Until the sight of one familiar face caused him to stop cold.

He pulled the folder out, looked at the name and the passport photo yet again, making sure his eyes weren't playing tricks on him. On the photocopied pages under the top sheet, black lines showed where the Paragon operative's biographical and job-history information had been redacted. After another moment of staring at the photo, Shaw copied the file like the rest and carefully replaced it in the drawer.

The file for the cyclist was near the end of the drawer. PAOLO, LOUIS. His curly mop of hair had been much shorter when the passport picture was snapped.

The bottom drawers held more blue-swathed contracts and red vendor invoices. There was no file for James Hargreaves. Maybe Hargreaves had erased his job records along with his history with the NSA or whatever spook incubator had spit him out.

As Shaw pushed the bottom drawer shut, it jammed on something inside. He pulled the drawer out again and bent low to look between the row of files and the slim steel length of the roller track. Just under the drawer was a flat sheet of metal, forming a raised bottom to the file cabinet half an inch off the floor. The sheet had tilted a fraction to one side, and the rolling drawer had caught on its edge.

Shaw reached in to press on the metal. It shifted a millimeter. Something underneath was stopping it. He took a penknife and inserted the blade between the sheet of metal and the cabinet to lift it.

Another golden folder lay on the floor beneath. Hargreaves's file? Shaw pulled it out.

It wasn't an employee record or anything else he'd found so far in the Paragon desks. The top sheet was a printout of a transfer of funds. He didn't recognize the name of the company sending the money, but the name on the receiving end made him look again. Linda Edgemont.

The next few pages documented more electronic transfers to a bank account in Edgemont's name. The earliest was four months prior.

Beneath the bank transfers was a different sheaf of pages. An employment contract between Droma International and someone named Kelvin Welch, hired on a contract basis as an "IT Engineer Level 3," whatever that was.

Shaw flipped back to double-check a date. Welch had joined Droma in February, the same month the first payment was made to Edgemont.

He looked at the next page on Welch. A nondisclosure agreement. Shaw felt like he was becoming a reluctant expert on those damned things. He had nearly flipped past it when he caught the name of the company who had engaged Welch for three months from Droma's pool of expert resources.

Avizda Industrial. In Dallas.

The same company where Nelson Bao had worked.

There were more pages. Too many for Shaw to photograph. He'd overstayed his time at Paragon already. He would have to take the file with him if he wanted to unravel what it all meant.

Worth the risk. He stuffed the file into his messenger bag before replacing the cabinet's false bottom and relocking everything.

As he exited the Paragon office, a bell dinged from the bank of elevators at the far end of the hall.

Shaw ran to the closest set of stairs, hearing the muted thump of the elevator doors sliding open even as he slipped inside. The stairwell door creaked softly on its hinges.

He descended half a flight and stopped. Something else was wrong. It took him a second to register the soft taps of shoes coming up the stairs. He leaned to look over the railing, down the sliver of space running along the center of the spiraling flights. A shadow, three floors below. The person continued ascending at the same measured pace. Maybe they hadn't heard Shaw. Maybe it was just some Jansson Building employee, getting his Fitbit steps on the way to putting in some hours on a Saturday.

Shaw didn't think so.

He silently backtracked to the eighth floor and up two more to the tenth. The footsteps below kept coming. There were cameras in the stairwell. Were the building security guards on his trail? He didn't want to risk opening the door to floor ten, not if it would make as much noise as the one on eight.

From below, Shaw heard the door to the eighth floor squeak open. He held his breath.

The door didn't close again. Was the bastard listening? Whispering to whoever had come off the elevator?

He waited, knowing that whoever was below him was waiting, too.

HARGREAVES HAD BEEN WATCHING THE Paragon cameras on his phone. He'd seen Shaw spend twelve full minutes in Chiarra's office, as much time as he'd spent searching Hargreaves's and Karla's offices combined. Had Shaw been planting a bug? A camera?

Or had he found something? Hargreaves's mouth tightened.

Hargreaves had texted Riley and Taskine updates on Shaw every two minutes. All the while silently cursing the pair for not getting there faster. When Shaw left Chiarra's office and headed for the door, Hargreaves had reached the end of his patience and called Riley directly.

"Shaw's leaving," Hargreaves said.

"We're headed up," said Riley's soft voice. "Hold."

Hargreaves checked the camera feed again, knowing it would tell him nothing. Shaw was out of its field and likely out the front door.

Riley came back. Hargreaves could tell by the sound that he was on the move. "Shaw's left the floor. Probably in one of the stairwells, going down. We'll take the elevators and pass him. Get a fix on him when he hits the street."

"There's a service entrance," said Hargreaves. "A garage door at the next building up Forty-fifth. If he's not headed for the lobby . . ."

"Roger that." Riley hung up.

THE MOMENT THE DOOR ON the eighth floor closed, Shaw exited onto floor ten and ran for the opposite stairwell. He didn't stop running for nine flights and half a block, to the service ramp where he'd first entered. He spared a glance outside and rolled the door up to slip underneath.

It had been close. The Jansson Building guards had come to investigate, or maybe he'd triggered something in the Paragon office that had alerted their people. At least he was out and clear now. The truck was four blocks away, and he wasn't going to waste a step in reaching it.

"WE'RE ON HIM." RILEY SAID. "Moving east on Forty-fifth."

They couldn't take Shaw on the street. "Transport," said Hargreaves.

"Already got some. Taskine's there now. If Shaw takes a cab or a train, at least one of us can follow him. If he goes to the airport, we'll find out what flight he's on and call you."

"He's a fugitive. If he takes a commercial flight, that means he's got fake ID good enough to pass." The mental image of Shaw traveling made Hargreaves realize something. "It's been four days since he escaped the cops. Plenty of time to drive to New York."

Riley's thoughtful hum stuttered a bit with the man's steps. "Hang on."

The silence stretched long enough for Hargreaves to pace his hotel room five times. He could picture Riley and Taskine striding a more direct path.

With his heavy black-rimmed glasses and thinning hair, Riley looked like any office drone who drove a computer every day. Until you noticed the smile. Like everything was funny and the worst things funniest of all. Riley could almost pass for sane. Taskine had no such disguise. He was an animal and looked the part.

"Right," Riley said, chuckling his soft laugh. "Your Shaw's a nervous boy. Stopped in a doorway for a while to check for a tail. Now he's doubling back."

"Did he make you?"

"Who you talking to? He's wandering in the wilderness, boss."

"His car," Hargreaves pressed.

"Yeah. There are two parking lots round the block. A garage farther up. Task will make a loop, get in front of him. If we can't take him quiet here, we'll follow him. The road is long, boss."

"If you need support . . ."

"We got this. Shaw's alone. And he's, what, twenty states from home? Call you later."

Tucker's men had been overconfident, too, Hargreaves was tempted to say. But Riley would just remind him once again that he and Taskine were different. And he would be correct. Different, and far more unhinged.

FORTY-SEVEN

Among the gear in the truck, Shaw had brought a prepaid mobile hot spot. Its boosted connection let him use his laptop while on the road. He set the open computer on the passenger seat. Each time traffic on the George Washington Bridge stopped, which was every fifty feet, Shaw typed a few words into a secure chat application.

The first to reply was Wren, just as the jam was beginning to disperse in the express lanes on I-80. She leaned in toward the lens, her black-coffee hair like a second frame in the chat app's window.

"Van?" she whispered.

"Where are you?" He had to turn his attention to the road. She would see his right profile, the one without the scars.

"I'm down the road from home, using Lettie's computer."

Shaw nodded. The odds that the SPD would tap a girlfriend's phone or Chromebook, on the chance that a fugitive suspect might call her, would usually be as low as a snake's belly. Warrants like that didn't come easy. Nor did the personnel hours. But Paragon would have no such limitations if they had managed to find Wren.

"I'm okay," Shaw said. "I'm safe. How are you doing?"

"Staying strong and going crazy, depending on the minute. This is . . . I hate worrying about you all the time. And then I feel guilty for not wanting to care so much. A bad spiral."

"I'm glad you care. I'm to blame for putting you in this spot."

Wren attempted a smile. "We'll flame out together." She glanced back over her shoulder. "Sneaking around is strange. It's as though I'm eight again and scared my parents will find me out of bed and stealing macarons from the kitchen. Are you used to this?"

Shaw wasn't quite sure how to answer. He'd had to go into hiding before. But breaking out of custody was new territory, as was being under the shadow of a homicide charge. Maybe multiple charges by now.

"No," he said, "and I hope this is over before the novelty wears off. Did you hear from Hollis?"

"He called Francine. She handed me the phone." Wren shook her head. "Does this make my roommates your accomplices? Or his? Hollis said to contact him if we see anyone hanging around the house. I could tell from the way he said it that he wasn't only talking about policemen."

"Just a precaution," Shaw said. "There's probably no reason to worry."

"I'm still going to look both ways twice before I cross the street. This must be what they call a healthy paranoia. Tell me something that I can do. Anything. I do not sit well."

Shaw had known Wren long enough to recognize her terse phrasing as a riptide threshing below the surface.

"Addy," he said. "And Cyndra. Cyn most of all. Addy will fret, but she's seen a lot worse than me going on a sudden secret vacation."

"About that. I spent the afternoon at Addy's house earlier this week, hoping to have some time with Cyndra. She barely came out of her room."

"I thought it was me she was mad at."

"She is. She's angry with everything. You and me, our relationship, that's . . ." Wren made a gesture that Shaw missed while driving. He guessed it was something Gallic and expressing her frustration. "That issue is just a way to divert herself. Addy had a better perspective. She thinks Cyn is mad because you might go away."

"Go away?"

"To prison."

Cyndra's dad had been a convict for most of her life. Absent.

"Goddamn, Wren."

"Yes. I want to hold her and tell her it will be all right."

"But we don't know that it will." Shaw's hands tightened on the steering wheel.

"She eats her dinner in three bites, Addy says. When she eats at all. I wish I knew what to do."

"If Cyn was like me, I'd say give her some space. Tell her . . . tell her I want to talk to her. Just her and me. Addy can figure out where and when."

"Like this? From the road?"

"I'll make it happen. Even if she wants to just hurl shit at me for an hour, at least that's something. Let her get some of the poison out."

"She loves you."

"I loved Dono, too. Doesn't mean I didn't want to brain him with a crowbar every second Tuesday."

Wren's laugh was one of Shaw's favorite things about her. Loud and unabashed. "I know what you're doing, making jokes. How can you be the cause of my trouble and the salve?"

"Is it working?"

"Yes. But salves are temporary. You'll have to come home to cure me."

"On my way. I'm going to sort this out, Wren."

Somehow.

After Wren hung up, Shaw had a mental vision of himself lighting fuses and running. The wick sputtering and sparking, inching ever closer to disaster. The women in his life left behind to deal with the wreckage.

EVEN BEFORE ESCAPING CUSTODY, SHAW had habitually scanned his rearview while driving for anything out of the ordinary. Checking for a car matching his speed too closely or suddenly reappearing after being out of sight for a time, which might signal two or more tail cars working in tandem. After nearly a week on the run, that practice had become as reflexive as pressing the brake pedal to slow. He knew that most of the vehicles behind him were the same as those that had been there five miles before. Nothing weird about that, not on a busy multilane just outside the nation's largest city.

So why couldn't he shake the feeling that someone was following him?

The Jansson Building, for starters. He wasn't certain that whoever had been coming up the staircase to the eighth floor had been hunting for him. But he didn't have to be certain. He had to trust his instincts. And his gut said that inside the building, and out on the street, and right now in the truck, he was being watched.

Not cops. Cops would have bottled up the Jansson Building or taken him on the street if they'd needed an extra couple of minutes for backup to arrive. Paragon's agents. Had to be.

Which meant his truck was burned.

The Ford's previous owner had sprung for the extra-capacity fuel tank, and Shaw had topped it up in Brooklyn. Enough gas to carry him over seven hundred miles. He could remain on the interstate all the way to Indiana and see which car or cars went the distance.

Of course, time for him meant time for them. They might already have reinforcements waiting ahead, multiple teams trading off the intensive work of surveillance. Ready to converge whenever Shaw dared to stop. Or force him off the road if he didn't.

It would be smart to pick the battlefield before they made their move. Shaw pulled up a map application on his phone and began to review the spiderweb of highways over the states ahead.

FORTY-EIGHT

The business had been a laundromat. Now it was vacant, with square outlines of ground-in dirt on the walls and linoleum to indicate where industrial-size washers had once sat. Electrical outlets remained on the floor, like droppings left by the machines. Either Vic or Tucker had plugged a hand drill into the outlet nearest to Ed Chiarra. It lay on the ground, a foot in front of the man's shoe, where the lawyer could see it—and dwell on it.

Hargreaves nodded to Louis, standing watch outside, and closed the front door.

"Ed," he said. "Sorry to keep you waiting."

Chiarra looked up from the chair. One of the stackable kind, molded from a single piece of plastic. So flimsy its legs would bend if someone shifted too far to one side. So cheap that not even the scavengers who'd gutted the coin-op laundry had thought it worth stealing.

"Please," said Chiarra. "James, please."

The men had taken Chiarra straight from his hotel room, knocking on the door before he was fully awake. Making him pack his bags, which now stood beside the wall next to Tucker.

Hargreaves looked at Vic, who was gingerly washing his face in the dented tub of a sink by the laundry's single restroom. Vic glanced back. Hargreaves saw that the swelling around his eyes had gone down. The flesh was still the color of a Gala apple, though.

"You have nothing to worry about, Ed," said Hargreaves. "If you answer my questions clearly and honestly, there's no reason that you can't be back in New York tomorrow. Do you understand?"

Chiarra nodded. Wanting so badly to please.

"Van Shaw was in our Jansson Building office this morning, Ed. Specifically, he was in *your* office." Hargreaves waited a beat to make certain Chiarra comprehended what he was saying. The man was near panic. "We have Shaw on camera. He took something with him when he left." That last was conjecture, but guesswork was sometimes necessary in an interrogation.

Tucker, understanding his role in their little scene, moved a step closer to Chiarra. Hargreaves's outward expression was one he had practiced, an equal mix of concern and compassion. His bedside manner, he called it.

"What did you tell him to take, Ed?" Hargreaves asked.

"I . . . Nothing. I never told him anything."

"Did you mention Paragon to him?"

"No. I swear, James."

"When he asked who sent you to the jail, what did you say?"

"I didn't. I avoided the question."

"Ed. Shaw escaped from custody. He left Tucker and Vic and Louis in the lurch after they took a tremendous risk to free him. And the very first thing Shaw does is travel all the way across the country, all the way to Paragon, and he goes straight to your office. Are you trying to tell us he did that on a whim, Ed? On a guess?"

"I don't know why—"

"Because I don't think that's the truth. I'm sure they don't either." Hargreaves glanced at Vic and Tucker, now both standing within ten feet of the chair. Chiarra leaned away. He would have squirmed over the back of the chair if he could, just to put another inch between himself and the men who stared ominously down at him.

"What was in your office, Ed?" Hargreaves said.

"Only what we needed. I'm being straight with you. Really."

"Needed for what?"

"For Edgemont. You said we might need to press her."

"Yes," said Hargreaves. "I did say that."

"You did." Chiarra lunged at what sounded like a way out, as Hargreaves had expected. So simple. "You said we might have to keep Edgemont quiet. Show her the bank transfers to her account and say we'd inform Rohner, or the cops."

"Go on." The payments to Linda Edgemont had been through a bank in Guyana. Completely untraceable to Paragon. "You had these records in your office?"

"I did. Hidden. If Shaw went through every one of my files, he still wouldn't find them. And they can't hurt us anyway." The lawyer nodded. Like that was any kind of conclusion.

"Why did you print them out?" Hargreaves said.

"Why? I told you. You said you—"

Hargreaves nodded to Tucker, who picked up the drill with impressive speed for someone so large. Vic pressed down on Chiarra's knee with one powerful hand and grabbed the lawyer's oxford shoe with the other. Chiarra's cry of protest became a scream with the same breath as the eighth-inch bit bore through his argyle sock and the anklebone beneath.

Two minutes later Chiarra's sobs had subsided to weeping. The drilling, the most intense part of the pain, had lasted only three or four seconds. Chiarra would even be able to walk—hobble at least—on that foot if they went no further, Hargreaves knew.

The pain wasn't the point. It was the fear that lasted.

"Why did you print those records out, Ed?" he said when he was sure Chiarra would hear him. "You could have shown Edgemont the transfers on any laptop, any phone screen. Why print hard copies and hide them in New York?"

"I can't . . . I can't breathe."

"Did you have another purpose for those papers? Were you going to send them somewhere?"

Chiarra kept shaking his head.

"Hand them off to someone?"

Hargreaves crouched down to watch Chiarra's face as it twisted.

"Were those the only documents you printed?"

"Not all." So softly that Tucker, a few feet away, tilted his head as if unsure of what he'd heard.

"What else, Edwin? What else did you keep with the transfer records?"

"Welch," Chiarra said, tears and snot mixing on the man's chin. Hargreaves's lip curled.

"Kelvin Welch? The hacker? What about him?" Chiarra was back to quaking in denial. Hargreaves glanced at Tucker, who reached for the drill again.

"Avizda." The word was almost a howl.

"Welch's contracts," Hargreaves said, filling in the blanks of Chiarra's gasping. "His papers for Droma and his hiring contract with Avizda."

Chiarra was back to nodding frantically. "That's all. Just those."

Those were enough to cause trouble, Hargreaves mused. Not with the courts. It would be an uphill battle for any district attorney to prove that Kelvin Welch's placement at Avizda through Droma's IT resource pool was anything more than normal business. Droma overlooking Welch's criminal record could be excused as a bureaucratic error. Rohner would pretend ignorance. And Welch was long past being able to testify.

But the revelation would set Avizda frantically searching for security breaches. Welch's black-hat work in their internal network might be uncovered. That could lead Avizda to check their labs for missing inventory, including testing samples. They might learn that their wondrous innovation was no longer solely theirs.

Ample cause for concern. And action.

"Which brings us back to why." Hargreaves patted Chiarra on the shoulder. "I know you were nervous, Ed. Nervous when Shaw killed Linda Edgemont. Nervous about helping us arrange for Shaw to be sprung from custody. You told me as much. You wanted something to protect yourself. To hand over to the police if this went the wrong direction. Yes?"

Chiarra didn't answer, which was answer enough.

"It's all right," Hargreaves said as he stood. "You had a crisis of faith. We can move past that. Just rest."

He looked at Tucker and Vic. The two men followed him to the front of the abandoned shop.

"You want us to . . . ?" Tucker angled his head toward the lawyer, now curled like a fried shrimp in the chair, not daring to touch his perforated ankle.

Hargreaves said no. "Too many people know he's here. We can't have anything happen in Seattle connected to us." He folded his arms. "Ed has family. His children's names are Junie and Ed the Third. I'll get you their schools and other background. Make sure Ed understands that the drill touches them next if he even twitches the wrong way."

The idiot, Hargreaves thought, looking at Chiarra. Probably printed out the records thinking he was being smart, creating physical copies that couldn't be hacked or erased. Where did that get you, Ed?

"Shaw is the problem," Tucker said. "If he goes to the cops . . ."

"The police can be managed. I'm more concerned that Shaw might contact Avizda. The whole point of hiring Welch was that Avizda can't know they've been taken until it's too late. Chen needs the lead time."

"So what does the freak want?" said Vic, his voice made adenoidal by clogged sinuses. Hargreaves's immediate thought was that Vic resided in a glass house, mocking Shaw's scarred visage. His own face might be permanently altered after Shaw's continued rearrangement of it.

"He's not playing defense," said Hargreaves. "Chiarra keeps employment records in his office. That means Shaw might have made each of you. He's clearly trying to return to Seattle. Rohner tried to pay him off before. Maybe Shaw thinks he still will, if he trades his information about Linda being our inside source." He shrugged. "But Shaw's intentions are moot. Riley and Taskine are following him now."

Vic twitched in surprise. "I thought you wanted him alive."

"I will take what I can get. If they capture Shaw, he'll tell us whatever he knows. If not." Hargreaves's gaze turned to Chiarra again. The blood had soaked through the attorney's sock, likely filling his wingtip shoe. "Death is better than Shaw deserves."

The thief had learned about Paragon from someone.

If not from Chiarra, then from Karla Haiden.

Karla had claimed not to have been in contact with Shaw since before the thief's arrest. Hargreaves knew that to be true, at least when it came to Karla's personal cell phone, her work phone, and her tablet. No calls had been routed to her room at the Crowne Plaza. Hargreaves had weighed the merits of bugging the room before her date with Shaw, but Karla was skilled enough to avoid talking—or anything else—in a potentially compromised room before she'd checked it carefully. She might have even found the bug and used it against Hargreaves. He'd hired the woman for more than her considerable looks.

Perhaps Shaw had told Karla more about the stolen chemical sample than she'd admitted. Perhaps the new lovers had gotten ideas.

"Get Ed cleaned up," Hargreaves said to Tucker. "Put him on a plane. We have work to do."

FORTY-NINE

Youngstown, Ohio. Shaw had chosen it before he was halfway across Pennsylvania. He'd never been through the town before, but it was a reasonable bet the two men in the white Jeep Cherokee tailing him hadn't either.

He'd clocked the Cherokee as one of a dozen cars keeping pace behind him on the same Jersey stretch of I-80. As the miles wore on, the other candidates had dropped out, either exiting the freeway or falling far behind.

Rounding a curve outside Lewisburg, Shaw had crossed quickly to the right lane and let the Ford coast. As the Cherokee came up the fast lane where he'd been moments before, he caught the dark outlines of two men in the front seats. They were experienced enough not to immediately slow to match Shaw's speed. The Cherokee drifted alongside. Shaw hadn't glanced at it, not wanting to reveal his interest. Over the next twenty miles, their vehicle had gradually faded back, almost out of sight.

They were good. It had taken him a lot of miles to be sure of their intent. And being skilled, they had to know he'd make them sooner or later. They'd be expecting him to run.

The next three hours had passed without change. His pursuers seemed to have started with a full tank, like he had. Shaw didn't want a war of attrition, letting his tank run low in the process. The Cherokee might be the heeler, the dog that stays behind the flock, driving it forward into the pen. Or into the chute leading to slaughter.

Shaw wouldn't wait for that moment. Youngstown would have to be the place.

The town was optimal. It lay at the intersections of multiple highways and interstates, leading to every point on the compass. Even if the men tailing him assumed that Shaw would still ultimately head west, he might go north or south or even backtrack for a short while before picking a state route or a suburban back road in that direction. Too many possibilities for even a large coordinated team to cover.

Eight miles over the state line into Ohio, he pulled off the freeway and headed south on a five-lane thoroughfare toward the city. A stretch of inns and strip malls, banks and family restaurants, with plenty of elbow room between each for abundant parking. All of them chain stores or franchises. The same street might exist in Fort Worth or Anchorage or Tallahassee. Apart from the telephone poles, the tallest things on the horizon were business signs on their posts, lining the thoroughfare like monuments to corporate logos.

The Cherokee followed him, keeping a hundred yards distant. Shaw might be preparing to stop for gas or food at any of two dozen places. He imagined the men in their vehicle flexing sensation back into their limbs, checking their weapons. Readying themselves to finally make the kill after their long chase.

When the upcoming light turned yellow, Shaw hit the gas through the intersection and then immediately turned left into the vast parking lot of a Walmart, a structure large enough to host a college football game. He accelerated, cutting a diagonal path across the empty acres of lot nearer the road.

In the rearview he caught the white flash of the Cherokee as it swerved around cars stopped in the intersection. They knew he was fleeing now. They had no choice but to run him down.

He kept pressure on the gas, roaring out the side entrance of the lot and onto a two-lane road to swing hard right, back toward the thoroughfare. A driver turning into the store stomped on her brakes, leaving rubber. A thick line of trees shielded the road from the Walmart lot. The two men in the Cherokee would have to slow, if only for an instant, to see which way he'd gone. Every yard Shaw could put between them counted.

The Ford was doing fifty miles an hour when he crossed the five-lane road, straight through a red light and over a flattened curb into what looked like a park. Car horns blared, too late to do more than announce their fury and fright. He braked and swerved, narrowly missing a tree. No sign of the Cherokee in his mirrors.

Not a park, Shaw realized. A cemetery. Beyond the spruces and oaks, a path formed a winding perimeter around a collection of low headstones and crosses, with dozens of other markers beyond. He veered to follow the path, the only safe way through the minefield of memorials.

Shit. He had hoped to haul ass directly through a field and lose himself in the streets on the other side. Maintaining speed was impossible here. He couldn't drive directly off the cemetery grounds; an ivy-covered fence ringed the block. He sure as hell couldn't go back.

Had they seen him enter the graveyard? The trees and fence would provide some cover. He would have to keep moving forward. Find another way out. The path curved gently every few yards, forcing Shaw as slow as fifteen miles an hour. People walking among the stones in the distance stopped and stared at the black Ford's intrusion on hallowed ground. He gritted his teeth and pressed on.

There. The mortuary office, a hundred yards away. The path would take him directly into its lot. He could cut around the building and escape.

Shaw heard the Cherokee's engine first. To his right, on the road running parallel to his path. Racing to get ahead of him, to beat him to the end of the fence and cut him off. The cemetery was nearly empty. An optimal place to make their move.

He glanced left, searching for an opening in the crop of tombstones. Nothing. The cemetery was old and had filled every available plot. Moss and water stains and crumbled corners on the markers for the dead. He might join their ranks soon enough.

The Cherokee reached the end of the fence line, forty yards ahead of him. It turned left, banging over the curb and onto the grounds. Shaw swerved right to skim the fence. His sideview mirror tore strands of ivy from the links. Maybe he could cut behind them, reach the open road before they could turn around in the tight confines of the cemetery—

No good. The Cherokee stopped abruptly, a wall ten yards from his front bumper. He had an instant's glimpse of the driver, a bushy black tangle of Viking beard and tattooed forearms like Christmas hams. He'd have to stop. He couldn't stop. Stopping would mean the end. He stood on the gas and hauled the wheel sharp left, away from the fence.

The driver saw Shaw trying to veer around them. Maybe he'd been waiting for just that moment, a chance to hit Shaw broadside as he passed and smash the Ford into the dragon's maw of tombstones. He punched the gas.

Too hard. Too eager for the kill. The Cherokee's front wheel spun for half a second on grass still wet from the afternoon sprinklers. It lurched forward just as Shaw's truck raced past. Their front bumper clipped the rear of the Ford. The impact knocked the tail of the Ford sideways. Then the Cherokee slipped free with a screech of tearing fender. Left without anything to impede its momentum, the charging vehicle flung itself across the path and into the gravestones beyond.

Shaw heard the agonized crack of something large and metallic snapping. He saw only the jostling view ahead as his truck fishtailed on the grass, finally gaining traction and bouncing over the curb onto the road. He floored it, roaring away into the residential streets on the far side of the cemetery. Only when he had ten blocks and two turns behind him did he slow.

No sound of sirens. But the cops must be close. With any luck they would arrest the two assholes in the Cherokee.

If any of the people at the graveyard got involved, they would report his black truck. A sharp-eyed witness might have noted the New York plates. Disposing of those was a priority.

Take the side roads, backtrack the few miles to Pennsylvania. Find plates there. And check the damage from the love tap he'd received from the Cherokee. Getting pulled over for a busted taillight would do him no good at all.

If Paragon sent more teams after him—and Shaw figured that was a given—his saving grace was that they wouldn't want the cops to find him before they did. If he put distance between himself and Ohio fast enough, he could hold on to the truck for another day, maybe more. Driving through the afternoon and all night and taking the state routes to avoid I-90 would put him somewhere close to Kansas City.

Eight hundred miles to figure out his next move. Which had better be good. The closer he got to Seattle, the greater the danger. They knew he was coming home.

FIFTY

Half an hour later, Riley made the call. Taskine had been driving when they'd splintered the Jeep's axle on that fucking granite slab, but it had been Riley's idea to take Shaw in the graveyard. The way Taskine figured, it meant Riley had to deliver the bad news. Riley knew better than to argue when Taskine was in the kind of mood that got people's eyeballs skewered.

"Yes?" Hargreaves said.

No point sugarcoating it, Riley thought. "Shaw got away. Outside Youngstown."

"So he made you," said Hargreaves.

"Just crap luck. We need a new car. We can grab one here, but the faster we swap it out for something clean, the better."

"Cleveland," said Taskine.

"Yeah," Riley said to Hargreaves. "Rent a car in Cleveland. We can be there inside an hour if we haul ass."

There was a pause, long enough for Riley to raise a doubtful brow to Taskine. He could read the vibe.

"No," said Hargreaves. "You've had your shot. Shaw won't get back on the interstate."

"Any spending on his cards?" Taskine asked, impatiently motioning for Riley to put the phone on speaker.

They could talk as loud as they chose. One look at the totaled underside of the Cherokee had been enough for the two men to grab their bags and quick-time it away from the cemetery. When they stopped, they were a mile down the road and drenched in sweat from the sweltering humidity. They stayed out of sight behind a Youngstown strip mall that had nothing in its windows but FOR LEASE signs.

"Shaw's too smart to be on the grid," said Hargreaves.

"The truck," said Riley. "A Ford F-250. Black with a silver toolbox in the bed." He recited the plate number.

"Wherever Shaw got it, it's not in his name. I'll run the plates, but odds are he stole the truck in New York. He'll probably steal another one now that he's shaken you two off his ass. If you don't have any better ideas, go home."

"He went to Paragon for a reason," Riley pressed. "Right? What was he looking for?"

"He's grasping at straws," Hargreaves said, "facing two murder charges and desperate to find anything he can swap for money. Including confidential client information."

"Which clients?" Taskine grumbled. "Could be he's headed for them next."

"Forget it. Shaw's been in jail and on the run for a week. He'll be worn out. Somebody in that situation goes to ground where he feels safest. For Shaw that's Seattle, or it's down in Georgia where he was stationed, or it's with some Army buddy. I'll make inquiries. If I can get a line on his old platoon, there might be something for you to do."

"Mr. Hargreaves," Riley said. "We can make this right. Give us a lead, we'll bag this bird."

Hargreaves didn't answer immediately. Riley grimaced. This assignment was in the toilet. If they were given another, it would probably be pushing around labor organizers in Newfoundland until Hargreaves counted their debt as paid.

"Get to Seattle," Hargreaves said at last.

The two men exchanged looks. More stunned than pleased.

"Sure, yeah," said Riley. "Pittsburgh's close. We'll grab a ride, catch a red-eye."

Hargreaves hung up.

"How you figure that?" Taskine said to Riley.

Riley stuck the phone in his pocket and frowned even deeper than before. "Not like Jimmy Boy to pass up a chance to stick this mistake up our asses and make us say Thank You, Sir. He must need all hands on deck right now."

"He's nervous. I can smell it."

"You think Shaw's holding something on him?"

"Don't know. Don't care." Taskine mopped his broad forehead with a shirttail already soaked through. "I just want to find this fucker and rip pieces off his face with pliers. Make him beg some before we start with the questions."

Riley had been around. For most dudes talk like that was just so much shit, a way to pump themselves up. Taskine was different. He was probably already imagining the feel of the rubberized grip in his hand as Shaw's nose or eyelid tore loose. Riley kept his mouth shut as they walked back to the main drag. Somebody would have to be a focus for his partner's fury. Better Shaw than him.

FIFTY-ONE

Shaw woke in the backseat of his truck. He knew it was midafternoon from the angle of the sun and that he'd slept for half the day, a consequence of his bone-deep weariness after driving nearly twenty hours straight with the frenzy in Youngstown smack in the middle of the trip.

He pushed the door open with his boot and climbed out. His side ached. Sometime during the chase, he'd torn the bandage and the healing scab beneath, only realizing the extent when he was a hundred miles down the state road and the gauze sagged heavy with blood. The next time he stopped to empty his bladder, he'd taped a fresh pad over his ribs, which had finally stopped seeping. Two steps forward, one step back.

The air outside smelled good. Soil and the wet heat of summer, with the hint of more, maybe rain from the clouds he saw in the northern sky. He'd parked the truck behind a silo near a soybean field on the outskirts of Hannibal, Missouri. Shaw knew next to nothing about farming, but the foot-high rows of leafy green plants hadn't looked tall enough or thick enough to harvest. Any workers would likely have started by nine in the morning if they were going to show at all. It was a reasonable guess that the field would remain untended through the day. Safe enough. He'd fallen asleep within minutes of curling up in the backseat.

Now, with the day starting its unhurried end, the crop fairly glowed in the sun. Orderly and peaceful. The path not taken. Shaw relieved himself, drank a full bottle of water and ate half a bag of trail mix, and did his best to stretch without disturbing his side more than it was.

Once he felt human, he dug his last burner phone from the truck's hidden compartment and called Karla Haiden.

"Hello?" she said.

"Can you talk?"

"Hold on."

Shaw waited. Five seconds. Ten. Maybe she was signaling some-one to trace the signal, if that was within Paragon's capabilities.

"I'm alone," Karla said. "Are you okay?"

"Surviving. Where are you?"

"Still in Seattle. I think I've learned the names and family histories of every staff person at the Plaza by now."

"So your company is counting on the deal with Droma and Chen Li."

She hesitated. "Yes."

"But the chemical hasn't turned up."

"No. It hasn't."

"What if I were able to make that happen?"

"How?" Karla said. "How could you do that? Do you have it?"

"What if?"

"Van. I need you . . ." She paused again. "I have to know. Did you have anything to do with Nelson Bao's death? Or Linda Edgemont?"

"I'm not a murderer. I've killed men before. In war or in self-defense and in defense of others. But never for profit. Never for hatred."

Karla exhaled. "Okay. I trust you."

That's the con, the cold voice said, *offering trust to get it in return.*

"Thanks," said Shaw. "That means a lot."

"If you somehow recover the sample," Karla continued, "I'm sure Sebastien Rohner would put all his efforts toward clearing you. The best lawyers. Somehow they can prove you weren't involved."

"And your company?" Bridgetrust. Paragon. Shaw left it unnamed.

"Of course. Everything we can. I'll force them to help if I have to."

"Can you meet me?"

"I . . . Yes. I will. Where are you?"

"Fly to Denver. Tonight, or the earliest flight tomorrow. Be in the terminal at DIA by nine in the morning."

"What happens at nine in the morning?"

"I'll be there. And I won't wait long."

"I understand. Will you have the sample with you?"

"See you there." Shaw hung up. He removed the battery and SIM card from the cheap flip phone and placed all three in the center console of the truck. The phone could stay invisible until Denver.

Karla would show. He was certain of that much.

He'd have to wait to find out who came with her.

HARGREAVES MET KARLA IN THE sitting lounge at the Mayflower Park, a carpeted flight of steps above the main lobby. When she'd called up to his room, he'd been showering after an hour on the treadmill in the hotel gym. The gravity in her tone was enough to make him move swiftly. He had told her where to wait, dried, then grabbed the clothes off the first hanger in his closet, slacks and a golf shirt. His stiff hair was damp, and his body temperature hadn't fully recovered after the run. Fresh beads of sweat rose on his arms, cold in the air-conditioned lobby.

"What is it?" he said, taking the seat to her left at the low, glass-topped table. An ingrained habit for Hargreaves. Karla was right-handed. Sitting on a person's weak side put them a tiny bit on the defensive.

"Van Shaw called me," said Karla. "Half an hour ago."

"Where is he?"

"He wouldn't say. He wants to make a deal for the chemical sample."

Hargreaves frowned. "After five days of silence, now he claims he has it. What's his asking price?"

"Freedom. He wants Sebastien Rohner to provide legal cover. Says he didn't have anything to do with Linda Edgemont's homicide, or Nelson Bao's death, murder or manslaughter or whatever charge the DA settles on."

When she was under stress, Karla talked like the cop she'd once been, Hargreaves had noted before. What was causing her anxiety now?

"Do you believe him?" he said.

"Yes."

"That makes one of us. Why did Shaw come to you? Why not Rohner directly?" Hargreaves said. He looked her up and down pointedly. "Or is that an obvious question?"

She stiffened. "He trusts me enough to start the ball rolling. Without giving him up to the authorities."

Hargreaves glanced around the lounge. One of his favorite places in the hotel. Luxurious. The floral patterns of the couch pillows and curved shape of the chairs both Asian-inspired but too subtle to make the place look like a restaurant. A colonial feel. He imagined this was how the Brits had lived when they had their grip on Hong Kong.

"I think Chen never lost the sample in the first place," he said. "If Shaw had the chemical, he'd have offered to sell it long before today." He stopped as though a new thought had occurred to him. "Unless, of course, Shaw had a buyer and it fell through."

"Then either way we win. Shaw will barter for the sample, or Chen still has it," said Karla, her expression flat. "Still leaves us without a suspect for Bao and Edgemont."

"Are you interrogating me, Officer Haiden?" Hargreaves smiled. "I was with Sebastien Rohner and Olen Anders the afternoon Linda Edgemont was shot. We had an early dinner at his club. And you know that I was meeting with them and Morton when Bao died."

"I didn't mean you personally, James."

"So someone else from Paragon killed them? What do you think we are, Karla? I realize pushing the envelope is our niche. We take care of what our clients can't handle themselves. Or what services they can't find elsewhere. But it's a long walk from that to homicide."

Hargreaves dabbed at his damp sideburn with a cocktail napkin. "Shaw's the one who had something to gain. He got the chemical by killing Bao, or he tried to and fucked it up, and then he went to Linda Edgemont's house. I don't know if he was looking to sell her the sample or whether he was just hoping to find something else worth stealing. He's a damn thief, Karla. Has been since he was a kid. You know his history."

She nodded. Skeptical, Hargreaves was sure, but willing to listen.

"Maybe Shaw imagines he can steal the chemical from Chen," he said. "And perhaps he can. He seems loaded with unpleasant surprises." He pointed a finger at her. "Did he say how to contact him?"

"No. Only that I should start the ball rolling and he'd be in touch."

"I'll contact Rohner. When Shaw calls, you let me know immediately."

"I will."

"Watch yourself, Karla. If I'm right and you're wrong, that means Shaw's killed two people so far. One of them a woman he might have been trying to negotiate a deal through. Just like you."

"I'll be careful." She rose and walked down the steps and away.

Hargreaves sat for a few moments at the table, looking at the green brocade curtain that could be drawn in front of the steps to hide the lounge from view. Like the stage of a theater.

Karla had been telling him the truth about Shaw's call. He'd checked the automated feed he'd placed on her phone records while he'd hurriedly dressed. A three-minute chat with someone calling from a Central California area code, though he knew full well Shaw was nowhere near Cali. A burner phone, or routed through VOIP, had to be.

Didn't mean she'd told him the whole truth, any more than he'd been fully honest with her.

She had been on her game, in a knee-length dress and a fitted suede blazer. Delicious legs. He fully understood why Shaw had contacted her.

Shaw would want to see her in person, of course. And maybe she wanted to see him. Karla had that look. Distracted.

He took out his phone to call Riley.

FIFTY-TWO

Addy called on the computer as Shaw was rolling past the endless fields and gullies of Interstate 70 toward Lawrence, Kansas. He had the visor lowered and his sunglasses on to stave off the glare of the setting sun. The laptop sat open on the passenger seat. He tapped the touchpad to accept the call.

"Van?" Addy's voice. Shaw was moving into the slow lane and couldn't glance her way. "All I have is your elbow on the screen."

"My elbow can hear you fine," he said.

"Where are you? Or can you tell me that?"

"I'm in Kansas. Heading west."

"Cyndra's here, too."

He'd asked Wren to set up a talk with the kid while he was on the road. He hadn't expected the timing would be so literal. He set the cruise control and let the Ford coast at a couple of miles over the posted limit of seventy-five.

"Cyn, how are you?"

No answer. Shaw hoped he'd at least gotten a nod of acknowledgment.

"What's it like there?" said Addy. "Can you show us?"

"Give me a sec." He set the open laptop on the dashboard, pointed outward. "Okay?"

"It's just the road," Addy said.

"Now you know how I feel," Shaw said. "You can see a long way 'cause there's nothing to see."

"You're spoiled, living around mountains and water," said Addy. "Are you all right?"

"Yes."

"We're with Professor Mills."

Surprised, Shaw turned the laptop around to keep the screen in his peripheral. Addy's and Cyn's faces, side by side on the screen. Cyndra's eyes looking elsewhere. They weren't in Addy's tidy little living room. Behind them he saw a bookcase packed with binders and academic tomes thick enough to work as tire chocks. Cyn squeezed closer to Addy as Jemma Mills came in from the left to peer at the screen.

"Van," she said. "I have news if you have the time."

"Only eight more hours until I get where I'm going," said Shaw.

"Eight minutes should do." Mills glanced at Cyndra.

"I'm staying," the teenager said.

Shaw nodded assent. "She's come this far."

"I made a few calls to colleagues who have contacts at Avizda. And to some industry journalists who keep track of what innovations are brewing. The short version is that Avizda has been investing heavily in sustainable recycling. Something of a holy grail for polymer research."

"Recycling? Like bottles and cans?"

"Like ninety percent of all plastics. Avizda is working on a bridging molecule between polyethylene and polypropylene. I don't know if they've actually succeeded, but if so, the potential applications are tremendous. It creates stabilization where there was little before."

"You lost me," said Shaw.

Mills chuckled. "I thought I might have. Soap is a good analogy. Dirt and grease are hydrophobic. They repel water. You can't clean a greasy pan just by rinsing it. You need a hydrophilic—water-loving—molecule to dissolve and grab on to the water. Soap is the bridge molecule that binds those two types together into a solid. Add water and one molecule holds on to water while the other holds on to dirt and carries it away. Do you understand?"

"Squeaky clean," said Cyndra from off camera. Not sounding sarcastic, Shaw noted.

"What Avizda is working on," Mills said, "is a soap molecule for plastics. Polypropylene and polyethylene are different types of plastics. When they're melted together and formed into a solid product, they tend to phase-separate, like oil and water. The resulting plastic is weaker as a result and can only be used in certain applications."

"So . . . this miracle polymer can create a stronger plastic?" said Shaw.

"Yes, but much more than that. The real benefit is when you go to recycle that new plastic. Every time a polymer is recycled, it loses integrity. More fresh plastic must be added to make it structurally reliable. There's no such thing as one-hundred-percent recycled material. After two or maybe three times, that's it. The polymers become unusable, forever. Permanent landfill."

"Unless . . ." Addy prompted.

"Unless there's a molecule that stabilizes the polypro and polyeth so that they can be separated cleanly. Recycled potentially dozens or even hundreds of times, each time as strong as before. I wouldn't use the term 'infinite recycling,' but in practical terms it might as well be."

"In practical terms," said Shaw. "What about financial?"

"Billions. Tens of billions annually," said Mills. "For one, cheaper production costs if you don't require as much new plastic every time. Far fewer units to produce overall if you can just melt them down and pour the result into a new mold. The industry won't change overnight, and a lot of companies will push back hard to keep the status quo. But an innovation this significant will win out eventually."

Especially if the government could make the rules for production, thought Shaw. Like in China. Chen would be giving his nation a massive head start.

"How sure are you that it works?" Shaw said.

"Are you asking for a probability? Like eighty percent? I can't say." Mills held up a cautionary finger. "I can make an educated guess that Avizda believes strongly in the *chance* that it will work. They think their research is onto something."

"They gave it a vote of confidence."

"Many millions of votes, in their corporate budget. This kind of trial-and-error experimentation requires a lot of dollars. No one knows that better than an underfunded research scientist like me."

"Impoverished but brilliant," said Addy.

"Agreed," said Shaw, taking the next off-ramp. "You told me that the GPC testing couldn't reveal what was in the polymer, right? Only help chemists make an educated guess?"

"Yes," said Mills.

"So if somebody had a small sample of the chemical and not much else, they might need more information to fill in the blanks."

"I'd say so. Especially with a newly engineered molecule. Think of it like looking at an X-ray. You'll recognize bone and tendon if you've seen those before. But if someone's cartilage was made of balsa wood, you might be in the dark."

Shaw nodded. "Until you opened them up."

Or had someone hack their corporate computers. Maybe an IT Engineer Level 3. Shaw had an inkling now of how Droma was involved and why Kelvin Welch had been placed at Avizda.

"Thanks, Professor," he said. "This is what I needed to know."

"Consider me reimbursed. I'm going out tomorrow and buying a few shares of stock in Avizda Industries. If they think it's worth the gamble, so do I."

Shaw pulled over and stopped the truck. The sun was below the horizon now, leaving a sky painted in mile-high stripes of orange and gold. Its final rays had been caught by the top edge of a low, thick shelf of cumulus. White light shone from every peak of the cloud, like a lightning bolt steaking horizontally across the prairie. He set the laptop in front of him on the dash.

"Hey, Cyn," he said. "You got a minute?"

Cyndra's pink hair and her eyes popped into view on the right of the screen.

"Kick the adults out," he said. "With the professor's permission."

"I'm closing up for the day anyway," Mills said. "Addy is taking me to dinner."

"You're paying," Addy said to Shaw. "Cyndra, let yourself out and meet us downstairs. Make sure to shut the door tight."

The two women stood, and after a moment Shaw heard the office door close. Cyndra sat in front of the camera, eyes wide.

"How you doing?" Shaw said.

"Fine."

"I'm sorry I'm not there."

Cyn didn't say anything.

"And I'm sorry if my being in trouble makes you worried."

"I'm not freaked."

"'Cause if it were me, and I thought you might have to go away for a long time, I don't know how I'd handle it. Probably not very well."

They sat for a moment. Cyndra looking somewhere below the screen.

"You remember when you first came to live with Addy?" Shaw said. "For a while there, we weren't sure we could talk social services in California into letting you stay. You were kinda stressed about that. You remember what Addy said?"

"Yeah."

"Could you tell me? I'm old and my memory isn't what it used to be."

Cyndra pulled a face. "You guys said we'd make it happen. No matter what."

"That's right. No matter what. That worked out, I guess."

"Uh-huh."

"Tell me something about summer vacation. Did you decide if you're doing that skate camp?" Cyndra, like a lot of kids, shifted her obsessions about as often as Shaw changed T-shirts. While she still declared her undying allegiance to roller derby, she had rediscovered her skateboard before school let out.

"Yeah. Mellie's going too. And maybe Bryce."

"Bryce? The camp's coed?"

"What's that?"

"Boys and girls together. I guess anyone who's in between, too. Everybody gets to sleep over?"

"Sure."

Shaw thought back to when he'd had his first real encounters with girls. Around the same age as Cyndra. Seemed young as hell, looking at it now.

"Don't get any piercings while I'm gone, okay?" he said.

"No promises," Cyndra said.

"I'll be there as soon as I can."

"Will you have to go to jail?"

Her eyes were shining. But she didn't look away. Guts.

Shaw hesitated. Whatever else, he shouldn't lie to the kid. Adults had been unreliable or apathetic or abusive to Cyndra her whole damn life until Addy came into the picture. Shaw was no kind of role model, but at least he could be straight with her.

"I don't know, Cyn," he said. "I'm fighting really hard not to. I didn't commit the crimes they suspect me of. It's important you know that much."

"Then why do they think you did?"

"The whole story is too long for a video chat," he said. "I'll have to explain it later. It's a thrilling adventure of thieves and mysterious islands and magic potions."

"The polymer isn't magic, Van. It's chemistry."

"My last science class was biology. We dissected prawns. I got a C-plus. Chemistry's magic to me."

Cyndra laughed. Finally.

"Look after Addy for me," said Shaw.

"Okay."

"I love you. Go make Addy buy you a huge dessert. Tell her I said so."

Cyndra ended the call. The window closed, leaving the black wallpaper image of the computer. The upper reaches of the sky and the vast expanse of land outside nearly matched its ebon hue, with a swath of brilliant crimson splitting the difference. As Shaw watched, the ruby horizon narrowed and grew deeper.

More of the picture was becoming clear. Bao, the Chinese agent, had ripped off Avizda for their innovation on infinite recycling. But not completely successfully. There were parts of the molecule that had remained a mystery despite their attempts at reverse-engineering the stolen sample. Chen, Bao's handler, had needed more information on the polymer's structure.

Rohner's company, Droma, controlled resource placement at Avizda. Chen knew that Rohner craved entry into the huge Chinese market. So they'd reached an agreement, and Droma had placed Kelvin Welch in Dallas. An IT expert who could steal the final pieces of that molecule puzzle.

And Hargreaves? Guessing by the papers Shaw had stolen from Chiarra's office at Paragon, the PI firm either had discovered that Linda Edgemont was taking bribes or were bribing her themselves through a shell company. Edgemont might have given Hargreaves inside information on exactly why Chen and Rohner wanted Avizda hacked. Maybe James Hargreaves had cut himself in on their billion-dollar deal. That didn't fully explain why he'd required the Bridgetrust cover, but it was a theory.

Bao was dead. Linda Edgemont was dead. Who else?

Shaw's gut turned over. He took the laptop off the dashboard and began a search for Kelvin Welch. He found what he was looking for on the first page of results. A news brief from the *Times-Picayune* in New Orleans, from the tenth of May.

TOURIST, 26, SHOT IN FRENCH QUARTER ROBBERY

A Florida tourist in New Orleans' French Quarter was shot and killed Saturday night during an apparent robbery, police have reported.

The victim, Kelvin Welch of Dade County, Florida, was found shortly before 1:00 a.m. by a server at Lanie's Bayou in the alley behind the bar, according to a statement by the New Orleans Police Department. The robber made off with the victim's wallet and cell phone. The alley gate leading to St. Ann Street was found broken, and police suspect that the unidentified robber might have fled the scene through the gate.

Police Superintendent Renee Jeffcoat urged anyone with additional information to contact NOPD Eighth District detectives or call anonymously to Crimestoppers of Greater New Orleans.

Bao and Edgemont and now Welch. Or Welch first. He had been killed more than a month ago. Shot to death, like Edgemont.

Bao, employed at Avizda. Welch, placed at Avizda by Droma. Edgemont, part of Droma's inner circle. All three stealing or selling secrets. All three dead.

Hargreaves was closing up shop. Was Karla Haiden another loose end the former government agent would cut? Or was Karla helping to wield the shears?

FIFTY-THREE

Denver," Louis Paolo said to Hargreaves over the phone. "She's taking the early Frontier flight. Plane lands at eight-thirty."

"You're certain?"

"That's their only flight leaving out of Concourse A in the next hour. I saw her at the ticketing counter and again in line for security. No luggage, just a purse and a shoulder bag. Moving fast."

Hargreaves nodded. Karla had used a prepaid debit card from First Citizens Bank instead of her primary accounts. Hargreaves had learned of her card application a year before, during one of his regular scourings of key employees' financial records. Since Karla met with Shaw, Hargreaves had set his trace programs to notify him of any transactions. His phone had pinged last night when she bought the ticket. Louis had been waiting at the airport this morning when she'd arrived.

"You're sure she didn't make you?" he said to Louis.

"Didn't give her a chance. I kept my distance. And it's crowded here."

"Shaw was driving west," Hargreaves said. He sat with Tucker in his rental BMW. "He could have made it to Denver by now, if he was determined."

"Karla told you he'd called her," said Tucker. "Why would she say anything if she was going to meet him?"

Because she's not a fool, Hargreaves thought. She suspects she's under watch.

She'd bought the ticket under her own name. So far as Hargreaves was aware, Karla didn't hold any false IDs good enough to allow her to board another flight out of Colorado under an assumed name.

That would limit her options. And perhaps Shaw's, if she were joining him.

Hargreaves considered the scenario for a moment before turning
to make sure Tucker understood that his instructions were for both
him and Louis. "Denver can't be his final stop. He might keep driving
whatever vehicle he has now. But if Karla's going with him out of Colorado, that might be his time to switch transport. Start with trains. If
Shaw's been driving as much as I suspect, he's going to want to sleep.
Buses next. Planes last."

Tucker agreed. He was skilled at pretending to be a federal officer over the phone. He had a list of legitimate credentials, and Louis
would back him up, fronting as the local FBI or Homeland field office
if required. "I'll describe the dirtbag we're after. Somebody at Amtrak
or Greyhound might give up the name Shaw's using."

"Don't assume they're returning to Seattle. That's probable—he's
been heading west for three days—but he could have changed his
mind."

"If Shaw doesn't have the chemical shit, why's Karla throwing in
with him?" said Louis.

Hargreaves didn't have a definite answer for that. He might have
misjudged, and Shaw truly was in possession of the sample. Or if
Hargreaves was right about Chen still holding it, perhaps Shaw had
somehow discovered where Chen had the sample hidden. If so, Shaw
would try to steal it. The man was nothing if not aggressive.

They could warn Chen that Shaw was coming. Maybe cut a deal,
team up with the Chinese agent to catch Shaw when he made his run.
Worth thinking about. The best case would be finding Shaw and that
bitch themselves and forcing them to surrender the sample. Second
place would be Chen's bodyguard, Zhang, putting a bullet between
Shaw's eyes. Threat eliminated.

"We'll have to ask Karla face-to-face."

"And then?" said Tucker.

"She's made her choice." Hargreaves inclined his head, a token shrug. "Her percentage is the same as yours. Yours to split, if you deliver."

"Hell," said Tucker. "I'll run after them on foot for that kind of money." He took out his phone and opened the car door. "Give us an hour to play *federales* with these Denver fools. If anyone's so much as caught a glimpse of Shaw's shadow, we'll know it."

FIFTY-FOUR

At ten minutes to nine in the morning, Shaw called Information Assistance at Denver International and explained that his sister had left her cell phone in the car before boarding her plane earlier that morning, and could she please be paged? He waited while the call went out over the airport speakers.

"Hello?" Karla said when she came on the line.

"It's me. Go out through Terminal West baggage claim. West Garage. Row K. Got that?" She did. "There's a woman there, standing by a red Impreza and wearing a Colorado Avalanche baseball cap. She knows where to go."

Shaw hung up. From the middle of the baggage terminal, he could see every exit. Karla would be coming off the train, taking the fastest route outside to the garage. That would put her on his left. The airport was in the middle of the morning rush, the first commuter flights landing and the second or maybe third wave of departures already lifting off. It was easy to fade in with the crowd, holding a discarded claim tag like he was waiting for the carousel to start spitting out luggage.

Five minutes later he spotted the sweep of Karla's red hair as she strode toward the exit, half a step faster than anyone around her. She had brought only a brown leather shoulder bag and a purse. He made a parallel path out the nearest sliding door and watched as Karla waited for the light and crossed the lanes to the short-term-parking structure. No one followed her. He watched for another two minutes before crossing the road to a different section of the garage and the truck.

He drove out of the airport toward the center of town. No need to follow the rideshare driver closely. He'd paid the fare and set the destination. Better to keep out of sight, in case Karla had been told to watch for a black Ford pickup. A team from Paragon might not be trailing her directly, but if Karla was acting as bait, she could summon reinforcements at any time.

The weekday morning traffic turned I-70 into a sluggish flow. Shaw got off the freeway and zigzagged through downtown streets until he reached a twenty-four-hour parking garage off Wewatta Street. He took his rucksack—clothes and gear already packed—and left the truck. He wouldn't be needing it again.

A juice bar occupied the corner of an office building in the middle of the block on Chestnut Place. The bar was airy and brightly lit. Its windows allowed views in multiple directions, one reason that Shaw had chosen it as the drop-off point for Karla's rideshare. He saw her inside, collecting a green-colored drink from the counter and moving to a stool where she'd be able to watch the street.

Shaw crossed to walk around the block to enter the building from the back side. The juice bar had a rear entrance for employees to take out the trash. Shaw popped the latch with a bump key and walked through the bar to occupy the stool next to Karla. She looked at him.

"Should have guessed you wouldn't use the front door," she said.

"Who knows you're here?" said Shaw.

"Hello to you, too. You look exhausted. I haven't told anyone I was leaving Seattle. I came alone."

Shaw didn't say anything.

Karla moved her drink to place her purse and shoulder bag on the narrow shelf in front of her. She unzipped them both and put her cell phone in front of Shaw. "Be my guest."

He left the bags where they were. "If you were setting me up, you're too smart to bring a tracker. Or to leave a trail on your phone."

"True."

"I can't trust you completely either. Not yet."

"You're the one who's a murder suspect, pal."

He watched the street as he talked. "You asked me if I had anything to do with Nelson Bao or Linda Edgemont. The only way for me to prove I didn't, to you or to the cops, is to find out who did and why. I have a pretty good idea. I have some evidence to back it up. Not enough to clear my name yet."

"Start with me."

He nodded. "That's the idea. And maybe if I persuade you, you'll be able to fill in some gaps in what I know."

"Which would show you I'm on your side," she said. "All right. Where do we start?"

"By leaving out the back," said Shaw, shouldering his duffel, "and catching a train."

FIFTY-FIVE

Union Station lay one block west of the juice bar. Shaw followed the signs under the white, wavelike roof to the designated platform. His electronic ticket noted the westbound Zephyr passenger train and car number. Karla seemed amused.

"I could have taken a train straight here from the airport," she said, "but then I wouldn't have enjoyed that matcha tea."

Inside the Superliner car, they walked upstairs to follow the narrow passage along the left side of the train. Theirs was the last compartment of five in the rear half of the car. A tag on the door noted the ticket holder and the final destination of Seattle.

Karla read the tag. "Who's Steven Ingram?"

"A guy taking an unexpected tour of the continental U.S." Shaw slid the compartment door open.

"Two passengers, three days and two nights to Seattle." She eyed the bunk bed, folded up and locked in place on the wall, as Shaw tossed his ruck onto the bedroom's settee. "You're sure of yourself."

"Options. If you'd said no, Ingram would have missed his train and I'd already be back on the road."

They spent a minute examining the tiny accommodations. The settee under the upper bunk. One chair by the window. A combination toilet and shower, and a slim hanging locker for clothes. Every piece built in and unadorned, just like on a ship.

"At least you picked a room with separate beds," Karla said. "A gentleman." She took the single seat and cracked open one of the complimentary plastic bottles of water. Shaw closed the door.

"Okay," she said. "Lay it out for me. What happened to Nelson Bao?"

"We'll get to that. Let's start with a game of true or false. Your name is Karla Lokosh."

She stared. "Why?"

"Not why. Yes or no."

He waited.

"False," she said.

"You work for Bridgetrust Group."

"False."

"Your boss is Bill Flynn."

"False."

"Your boss is James Hargreaves."

She frowned. "True."

"What's your job?"

"That's not a binary question. But let's bend the rules. I work in business intelligence."

"A private investigator."

"How do you know that?"

"A few more questions and it'll be your turn."

"Okay." She inhaled. "I was a PI. What I do now . . . is more variable, depending on the client."

"Assumed identities. Cover stories to gain information."

"Sometimes."

"Corporate espionage."

She hesitated. "We guard secrets, too."

"But spying is what this is about, with Droma. And Jiangsu Manufacturing."

Karla closed her eyes for a second. Guilt. Or just an acknowledgment of being cornered.

"Yes."

"Your target was Avizda, in Dallas."

"God. How do you know these things?"

They were interrupted by the conductor, tapping on the door for Shaw's ticket. Shaw held out his phone with the QR code for the conductor to scan and drew the navy-blue privacy curtain before sitting back down.

"I'll cover the what before the how," he said to Karla. "Nelson Bao worked as a chemist for Avizda before he went to work for Chen Li. Or maybe he was already secretly working for Chen. The chemical sample that you told me was Jiangsu's great innovation isn't actually theirs. Bao stole it from Avizda. Right?"

"I haven't been told directly that Bao stole it, but it's implicit."

"And for some reason, Bao's sample wasn't enough on its own. Chen needed more."

He waited, until Karla picked up the thread.

"Avizda is very careful about intellectual property," she said. "The chemical's structure and the different stages of the process are split across different dedicated computers, accessible only within the company property. Even the teams that create and test the physical samples are kept separate to reduce the chance that one employee might learn every facet. The polymer sample Bao stole couldn't be reverse-engineered, not entirely."

"Which is why Chen needed Droma. And Paragon."

"You know about Paragon, too."

"I've been in your office. Your mom and her husband make a nice couple. A little stiff in the studio portrait, though."

"Lord."

"Keep going."

"Droma was in charge of resourcing for Avizda. They could place anyone there, claiming that all background and criminal-record checks came back clean. What they needed was someone skilled in hacking to break into the internal servers without leaving a trail and obtain the portion of the molecular structure Chen needed to complete the polymer."

Shaw drummed his fingers on the window. "Skilled like an IT principal consultant. Kelvin Welch."

"You have to stop that. It's scary. Am I telling you anything you don't already know?"

"You are. And what I've already guessed, you're confirming. Rohner needed a hacker. Paragon had one. Welch."

"Yes. Sebastien Rohner has hired Paragon before. For business intelligence research and to gather ammunition for his divorce from his former wife."

"And he knew that Hargreaves was willing to break a few laws. That's Paragon's whole sales pitch."

Karla looked out the window. The train was beginning to move out of the station, picking up speed rapidly.

Shaw continued. "Paragon supplies Kelvin Welch. Droma places Welch at Avizda, and he hacks their system for the missing information. In exchange Droma gets to do business in China. So why isn't Chen sitting fat and happy back in Beijing? Why the big meeting on Rohner's island?"

"James Hargreaves," Karla said. "He guessed there was more than what Sebastien Rohner was telling him. He's holding on to the information that Welch hacked, and he won't give it up without a substantial payoff from Rohner. The meeting at the island was to confirm that the polymer is legit and for Hargreaves to collect, while Droma negotiated the public deal with Jiangsu."

"You brought Morton. Your own chemist."

Karla nodded. "And Chen Li had Bao. Both sides with their own expert to verify that the pieces of the molecule fit together."

"Why the smoke and mirrors with Bridgetrust and the false names? Why not just show up as Paragon and get paid?"

"Bridgetrust is our front for business intelligence work. It helps to have an established company for false job histories when you're investigating other corporations."

"Infiltrating, you mean."

"Or that. We made use of Bridgetrust as our cover on the island for two reasons. One was so that Rohner's payment to Paragon would be disguised—laundered, really—through Bridgetrust. He'll use Droma funds and call it an investment, one that will never pay out and be written off as a loss. The other reason is to keep Chen from knowing about Paragon's involvement."

Shaw looked at her. "Because Hargreaves is former NSA or CIA or whatever. Right?"

Karla seemed to be growing accustomed to Shaw's knowing things; she barely seemed startled this time. "Right. Any hint of government involvement might spook Chen. He's no more interested in serving twenty years for espionage than any of us."

Shaw gazed out the window. It all fit. Hargreaves had obtained the missing part of the polymer. But he didn't dare approach Chen directly. He still needed Droma to complete the deal. The Bridgetrust cover allowed Hargreaves to be on the scene when the polymer was verified and make sure he got his money.

The train was speeding through the outskirts of Denver now, the long, flat walls of warehouses rushing past and the towers of the power lines running parallel to the tracks marking progress at one every two seconds.

"You realize Chen's not a chemical-company CEO," he said. "Or not only that."

"Chinese intelligence?" she asked. "I do. China's had a major espionage push for more than a decade, recruiting foreign experts or paying them for proprietary secrets. The 'Thousand Talents,' they call it."

Shaw leaned back in his seat. "But you were willing to look the other way."

She gazed at the water bottle in her hands as if she'd forgotten it was there. "More often than not, I am."

"I don't care much," said Shaw. "I've lived by stealing before. Maybe I'll have to again someday. I wouldn't do what you do, and I don't pretend it's right. But I don't give a damn what companies and governments steal from each other. It's been happening forever. It'll go on forever."

"That's . . . nihilistic."

"Or realistic. Sometimes the stealing is direct, like yours. Sometimes it's done by squatting on patents or price gouging or just refusing to pay the other guy because you know he can't afford to sue. It's all theft." Shaw looked at her. "What I do care about is people getting hurt. Nelson Bao was a thief and a spy, but he probably didn't deserve to have his head bashed in."

"I don't know why he was killed. Or Linda Edgemont."

"I don't either. But Hargreaves didn't simply guess why Rohner wanted Avizda hacked. He had an inside source."

Shaw opened his duffel, drew out the file he'd taken from Chiarra's office, and handed it to her.

As Karla paged through the records, he watched the morning blur past the window. He was tired. Too many miles, not enough real rest. He knew from experience that he could keep going, keep functioning effectively, for a long time at this pace. Didn't mean the fatigue wasn't real.

Karla stared at one sheet. "I know this shell company. We've used it before, for transactions we don't want linked to Paragon." She held up a page. "If this is what you say, a bribe to Linda Edgemont, then the first payment to her was made at nearly the same time as Kelvin Welch joining Avizda. James was working both angles from the start."

"Linda was the person who recruited me, too. She probably told Hargreaves that Rohner was hiring a former thief." Shaw leaned his forehead against the cool glass. "I was burned before I started."

"Where did you find these papers?"

"Ed Chiarra's office."

"I know how James works. He would have approached Linda or had Ed do it for him. He'd say he was worried about whether Avizda was involved in work for the U.S. government. A Paragon operation that interfered with a military or federal contract could blow up in our faces. It might even be considered treason. He'd ask Linda for assurances, covertly, on what Droma was looking for. And he would let Linda know that in return he'd pay a consulting fee."

"And once she accepted the money, he'd own her." Shaw stood up and stretched, more a reaction to his agitated thoughts than to exercise his limbs. "Is James Hargreaves his real name?"

"It might be his real name now. The one the government created for him when he left."

Shaw grunted. Hargreaves's whole life had been redacted. No wonder Chiarra hadn't had a file on him.

"I've got a lot of guesses about what happened, theories that fit the facts," he said. "Bao's death had no premeditation. Everyone thinks he was killed for the chemical sample. Everyone figured me for the crime. Rohner offered me a guaranteed job and a trip around the world as incentive to hand over the chemical. A team of thugs has been trying to grab me off the street. *Give us the sample or else.* But I don't have it."

"Well, *someone* killed him."

"Yeah. The idea I keep coming back to is that Bao was murdered by mistake or out of panic. Maybe he saw something he shouldn't have. Someone poking around where they shouldn't be. And Chen was left with his chemist dead and maybe feeling he was in some danger himself. So Chen decided to tell Rohner and Hargreaves that the magic chemical was missing."

"When he had it all along. That makes sense. Everyone else has been setting fire to the brush, trying to flush out whoever has the sample. Chen's the only one who seems calm."

Shaw sat back down. His ribs objected to the movement.

"Linda Edgemont's death is easier to guess," he said. "Bao had been murdered. Maybe she got nervous. Or Hargreaves was just eliminating a potential risk."

"You think it was James?" Karla smoothed her pant leg, as if wiping away the thought. "He can be cold. Even ruthless, in business. But that level of brutality . . ." She shook her head.

Shaw took out his phone and held it up to flip through personnel photos. "Vic Urbaniak. Louis Paolo. Emmet Tucker. There's your brutality, times three."

She looked at the last picture, the one of Tucker staring stolidly from his driver's license.

"I've seen them. Not often, but they've been around the Paragon office. Field operatives. They've worked for James for a long time, from what I hear. They're the men who attacked you? After . . . after you left my room?"

"And the ones who broke me out of the cop car at Westlake. With the intention of finishing what they'd started outside your place." Shaw tapped at his phone. "I don't know if one of them pulled the trigger on Linda, but they're my first pick in that draft. And there's this."

He handed the phone to her. The screen showed the news story of Kelvin Welch's murder in New Orleans.

Karla stared. Long enough to read the article three times over if she chose to. She didn't say anything.

"You're in with bad people," said Shaw.

She turned to the window.

"Maybe you already knew that."

They sat for a time as the buildings flashing past the window became fewer and farther between. The train slowed and stopped at a station for a few minutes. The announcement warbled over the car's speakers. Then the train gathered speed again. Karla stayed silent. Shaw felt the weight of the quiet in his shoulders and neck.

"I told myself it wasn't much," she said at last. "That if I broke any laws, it was just one megacorporation stealing from another. That they probably deserved it."

Shaw waited.

"And I wanted the money."

He nodded.

"Maybe I knew the truth then. But . . . I'd gotten used to not asking the follow-up questions. Not looking too close." She regarded him. "Did you think that I set you up?"

"I knew it was possible."

"You called me here."

"Yes."

"Do you still think I'm on his side?"

"Less than I did then."

She sighed. "I'd feel that way, too, if our positions were reversed. Worse. I would have assumed you were my enemy right away."

"You came here. Alone."

"Yes," she said.

"Did you tell Hargreaves you were coming?"

"No. He knows you contacted me. He would have known even if

I hadn't told him. I doubt there's a single line of communication to a Paragon employee he doesn't monitor, at least while we're in the field."

"Why'd you keep it a secret?"

Karla was still holding his phone, turning it over and over in her hands. She might not realize she was doing it. "I knew it was time to choose."

Shaw raised an eyebrow.

"I didn't sleep with you to trick you," she said, "or to find out if you had the missing sample. By that point I was pretty certain you weren't the thief."

"Why?"

"Because of the way you talked about finding Nelson Bao. You had empathy. More than someone who'd murdered him for some chemical could muster. Also because of all the people on that island, you seemed like the only one without a map to what was really happening. I couldn't fit that together with you killing someone for profit."

Shaw smiled. "So why did you seduce me?"

She laughed. "Oh, that was mutual, and don't try to tell me different." She leaned back in the compartment's lone chair, the first show of relaxation since they'd arrived. "I went to bed with you because I wanted to. Because we'd had a nice night and you'd made me laugh and I thought we'd be damned good together. In case you thought I had any other motive."

"Crossed my mind."

"That's the only reason I sleep with anyone. I don't use sex to advance my career. Or play Mata Hari with investigation subjects. Ever."

"Okay," said Shaw, hearing the force behind her words.

"Every woman gets accused of shit like that. Even if her work isn't dealing in secrets and lies." Karla brushed a hand over her cheek, wiping at a flush that was just beginning to bloom. "And I'm well aware that drawing a line at using my body while I'm bartering for trade secrets from Avizda might be fatuous. And hypocritical."

"I wasn't going to say anything." Shaw stretched to prop his feet on the sink counter. "I grew up burgling houses and stores. Doesn't mean I was a street hustler. And the kids who were hustlers and pros around Broadway probably wouldn't break into houses to steal either. Everybody chooses their own limit."

"You knew prostitutes? When you were a child?"

"I knew kids my age. Home lives worse than mine, and mine was all kinds of fucked up. A few of them hooked part of the time." He shrugged. "Survival."

The morning sun was bright. Shaw closed his eyes.

"What do we do now?" Karla said.

"Now," said Shaw with his eyes still shut, "I'm going to sleep."

"I mean after that, smart guy."

"We fight. We kick them right in their shiny white teeth." His voice seemed a long way off. "Wake me when we hit Utah."

Bridgetrust and Jiangsu and Lokosh and Hargreaves. Shaw fell asleep. He dreamed of rows upon rows of porcelain masks, all staring balefully at one another, waiting endlessly to see who would be the first to blink.

FIFTY-SIX

The smell of coffee woke him before the click of the train compartment door closing. He rose from the settee. His coat was off. He vaguely remembered removing it before lying down and peeling off the curling bandage under his T-shirt to toss it in the trash. Karla extended the miniature table from the side of the compartment and placed paper boxes with the Amtrak logo on it.

"Dinner," she said. "I guessed you might not feel up to visiting the dining room."

"Thanks."

Karla was right, but not because Shaw still felt tired. He wanted to keep his face with its memorable scars away from as many eyes as possible. Hargreaves's net might be wide.

He checked his watch. Five o'clock in the afternoon.

"You had to rest," she said by way of explanation. "You didn't tell me you were injured."

"A mere scratch." Shaw touched his ribs under the shirt. It didn't twinge at the pressure, which he took for a good sign.

"Well, that scratch is flirting with infection. Here." She motioned to a small pile of gauze and tape and antibiotic ointment packets in the sink. "I told the conductor you had scrapes from a motorcycle spill. He raided the train's first-aid kit."

Shaw saw her phone on the little seat. Had she contacted anyone while he was out?

"I've kept it off," she said at his look. "Gave me a chance to catch up on what was happening at the Battle of Monmouth." She held up her thick paperback.

"History buff."

Karla smiled. "It might have been my major, if dance weren't such a lucrative field."

"And an M.B.A. And a PI license. You keep busy."

"I might have a lot more time to read soon," she said, her smile vanishing as quickly as it had come. "We have to go to the police. *I* have to go to the police. With or without you. I need to come to terms with this."

"Even if that means prison?"

"Even if."

Outside, a field in the full burst of summer made a haze of emerald green past the window. With Karla's red hair and the sound of the wheels on the track, Shaw had the impression of another era, another continent, an early diesel locomotive driving the train past farm country where his grandfather would someday be raised in County Antrim. Another time. Not a simpler time. That was an illusion, he knew.

"Okay," he said. "If you'll give me a couple of days after we reach Seattle, I might be able to help. Put the cops in a better frame of mind to hear you out."

"How?"

"You'll have to give evidence."

"I assumed as much," she said.

"And someone else will have to join you."

Shaw told her what he had in mind, or at least as much plan as he'd formed so far. She thought he was crazy, which was no surprise. He thought the scheme was more than halfway to howling at the moon himself. But better than walking into SPD headquarters and placing his head on the chopping block.

BY THE TIME THEY'D TALKED it through, night had fallen and Karla's jaw creaked with yawning. Shaw pulled the bunk down, and she went into the bathroom. When she came out, she was wearing shorts and an extra-large pink T-shirt with KILLINGTON RESORT over a picture of snowy peaks. The shirt so old and softened from countless washings that the cracks in the printed image looked like huge crevasses in the mountains.

She climbed up into the bunk to lie on her side and regard him with her hazel eyes. With Shaw standing, their faces were nearly even.

She smiled. "Thanks. For talking it out. And giving me a chance."

"Same here."

Her fingers curled over the crisply folded top edge of the bedsheet beneath her. "I'd invite you in, but . . ."

"Yeah," he said. "Maybe when we're on the other side of all this."

Shaw picked up his jacket to step out into the corridor. He drew the compartment's curtain closed again and shut the door. The passage lights had been dimmed for the night, save for a line of safety bulbs running along the edge of the floor. Their bedroom was at the end of the car, next to a luggage rack. The only occupied room in this half. At the front end, past the public toilet and the cramped stairwell at the car's center, was a row of unoccupied roomettes. Shaw stepped to lean against the wall by the rack.

His first call was to Professor Jemma Mills. He got her voice mail and described in detail the favor he needed. A tiny batch of chemical to mimic the sample he'd seen in Bao's apartment. Any mixture would do, so long as it looked the same. He said he couldn't be reached directly but that he would call back tomorrow.

Hollis picked up his own burner phone on the second ring.

"Van. You all right?" he said.

"Enduring. Maybe even turning the tide. I need some transport, if you can stand a long drive."

"I can leave straightaway. Where?"

"Reno. That's twelve hours of road. If you leave now and don't spare the horses, we should hit the Amtrak station about the same time as you."

"We?" said Hollis.

"Me and the redhead. I'll explain everything on the drive."

"Should be a tale. See you there."

Shaw's last call was to a number in San Francisco. He'd looked it up outside Kansas, memorizing it in the event he needed to take a wild swing.

"Good evening, Consulate-General of the People's Republic."

"Good evening," said Shaw. "I have an unusual request. I'm trying to get a message to one of your citizens currently traveling in Seattle."

"I'm sure we would not know how to reach them, sir." The young man sounded offended. This American oaf expected all Chinese people to know one another.

"No, of course. But Mr. Chen may reach out to you. Most likely to your section in charge of business affairs. Mr. Chen Li is chairman of Jiangsu Special Manufacturing. He will have made your consulate aware of his important visit to the United States."

"Perhaps." The consular officer sounded slightly mollified.

"Would you be good enough to let your section head know of my request, on the chance Mr. Chen should call?" Shaw realized how much he sounded like Wren when she slipped into overly correct phrasings.

"Your name, please?"

"Van Shaw. Here's an e-mail where I can be reached at any time." Shaw read him the address. The young man repeated it back, letter by letter, as if afraid he might get it wrong.

"Thank you," Shaw said. "I'm certain Mr. Chen greatly appreciates your assistance."

A Hail Mary pass, Shaw thought as he hung up. But no harm in trying. If Chen and Zhang were Chinese agents, his inquiry would find its way to them. And if Chen's assignment was as important as Shaw suspected, whatever section chief at the consulate acted as their messenger boy for spies might be on the horn to his higher-ups right this minute.

Deceptions upon evasions. Dono would have rolled his eyes at all the chicanery these intelligence firms and foreign operatives got up to. The old man liked his crimes simple and direct.

Shaw stayed in the train corridor watching the trees and rocks of the Utah mountains speed past the windows. Even at night the terrain had a kind of grandeur. Shaw liked the mountains. The terrors and trials of the Afghan peaks hadn't spoiled that for him. He'd spent most of his life near the water, but when he thought of building a home somewhere, a place to stay for more than the length of a lease, he always imagined it at elevation. Where he could see the snow and smell the evergreens in his retirement.

Of course, he'd have to have a job to retire from. And he'd have to live to reach old age.

The land outside became flatter. The Zephyr was pulling in to Salt Lake. Shaw watched from the darkened corridor as the train slowed and stopped. At well past midnight, the station was quiet. A few passengers disembarked. A luggage carrier not much larger than a golf cart pulled alongside and began to load bags onto the train. Conductors and other Amtrak personnel walked the length of the cars, talking quietly so as not to wake people aboard. After ten minutes the group split up to go to their individual cars or back into the station. Readying to go.

Two men walked quickly from the station to the waiting train. They wore long rainproof coats and carried duffel bags over their shoulders.

Shaw had seen the larger of the two before. That bushy black Viking beard was unmistakable, even though he'd only glimpsed it for an instant through the open driver's window of the Jeep Cherokee that had tried to run him to ground in Youngstown.

The Viking's brawn was apparent even through the raincoat. He rolled a little as he walked.

His partner's movements were more fluid, even snakelike, bobbing his head to unheard music as he walked. As Shaw watched, the partner adjusted his heavy-framed dark eyeglasses and looked up to the second level. Shaw faded back from the window.

The men boarded their car. Shaw had the SIG in the pocket of his jacket. He kept his hand on it as the train doors closed and the Zephyr began to pull away from the station.

A minute passed. Then five. No one came up the stairs.

Shaw removed the tag with Steven Ingram's name on it from their compartment door and walked silently down the corridor to place it on the empty room three doors down. He drew the room's curtain and used his picks to lock the door. Then he retreated to their room and kept an eye on the stairs as he reached in to shake Karla's foot until she woke and stared at him confusedly.

"Get up," Shaw said in a whisper. "We're in trouble."

FIFTY-SEVEN

Shaw recalled the map of the Zephyr's route. Elko, Nevada, would be the next stop. Five hours away. If the two killers wanted them alive, that would be where they'd force Shaw and Karla off the train. Likely making their move just before the train hit the station so they wouldn't have to hold their captives at gunpoint for hours.

If the plan was to kill them, the men would still strike in the minutes before Elko. Shaw and Karla were alone on the upper level. No witnesses. The killers could off them in their compartment and make a quick exit before their corpses had cooled.

Better to guard the stairs—the only approach from the lower level of the car—than to wager on the two killers being cautious. Shaw stayed near the luggage rack and watched the corridor while Karla packed their things. Then there was nothing to do but wait.

"You're sure?" she whispered. She had her shoes and jacket on and her shoulder bag over her back, poised as if to sprint from the room.

"I'm sure. They tailed me from New York. Maybe from the Paragon offices. I lost them in Ohio." Shaw described the two. "You know them?"

She shook her head. "God. I'd remember men like that."

He nodded. The bigger one with the beard looked like he could make a fair attempt at benching the train car. The other might slide right under the wheels without a scratch.

"Sit," he said. "Rest. Odds are we won't move for four more hours."

"If they come sooner—"

"I'll stop them."

"How will we get past them?"

Shaw didn't answer. He knew they wouldn't. There was no way off the train without the two knowing. The killers would be watching as closely as he was.

AT FOUR O'CLOCK IN THE morning, Shaw moved down the corridor to the center of the car. The narrow stairwell to the lower level was empty. He motioned to Karla, who walked with their bags down the row of bedrooms and past Shaw, into the nearest roomette in the front half of the car. She shut the roomette's door and drew the curtain. Shaw stepped into the public toilet and hooked a finger over the handle to pull the metal door shut, but not latched.

He waited in the dark. The tight space smelled of antiseptic cleanser and a plug-in air freshener doing a sickly imitation of gardenias.

After forty minutes the sound of the train changed. Or its surroundings had changed. Closer to the tracks. Buildings instead of open air.

Shaw let the door ease open a millimeter. He could see only a dim sliver of the corridor, a line of light gray in the black.

Outside, the train rushing by the buildings created a hollow moan. Shaw remained as he was.

They had made no sound as they came up the stairs. Shaw's only warning was the slice of gray light from the corridor going black and then gray once more, as someone moved past his door into the row of bedrooms. A second person passed.

Shaw opened the door another finger's width. He found himself looking at the broad back of the Viking, still in his long coat, standing at the top of the curving stairwell. Visible over the Viking's shoulder was the killer with the eyeglasses, moving silently away, toward the room where Shaw had placed the Ingram ticket tag.

Shaw stepped out from the bathroom. He put his left palm on the right side of the Viking's head and his other hand holding the SIG against the man's bowling-ball shoulder and heaved to his left with all his strength. The Viking toppled into the stairwell, a gun in his hand striking the wood-veneer wall and clattering to the floor at Shaw's feet. The big man crashed into the side of the landing six feet below with an almighty bang. Shaw aimed his SIG at the one with the glasses, who had spun at the sound.

"Don't," Shaw said as the killer's hand moved toward his jacket. "Turn around."

The man complied. His expression had hardly changed.

"Back up to me," Shaw said. Below him the Viking was clambering to his feet, not an easy maneuver in a stairwell barely half his width. When the one with the glasses reached him, Shaw quickly frisked him and removed a pistol from his raincoat pocket. He handed it to Karla, behind him.

"Cover that one," he said, tilting his head toward the Viking, who had regained his feet on the tiny stairwell landing below them. His blueberry eyes, incongruous over the rage of black beard, glared murderously. "If he twitches, put four in his center mass."

"You all right?" a voice called from the floor below.

"Yeah, thanks," Shaw called back. "Just dropped my bag."

"Easy, buddy," said the guy with the glasses, craning his neck to keep Shaw in his peripheral vision. "Just a mix-up. We're here to talk."

Shaw rabbit-punched him in the back of the neck. The glasses flew off and the man dropped to all fours.

He saw what the Viking had fumbled by his feet. A KRISS Vector submachine gun. A squarish black chunk sixteen inches long without the stock and probably capable of killing every person in the train car with a single clip, doors and walls be damned.

Shaw scooped up the gun with his left hand. He looked at the Viking and motioned to his dazed partner. "Get him up."

The man lumbered to the top of the stairs. Shaw stepped back, out of reach. He waited as the Viking placed his hands under the other man's arms and hefted him to his feet with ease. The train was slowing now. Drawing into the station at Elko.

Shaw nodded to the toilet. "In there. Both of you."

"Fuck off," the Viking rumbled.

Shaw pointed the SIG at the man's right leg. "Door Number Two earns you a prosthetic knee."

The Viking sneered but moved. He and his partner squeezed into the toilet room, chest to back, like a compacted conga line.

"Romantic," Shaw said. "Don't fucking blink."

He shut the metal door. As Karla covered it, Shaw used his picks to lock the toilet's dead bolt through the access keyhole, there for the train staff in case some toddler locked himself in. He jammed the slim pick inside the lock's workings and bent the metal until it snapped. He tried the handle. It barely budged.

"Let's go," he said, stuffing the submachine gun into his rucksack. Karla followed him downstairs. They were the first passengers off the train when the doors opened, and they beat the dawn to the streets of Elko, Nevada.

FIFTY-EIGHT

Putting distance between themselves and the town was the top priority. The train had pulled away from the station with the two killers still inside; that didn't mean Shaw and Karla were safe. Once they were freed, the two might spin a story to the Amtrak people that would set cops on their asses.

Searching on Shaw's phone, they found a large new-and-used-car lot less than half an hour's walk away. They crossed the Humboldt River at a fast clip. Shaw felt uncomfortably exposed on the wide, empty road. He swiped the license plates off a Dodge parked on the gravel curb outside a housing development, and when they reached the auto dealer, he compounded the crime by boosting a used Toyota 4Runner from a row of half a dozen of the same model on their back lot.

Within five minutes they were on Interstate 80 with the sun at their backs. The morning was clear and promised heat. The tall piles of clouds in the endless sky looked as clean as angels' dreams.

Shaw called Hollis on speaker. "Where are you?"

"I just passed—hold on—Chemult, Oregon. Making good time in the Caddy."

"You'll have to make it in a different direction. Sorry. Our plans are shifting."

Karla held up Shaw's laptop with the map on it for him to see. He nodded.

"Turn around and go back up 97 and cross Oregon on Route 20," he said to Hollis. "We'll be coming straight north out of Nevada. Probably meet you somewhere around Steens Mountain in four hours."

If we don't get busted for grand theft auto for a damn 4Runner, he thought.

"Never dull with you, Van," said Hollis.

"I do what I can. See you soon." He hung up.

"A friend?" said Karla.

"Best kind," said Shaw. "I hope you like him, too, because he's going to host you aboard his boat for a couple of days while I work things out. If I can convince him. And maybe his lady friend. Do you get seasick?"

"Not much."

"Good. The safest place to be is offshore."

"Your friend is right. You are *not* boring."

"After the gruesome twosome on the train, boring sounds great right about now."

His phone pinged. A new e-mail on the address he'd created specifically for Chen Li.

Thank you for your interest. Please contact the number below soon.

A number with a western Washington area code followed. He wondered why Chen hadn't simply sent the number on its own and concluded that the key word was "soon." Maybe Chen was under some pressure. The polite tone implied a willingness to discuss terms.

Shaw would have to let Chen bite his nails for a while. He checked the rearview. Nothing in it but the morning sun. Before it set again, they would be home. And then he'd see what kind of storm he could create for Chen, and Rohner, and especially James Hargreaves.

FIFTY-NINE

Hollis had stashed the *Francesca* in a friend's empty moorage slip in Tacoma, along with Shaw's speedboat, which Hollis and his lady friend, Dr. Paula Claybeck, had towed from Shilshole. When the Cadillac returned from its long road trip, the doctor told Hollis that he'd received three calls from Ephraim Ganz that day. The criminal defense attorney had refused to specify what he wanted, just that he'd call again.

Hollis had looked at Shaw. His pink face had unfamiliar bags under the eyes. He'd been in one seat of his Cadillac or another for nearly twenty-four hours. "Trying to reach you, I'll wager," he'd said.

And being cautious about it. Shaw was still a fugitive and a murder suspect.

He had bid Karla and Hollis and Paula farewell and driven his speedboat north of Seattle, to dock in a little-used boatyard. The yard smelled faintly of rancid seaweed that had been stranded in the barnacles and splinters of the older, shorter dock, which had been left to rot when the new one was built above it. Tiger stripes of rust streaked the corrugated-steel walls of the boathouse, two decades of gutter wash.

Home and hiding place for a few days, while he made preparations.

He called Ganz's office. It was after business hours, but that rarely meant much for the energetic attorney.

"Ephraim Ganz," the receptionist said.

"Hey, this is Mr. Ganz's plumber. We're looking at the house now, and we'll have to tear out most of the second-floor bath to get to the problem. If Mr. Ganz can call me back quick, we might be able to save the Jungle Room."

"Oh, my. Yes. What is your number?"

Shaw gave it. His phone rang within five minutes.

"How is it you announce yourself without ever leaving your name?" Ganz said.

"I figured it was supposed to be a secret, you talking to me."

"It is. Just like I'm supposed to tell you to turn yourself over to the authorities. But before you rush out and do that, Sofia Rohner has been calling me every day. Trying to reach you. She insists she knows something that can help your case. Given it might encourage you to do the right thing, legally, I felt bound to pass the news along." He read off a phone number to Shaw.

"Thanks. And, Ephraim. I didn't get the chance to say before, I'm sorry about Linda."

"Not your doing. You're a maniac of the first order, but you aren't that kind of crazy. I should never have gotten you involved in this, kid."

"I walked in eyes open. Ignoring every red flag. Next time we'll know better."

"Sure we will," Ganz said.

Shaw stepped away from the boat to call Sofia Rohner. Restless. He needed to move. To engage with the enemy.

"This is Sofia," she answered.

"You wanted to talk to me," he said.

"Yes," she said without pause. Maybe she had reserved this number solely for his call. "Thank you. Can we meet?"

"You said you had information that could help me."

"I do. But I would prefer to speak with you in person."

Shaw was about to tell her how much her preference was worth when he realized that an in-person meeting might have another advantage.

"Have Rangi drive you south of downtown tomorrow at ten," he said. "I'll call this number and tell you where to meet me. And I want you to give me something for my risk and trouble."

"I see. How much did you want?"

"Not money." He told Sofia what he wanted her to bring. After a moment's surprised hesitation, she said she would see him in the morning.

Shaw sat on the railroad ties that edged the high dock, looking out at the water. The wooden pilings that had once served as tie-ups for ships awaiting dock space had rotted and splintered, their jagged tops poking above the water like the spiny hide of some gigantic submerged crocodile.

A sliver of Shaw's heart yearned to talk to Wren, to hear her voice and her laughter. But the colder part of him prevented it. He knew why. He'd had the same inclination before deployments. Not going out on the town, not visiting the fighting gyms that were his usual hangouts off base. Limiting human contact. Removing himself, bit by bit, from the comforts and distractions of the civilian world.

Narrowing his focus to what was to come. And how best to survive it.

SIXTY

Shaw talked Rangi through the turns as the big man drove Sofia Rohner through the lot of a giant Home Depot and onto a side road that ran parallel to the railroad tracks. The silver Lexus sedan circled and crossed the tracks on Hanford to turn at a skate park where Shaw had taken Cyn a few times. The sedan followed a line of freight companies until it came to where Shaw waited at a repair shop for big rigs.

A winding enough route to reassure him that the Lexus hadn't been followed. If the police should show, his speedboat was waiting a quick sprint across Route 99, on a side pocket of the waterway. He wouldn't be caught. Not now, not when he was so close.

He stepped out from behind a row of food-hauling trailers, standing lonely on their slim landing-gear posts. All the tractors were across the lot in front of the repair building, noses in, like hogs at a trough. The Lexus parked ten yards away, incongruously sleek and gleaming.

Rangi got out first. He wore his usual black suit and tie for shore work. Shaw held up a hand in greeting. Rangi just shook his head, like he couldn't believe he'd been dragged on such a fool's errand.

Sofia Rohner stepped out from the backseat and closed the door. To ward off the morning chill, she wore a dove-gray topcoat over her midnight business suit. Her blond hair was wound in a complex twist that lay almost flat against the back of her head. She held the tablet computer with the gloss ivory cover that Shaw had seen on the island.

"Thank you for meeting me," she said. Her accent was more pronounced than at the island. Tension, Shaw supposed. "I have some questions. And in return I hope I can help you."

Shaw had anticipated there might be more to Sofia's fervent need to see him than philanthropy.

"What is it you want to know?" he said.

"My father offered you a position with Droma, before you were arrested. Head of security in place of Warren Kilbane."

"I didn't take the job."

"I know that, too. My question is why. I found a draft of his offer to you in the Droma employment system. He had deleted the final copy but failed to remember that our system automatically saves a backup of every document in progress. Why would my father offer you a job and try to keep it off the official record? Why didn't you accept?"

Shaw looked at her, then at Rangi.

"Here's my dilemma, Ms. Rohner," he said. "You love your father. You probably love Droma, too—you've invested a lot of your life into it. If I tell you what I know or what I suspect, then I've shown my cards to somebody whose loyalties lie elsewhere."

"You think you can't trust me."

"I think your father can. It amounts to the same thing."

"I'm not your enemy. Why do you believe my father is?"

"He's sure as shit not an ally. You said something about information for me. Let's start with that, and then maybe I'll trade a little in return."

Sofia hesitated.

Rangi nodded toward the way they had come in. "I can take a walk if you want, Ms. Rohner."

"No. It's better that you stay," she told him. "I may want a witness to what's said. Thank you."

She turned to Shaw. Her shoulders drew back, as if she were bracing herself against a strong wind.

"I only know bits and pieces," she said. "Linda Edgemont sent me a message after she returned from the island. Wanting to speak to me urgently. I didn't receive it until after . . . until it was too late."

"What did she want?"

"She didn't elaborate. But she was very distraught about Mr. Bao's death. I know Linda was the one who recruited you. I asked my lawyer—who has some friends in law enforcement—about your background."

"My rap sheet."

"Yes. And your grandfather's. You were a burglar once."

"And you want to know if Rohner and Anders hired me to steal for them, is that it?"

"No. I don't believe that's the case. My father and Olen had no need for your help."

"Because they wouldn't need a thief to get into the gallery themselves," said Shaw. "That's why they put the laboratory there."

Sofia blinked. "You know about the tests."

"I've had a busy week, kicking over rocks and seeing what squirms."

"My father is counting on this deal. Depending on it."

"So he aimed to steal Chen's invention, to make sure he didn't get cut out. I'm ahead of you on that one." Shaw nodded. "Your father and Anders hired me because I was conspicuous. To be a smoke screen. It didn't work out."

"He's only trying to survive."

"Me, too. But corporate secrets aren't what you're really worried about, right? You asked about Linda."

A diesel at the repair bay came to life with a loud stuttering thrum. If Sofia heard it, she gave no sign.

"Linda was my friend," she said. "She was a good person. I want . . . I need to know what happened."

Shaw waited.

"Was my father involved in her death?"

It might have been the first time Sofia had given voice to a fear she'd been holding for days. Her eyes were bright with tears that refused, perhaps by some force of her considerable will, to fall. Rangi stared at her, too, his routinely doleful face slack with surprise.

"If Linda knew he was planning to steal from Chen, if she knew why they were hiring you, perhaps my father thought she was . . ." Sofia reached for the words.

"A liability."

"Hey, I've got a piece of this," said Rangi. "I'm the guy who dropped

Ms. Edgemont off that day. I was the last one to see her before it happened, the cops said."

Shaw's fists balled in his pockets. Anything he told Sofia and Rangi might ultimately get back to Rohner. It could upset the delicate scheme he'd just begun to set into motion. Exhaust from the running tractor wafted across them, sugary sweet in the chill morning air.

He sympathized with Sofia's grief, too. Her drive. That hunger for answers to fill the painful void inside.

"I don't think your father's that far gone," he said. "He's not clean, and maybe a lot more trouble is coming to him, but if I'm right, he didn't have Linda killed. It's not his way."

Sofia nodded, and after another moment she gave out a brittle sound that might have been a laugh. "How can words like that be comforting? Yet they are."

"D'you know who did kill her?" Rangi asked.

"Yeah," said Shaw. "But that's my problem to worry about."

Sofia looked like she was about to protest. Perhaps the expression on Shaw's face stopped her.

She held out the ivory tablet. Shaw stepped forward to take it.

"I don't know if the software will open the gallery," she said. "I tried again without success before leaving the island."

"It'll do."

"What happens now?" she said.

"You run your company. I handle my own business. If we're lucky, neither runs into the other."

She got back into the car. Rangi raised a heavy palm off the Lexus's roof in farewell, or maybe resignation, and lowered himself into the driver's seat. They were gone in seconds.

Sofia had to suspect, Shaw mused. Had to have at least guessed that Chen's scientific miracle wasn't his own invention. That her father was colluding with a foreign power. It was all there for her to see and make her suppositions, even if she couldn't prove it. Or didn't want to.

But murder was beyond the pale. More than Sofia could rationalize or sidestep on behalf of her family.

Dono had felt that way, too. Being a thief was the way of the world. Stealing a life, however, was left for some higher power.

The tough old bastard had raised Shaw to believe that. And for a long time, he had. Before war and other ordeals had begun to steadily chip away at Shaw's conviction. Ethics were situational, he knew now. Killing, too.

Soon he'd know what the situation with James Hargreaves demanded.

SIXTY-ONE

Detective Neal Kanellis lived in a condominium a few blocks off Green Lake. Close enough to walk to the lake but far enough from the water that the real-estate agent had stretched the truth if they'd claimed that the listing was part of the neighborhood. The building was three stories tall in a courtyard style, with its interior balconies facing the amenities, including a fitness center and a rec area with a barbecue. Appearance-wise Shaw thought the place was the architectural equivalent of a saltine cracker.

The detective's one-bedroom unit took up a corner on the second floor. Easy to scale from the ground. Easier to open the sliding glass door. The interior was less cluttered than Shaw had expected, though it was impossible to tell without the lights on whether the place was really clean.

Shaw stepped past a framed Claude Lemieux San Jose Sharks jersey to tap Kanellis's shin with his boot. "Wake up."

Kanellis bolted upright, his right hand flying toward the nightstand as if it had its own mind. When the hand didn't find what it sought, Kanellis's head turned in that direction to see for itself.

"Take it easy," said Shaw. "I come in peace."

"The fuh you doin' 'ere?" Kanellis sputtered through a mouth that sounded as dry as rice paper.

"Let's talk."

"Crazy fug." Kanellis wiped his mouth. "You're dead. Breaking into a cop's home. I'll throw your ass off the friggin' balcony."

"Be reasonable, Neal. I've got forty pounds and a whole lifetime of knocking guys slantwise on you. Plus, I'm wearing pants. Pull the sheet up, wouldja?"

Kanellis did. "You're under arrest."

"Sure. But hear me out. Major busts could be yours."

"What kind of busts?"

"Economic and industrial espionage. Multiple counts. Assault with intent. Attempted kidnapping. Plus, if I'm right, a better lead on the killer of Linda Edgemont. Promotion material."

"So spill it."

"Pay attention. This is too long to go through twice."

Shaw talked for fifteen minutes, recapping some of what Kanellis already knew from Shaw's time in the interview room at SPD headquarters. He described each of the major players he'd met at Briar Bay Island, finding Nelson Bao's body, and his assumptions about the connections between Rohner and Hargreaves and Chen Li. He had to muddle a few details. He said he'd gone to look at Bao's apartment and found the remnants of the chemical sample in a Hefty bag in the Dumpster outside. When he came to the part about Chiarra, and the Paragon team busting him out of jail, Shaw hedged.

"Their team set off the flashbangs and smoke by Westlake Center. They yanked me out of the cop car when you went to check on the bystanders," Shaw said.

"You shit."

"They insisted. Herded me to the rail station underground and shoved me into a car. I got away when they came up for air by the stadiums."

"I know. We found the Chrysler crashed there. Smoke-grenade residue all over it, along with your prints. One of their crew practically gave the transit joe a cerebral hemorrhage, knocking him out."

"To lower the barrier on the tracks?" Shaw felt a relief so palpable the hairs on his arms rose. They hadn't killed the guard. "Was it a woman who attacked him?"

"Now, how did you know that? He only got a glimpse before she walloped him with a sap, but yeah. Younger woman, sunglasses and a hat, dark hair mighta been a wig."

"Glad he's okay."

"You should have turned yourself in, asshole," said Kanellis.

"Would you? I hadn't been charged with Edgemont's murder, but I knew that was right around the corner. You weren't looking hard to find other suspects. Besides"—Shaw lifted his shirt to show Kanellis the laceration on his ribs—"I didn't think jail was a safe place to be. These guys have reach."

"You're in deep shit, Shaw."

"I know it. But I've got a shovel now."

Shaw held up a thick manila envelope. "This is evidence from Paragon's home office. It links Chiarra and the private intelligence firm he works for to Linda Edgemont, and to a hacker named Kelvin Welch. Welch was shot to death in New Orleans a month ago. The news didn't say, but I bet if you ask NOLA, you'll find out the weapon was a suppressed .22, same as the kind that killed Edgemont. They all stole trade secrets from a company called Avizda Industries in Dallas, on Rohner's dime, with the intent of selling those secrets to a foreign power."

Despite the detective's scowl, Shaw was fairly sure he saw Kanellis's eyes glitter greedily in the half-light.

Shaw tossed the envelope onto the bed. "There's everything I got from Paragon. You'll also find four pages written and signed by me. My confession to B&E in New York City and my statement of everything that's happened, along with my best guesses as to how it all fits together."

"It's not enough. The word of a fucking fugitive."

"No," Shaw admitted, "but there are plenty of threads to pull. I'd start with Ed Chiarra. He's a weak link."

Kanellis grimaced. "Like I need your help to do my job."

"You'll get it anyway." Shaw took Kanellis's Glock and phone from his pocket and placed them on the detective's dresser next to a football autographed by Russell Wilson, standing upright on its tee. The loaded clip from the gun he tossed underhand out of the bedroom and behind Kanellis's sectional sofa. "I got your number. I'll contact you."

"The hell. You're gonna wait in a cell while we sort this out. If what you say is true, you'll get a fair shake."

"Three months from now, maybe. After Rohner's fled the country and Hargreaves has covered every track. No. You need to catch them in the act of selling secrets." He moved to the bedroom door.

"Don't be an idiot. Giving yourself up would show you want to make this right. A judge will go easy on you."

"Get some rest. Big day tomorrow."

"Shaw," Kanellis called after him. The detective's quieter tone made Shaw pause. "Why bring this to me? Why not Guerin? You two got more history."

"You're hungrier. You can talk Guerin into waiting for the right moment and make sure you've got more than just my typing to go on. Besides"—Shaw smiled—"Guerin has his own copy of my statement waiting for him when he wakes up. The man's got family. I didn't want to scare his wife and kids."

"What if I'd had a girl here? You think about that?"

Shaw looked at the hockey jersey on the wall. "Not once I saw your place."

SIXTY-TWO

Midday on a sunny Thursday in July, an early start to a holiday weekend, meant the main drag of the Market was as packed as it was possible to get. The most crowded place in the city at that moment. Possibly on the entire West Coast.

Shaw shuffled along with the mob. He had a feeling of unreality, being in proximity to so many people after over a year of social distancing. His face was obscured by a Seahawks cap pulled low and a bandanna across his face, still a common sight even after the pandemic. The scarf did little to dilute the competing scents of freshly caught fish from the vendors on the right-hand side of the row and from ten thousand flowers to his left. Carnations and sunflowers and chrysanthemums and lilies.

Shaw would have been happy to skip the lilies. This meeting would be hazardous enough without a reminder of funerals.

He cut right, weaving his way out of the crush and across Pike Place to continue walking along the row of shops on the opposite side. Most had open fronts to sell directly to passersby on the sidewalk. Baklava, fish and chips, wheatgrass juice. Shaw circled the knots of customers waiting to be next. Cars driving down the street had to inch through the throng. Regret showed on every driver's face for having made the wrong turn downtown and getting mired in the morass of people.

Next to a cinnamon-roll bakery was a stunted hallway leading to back doors and an elevator for the vendors' use. The official name of the century-old structure across from the Market's main drag was the Silver Okum Building, but every vendor Shaw had ever met called it the Triangle, because that was its shape. The sharpest end pointed south, while the base ran parallel to Pine Street at the north. Its two elongated sides faced Pike Place in front and Post Alley behind.

Shaw ducked into the Triangle's blunt hallway, returning to the sidewalk two minutes later. It was time.

He stayed close to the hall, among shoppers browsing a display of olive oil and salad dressing in the shop next door. Syrupy wafts of cinnamon and baked cookies suffused the walkway.

The Market's outskirts had expanded while he'd been off at war. All part of the massive reconfiguration of the waterfront that had peaked with the demolition of the old viaduct. But Pike Place's center still looked as it had when he was a kid, from the stalls selling watercolor paintings of Rainier to the bronze pig the size of a recliner. Shaw couldn't see the pig now through the multitude, but he liked knowing it was there.

He spotted Zhang first. Under the green metal roof of the Market, walking with the idling tourists but looking outward. Surveying the street. The Chinese agent wore black running pants and shoes and a jacket the color of modeling clay. The jacket was unzipped most of the way. Shoulder holster, Shaw assumed.

Zhang scanned the street for another ten seconds before his eyes found Shaw in the background, on the sidewalk. Shaw nodded to him. Zhang looked to his right and scratched his head. A signal. Shaw looked in that same direction to find Chen on the street, moving along with the heavy traffic in their direction, like a round rock tumbling in a river.

Zhang crossed to join Shaw. He stared silently, his mistrust evident. Shaw smiled back.

"Okay?" he said when the shuffling flow brought Chen to them, motioning to the surroundings.

Chen nodded agreement. "You said you had information."

"To trade."

"Within reason I can answer questions. Please show your pockets. And under your shirt."

Shaw held up his phone so they could see it wasn't recording. He flipped up his shirt to prove the absence of a wire.

"You are injured," said Zhang.

"Tough week," said Shaw. "I've got three bits of knowledge for you. The first is for free. I know about Avizda, and your chemist Nelson Bao working there, and why Paragon was hired to get what Nelson couldn't. So we can skip the pretending and protestations of innocence."

"Sebastien Rohner told you this story."

"No. I had to do the legwork my own way." He tapped the bandage on his ribs. "Item two: Rohner was going to cheat you of your prize, Mr. Chen. He hired me as a distraction. Once your tests proved that the sample molecule was complete, Rohner would make the final product disappear. And me along with it. While you were chasing me, he'd be selling the goods elsewhere."

Chen watched the people passing as he seemed to think. "Not completely unexpected. You appeared to me to be . . . an odd choice to manage the island's estate."

"Your turn. Why did you tell Rohner and Hargreaves that your chemical had been stolen?"

A slight shrug. "Why not? I would have to spend the time to acquire another chemist from China. Perhaps their reactions might reveal something."

"Did they?"

"That is a different question. It is your turn again."

Shaw held up the black-capped sample vial that Professor Mills had given him the evening before. The vial was filled with brown syrupy liquid. A white label with tiny print made a stripe on one side of the vial, like the pale underbelly of a fish.

"You're not the only one holding the chemical now," said Shaw.

Chen frowned. "No. I do not believe that is real."

"A bridging molecule with one part to bond to polypropylene and another intended for polyethylene, to allow pure separation while recycling? In a suspension that smells like chlorine? Yeah, I got that."

Zhang said something that Shaw assumed was highly derogatory.

"How?" said Chen.

"I've been doing a lot of driving this past week. Across the country and back, with a few stops."

"You went to Dallas?"

"Dallas. Armbruster Road. Test Lab 146. Avizda's security is decent, but nothing I haven't seen before."

Chen exhaled slowly. Almost a deflation.

Shaw could sympathize. The Chinese operative had been working on this for months, maybe years.

If his deception worked, it might hang on Chen's own fears that all his efforts were coming to naught.

"Are you wanting payment?" said Chen.

"We haven't finished our game yet. Last question: Who's your guess for killing Nelson Bao?"

Chen hummed thoughtfully. "You asked what I learned from claiming that I no longer had the sample. Sebastien Rohner told me that he would attempt to buy your loyalty and the chemical from you. Did he do so?"

"He tried."

The older man nodded. "Money is Sebastien's only tool and only measure of success. I did not have to ask James Hargreaves what he intended."

Shaw stared poker-faced at Chen for a moment, until his admiring grin could no longer be suppressed.

"You knew that Flynn was James Hargreaves all along," he said.

"Mr. Hargreaves, and his guise of Bridgetrust Group, yes. Violence and coercion are his way. Sebastien had offered Hargreaves a substantial fee to obtain the missing portion of the molecular structure. I had already guessed that Hargreaves might demand more. Or even that he might attempt to take the completed solution by force from us."

"Sounds like Big Jim."

"He has been my leading suspect for Nelson's murder from the beginning, although I do not have a reason as to why he would risk a very profitable deal on such a clumsy attempt at acquiring the chemical sample. When the attorney Linda Edgemont was murdered, I became certain that it was on Hargreaves's order. And"—Chen tilted his head at Shaw—"that you were most likely innocent."

"Thanks for the vote."

Chen nodded to Shaw's pocket. "What is your intention with the chemical?"

"I'm going to squeeze Rohner and Hargreaves until they pop."

"It would be simpler, and safer, to accept a sum from me to stay out of the proceedings."

"Like you said, money's not the only measure of success."

"You wish revenge?"

"I wish to see their guts spilled on the floor. But I'll settle for prison time."

"Sebastien Rohner is too wealthy for America to convict. If they detain him at all."

"One fight at a time. And yours is done. You're out, Mr. Chen. Time for you and Zhang to go home."

"No," said Zhang. "You will give us the chemical."

"Or you'll draw your gun and shoot me? There's a security camera ten feet from your head, friend. Not to mention all the tourists taking pictures and walking around with GoPros. And then"—Shaw inclined his head northward, to the riot of flowers in the market stalls—"there are the cops."

Zhang and Chen glanced subtly where Shaw had indicated. Not broadcasting their sudden interest. They were professionals.

"See the guy with the overly shaped chin stubble hiding behind the carnations? That's Kanellis. Seattle detective. He'll have backup."

"Here to arrest you," said Chen.

"Yes. They're waiting until we split up. I'm considered armed and extremely dangerous." Shaw shrugged with false modesty. "Regulations tell them not to close in until I'm away from the crowd or unless I offer some sort of threat."

Shaw tapped the pocket holding his phone. "I texted Kanellis before you arrived. The cops will have questions. You won't answer them, I know. Maybe you've got some sort of diplomatic shield to hide behind. But sure as shit the attention can't be good for you. SPD will have to tell the FBI, and the Feds will probably have to tell the CIA or whoever. I don't know a ton about spies, but I have to figure your mission here is as fried as crispy bacon. They'll be watching you every minute now."

"I can offer you more than remuneration," Chen said. "You face a life in prison in America. In China you might be free."

Shaw smiled apologetically. "That's a thorny topic. Patriotism."

"You will not?"

"I will not. Aiding a foreign power is a step over the line, even for me. But I appreciate the offer."

Chen nodded. "One loyalist to another, Mr. Shaw."

"Have a good flight home, Mr. Chen."

Shaw turned and walked down the short corridor. He removed the makeshift key he had taped in its keyhole a few minutes before to hold the elevator in place, and stepped into the car as the door automatically began to close. Behind him, from the street, he heard a shout.

There were only two buttons inside the elevator. Shaw pressed the button marked 1, and the elevator began to descend. He took off his light blue coat and Hawks cap and bandanna and left them on the floor.

Below the Triangle building was a rabbit warren of storage lockers and cages where Market vendors kept their goods overnight. Shaw had first seen the subterranean passages as a teen, when one of his schoolmates was working at her family's stall selling ceramic flutes and ocarinas. She'd brought him along as she locked up the bins of instruments one evening, showing him the loop of cages made of plywood and chain-link. Vendors had decorated the gloomy maze, drawing and writing jokes in ballpoint pen all over the plywood walls. Shaw and the girl had paused halfway through the tour for a quick make-out session. If not for that, he wasn't sure he would have remembered the hidden labyrinth.

The plywood was gone now, replaced by sturdier metal fencing. But the layout was the same. He pulled a loading cart to block the elevator door from closing again, in case Kanellis found someone with a key to call the car back.

From an unused storage locker, Shaw removed a motorcycle helmet. He put it on as he hurried down the underground hall and up two flights of stairs to emerge onto Pine Street by the corner of Post Alley. Vaulting the railing, he strolled up the hill to the dinged-up Yamaha MT-03 he'd left parked sideways between cars at the curb. A Craigslist purchase from a dude in Renton the evening before.

A pair of bike cops sped past him, heading for Pike Place. The Yamaha started on the first attempt. Five seconds later Shaw was gone.

SIXTY-THREE

That afternoon Shaw called the main line for Seattle PD and claimed to be a detective from the North Precinct calling on his mobile. The operator put him through.

"John Guerin."

"It's Shaw."

"You son of a bitch."

"Yeah, yeah. Let's skip the recriminations. Did you and Kanellis talk to our friend from China?"

"About three sentences before he referred us to the chief consulate. He claimed he'd never seen you before today and that you accosted him while he and his junior associate were shopping."

"Which we knew he would."

"Sure. I asked the consulate for information on Chen's visit to Seattle, and they directed me to the State Department. I expect I'll get answers about the time that Chen Li's grandchildren die of old age."

"The asking is enough."

"For you, maybe. For me it's zero. I put a request in to a contact at the FBI—they have a watch on Chen's passport. We can't stop him from traveling, but we'll know if he does."

"Bet you a penny he's out of the country by end of the week."

"You already owe me a hell of a lot more than you can afford. You need to turn yourself in, Shaw. Now's the time. Our witness on Edgemont's murder turned out to be a false lead."

"They recanted?"

"Ghosted. The name and contact information she gave Officer Beatts were fake. Said she lived just down the street. That was horseshit, too."

Shaw was silent for half a beat. "This woman a redhead?"

"What's that have to do with anything?"

"Humor me."

"Hold on." The line went quiet for a second, and then a recorded message about SPD's commitment to community involvement began playing. After a long-winded sentence and a half, Guerin returned. "No, not a ginger, Beatts says. Brunette. Athleisure type. Said she was out running when she supposedly saw you. Why'd you think our slippery witness might be a redhead?"

"Healthy paranoia. Forget it. Sorry you're stuck working the holiday weekend."

"You're the cause of it. You and these pages you wrote of what's probably ninety percent fiction."

"Only ninety? Sounds like you're starting to believe me, Lieutenant."

"Let's talk about that in person. I can't do anything to help until you meet us halfway."

"There's somebody else you need to meet first. One of Hargreaves's lead operatives."

"Christ, Shaw."

"She'll talk. In exchange for immunity."

"Immunity from what?"

"Accessory after the fact on the corporate theft from Avizda. Probably some other minor charges. Nothing with real weight. She's white-collar, not a thug."

"Not like you, you mean. What's her name?"

"There's more I need done."

"You're dreaming. Give me her name."

"Rohner has to incriminate himself for you to have any hope of charging him. I've got an idea to make that happen. But it'll take her help, and yours, and some official pressure. She'll lay it out for you."

"Start with your witness and we'll see."

"Karla Haiden. New York resident. PI license. I've got her stashed

away. Hargreaves's men already tried to kill her once." Shaw gave
Guerin the number of Hollis's burner. "Get her to a safe house and
she'll cooperate."

"You better be sure on this."

Shaw had been thinking much the same thing. He was taking a
big risk on where Karla Haiden's loyalties would land when the wheel
stopped spinning.

SIXTY-FOUR

Shaw dropped anchor fifty yards off the shore of Briar Bay Island. The blunt western tip of its crescent formed a misshapen half circle topped by thick forest. Completely black in the night, with only the stars and the almost tangible presence of the landmass to distinguish it from the sky. To Shaw the island looked like the shaggy head of some vengeful giant, a colossus emerging step by league-spanning step from the deep sea.

From the cabin of the speedboat, Shaw removed an inflatable Zodiac dinghy he'd borrowed from Hollis's dock locker. Its rubbery skin was empty of air, its PVC hull wrapped neatly around the only rigid piece of the craft, a two-foot aluminum transom to allow for mounting a small outboard engine. Shaw spread the Zodiac out on the speedboat's bow. He plugged a battery-powered pump into the inflatable's socket and switched it on. Compared to the soft lapping of the waves on the speedboat's hull, the pump's motor sounded as loud as a referee's whistle, though Shaw knew that the high-pitched whine would scarcely carry as far as the shore.

The pump worked fast. By the time Shaw had gotten his wet suit over his legs, the boat was fully inflated. He switched off the pump and finished wrestling his upper body into the neoprene suit.

Once filled, the inflatable was eight feet long with rounded sides and a blunt wedge of a bow. He fastened the little three-horse Evinrude onto its transom before pushing the boat's bow over the side, holding on to the engine to lower the craft into the chill water.

Shaw set a small rucksack of gear in the dinghy, along with a life vest, two oars, and a pair of swim fins. He made a last check of the anchor—it would be a long night if the speedboat drifted out to sea while he was gone—before untying the inflatable's line and stepping down to its yielding floor.

The outboard engine was for later. The oars would bring him silently to shore tonight. It had been years since Shaw had rowed, but the motion came back to him easily. A twist of the wrists to dip the oars below the surface, a smooth pull and twist again to skim their blades over the water. The flesh over his ribs finally felt whole after three days without reinjury.

In the shadow of the island's bulk, the waves were gentle. Still, the current carried him south between every stroke of the oars as he closed the distance. When the inflatable's bow touched shore, he was fifty yards downstream of the speedboat. He reminded himself, not for the first time, to account for the current when swimming back. Even with the fins boosting his speed, missing the boat on the first try would be bad news. His next stop might be Vancouver Island, fifteen nautical miles away. Or Japan, if he were swept out of the straits entirely.

Shaw stepped out to pull the inflatable farther up the beach. High tide had reduced the shore at the tip of the island to a strip of weathered stone. The smells of algae and eons of dried seawater filled his nose. Barely thirty feet separated the water from the vertical bluff that marked the inland boundary. He looked up at the wall of rock. Grasses and two or three small trees grew from its crags, high enough and hardy enough to survive the winds and salt spray. It was difficult to discern the height of the bluff in the dark. It seemed to go straight up for a few yards before its slope gradually leveled out nearer the top. Shaw could see the upper reaches of the forest atop the cliff nearest him.

He walked in each direction, gauging where the cliff's irregular face might be scaled or where someone might be able to jump partway down and land without snapping an ankle on the pitted beach. He expected to be climbing down the cliff at night. He wanted every element in his favor.

On his walk to the east, he found a cleft in the sheer face of the bluff. Only a yard from edge to edge and no more than twice that much deep. But on the barren shore, the closest thing to a hiding place.

Shaw returned to the boat and set the rucksack and the oars and fins aside to carry the inflatable to the narrow cleft. It was awkward work, hefting fifty pounds of balloonlike boat with another fifty of gas-filled outboard weighing down one end. He took his time, not wanting to risk rupturing the boat's PVC skin on a jagged bit of shore.

With the inflatable tilted on one side, most of its length fit into the cleft. The stern and engine stuck out three feet. It couldn't be seen from above, not over the long incline of the bluff. But anyone passing within a quarter mile offshore during the day might easily spot the dark gray boat.

Shaw looked up the cliff once again. A stunted tree, thick with the leaves of early summer, grew from a split twenty feet up and to his right. He began to climb. The cliff's protrusions made easy handholds. His wet suit's boots provided protection and traction.

Within two minutes he had reached the tree. Its trunk was no thicker than his wrist and curved upward toward the sky. He placed a hand on the spiny bark and pulled. It bent easily, its roots tearing within the split in the rock. Another yank snapped more of the plentiful but slim fibers and the tree came loose. He dropped it to the beach and carefully made his way back down.

The trunk and its green branches were long enough to cover the stern of the inflatable. Shaw draped it over the outboard. Moderate camouflage at best. Once the leaves dried and curled, the tree would barely disguise the boat at all. But it needed to serve for only a day or two. After that, Shaw would either have sailed away, be in jail, or be in the morgue.

He placed the ruck and the other gear inside the upturned boat. The ruck contained all the essentials for a brief voyage. Clothes and rain gear and food and water bottles and his SIG pistol with a spare clip. So long as the weather held, the Zodiac could carry him to any of the nearby islands or the mainland.

The breeze had shifted. The anchored speedboat's bow pointed northwest now. Shaw walked a hundred yards upwind and sat to pull on the swim fins. He hadn't bothered to bring a mask. This would be a quick sprint on the surface. A mask and snorkel would only slow him down.

He waded in. The water hadn't gotten any warmer since he'd come ashore. Rather than dwell on the cold seeping between the wet suit and his skin, Shaw dove into the sea and began to swim.

SIXTY-FIVE

When his phone rang, Olen Anders was at his desk on the Droma campus, in the executive office allocated to him while he was in the United States. An open-ended duration of time. Its desk and cabinets were what he assumed passed for quality in this country, an artificial dark walnut shell glued over some sort of resin core, and a chair that had more adjustable functions than actual comfort.

Anders did his best to block out his surroundings, focusing instead on a multiyear agreement with a Mexico City venture firm, clearing it for review by Droma's Legal & Regulatory department. This sort of appraisal, making sure a contract lived up to the spirit of what had been stated between CEOs around the negotiating table, was a task Sebastien usually preferred to do himself. But Sebastien had been distracted lately. So had Anders, but as the Americans said with their national penchant for vulgarity, shit rolled downhill.

He took his attention from his computer screen just long enough to tap the phone's speaker button. "Yes, Sofia?"

"No Sofia," said Shaw.

Anders looked again at the phone display. Sofia's name and number, as he'd first thought.

"An interesting trick," Anders said, "or do you actually possess her telephone somehow?"

"What I have is an offer. Take a look."

The phone beeped. An SMS message. No, a photograph. Of a clear container with a black screw cap, inside of which was a thick golden-brown liquid. As Anders looked, a second photo arrived. He had to expand the image to read the opening lines of the page. The Droma employment contract for Kelvin Welch.

Anders had never met Welch in person, of course. But he knew the name. Knew why the man had been hired. He stared at the photograph for a long moment before Shaw broke his reverie.

"Chen's out. I'm in. You'll pay me for the chemical sample and for my silence."

"You . . . took the sample from Chen?"

"Does it matter? I want six million dollars, transferred to an account I'll specify at the time. Cheap for cornering the market on infinite recycling, I think."

Anders felt slightly dazed. How the hell did Shaw know these things? Only four men outside Avizda's top executives—Sebastien and Anders and Chen and Hargreaves—knew the full extent of the Dallas firm's innovation, and its potential.

And now, apparently, Shaw made five. Who else might he have told?

Shaw continued. "What you do with the glop after that is up to you. Hell, you could even sell the stuff back to Chen."

"I will have to talk to Mr. Rohner," Anders said. "And we must have proof, Shaw. If the solution is not viable, there can be no deal."

"Fire up your Bunsen burners. The island, tomorrow night. I'm guessing your testing equipment is still there."

"The island, yes. But one day is insufficient to acquire such a substantial sum."

"It's not a suitcase full of small bills, Anders. Transfer the money from whatever slush fund Droma uses for bribing politicians and cover your tracks afterward. Take it out of Hargreaves's cut, if you want."

Anders paused in astonishment for an instant before berating himself. Of course, if Shaw had found Kelvin Welch, he might also know of Paragon and Hargreaves. The man was a menace.

"Is anyone else aware of the chemical?" he said. "If word escapes, the value could plummet. For all of us."

"That's the trouble with trade secrets. You have to make sure they stay secret if you want to trade them. I'll want a plane to take me to and from the island."

"That's . . . possible. We can arrange for a seaplane, as before."

"The dock at Magnuson Park. Eight o'clock tomorrow night."

Shaw hung up.

Anders looked once more at the photograph of the sample vial the man had sent him. Feeling slightly winded. Was it real? And if it were not, what was Shaw's ploy? He must expect they would verify the chemical's structure before any money would be exchanged.

Anders had tried to reach Chen three times during the past two days, through the secure channel the Chinese intelligence agent had provided. He had received no response. Not even a cursory affirmation that Chen was still awaiting word about his replacement chemist. Anders was not even sure that Chen was still in the United States. Perhaps now he knew why.

He stood and paced the office as he called Sebastien Rohner.

"Are you where you can speak?" Anders said.

"I'm at home," Sebastien said. He meant the Rohner apartments in the center of the city. Sebastien called the Briar Bay Island estate "the island," or sometimes "the house offshore." If they were in Europe, "home" would have meant the family dwellings in Bern.

"We have a new development."

Anders described the conversation with Shaw.

"A trick. To steal from us when we arrive," suggested Sebastien.

"Perhaps not. He may have the actual chemical. He has learned its history and its worth, though how, I do not understand."

Sebastien didn't reply.

"If Shaw somehow reached the same conclusion we did—that Chen was in possession of the chemical all along—he might also have found an opportunity to steal it from Chen. And to force Chen to tell him what it was. Shaw has proved to be imaginative where criminal feats are involved."

"And he's willing to come to the island?"

"He is a fugitive from justice. I imagine his prime concerns are getting the money and escaping prosecution."

"Overconfident," Sebastien murmured.

Anders waited, knowing that his friend was thinking. He glanced out his third-floor window. Today was a Saturday, and the day before the American day of independence, which left the campus all but deserted. Sparing Anders the sight of employees streaming from the buildings at this hour, funneling into the stairwell to the below-ground parking structure like so many sheep. Eager to return to their reality-television programs and frozen meals. Anders was counting the days until his return home.

"Shaw must have something more," said Sebastien after another moment. "Something that in his mind will guarantee his safety and ensure that we will pay his price once the solution is complete."

"He was a soldier for his entire adult life. Trained in gun-barrel diplomacy. That will be his reflex."

Sebastien hummed agreement. "Working with a team as well. He may have accomplices."

"Enlisting friends from the military, you mean." Anders contemplated that. He had initially thought Shaw was being reckless, rushing into a situation where he would be vulnerable. Sacrificing safety for speed. But now he wondered if the island's isolation might work more to Shaw's advantage. If the former soldier did arrive with a boatful of heavily armed and mindlessly aggressive cohorts, what would be their recourse?

"We will require Kilbane," Anders said finally. "I've already spoken to him about the need for greater physical security after Linda's murder. He and his men can protect us on the island. We'll have to explain about Hargreaves. He's as much a danger as Shaw."

"Very well," said Sebastien. "Time is short."

"We'll fly to the island in the morning and make preparations."

"Once Hargreaves knows Chen is gone, he may entertain thoughts of taking the goods for himself."

"That had occurred to me as well," said Anders.

After Sebastien rang off, Anders stood at the window for a time, looking at the empty grounds of the campus.

He knew he was not without courage. He had completed his compulsory service in the Swiss mountain infantry when he was hardly more than a boy and had acquitted himself well. But he'd regretted Sebastien's choice to pursue the deal with Chen Li almost from the beginning. Over time he had come to recognize the wellspring of that regret as fear.

Some of that fear was natural. Concern that they were overreaching, that there would be legal or governmental repercussions if Droma were caught engaging in corporate theft.

Since Linda Edgemont's death, a more visceral dread had snuck in around the edges. Anders found himself checking the locks of every window and door in his rented home at night. He'd begun keeping a firearm by his bedside, a choice that felt as though he had already lost some battle of principle. Anders preferred that his first and best defense would, as always, be his mind.

But the choice had been made. They would be ready if Shaw or Hargreaves came with violence in mind. He picked up the phone to call Kilbane.

HARGREAVES, IN HIS HOTEL SUITE, listened a second time to the playback of the conversations between Olen Anders and Shaw, and Anders and his boss, Rohner. Or to one side of the exchanges. The bug Louis had planted in Anders's office was good enough to pick up every word from the Droma chief of staff. Tapping his mobile device had proved out of reach. But one side was enough.

"It's on," he said to Tucker and the others. "Tomorrow night on the island."

"Shaw ripped off Chen." Tucker shook his head. "That slick shit."

"Fortunes turn. We'll have everybody in one place, away from the city."

"How much time does Morton say it'll take to test the chemical process?" asked Louis.

"An hour, if he cuts a few corners."

Tucker scowled. "That's a long damn time to be staring at one another across a room, everybody with one hand on his gun."

Hargreaves saw Tucker's point. He drummed his fingers on the suite's French Provincial coffee table. "I think Rohner's wrong about Shaw recruiting a team of Army grunts, all yelling 'Hooah' and looking to kick ass. If he were to enlist help, he'd have done so when he escaped the police. Shaw's more subtle than he seems at first."

"You said he asked for a plane to the island."

"Yes," Hargreaves said. "That's good luck for us. We can stack the odds in our favor ahead of time. I'll make the call."

"What about Rohner?"

Hargreaves thought about it. "Rohner and his team are a known quantity. But we can improve our situation there, too. Louis, is your pilot rating still up to snuff?"

"Yeah."

"Okay. Half our team on the island, as they expect. The other half arriving after the festivities have started. We'll use Taskine and Riley. They're frothing for another chance at Shaw."

"Keeping them on a leash might be tough," said Tucker.

"By that stage"—Hargreaves smiled—"the last thing I'll want will be to hold them back."

SIXTY-SIX

Shaw watched as a dot in the sky resolved into the familiar blue-and-white seaplane. It banked low, as if to duck under the rays of sunlight still streaming from the west into the shadow of the land. The Otter touched down and immediately turned toward the boat launch at Magnuson Park. Shaw walked out to meet it.

The plane came alongside the dock and slowed. From the pilot's seat, C.J. waved hello. Shaw made a keep-going motion. He ducked under the wing and stepped smoothly onto the float with his duffel bag to open the rear door. He placed the duffel gently inside before climbing in after it.

"I figured it would be you," Shaw said.

"That's the job," C.J. called back over the thrum of the engine. "On call twenty-four/seven. Happy Fourth of July. Another hour and I'd have had to dodge the fireworks."

Shaw looked into the storage area at the back of the plane. A milk bin full of different lengths of quarter-inch galvanized chain had been strapped firmly to the lower stanchions of the luggage rack. He picked up the duffel and hunched to walk between the passenger seats. The duffel went under the first seat on the starboard side, where it would be secure from turbulence. Shaw settled into the copilot seat and put the headset on.

"What did Rohner tell you about tonight?" he asked. "Or was it Anders?"

"Mr. Anders. He said they're having a business meeting at the last minute because one of the partners has to go out of town early in the morning. That Mr. Rohner wanted them to have a last look at the estate."

"Did you fly them all to the island earlier?"

She nodded. "The Droma team and Mr. Hargreaves's people. About four hours ago."

"How many?"

C.J. gave him a sideways look as she steered the plane to face away from shore. "How many on the flight?"

"Yeah. Rohner and Anders and who else?"

"Warren Kilbane and Mr. Castelli and Ms. Pollan. Plus Mr. Hargreaves and three others."

"Morton, the weedy guy. He's one of Hargreaves's bunch," said Shaw. "Did you know the other two?"

"Nope."

"Bigger guys? One black man, one white with a busted face?"

She gave him that quizzical look again. "Sounds like you didn't have to ask."

Tucker and Vic. Leaving their curly-haired buddy Louis elsewhere. And the two hitters who had chased him across the continental U.S. Where were they?

"Mr. Anders sent me back here to pick you up," C.J. said.

"Another private trip."

She smiled softly. "I don't mind."

The summer holiday had lured plenty of boaters to the lake, but the Otter had an unobstructed path straight out from land for a quarter mile or more. They picked up speed and were airborne within another minute.

"Your bag okay there?" she said as they banked softly left. "You can strap it down in the luggage compartment in back if you want."

"Should be fine."

"'Cause I am expecting a few bumps. We've got rain coming in."

"What's the box of chain for?"

"That? New anchor chain for the boat."

"Pretty lightweight for a yacht that size."

She shrugged. "Maybe it's for the lifeboat."

Shaw unzipped his jacket and settled in. The view wasn't as clear as it had been the morning C.J. had flown him over the northern reaches of the city, but the hills and islands gained extra definition from the low sun and the promised clouds far ahead.

They sat without talking for the rest of the trip, C.J. perhaps catching Shaw's quiet mood. He remained focused on the horizon through the windshield, half his mind occupied with what was to come.

He couldn't match the enemy for firepower. Not even close. He'd have to rely on the preparations he'd already made, already checked over in his mind two dozen times. They would be enough, or they wouldn't. The time for strategizing was done. Now there was nothing left to do but act and react to what came, like a boxer after the bell rang.

C.J. followed as straight a route as regulations allowed, along the diagonal length of Whidbey and on up into the islands. The hour's flight passed swiftly. They seemed to be racing the sun for which would touch the water first. The forested islands became a richer green, the straits deeper blue. As if not to be outdone, the western sky took on the sheen of polished topaz.

All the colors were momentary. Even as C.J. banked around the northern tip of Orcas, the first fingers of night crept in, robbing hue and tone in equal measure from everything. The plane dipped lower, until Shaw could see the whitecaps on the waves below. Large swells, growing larger. The Otter shuddered in the headwind. To the north, a wall of clouds loomed.

Briar Bay Island was a torch. Dark along its fat cigar length until the very tip, where Rohner's showpiece pavilion blazed with light. The spikes and spires of the glass enclosure looked as though each sharp point had skewered a tiny sun and held it trapped.

"Whoa," said C.J. "I've never seen it from the air at night."

The pavilion was bright enough that as their plane passed Shaw thought he could make out figures moving within. A large table had been placed near the center of the structure, an image fragmented by the dozens of crooked windowpanes.

The lab, Shaw was certain. Relocated to the pavilion from the art gallery. Maybe Rohner couldn't resist the spectacle or Anders had

thought the huge pavilion and its multiple exits made a safer place for
the exchange than the confined gallery.

C.J. brought the plane in. Compared to the brilliant pavilion, the
solar lamps on the maintenance sheds and dock were mere specks of
gold leaf, the helipad's light a square of candles. Everything else on the
island—the paths, the wings, and the main house—was dark. Doused.
All attention on Rohner's star attraction.

They landed on choppy seas. C.J. gripped the yoke tightly, letting the plane tap each successive wave until its speed lessened and
the floats eased into a rumbling and rapid deceleration. The slender,
crooked finger of dock was empty. C.J. steered the Otter in a wide circle around the dock's end, the plane rocking on the waves as she made
a loop to bring the starboard side in first.

Shaw took off his headset with one hand and hung it on the dashboard hook. He unclipped his seat belt.

"Mind stepping out and tying us off?" C.J. said over the idling
engine as she removed her own headset.

She turned to see Shaw pointing a gun at her across the cockpit.

"What are you doing?" C.J. said, her eyes suddenly wide.

"Testing my psychic powers. Keep both hands on the wheel. And
keep us next to the dock."

Shaw moved behind her, making sure she felt the muzzle of the
Browning touching the back of her hair. He reached down to run his
left hand along the edge of the pilot's chair, between C.J.'s leg and
the door. His fingers touched metal. He wrapped his hand cautiously
around the length and pulled. With the whispery sound of tearing
tape, it came loose.

A Ruger Mark III .22-caliber. A shorter-barreled version, but with
the added suppressor the weapon was more than a foot long.

"You drill the baffles on the suppressor yourself?" Shaw said.

C.J. was silent.

"Sure you did." Shaw sniffed the gun. It didn't have the scent of
being fired. He would have been surprised if it had.

"I just have that for safety," said C.J.

Shaw grunted. "I don't feel safe at all." He set the Ruger down and felt her shins and ankles and forced his hand behind her to check between her back and the seat.

"That hurt," she said.

Shaw picked up the Ruger again and sat sideways in the copilot's seat. He glanced toward the bin full of chain. "I'll play fortune teller again. It would go like this: I step toward the back of the plane to open the door. You shoot me. You wrap my body with chain and drive the plane out into the strait half a mile or so, or as far as you can get with the weather like this. Then you shove me out the door. Hard work. But clean. Nobody would ever find me, except the crabs."

"What? No. I only keep the pistol—"

"This gun's not the same one you used to shoot Linda Edgemont, right? You're a pro. You'd have tossed the murder weapon as soon as possible. But I'm guessing you made this"—Shaw tapped the suppressor with the barrel of his own gun—"the same way. Titanium baffles. The cops will compare the materials. They took flecks of metal off Linda." Shaw removed the Ruger's clip and pocketed it before ejecting the round in the chamber and tossing the gun onto the seat behind him.

"I got the pistol at a swap meet. I don't know about baffles or anything like that. I haven't *killed* anyone, for God's sake."

"Rangi dropped Linda off at home. You knew exactly when. All the Droma executive-transport schedules are linked online," he said. "Planes and trains and automobiles, so you and Rangi and others can coordinate. Linda got home and you knocked on the sliding glass door in her backyard. She must have been very surprised. Maybe she thought she'd forgotten a plane flight or had left something on board. But she knew you. Trusted you. She opened the door, and that was that."

"You're wrong. Please listen to me."

"You had lousy luck. A patrol cop named Beatts happened by after you left the backyard. Maybe later he'd remember you as being on the scene. So you thought fast and went from possible suspect to witness in one go. You flagged his car down and told him about a scarred man coming out of Edgemont's yard. I don't know if the plan had been to frame me all along, calling nine-one-one once you were clear, but you grabbed the opportunity and Beatts fell for your story. You had to give him a fake name and address. He'll remember your face, though." Shaw took out his phone.

"You're crazy. I swear I didn't kill anybody, Mr. Shaw. I'm just a pilot. Please let me out of here."

"Sure thing, Jane."

Her face went blank. "Who?"

Shaw held up the phone, letting her see the photo he'd taken of her personnel file in Chiarra's office at Paragon.

"Jane Calloway," he said. "J.C. C.J. Kind of cute."

She said nothing.

"With Paragon four years. Your job history before that is mostly redacted, so I suppose you're a graduate of the same spy factory that produced Hargreaves, or whatever his real name is." Shaw shook his head. "You people have a lock on infiltration, I'll say that. You came to work for Rohner only a month after Linda Edgemont started selling secrets. Great placement for keeping tabs, being the go-to girl for flying Rohner's people to and from the island and anywhere else."

"What is it you want?" she said. "We can pay you."

Her voice was the same, yet completely different. Better enunciation and absent any hint of C.J.'s levity.

"I want to stay alive," said Shaw. "Your job description bumps against that. Kelvin Welch was shot in New Orleans a few weeks ago. Suspected mugging. If the cops check the dates, would they coincide with vacation days you took from Droma?"

She didn't answer.

"Kill the engine."

She flipped switches. The pitch of the whirling prop deepened immediately as it began to coast to a stop.

Shaw stood and motioned her out of the pilot's seat. "Move."

Her eyes flashed to the useless Ruger as she climbed from the cockpit. Shaw nodded to the rear door.

"Onto the dock."

"Are you going to shoot me?"

"Tie off the plane." Shaw grabbed a twenty-foot coil of chain from the bin in the luggage compartment, hooking it over his shoulder.

While she moored the aircraft, he gave the surroundings a closer look than the plane's windows had afforded. Only the shining upper spires of the pavilion could be seen from the dock. The rest of the island seemed even darker than it had from the air. The wind gusted, throwing bits of spray off the choppy waves over his pant legs.

"I wasn't lying about the money," she said. Her hands were shaking, though the night still held on to vestiges of warmth. "There'll be plenty of it to go around. I can help you."

Shaw spun her around and bound her hands behind her with a zip-tie from his pocket.

"Where are the rest of Hargreaves's people?" he said.

"I flew them here. I told you."

He hauled her to the end of the dock. To the edge. Shaw held her by the collar at arm's length, so that she leaned out over the chill water, up on the balls of her feet. He draped the heavy coil of chain over her head.

Thirty pounds at least. No chance of staying afloat, no matter how hard she kicked.

"Don't," she said, her feet trying to inch back from the edge.

"Tucker. Vic. Morton. They're here. What about the others?"

"Louis," she said. "He's bringing a helicopter. That's how we're leaving. You can leave with us."

"We?" Shaw shook her.

"Me and Vic and Tucker and Hargreaves. Maybe Morton, too, I don't know."

"There are more," he said. "A big shooter with a beard. His partner, a slimy guy with glasses. Where are they?"

"I don't know them."

"My arm's getting tired," said Shaw.

"I *don't*. Hargreaves uses contractors sometimes. If he's in a hurry or if . . . if he needs specialists, for tough jobs. Please."

"Tell me about Nelson Bao."

"What?"

Shaw released his grip, just for an instant. She screamed. As his fist gripped her shirt again, he had to pull back hard to keep her momentum from dragging them both in. She was leaning out over the water now. The toes of her running shoes dripping with sea foam. The chain hanging from her neck swayed side to side.

"Bao," he repeated.

"It . . . it was an accident. Hargreaves told me to try to find the sample. He knew that Rohner had hired you. He wanted us to steal it first. I went through Bao's room and found a jar of chemical. I thought it must be the sample, and I took it. But he saw me leaving. Chased me down to the beach."

"And you beat his head in with a rock." Shaw let her tilt another inch toward the black water.

"He grabbed me," she said, as if the wind had whipped the sound from her. "It was self-defense. Please don't kill me. I can't drown. I can't." The last words were almost gibberish, choked by sobs and snot.

Finish the job. That would be Hargreaves's way, to wipe the slate clean of all potential risks.

Shaw pulled her back. She collapsed on the dock, the weight of the chain toppling her as the metal links rattled on the planks. He felt a cobweb's touch of compassion before thinking of Linda Edgemont and Kelvin Welch. Had either of them had an instant's horrified realization of what was happening before this woman pulled the trigger?

At the midpoint of the dock was an all-weather storage box, like an oversize footlocker. Shaw flipped open the lid. A pair of moorage lines lay at the bottom, along with clean rags and a single life vest. He grabbed a handful of rags and walked back to where Jane Calloway sat on the dock. He removed the chain from her neck, stuffed a rag in her mouth, and tied two others around her head to hold it in place. Then he hauled her to her feet and over to the storage box.

"Get in," he said. She lifted one leg and then the other to climb over the box's side. Willing to cooperate while it appeared that Shaw might not end her life.

"If you're smart," Shaw said, "you'll stay very quiet. Hargreaves is planning to kill everyone here, right? You know that's his MO."

She nodded slowly.

"How long do you think you and the rest of the Paragon hired help will survive after tonight? Hargreaves will be sitting on a trade secret he can sell for ten figures. He's not going back to bugging telephones and bodyguarding tycoons. Anybody who can place him at the scene is an unacceptable risk."

She stared.

"Lie down. Stay put."

She curled up in the bottom of the box. Shaw zip-tied her feet and knees together and closed the lid. As a final assurance, he knotted the chain through the big box's padlock hasp.

He returned to the plane and the duffel. He debated taking the Ruger—an extra gun might be useful—but ultimately decided to leave it. Better that the Ruger became evidence, to help ensure that the lethal Jane Calloway didn't fly free.

No reason to leave a loaded gun around, however. Or a working plane. Shaw replaced the clip in the Ruger and fired five aimed shots into the instrument panel, blowing apart the compass and the altimeter and airspeed indicator and a few gauges he didn't know. The pistol's remaining rounds shattered the plane's twin yokes beyond repair.

The woman had known her business, Shaw had to admit. The suppressor worked just fine. Each shot had been barely louder than the click of a metronome.

SIXTY-SEVEN

Shaw walked up the dock and onto the island. He carried the duffel mindfully, keeping the bag from bumping against his leg. No one was in sight. Hargreaves and the rest would have heard the plane landing, but they wouldn't expect C.J.-slash-Jane to arrive until after she had disposed of Shaw's corpse.

He stopped when he came to the helipad. C.J. had said Louis would be arriving by helo. That could be a problem, especially if the curly-haired killer brought reinforcements. The American flag at the top of the nearby pole lashed to and fro in the wind, as if frantic to escape the coming rainstorm.

Shaw set the duffel aside and went to take a closer look at the helipad lights. Each squat cylinder in the rough square shone its beam directly upward, every lumen intended for a pilot's eyes. The string of lights had been set on the earth around the slab of concrete, awaiting the day when they would be bolted permanently in place. Shaw reached down to heft the first light and considered the flat ground surrounding the pad.

After a few minutes, he continued on his way.

He walked up the slope and into the patch of forest behind the main house. Thorns clutched at him as he moved slowly through the low brambles and weeds, until he could make out the looming back of the dark house.

Sheltered behind a gigantic evergreen, he removed Sofia Rohner's little ivory tablet from his pocket. He'd turned the screen's brightness down to the minimum. It glowed just enough to reveal its soft image, a simple map of the estate outlined in gold.

Shaw touched the octagonal outline of the pavilion. The shape expanded to fill the screen. A menu to one side noted options of

LIGHTS-SECURITY-CLIMATE-PRIVACY. Shaw tapped SECURITY. The shape turned blue, denoting that the pavilion's alarms were currently off. Each door around the perimeter of the shape was green. Unlocked. He tapped PRIVACY, and a sliding bar appeared at the side with CLEAR at one end and FULL at the other. He turned off the tablet and slipped it into his pocket.

There were two items in the duffel. The first was the KRISS submachine gun he'd taken from the bearded killer on the train. Modified for full auto, the KRISS carried more bang than any firearm in Shaw's eclectic arsenal. And just as important for tonight, the boxy weapon was also the most intimidating.

He removed the gun and checked to make sure the padding was secure around the duffel's bulkier contents. It wouldn't do to have them disturbed before the time came.

With the open duffel in his left hand and the gun in his right, Shaw walked around the north edge of the house and around the outside of the art gallery, down the slope to the shore. He kept close to the rise, to be under the line of sight from the dark estate. Waves rolled to shore, borne on the powerful current. He heard the sizzling of spray tossed high by the crevices and splashing down onto the rock. Perhaps the same cleft that had held Nelson Bao.

Near the end of the north wing, the pavilion came dazzlingly into view. It took Shaw's eyes a moment to adjust after the long minutes in darkness. Some psych game of Anders's invention, perhaps, turning on every light. In the vast crystalline pavilion, there was nowhere to hide. Maybe Rohner's guests would feel less inclined to start trouble.

He walked along the shore until he had neared the tip of the island, then crouched to edge forward, higher up the rise to where he could see the interior. A first tiny droplet of rain touched his cheek.

The teams had chosen sides of the playing field, with the laboratory table at the center. Hargreaves and Vic and Tucker stood on the southern half, spread out from one another. Closer to Shaw was Sebastien Rohner's bunch. He saw the backs of Anders's bald head and Rohner's silver-blond one. In front of them stood the bodyguards,

Kilbane and Castelli. Shaw guessed the female member of their team, Pollan, would be just out of his sight behind the entrance wall. Morton was hard at work at the GPC machine on the table, the lone figure in the center of the room.

Shaw shouldered his duffel, raised the submachine gun, and walked to the nearest door.

"HEY," SAID RILEY INTO HIS HEADSET. He watched a dark figure move from the shore toward the pavilion, almost directly ahead of where Riley knelt on the blue metal tiles of the north wing's roof. "Outside the building, eleven o'clock. Is that Shaw?"

Taskine responded from his position on the beach, his lowered voice coming through the earpiece in Riley's left ear. "I don't see him."

"He's going inside now."

"Got him. That's the fucker. Hargreaves said he'd be taken care of."

"Guess ol' Jimbo was wrong. Not his first mistake this week."

Riley debated for a moment whether Taskine should check on the plane and its pilot, then decided it would be pointless. If the stupid bitch was dead or bleeding out, that was on her.

"This change our priorities?" Taskine said.

Riley looked through his telescopic sight at Shaw. At this range, barely a hundred yards through the pavilion's glass wall, the Leupold scope showed Shaw's entire chest and neck. As good as point-blank.

Both Riley and Taskine had been given M2010 sniper rifles, courtesy of one of Hargreaves's shadowy friends. Riley figured the friend must have connections in the military. Both rifles showed signs of regular use, scratches on the stocks and wear on the grips. The weapons were probably due to be sold off to some mudhole nation's token defense force before Hargreaves made an offer.

Neither Taskine nor Riley was a trained sniper. But they could both zero a scope, and they'd had three full hours alone on the island to work with the rifles before the seaplane had arrived with Rohner and the whole party. The guns had been fitted with suppressors that extended their total lengths over four feet. Awkward, especially when it came time for Riley to climb up onto the roof, but at least the sound of their practice shots hadn't carried to some asshole sailing past on his yacht.

No night optics, though. And no jacketed slugs either. The thick panes of the pavilion walls would deflect the .300 Magnum rounds at least a couple degrees. Couldn't be helped. In the end it would make no difference. He and Taskine had the place as bottled up as cheap beer.

They'd ranked their targets in order of potential threat. Rohner's bodyguards first. Taskine would go west to east and Riley east to west, firing until each hostile was down. Then the tall, bald cock who seemed to be around to make sure Rohner didn't have to do any heavy lifting for himself. Between Riley and Taskine outside and Tucker and the others inside, the rich prick's team would be dead before they cleared their holsters.

Shaw, though. Easily the most dangerous. But he was alone, and a wild card. When Hargreaves gave them the signal and the shooting started, which team would Shaw be aiming at? Riley didn't give a crap if Vic or Tucker caught a bullet, but Hargreaves had to be alive to pay them.

"Stick with Rohner's crew first," Riley said. "Then Shaw. Then the bald butler dude."

"Copy that. Rain's coming in."

"Yeah." Riley pulled his cap a little lower. Sometimes he hated wearing glasses. Being out in the rain was for shit. He watched the people inside, everybody's attention on Shaw after the dude's surprise entrance.

"Hey," said Riley as a smile creased his face. "Shaw's got your machine gun."

There was a pause. Riley knew Taskine was finding Shaw in his own scope. He imagined his partner's face on seeing the KRISS in Shaw's hand and grinned even wider.

"That motherfucker," Taskine said, his voice thick. "Stuff priority. This goes down, I'm going to blow that shitbird's spine apart, first thing."

"He's all yours, brother," said Riley.

SIXTY-EIGHT

Rohner and Anders and the rest turned quickly at the sound of Shaw opening the door. Kilbane and Castelli both reached for their hips.

"Everybody stay cool," said Shaw.

Kilbane moved to put his bosses behind him. His hand still on his holstered pistol.

"Drop the gun," Kilbane said.

"You have to be kidding," said Shaw.

Anders raised a hand. "It's all right. Let him in."

Pointless, as Shaw was already inside. He moved around the inside of the transparent wall, to where he could keep both teams in view.

"Do you have the sample?" said Rohner.

Shaw set the duffel on the floor and unzipped it without taking his eyes from the room. No one had a gun in his hand, but so far as he could tell, only Rohner and Morton weren't packing. Even Anders had a pistol on his belt.

By feel he unwrapped the last item in the duffel and gripped the handle to hold it up.

A clear gallon jug filled with yellowish gel. Black shrink-wrapped packets had been taped around the jug's middle, like a winter coat for the thick soup within. Wires connected each brick-shaped packet to the next.

"Damn me," said Tucker from across the room. The others were already edging back, seeking what shelter was offered by the planter troughs.

"Insurance," said Shaw. "White phosphorus plus some accelerant, just to be nasty. Bad enough for anyone in here, even worse for your miracle goop."

He flipped a toggle switch taped to its surface. A light atop one of the packets of phosphorus glowed red. Unnecessary for the bomb's function, but an effective visual reminder of its menace.

"You're psychotic," said Kilbane.

"It's bullshit," Vic said. "He's scamming us."

Shaw looked at Hargreaves. "You know my history by now, I'm guessing. Half a dozen courses in demolitions and combat engineering. Not counting refresher study and on-the-job training in IEDs in Iraq and Afghanistan. Even before the Army I was building shape charges with my grandfather to blow safes. I could probably make a decent bang out of the stuff in Paragon's coffee room."

Hargreaves's mouth twisted. "Not a bluff."

"Right." Shaw looked at Morton. "Come get it."

"I can't work with that around," Morton said, his eyes on the red light.

"You can and you will," said Hargreaves. "Take it."

Morton walked toward Shaw as if he were stepping on thin ice.

Shaw removed a radio transmitter from his pocket. "Remote trigger," he said, holding it up to the room as well.

He handed the jug to Morton before tucking the black-capped sample vial from Professor Mills into the chemist's chest pocket. "All yours, chief."

Morton retreated to the table, staring at the bomb the whole way.

Hargreaves looked at Shaw. "Where's the woman? The pilot?"

"I didn't like the in-flight entertainment."

"What did you do to her?" Kilbane said.

"Focus," said Shaw. "How long will it take you to test the stuff?"

Morton realized that the question was directed at him.

"We're skipping the practical tests," said Morton. "I just have to verify the molecular structure. An hour. Less." He looked back at Hargreaves, as if making sure he'd followed the script right.

They all watched as Morton became absorbed in readying the tiny sample for testing, dissolving it into a liquid. Shaw wished there'd been time for Mills to give him a crash course on molecular synthesis when he'd picked up her facsimile of the Avizda chemical. He had no idea if Morton was following procedure.

The minutes ticked by slowly. Shaw stood near one of the exit doors. He held the remote trigger and the KRISS and watched the others. Rohner's team was the more nervous of the two. Shifting their feet and changing position every few minutes. Hargreaves and his bunch, maybe more accustomed to armed conflict, stayed put. But Tucker blinked a lot. Vic's hands shook a fraction when he sipped from a plastic water bottle. Only Hargreaves seemed completely cool.

"The machine gun," said Anders. "It's not necessary to brandish it so."

"It's my security blanket," said Shaw. He looked at Rohner. "Time to set up the transfer."

"Premature, Mr. Shaw." Rohner shook his head as if he were disappointed. "First let's be certain you've brought what we need."

"No. Get it ready. I'll give you the account. You transfer one dollar as a test. As soon as Morton there gives you the thumbs-up, you pay the remaining five and six nines."

"Or you'll set off your toy?" said Hargreaves. "You're not that stupid."

"I'm also not dumb enough to trust anybody in this room." He indicated Anders and Rohner. "They hired me to guard against a thief stealing the art. Setting me up as the fall guy when the completed polymer would suddenly disappear."

"That's distorting the truth," said Rohner. He looked at Hargreaves. "I never had any intention of cutting you out of the deal, James. I was only looking to protect my interests."

Shaw smiled maliciously at Rohner. "The big joke was that there really was a thief, and it was you."

The magnate managed to look indignant. "If you had been reasonable, all this trouble could have been avoided."

"Our friend here is even worse," Shaw said, nodding to Hargreaves. "His pet freaks chased me all the way across the country. Dead or alive."

"A misunderstanding," Hargreaves said. "We thought you had stolen the chemical from us."

"And now that I've stolen it from Chen, all is forgiven." Shaw looked at Rohner. "Transfer the dollar. Call it a good-faith gesture. Try to cheat me and I'll sell the chemical back to Chen. Or Avizda. Or whoever will pay, I don't give a shit."

Rohner frowned but nodded to Anders, who removed a phone from his pocket.

"National Bank of Manila," said Shaw. He waited until Anders was ready and recited the routing and account numbers from memory. Anders typed them into his phone.

Within a minute Shaw's own phone chimed from his pocket. A tone he'd assigned to the bank's incoming notification of a deposit.

"Good." He nodded. "Now we wait for the happy news."

They all looked to Morton, who opened the front panel of the machine to inject the liquid with the sample into a port.

Anders conferred quietly with Rohner. Kilbane and Castelli and Pollan watched Hargreaves and Tucker and Vic, who watched them in return. Shaw merited only the occasional glance.

James Hargreaves was very different from the boisterous guise of Bill Flynn, Shaw had noted. No talking with his hands or excited stories. Flynn's snappy blue suit had been set aside for something less obviously tailored, in pearl gray. Hargreaves's real voice, if he had a real voice, was cold and flat. As if the personality of Flynn had been set aside, leaving an icily smooth surface for the next identity, the next op.

The Paragon team had slowly moved closer to the walls, and to the waist-high troughs of ferns and flowering bromeliads that were the pavilion's only furnishings. And only cover.

"What's your plan after I leave?" Shaw said to Rohner. "Everybody shakes hands and toasts with Dom Perignon?"

"That's not your concern," Anders said.

Shaw looked at Hargreaves. "How much are you getting?"

Hargreaves stared back. "Enough."

A sudden whirring from the lab table made everyone flinch.

"Sorry," Morton said, realizing. "The pump. It's pushing the solution into the columns." He pointed to a pair of slender metal tubes in the machine.

Tucker had an obvious shoulder rig under his suit coat. Vic's windbreaker was a loose fit, and Shaw speculated whether he might be carrying something larger, like a machine pistol. He supposed the goon's aim might not be at peak condition, even though the swelling around his raccoon eyes had gone down.

Vic caught Shaw looking.

"Asshole," Vic said.

"At least you'll be able to afford a face job," Shaw said over the sound of the pump. "Maybe get that nose back to three dimensions."

"Ease off, Shaw," said Tucker. "No reason to break anyone's balls now."

"You, too, Vic." Hargreaves spoke without taking his eyes off Shaw.

"Not when we're so close," Shaw agreed. "If Rohner pays me, he's got to pay you, right?"

"Shaw," Anders said. "I don't see why you're trying to make trouble."

"A fixation," said Shaw. "Everybody here's tried to frame or kidnap or kill me. Guess I have difficulty letting go."

"You'll be rich in . . ." Anders looked at Morton. "How long, Mr. Morton?"

"Huh?" Morton, distracted from his task of extracting liquid at the bottom of the tube. "Oh. Not long."

"Minutes," said Hargreaves. He had his phone out. Shaw watched as he typed with one thumb. Signaling Louis in the helicopter?

"Twenty minutes," said Morton. "Less."

Rain began to fall in earnest. The first drops flowed down from the pavilion's icicle spires into rivulets that collected in the slim gutter at the upper edge of the roof. Instead of funneling the water into downspouts, the gutter released it in minute amounts all along the glass wall, so that an even sheen of rain covered the glittering surface.

A beautiful effect, Shaw acknowledged, though no one in the pavilion paid it much heed.

"It's completed diffusion," Morton said, peering at the machine.

"What does that mean?" said Anders through clenched teeth.

"I can check the results." Morton typed on the keyboard in front of the computer monitor. "To see if the known molecules in the polymer match the structure Bao was able to describe. For the unknown portion, I compare those results against the element structure information Mr. Hargreaves has, to see if it's accurate."

"Of course it's accurate," said Hargreaves. "Get to it."

Morton kept typing. Shaw imagined that the rigid focus helped the chemist keep his cool. Cannon to the right of him, cannon to the left.

Shaw kept his eyes moving over the men on either side of the pavilion, while his ears strained for any sound of the helicopter. Would Hargreaves have it land before the deal was finished? If Louis was bringing reinforcements, now would be the time.

Morton looked up from the screen. "It's good to go."

"Say more," said Hargreaves.

"We have a complete definition of the new polymer. We'll have to stress-test it, of course. A lot of different applications. But it's what Chen advertised. A stable bridging molecule." Morton tried to smile but it slipped from his face like the rain off the glass. "We're good to go," he said again.

The light atop the packets of phosphorous began to blink. Red. Black. Red. Black.

No one moved. Then all heads turned to Shaw, who had the remote trigger raised.

SIXTY-NINE

Half a mile off the southern shore of Briar Bay Island, Lieutenant John Guerin and Detective Neal Kanellis sat in the cabin of an SPD Harbor Patrol launch. The boat had been pressed into service by the FBI, who, after a lot of arm-twisting above Guerin's pay grade, had permitted the Seattle officers to be on board strictly as observers. It was Guerin who'd brought the case to the FBI's attention, along with the informants and the evidence. Somehow the Feds had managed to be generous in return.

The cabin was cramped and quiet of any noise beyond the launch's engine and the rainstorm. Cramped because the six members of the FBI's tactical team aboard had gathered inside once the rain began falling in earnest. With Guerin and Kanellis and the Harbor Patrol pilot, a veteran SPD sergeant named Fajula, that made eight men and one woman in a space hardly big enough for five.

Quiet because they were all listening intently to a receiver, which was crudely secured by strips of electrical tape to the boat's dash. Fajula had handed Guerin the tape after the swells on the strait had threatened to pitch the receiver onto the floor.

The tactical team in their armor and helmets stood gripping tight to the handrails on either side of the cabin's ceiling. Their carbines were slung over their shoulders. Two of the team had vomited on the crossing from Roche Harbor. Guerin felt slightly queasy himself, but he chalked that up to stress.

A second HP launch idled unseen a quarter mile to their starboard side. Its running lights doused, just as the lights were on their own craft. Fajula and another pilot had brought the boats up from Seattle early in the day to wait for the FBI team to arrive in Roche. Six more members of the tactical team stood ready aboard the second boat.

It's good to go.

The words came from the receiver. Not the first they'd heard that night through the transmitter taped under Avery Morton's sweater, but the ones they'd been waiting for. The tactical-team leader held up a hand for silence, even though no one had spoken.

It's a stable bridge between polymers. We'll have to stress-test it, of course.

The team leader nodded to his men and to Guerin.

We're good to go.

The signal phrase again. Guerin hoped to hell that Morton wasn't losing his cool. The next ten minutes would be dangerous enough without the chemist giving away the game early.

Without being told, Fajula pressed the throttle, and the launch picked up speed. The FBI team tilted backward, hanging on tight as the bow lifted. One hand to keep themselves upright, the other reflexively gripping their weapons.

Shaw would be right in the middle of it, Guerin knew. Perhaps even enjoying himself. Sometimes he wondered about Shaw's sanity. Being brought up by a hardcase like Dono Shaw could knock anyone's psyche sideways.

His stomach lurched. Not the waves, he decided. Not the stress either.

Shaw did this to his gut, every time.

SEVENTY

On the roof of the north wing, Riley swiveled the sniper rifle on its bipod, peering over its sights at the assemblage inside the pavilion. No one had changed places, but something was different. Everyone looking at Shaw instead of at the geek playing with the chemistry set.

"What's going on?" he said to Taskine over the comm.

"Dunno. I'm moving to a better position."

Riley waited.

Taskine's rumbling voice came back. "There's a light flashing on the thing that Shaw brought. Ordnance. Has to be."

"Shit," said Riley. "He's going to blow the place."

"I've got the shot."

"No," said Riley. He didn't directly contradict his partner often—he was reminded of some old line he'd heard in high school about getting between dragons and their wrath—but he knew when a move was wrong. "No sign from Hargreaves yet. He needs Shaw alive."

"Fuck," Taskine spat. Riley could feel Task's frustration through the radio link.

"Give it a minute," Riley said. He trained the crosshairs of his scope between the shoulder blades of the easternmost target, one of the rich dude's bodyguards. The guy was close to the wall, almost perpendicular to Riley's line of fire. Perfect. The deflection from the glass would be insignificant. His first .300 round would smack dead center.

"Got them cold," he said, as much to himself as to Taskine. "Wait for the signal."

Then Riley's head jerked up in shock. His slam-dunk shot had vanished before his eyes.

Every pane of glass in the entire pavilion had just turned stark white.

"WHAT IN GOD'S NAME ARE you doing?" Anders said to Shaw, who held the remote trigger high. The incendiary device continued to flash ominously. All of them had taken at least one step away from the table. Morton had fled to the closed entrance door that led to the passageway.

"A dead man's switch," said Tucker.

"Gold star," said Shaw. "Shoot me now and this room gets very hot, very fast." He regarded Rohner. "I've delivered what you want. Move the money."

Anders looked to his boss. Rohner stared at Shaw as if trying to read his mind. Shaw knew the dilemma the billionaire was weighing. If Rohner paid, he lost some control over the situation. If he refused, how could he know what Shaw would do?

"Two million," Rohner said to Shaw, "and four more after we leave here."

Shaw removed Sofia Rohner's ivory tablet from his pocket.

"Where did you get that?" said Anders.

Shaw set the tablet on the plant trough and touched it with his thumb. A moment later a series of soft thunks echoed from around the walls. The locks of each door but the one behind Shaw engaging.

"Nobody leaves," Shaw said, raising the barrel of the machine gun. "Not until I'm paid."

He touched the tablet again. The towering pavilion walls changed to a milky white. Even the rain flowing down the outer surface of the glass disappeared from view. The giant room seemed to instantly shrink to a fraction of its former size.

Morton turned and frantically pulled at the entrance door. It didn't budge.

Shaw watched Hargreaves. If this was going to escalate further, it would be the Paragon chief who lit the fuse.

Tucker and Vic had eyes on their boss as well. Waiting for a signal. They could fall behind the plant troughs, count on having at least some cover from a blast.

Kilbane and Pollan had their hands on their holstered weapons.

Castelli had moved closer to the wall, maybe trying to find a position where he wouldn't be the first to get shot by either Shaw or Hargreaves's men.

"Yes. Very well," Rohner said. He held both hands out at stomach level, palms down, in a gesture intended to be calming. It looked more as though the tension in the room were causing him to levitate a fraction. "Please don't do anything." An entreaty intended for everyone in the vast room.

Anders, his long face stony, began typing on his phone once more. Within thirty anxious seconds, Shaw's phone chimed in answer. He was suddenly six million dollars richer, if he lived to see it.

"Right," said Shaw. "Here's what happens now. I leave. I deactivate the trigger." He held up the remote. "Anyone follows and I shoot them and maybe I decide to set off the bomb, too, just out of spite."

Very faintly, another sound made its presence known in the room over the soft patter of rain. The low buzz of a helicopter in the distance. Coming closer.

"No," said Hargreaves, slowly drawing a pistol from the small of his back. "Hand over the remote. We're not trusting you not to blow us all to hell."

As if attached by strings to their leader's movement, Tucker and Vic drew their own guns. Shaw had been right about Vic. The battered thug had brought a Micro Uzi. Twelve hundred rounds a minute, with a recoil that all but guaranteed each bullet would spray without much partiality as to target.

Across the room Kilbane and his team fanned out. Pollan motioned to Rohner and Anders to move back, an unnecessary command as Anders was already tugging his boss toward the nearest plant trough. Morton cowered by the entrance, still tugging at the door as if it might magically open.

The low, whipping roar of the helicopter was much closer now.

"If he moves," Hargreaves said over the noise, nodding to Shaw, "kill him."

SEVENTY-ONE

Louis Paolo gripped the stick of the Bell 427 helicopter and swore softly to himself. He'd been cursing almost constantly since he lifted off from the field at Anacortes. The dickwad whom Hargreaves had arranged to borrow the helo from had been an hour late, making Louis late in return. The sun would be down by the time he reached Briar Bay Island. Before he'd finished his preflight check, the rain had added to his problems.

He was out of practice. He'd known it, and now he was bitching himself out for the lack. After leaving the Army, Louis had jumped through all the dull civilian hoops to get his private and commercial licenses. He'd been diligent about maintaining them, too. But making daytime hops between airports just to rack up the required hours hadn't been enough to keep his edge. Flying in this visibility was just the kick in the balls to remind him.

At least the Bell was up to date. Louis had filed a Special V flight plan with Anacortes before taking off, only to cancel the clearance when he was away from the control tower's airspace. Once he saw that ATC had stopped following his flight path, he changed course and kept the craft at an easy three thousand feet over the San Juans.

He hoped he wouldn't have to regret that sneaky move. Nobody watching meant nobody coming to his rescue if things turned to dog shit.

Before long he was relying solely on the instruments to guide him. The rain and wind were coming almost straight on. Looking out the windscreen was like staring into a shower nozzle.

On approach to Briar Bay, the island might not have existed at all. Black on black obscured by a downpour. He slowed as the GPS indicated he was close. Still he saw nothing. Only when he was within a few hundred feet did he see a glimmer that revealed itself to be a large building, heavily lit from within. Shit. The thing looked like a giant spiky crown. So out of place in the storm it might as well be a hallucination.

The island's helipad was on the western side, Hargreaves had said. Closest to him. He slowed the Bell's approach to hover two hundred feet above the waves and off what little he could make out of the shoreline. He'd been warned that the pad was a work in progress—no ILS, no pilot-controlled beacon. Not even an illuminated letter *H*.

Louis switched on the helo's landing and search lights and gave the stick an ounce of pressure.

He started at the midpoint of the island and traced its coast north-northeast, toward the shining building. It followed that any landing pad would be near the island's main structures. Waves rolled past under the beams of his lights. Swells going south, choppy as fuck. At least he wasn't coming in by boat. That would have made for a long damn day.

The dock appeared in the beams first, with a seaplane moored on its interior side. Then Louis caught a glitter of white in his peripheral. Almost directly inland at his nine. He pivoted the Bell to shine the lights in that direction. There were the perimeter lights. Crap, a bunch of ground crew standing with flashlights wouldn't do much worse. Plus, the idiots had put the pad too close to the trees.

He grimaced and brought the Bell in. Slowly. He hoped the land was solid after all this rain. He could just see the skids getting stuck in the fucking mud—

BANG

The Bell shuddered as if shaken by a giant's fist. Louis's head whipped around toward the noise even as the helo yawed suddenly right and his body lurched with it. The tail rotor. He'd hit something. A high-frequency hum like a tuning fork wedged in his skull made his teeth rattle. *Fuck* the helo was going sideways and up. He pushed at the stick, trying to even her out, but *shit* he'd lost it somehow maybe the rotor was broken and *shit shit shit* the massive blazing glass building was RIGHT THERE RIGHT

SEVENTY-TWO

When it happened, it happened fast.

The pitch of the helicopter's roar changed, heightened, shrieked.

Nearly every person in the frost-white pavilion looked up, toward the banshee wail. All but one.

Shaw had the advantage of knowing he had repositioned the helipad lights. He realized almost instantly what was about to happen, even if it hadn't been what he'd intended. He'd hoped that the helo's rotors might strike a tree branch or one of the flagpole's guy wires. Enough damage to keep it from taking off again, eliminating Hargreaves's escape route if he were lucky. Somehow, with the storm, his small trick had taken a bad turn.

He dove for the floor.

The Bell hit one sharp spire of the pavilion, impaling itself. Its whirling rotors sliced through another spire an instant before the falling aircraft shattered the ceiling entirely. Shaw felt the impact in his bones. Every pane in the pavilion splintered.

He rolled for the nearest plant trough. An eight-foot wedge of glass hit the floor behind him, bursting into shards. The helo came down hard, sideways, right in the center of the huge room. It crushed the laboratory table and GPC machine even as its rotors tore into the pavilion floor with a piercing squeal, instantly launching the fuselage across the room nose-first. A panicked bird thrashing itself to death in a glass cage. Shaw heard the first scream. Or at least the first that had carried over the throes of the Bell.

The helicopter's tail struck the wall, sending a new explosion of glass and jagged metal. Shaw was already moving, crawling along the edge of the room. Rohner's team was closest. Castelli saw him, stood from his kneeling position. The broken glass wall next to the man shattered, almost an afterthought to the round that blew out the front of Castelli's chest.

Sniper. Shaw hit the floor again as another shot cracked the glass above him.

The best cover in the room was the newly dead helicopter. He jumped up and sprinted for it.

Two more shots, a handgun. From inside the pavilion at eight o'clock. Aimed at him? He didn't pause, ducking under the twisted tail of the helo and behind its fuselage, into a reek of fuel and torched electrics.

He stumbled over something. A leg. The rest of the body was tucked under the fuselage. He recognized the bit of windbreaker just north of the appendage. The luckless Vic.

Shaw looked above the wrecked shell of the aircraft and saw Hargreaves and Tucker far across the room, behind the broken halves of one of the troughs. Pistols turning in his direction.

He fired a short burst from the KRISS, but the two men had already ducked back. A shot cracked from Shaw's left, on the other side of the helicopter. From behind the spilled soil and plants of the cracked trough, Hargreaves and Tucker returned fire at the new threat.

Crouching low, Shaw moved to the helo's crushed canopy. Louis lay inside the cockpit, buckled into his seat, headset askew on curly hair sodden with blood. The pilot's right eye was half closed. A wink to those still living.

Morton had been huddled near the pavilion's entrance. There. By the trough on the other side. Maybe too panicked to realize that with half the walls in the pavilion destroyed, he could flee in almost any direction. The lab table and the gallon jug of accelerant along with it had been squashed almost flat. The remnants of the chemistry equipment lay among the larger debris of the demolished walls and ceiling.

Shaw realized he was still clutching the remote trigger. The deadman's switch. Would it still work? Or had the packets been torn apart?

He tossed the trigger away and ran for Morton.

Shaw hadn't been lying to the others about the white phosphorous. Professor Mills had given him a three-pound bag of the powdered element along with the fake polymer sample. Shaw had Tucker and his tactics at Westlake Center to thank for the idea.

White phosphorous made for one hell of a good smoke screen.

The center of the room erupted into huge billows of gray. If the room had been intact, the clouds would have engulfed the entire space within seconds. But the wind pouring in through the pavilion's shattered walls caught the smoke and pushed it toward Shaw and Morton.

The chemist cringed away from him.

"I'm on your side," Shaw said, as loudly as he dared. "Karla sent me. Come on." Morton's eyes widened, and he nodded frantically.

Shaw hauled Morton up and shoved him out through the destroyed wall, into the night. The man moved. Too slowly. Shaw grabbed him by the arm and forced him into a run.

More shots, behind them. Shaw kept moving. Morton had the pace now and sprinted ahead, terror lending him wings.

SEVENTY-THREE

This whole thing is a clusterfuck, thought Riley. He was still stunned from the helicopter's crash. He'd heard the bird's straining engine, realized something was funky a moment before he saw the Bell rise up over the buildings, already tilted sideways and slipping fast.

The next two minutes had been the craziest show he'd ever seen. The helicopter came down and tore the shit out of the building and probably half the dudes dumb enough to be inside it. Then the Gunfight at the Glass Corral had started, muzzle flashes hot in the sudden dim after most of the lights had been smashed.

Now smoke. A lot of smoke. Riley figured the Bell chopper was burning and taking what was left of the pavilion with it.

"We got cops. Police boats. Coming up on the dock," Taskine said in his ear. Riley could tell from the stuttering beat of Task's words that his partner was moving fast.

"Fuck. I can't see shit inside. Is Hargreaves still alive?"

"He was twenty seconds ago. I'm getting into position."

"For what?"

"What do you think? These mothers get to the dock, they're meat. I'll take 'em like tin cans off a fence."

Damn it. Riley didn't mind Taskine shooting cops. But it would require time to get to their own boat and exfil the hell off this island. Maybe these two police boats were just the first to arrive. Could be planes watching from the sky or helicopters dropping SWAT teams next. Even the fucking National Guard.

"How many cops on the boats?" he said.

"At least a dozen jagoffs. Tac gear and rifles."

"Keep them offshore. Make 'em scared to even look at the dock.

Buy me ten minutes and I'll put our boat in the water. You come on the run, we get the fuck out of here before they know you've left."

Taskine was silent. Riley knew that his fearsome nature was at war with his logic.

"Yeah," he said. "Go."

Riley started to do just that. He was on his feet before he saw two figures hurrying from the smoke-shrouded pavilion. Visible in the weak light still shining through the pavilion's former walls.

The geek. And Shaw.

No time for the scope. Riley knelt and aimed over the barrel. Shaw and the geek were almost under the shade screen of an outdoor patio between the pavilion and the north wing.

Got you. He grinned as he pulled the trigger.

SEVENTY-FOUR

Something ripped the machine gun from Shaw's grip. The pain in his right hand was immediate and almost a blessing, as he barreled reflexively in that direction, slamming into Morton and sending them both tumbling over the slope. They skidded through the muddy earth and grass to the rock shore.

Sniper. Again.

But not the same one.

The shot that had killed Castelli had come from the beach. This new bastard was somewhere farther up the estate. Shaw grabbed Morton before the chemist stood up.

"Did Hargreaves tell you about more men on the island?" he rasped into Morton's ear. "More shooters?"

"What?" Morton's eyes were wide. Shaw wasn't even sure the man realized that he was trying to pull himself from Shaw's grip. His lizard brain said run, so his body tried to run.

Escape was a fine idea. Shaw had stashed his inflatable Zodiac at the far tip of the island. A mile's fast run on the beach, so long as no one was trying to blow your head off.

The forest. In the cover of the trees, they could work their way toward the far end. But the forest was two hundred yards away, past the entire length of the north wing and the main house. And the sniper, wherever he was concealed.

Morton continued to twist in Shaw's grasp. Shaw shook him. "Stay down, idiot. They're shooting." Morton sagged into the dirt.

The sniper, or maybe both of them, would be on the move. Looking for a line of fire. Now that Shaw and Morton were out of the pavilion and its thick smoke, they were wide open. If the enemy had night optics, even worse.

More pistol fire from back near the pavilion. Where the hell was Guerin? He was supposed to be offshore with the Feds. They should be storming Rohner's fucking castle by now.

SEVENTY-FIVE

Sergeant Fajula brought the police launch straight into the dock. Coming ashore with all possible speed. Guerin braced for the sharp turn and sudden reverse of the props that would expertly touch the side of the launch to the dock. The FBI team shifted, impatient to surge ashore.

Maybe there was someone still alive after the helicopter crash. Though from what they'd seen, Guerin wasn't optimistic. The sound alone had been like a monster howling in fury. With the pavilion's lights destroyed, the brightest things on the island were the white clouds filling the crushed structure. The place must be on fire.

The tactical team assembled on the starboard side, causing the launch to heel. Kanellis clutched the handrail and made a face. "Observers. Shit. We should be in on this."

"Apply for SWAT if you want to," Guerin said. His time in the Marines had stripped any need to prove himself by being first through the door.

Kanellis seemed ready to retort when the right half of the boat's windshield exploded and the rear window along with it. Fajula cried out a warning even as she swerved to starboard. Guerin and Kanellis both ducked.

Fajula kicked the throttle to full. The Feds dove, one by one, into the open-air deck at the rear of the launch. Guerin heard the second shot hit, a firecracker snap as the round struck the boat's hull on the port side. The FBI men kept flat in the shallow well of the rear deck, piled up like young turtles in a nest.

"Rifle," Fajula yelled to him. Guerin nodded, though all the pilot's attention was on driving her boat over the swells. He had to figure the rocking would at least make them a tougher target. Rain and spray from the bow wake came through the broken windscreen.

"I need to take us farther out," she said. "Out of range. We can circle and try to beach once we find sand."

Guerin wasn't sure how Fajula would be able to tell sand from stone. The island was darker than ever. Even the pavilion was engulfed in gray.

Their informant, Morton, would have been in there. Shaw, too. Maybe they still were.

God save them, Guerin thought. Or at least make it quick.

SEVENTY-SIX

Shaw drew the Browning from under his coat. Gingerly. His right hand was numb. He'd have to shoot left. If it came to having to shoot at all, they were down to their last option.

He crawled sideways along the muddy slope for ten yards and up to the top to take a cautious glance. Only a handful of lights remained shining in the pavilion, most of them low and toward the entrance. Smoke billowed from every wound in its glass skin.

He looked to his right. Gauging what position he would choose, if it were him holding the rifle. The snipers must be Hargreaves's backup for the big show. The beach here offered no vantage on the pavilion.

The roof. Had to be. On the north wing, with the guest rooms. High enough and relatively flat. Was the shooter still there? Still watching the pavilion? Or waiting for Shaw and Morton to reappear?

"We have to move," Shaw said. He pointed to the path from the beach to the estate. "Inside will be safer. Run to the door at the end when I say. Ready?"

Morton nodded. Shaw said go. They sprinted for the north wing.

Shaw had a moment's fear that the door would be locked. That the destruction of the pavilion had somehow activated the security measures. If he had to stop and pick the lock, they would be easy game. But the door swung outward at Morton's first desperate pull on the handle. They rushed inside.

The dining area was dark apart from the green of the battery-powered exit signs and the red dots on the smoke detectors. Shaw walked silently through the room to the wing's main corridor. Morton followed, almost tiptoeing.

Shaw listened. When he was as sure as he could be that they were alone, they moved down the long corridor to the exit, which would take them into the glass passageway that led to the western side of the main house.

He didn't like the idea of taking the passageway. An enclosed space, transparent on both sides. Scarcely better than being outside. But scarcely better was still an improvement. They had to reach the forest to make it to Shaw's inflatable boat. And they had to reach the main house to have a prayer of reaching the forest.

The thought of the inflatable Zodiac spurred another idea. It was a reasonable guess that the snipers were Hargreaves's two hitters. The Viking with the beard and the snaky one with glasses. They hadn't flown in on C.J.'s plane with the rest. They must have arrived another way. On a boat. A boat that would have to be beached somewhere on shore.

Their deal for the polymer had gone to shit. Hargreaves had lost the helicopter that was supposed to extract them. And if their backup plan was to fly away in the seaplane, they would quickly learn they had neither plane nor pilot. Leaving only the possibility of the snipers' boat for Hargreaves and his remaining men to escape.

Their craft could be almost anywhere along two miles of shoreline. If the enemy was falling back, Shaw and Morton might accidentally cross paths with them. They would have to watch their every step.

Shaw said, "Let's go," and opened the door to the passageway. Morton followed him on the run. They reached the far end, and Shaw held up a hand for the chemist to keep quiet. He turned the knob on the gilded door to the house and gently tugged it open a crack.

Still dark within the manor. He slipped inside and made room for Morton to follow before closing the door just as softly.

They were in a stone-walled foyer, a smaller cousin to the one Shaw had seen when he'd talked with Sofia Rohner. He stepped silently to the opposite end. No sound and no light within the big house.

"Where are we going?" Morton whispered.

"A boat. Other side of the woods."

"But the cops. Can't we just wait for them?" Morton untucked his shirt. The tapes holding the wire around his middle had torn loose during their escape. The transmitter had been lost. Who knew how much Guerin and the others had heard. Maybe nothing.

Morton tugged the wire off his belly and dropped it onto the tiled floor. Karla had done good work convincing Morton to turn informant. The chemist had been smart enough to take the deal. Immunity on one hand, the probability of winding up like Kelvin Welch on the other.

"They're coming, right?" Morton said.

"I don't know." Feds would announce their arrival as loudly as possible. Intimidation tactics. Shaw hadn't heard so much as an air horn.

But he did hear something else. Movement, from within the dark house. Near the central stairwell.

Shaw motioned for Morton to wait. He moved past a dining area with a sideboard and a china cabinet and ten seats at the elongated table. The sound was footsteps. More than one person, descending the central staircase.

He looked around the corner. It was Rohner, and Anders, the latter's tall frame obvious even in the dim space.

"Hold it," he said, training the Browning at a point between them. "Drop the guns."

They turned. Shaw saw that their hands were empty. Anders's right hand was wet, a black sheen. His arm hung limply at his side.

"Don't shoot," Anders said. "We're not armed."

"Shaw?" said Rohner.

"Move back," Shaw said, "into the kitchen."

"Shaw, get us out of here."

"Move."

They went. Anders walked very slowly. Rohner, as if to compensate, could hardly stand in one place. Shaw came up quick behind them. He patted each of them down, the jumpy Rohner first. Patches of blood, seeping from the arm beneath, had stained Anders's suit sleeve. The tall man leaned against a monstrous Liebherr refrigerator.

Rohner clutched at Shaw's arm. "You made the right decision, coming back. You won't regret it."

Morton, attracted by the voices, had come to the stairwell. "Come on," he whispered. "Before they catch up."

"Where?" said Rohner. "Do you have a way off the island?"

"A boat," said Morton.

"Then we'll go together," Rohner said. The confidence of the statement undercut by a quaver he couldn't quite stifle. "All away from here."

"Too small a boat for four of us," said Shaw. "And besides, no one gives a shit."

"We can make it," Rohner said. "Name your price."

Shaw almost laughed. Second time tonight that someone had offered him a blank check. Shaw didn't believe Rohner any more than he had C.J.

"He can't take us, Sebastien," Anders said.

"He can. He will," Rohner said, blinking furiously.

The tall man stared at his employer. He pushed himself upright, his palm leaving a wine-red smear on the brushed-steel face of the refrigerator.

"Sebastien," he said.

Rohner looked back. Finally focusing on something. He was in shock, Shaw realized. Death had walked right up to spit in his face. Impossible to ignore. An adventure that Rampage Rohner could not command or control.

"It's over," said Anders. He sat down, or his legs gave out, depositing him on a kitchen chair.

Rohner blinked once more. He took a step toward the table, wavered, then finished crossing the room with three increasing sure strides. "Take Olen," he said to Shaw. "My offer stands. Take him."

Anders sighed. "No."

"I'll hide in the house," Rohner said to him. "They won't find me."

"I can't make the journey, Sebastien."

Rohner put a hand on Anders's shoulder. Maybe to offer comfort. Maybe to steady himself.

"Who's still alive?" Shaw asked Anders.

"Kilbane was shot dead. By Hargreaves or someone else, I'm not sure. I don't know about the rest."

"Castelli was killed, too. And at least two more on Hargreaves's side."

"The helicopter," Rohner said with that tremble again. "Came right down on one of them. Oh."

"Hang on," Shaw said. "The cops will get here."

"I could help," Morton said from the corner of the kitchen. "I have EMR training. I could stay. Stanch your bleeding."

They looked at the chemist.

"For money?" Anders said to him.

"Well, sure. Yeah. Since I'm risking my life, why not?"

Anders turned to Shaw. "And you?"

Shaw shook his head. "I've done enough business tonight."

He went to the rear door to peer around the curtain covering the window on the upper half. The few yards of grass separating the house from the forest were empty. The stygian black of the woods looked inviting. Safe.

"Good luck," he said, and ran for the tree line.

SEVENTY-SEVEN

Riley radioed Taskine. "I'm at the boat. Ready to leave in three."

"On my way," the reply came back.

Riley pushed hard on the bow of the twelve-foot speedboat. The thing looked like a toy, and it weighed less than Riley and Taskine put together, even with its twenty-horse engine. But it was fast. Reaching civilization quickly would be worth getting soaked again out on the waves. He and Taskine had beached at low tide and hauled the boat high onto the shore to camouflage it with a tarp. Now, with the waves lapping at the edge of the green plastic, it required only a few hard shoves from Riley, the hull scraping over the rock, before the transom was in deep enough water to lower the outboard. Holding the boat's bowline to keep it from floating away, Riley waded back ashore to collect his rifle and other gear.

Over the steady patter of rain on his cap, Riley heard a rustling sound from up the beach. He dropped to one knee, drew his Colt from his hip, and aimed in the direction of the sound. The rustling happened again, simultaneous with a gust of wind.

Jumpy, he chastised himself. But it was a good night to be on edge. He waited until he was sure the sound wasn't caused by anything living. A heavy rock pinned the bowline as Riley went to see what was making the noise.

A tree branch. He looked up the short bluff to the forest above. Even in the night, he could see scrub growing from the cliff face. It looked as though the branch had fallen over a lump in the rock. When the wind gusted, the leaves crackled against one another.

In another ten paces, Riley recognized what he was seeing. An inflatable lifeboat, up on its side, with a tiny engine. He stared at it for a long moment before his face split in an irrepressible smile.

Shaw. No damn way this boat wasn't the Ranger's. He might have stashed it here days ago. And Riley and Taskine had beached their own boat barely fifty yards away.

A new realization dimmed his mirth. If that cockroach Shaw was still alive, this would be where he was headed.

He edged back, slowly, listening for other signs of movement. When he heard none, he unsheathed his ASEK knife and plunged it into the rubbery inflatable. The first rush of escaping air made a juddering moan around the blade. The boat sagged into the split in the rock as it deflated.

Wait for Shaw to show up and blow him away? Or count on Taskine making it here first? They could be gone inside a minute.

Riley's habitual grin was back. Leave it to chance and see which one wins the race. It would be slow and noisy work to hide their speedboat under the tarp again. He left it where it was, bobbing on the incoming waves.

There wasn't much cover on the beach. But in his black waterproofs, he'd be obscured if he stuck to the cliffside. He picked up his sniper rifle.

On the opposite side of Shaw's shredded inflatable, the face of the cliff was extra rough. Plenty of concealing juts of rock to let him hunker down and wait.

If Shaw came around the tip of the island to his right, Riley had the Colt. Otherwise the rifle. From two hundred feet away, he heard the low thump of their speedboat, borne on a wave against the rocky shore.

Perfect, Riley thought. Perfect bait.

SEVENTY-EIGHT

Shaw moved through the dark forest. Without a flashlight the going was slow. Because he was making as little noise as possible, doubly so. His normal footfall was very quiet, but in the woods he could hear every pebble that shifted under his soles.

His weren't the only sensitive ears. A crunch of moving brush came from the trees far to his left. Blacktail deer, or raccoon, or something else with enough heft to broadcast its hasty exit from his presence. Shaw stopped and listened until the patter of the rain on the branches was once again the only sound.

He'd tamped down the instinctive urge to rush through the trees, reach his boat, and get gone. Short of offshore the woods were the safest place he could be. Even if the cops never showed, he could hide in the dense brambled acres for hours or even days.

Tucker and Hargreaves and the two shooters with their sniper rifles. Those were the remaining hostiles. Maybe Pollan, the female member of Kilbane's team. No one seemed to know what had happened to Pollan.

Five left, then, to be safe. Some of them maybe fleeing. Maybe under arrest.

Maybe hunting him through the woods, right this minute.

He kept going. The scents of fresh pine sap and decaying bark suffused his nose. The alpha and omega of forest life. He came across a trail, or at least a line through the trees a little wider and clearer of vegetation than the woods around it. Shaw followed its path west.

A piece of wood snapped, somewhere behind him.

Shaw ducked low and froze.

Breaking wood was not an animal noise. Not of the light-footed beasts of the San Juans.

He waited. The snapping sound didn't repeat. He moved off the trail, very carefully, feeling with his foot before each step to be sure there was nothing beneath his boot but moss and sodden leaves.

Ten feet from the trail, he crouched behind the rotted shell of what had once been the trunk of a massive hemlock. Shaw's eyes had long since adjusted as much as they would to the deep black under the forest canopy. He could make out the trees and the larger bushes. Looking upward from his crouch, he could see individual branches outlined against patches of overcast sky. Rain was still falling. More heard than felt, an arrhythmic tapping on leaves and in puddles.

Over the raindrops Shaw caught another noise from down the trail. Closer this time. Within half a minute, the new sound had divided in two: the repeated beat of footsteps and the soft rasp of waterproof fabric moving against itself.

Someone coming. Along the same path Shaw had found. Moving faster and consequently less quietly.

The person neared. A large man, hooded and holding a long rifle, its barrel down and to the left. The man's breath hissed through his nose. In and out, a quicker rhythm than his steps. He was pumped up and alert.

One of Hargreaves's hitters. The bigger of the two, the bearded Viking. Not searching for Shaw. His attitude and attention were focused on covering ground through the dark with speed. Heading for whatever extraction point he and his partner had arranged.

Without conscious thought Shaw raised and aimed the Browning. One less enemy. He didn't even have to kill the man; putting a round through the killer's leg at this range would be as easy as through his heart, even in the gloom.

But the shot would be heard by every person on the island. The rest of the Paragon team might be in the forest, or on the shore to either side. Giving away his position would be giving away his primary advantage.

Hargreaves's people could scatter. They could run as far as they chose, pick new names, new faces, even. If the law didn't find them, he would. Shaw made that promise to himself as he let the man pass. *In order* to let the man pass. Feeling his teeth clench tighter with every fading step.

After a count of fifty, he carried on. The map in his head told him the forest extended another quarter mile before the steep bluff and the shore beneath, where he'd concealed the Zodiac in the rocks.

A hundred yards along, he heard a drum's low beat far off to his eleven o'clock. Seconds later the same thump. And again. A familiar sound. The hull of a lightweight boat bumping against land.

That must be their escape route. A boat not far from his own. Had someone found the Zodiac in its hiding place?

He should hang back until he heard their boat leave. There was nothing to be served but his own ego from going after Hargreaves's hired killers now. Pride could get him killed, and quickly.

Better to let them escape. Absolutely.

Shaw turned off the path and headed toward the sound.

SEVENTY-NINE

Hargreaves pointed, and Tucker ran to the nearest outcropping of rock on the shore. When Tucker waved, Hargreaves moved past him to the next. Leapfrogging positions as each covered the other. They had made fast progress up the bare southern shore. Less than five minutes before, they'd spotted the FBI tactical team leaping from the beached police boats near Rohner's personal art museum.

The two men had cut across the estate, seconds ahead of the Feds. Getting soaked to the bone by the frigging rainstorm.

Tucker had nearly tripped over something that turned out to be a chunk of aluminum flagpole, one end of it flattened and torn. The helicopter's doing. Louis's final flight. The night had gone to hell fast after that.

Was Rohner dead? Hargreaves hoped not. He wanted his own chance to end that Swiss prick. And Karla. He was sure the whore had been behind the cops showing up. She and Shaw must be working together. They'd convinced Rohner to pay up and then bolted before the trap snapped shut.

It had been slick, Shaw's thing with the bomb or the smoke grenade or whatever that had been. And Hargreaves knew that the polymer invention was viable now. Morton had done at least that much good. That knowledge was worth something. He could get another operative inside Avizda. Take another batch of the chemical, by force if they had to.

There was a way off this island. The boat he'd arranged for Taskine and Riley. Had they cast off already?

Speed counted. If he and Tucker could beat them to the boat—or better yet catch them there by surprise—then finders fucking keepers. Those two psychopaths had exhausted their usefulness.

EIGHTY

The cliff wall lent Riley some shelter from the rain. He'd decided on a sitting position, one knee up to support his arm, the rifle nestled easily into the crook of his elbow. Not quite textbook, but more comfortable. He watched the little speedboat bob on the waves.

Riley didn't know fuck-all about the tide tables in the Northwest, but the waterline had been much lower when he and Taskine first arrived on the island. The tide had come up far enough to fill the pools near the cliff since then, and it seemed to be retreating now. The boat floated when the waves came in, thumped the rock when they went out. Wouldn't be long before it was aground again.

"Hey," said Taskine over the radio, "I'm at a damn drop-off. Way above the beach."

Riley spoke low. "Where?"

"Maybe half a klick from you. The woods were so dark I couldn't hardly see my feet."

"Follow the cliff west. Find a place to climb down."

"Copy."

"And keep quiet. We might have company comin'."

Good. Taskine was close. Five minutes, maybe less, and they would be gone.

And just like Christmas, another present arrived. A big, broadshouldered shape, one shadow splitting off from the others near the cliff. Moving to the boat as it nodded hello on the waves.

Riley smiled wide, his cheek pressing against the rifle's stock. Howdy-do, Shaw. Ran like a rabbit across the whole country from NYC. All that way just to get dead at home.

He took a deep breath and let it out slow. When the walking

shadow was calf-deep in the water, reaching to grab the boat's bow, Riley squeezed off one round.

Dead center. The bullet spiraling through breastbone and organs and spine so easily that it was an instant before the dead man collapsed, his arm skidding along the boat's hull and pushing the little craft aside.

The body lay facedown. Riley sat for a moment to watch with satisfaction as the tide lashed around the slack limbs. Fish food.

He stood up and walked toward the corpse. Maybe he should take a trophy. Wasn't normally his thing—Taskine liked souvenirs when he played with marks, especially women—but Shaw had required some goddamn effort. He should remember this victory.

Four shots came out of the darkness. Two taps of two. From low to the ground. Forty yards off, maybe fifty. Riley's senses noted all these facts even as his eyes were dazzled by the muzzle flare and a pain like a flaming sword sliced through his left shoulder, or neck, or both. Blood splashed over his face. His own. He fell to one knee, rolled, and somehow managed to keep rolling in his panic, more pain as he banged over the rocks. Scrambling for the cover of a boulder near the cliff face.

Shaw had a partner. Somebody planted early on the island, just like he and Task had been. Goddamn it. They should have guessed that.

Riley's left arm was limp. He pushed himself up with his right to lean back against the boulder. He drew his Colt with his good hand. His shooting hand. He'd lost the rifle.

And he was bleeding. A warm flow down his chest and belly. Scary fast. His trap muscle, he could tell now, just a couple inches off his neck. How bad? He wanted to reach to feel, but not so much that he wanted to let go of the Colt. His left hand lay useless in his lap, fingers curled like a shriveled spider.

The sneaky shit might think Riley was finished. Might show himself. Riley hoped that happened fast. Or else he was fucked up one side and down the other. Another warm pulse spread down his chest.

Where was Taskine? Riley didn't want to risk talking out loud.

He couldn't reach his left hand to tap the comm and signal distress. Screwed. He'd have to hope Task had heard the gunfire. Was coming to take this mother out.

Leaning against the boulder felt good. He wanted to rest. Instead he bent his left leg and braced his foot against the ground so that he could prop his right arm on his knee. The Colt in his hand and pointed down the beach. Ready to take the shot the instant Shaw's buddy showed an inch of himself.

Come on, you fuck, Riley breathed to himself. *Gimme one chance. I'll send you on ahead to hell. You can hold the door open for me.*

EIGHTY-ONE

Shaw instinctively ducked at the echoing cracks of the shots, although he knew immediately that the weapon had been fired from somewhere down on the shore. At least fifty yards ahead and another forty feet below the edge of the bluff.

Pistol shots meant a hostile. Any police tac team would be using long guns. Shotguns, M4s, maybe submachine guns like the one Shaw wished he still held right now. There'd been no answering volley. Return fire would have followed like a swarm of hornets if the pistol shots had been aimed at cops.

One enemy shooting at another. Had he hit what he'd aimed at?

The bearded killer who'd passed him in the woods had likely been drawn by the sound of the boat thumping against the shore, just as Shaw had. If so, the man must be close. Either just ahead, in the expanse of wind-scoured grass that rapidly sloped to the final short cliff, or working his way along the upper edge, searching for a place where he could climb down.

Shaw moved forward in a crouch. Keeping low so that his silhouette would merge with the mass of trees to anyone looking up the slope from below. The rain drummed on his hood and shoulders. Hearing movement, as he had in the forest, would be next to impossible.

He descended a step at a time. After ten paces he could feel the angle of the hill increasing beneath his feet. After twenty he was pressing himself back against the pull of the drop.

Ten yards in front of him, the grass abruptly ended. The cliff's edge. Beyond that he could see only waves.

The killer wasn't here. But the insistent, erratic bumps of the small boat against the rocks continued from Shaw's right. A small rise in the landmass blocked the view in that direction. Shaw got down on his knees and crawled to the peak of the low hill, the Browning in his hand.

He lifted his head above the rise. On the other side, nearer the cliff, he saw the broad shape of the bearded killer. The Viking stood tall, his rifle aimed downward at the beach. As Shaw watched, the barrel moved slightly left, then right. Seeking a target.

Most of Rohner's people had been accounted for. Had the cops arrived without Shaw hearing them? The brawny killer might be waiting for Guerin or one of the Feds to show themselves. That rifle had enough range to pick them off anywhere on the beach, even through the rain.

The man was right-handed. Aiming down and to the left, his front facing the cliff so that his back was angled toward Shaw.

Take this big son of a bitch out, quietly. The rain would cover his approach. A hard crack over the head and a choke hold. Take the rifle. Then deal with the rest of them, however he had to.

He crawled over the rise. Down the other side. The Viking continued to aim at the shore, intent on finding his quarry. Shaw placed one hand down, one knee, one hand. Twenty feet from the man now. Fifteen. Watching.

Shaw hadn't made a sound. He was certain of that. But the Viking suddenly knew. His shoulders tightened, thick trapezius muscles squeezing reflexively to protect his vulnerable neck a split second before he began to turn. Shaw was already launching himself upward. The killer spun, the barrel of his rifle swinging around to meet the new threat. Too high. Too late. Shaw was underneath, driving forward, slamming into the killer like a runaway train hitting the end of the line.

They fell. Down the slope. The incline so sharp that their fall stretched an extra yard, the impact a millisecond later than Shaw expected it. They hit and bounced. The Viking's breath exploded from his huge chest with a grunt. Shaw was thrown aside, tumbling along the slope. His leg came down onto nothing. Dropping off the cliff's edge. He let go of the Browning to claw desperately with both hands at the sodden ground, tearing away clumps of dirt. He managed to roll himself back the other way and up onto his knees.

A huge form, rushing. The Viking's kick hit him high on the shoulder. Spun him back toward the drop. He went with the force, rolled to the ground again. A second kick, trying to punt Shaw right off the edge, glanced off his hip. Shaw punched upward, aiming for the killer's groin and hitting his ribs instead as the man stumbled to one knee. He grabbed at Shaw, one spade hand clamping over Shaw's throat and pinning him to the ground. Bared teeth showing white in the black beard.

The crushing fingers closed. Trying to tear out Shaw's windpipe. The world went bright around the edges of his vision. Shaw coiled into a ball, lashing out with a kick. The sole of his boot smashed into the man's jaw. The Viking heaved up with the force of the blow, took one step back.

Disappeared. There and then suddenly not there, like a magic trick. Shaw rolled onto his stomach and crawled to the cliff edge.

Below, the shimmering water lapped at the narrow strip of shore. The Viking's body lay in a twisted X halfway between the cliff and the latest receding wave. Shaw could see his white face in profile. The head nearly submerged in a tide pool, the riot of beard floating on the ripples.

A muzzle flash blazed from Shaw's right, down on the beach. He ducked back. The Browning was somewhere in the patchy grass. He went looking on his hands and knees, with the afterimage of the flash still floating in his vision. His pistol lay a yard from the drop, along with the killer's rifle. Shaw slung the long gun over his shoulder and crawled to the cliff to cautiously look over its edge once more.

The single shot had come from only twenty feet down the shore. Near the cliff itself. He could see nothing in the deep shadows. The horizontal length of the flash made him guess that it had been aimed along the beach, not upward at him.

Aimed at what? He looked down the beach to his left. After a moment he heard a splash. A figure ran from the cliff to a spot where the shore dipped a few feet, just above the tide line. The running man ducked below the lip of rock.

The rainy night greedily leached color from the world, but Shaw had been certain that the figure was wearing a suit of pearl gray. Hargreaves.

He was trying to reach the boat. Pinned down by the man shooting from the cliff face.

Shaw's Zodiac, if it was still where he'd left it, was a few short yards behind the shooter. Along with the spot where Shaw had ascended the cliff face to tear the tree from its roots. He could climb down to the shore there. He crawled in that direction. Rainwater flowed from his muddy arms and legs to the wet soil and grass beneath, as if he were melting into the island.

EIGHTY-TWO

Hargreaves knelt beneath the rocky overhang. His hands had been scraped bloody by the barnacles and the stucco texture of the shore. The knees of his suit pants were ragged and the skin below torn as well. He'd seen Tucker die. The round had blown half the man's back away. A ribbon of hot liquid had lashed through the rain to join the surf.

Riley or Taskine. He'd known immediately by the sharp spitting noise of the suppressed round. Using the rifles he had given them himself. Traitorous shits.

He'd returned fire. Maybe hit one of them. There hadn't been an answering shot. Still, he'd lain flat for a full two minutes before daring to move. If both those madmen were on the beach, he was outmatched.

Then, as if the gods were granting him a gift, Taskine had appeared. Splat. It was darkly funny, the way the pumped-up ape had hit the rocks thirty feet from where Hargreaves lay, his head leading the charge by a fraction of a second.

He was dead. No question about that. Taskine's skull must be halfway to two-dimensional after that impact. The monster must have slipped while trying to clamber down the cliff.

Which left just Riley.

Emboldened, Hargreaves dashed for a closer position, a low spot he could duck beneath.

Riley fired once. A pistol this time.

Hargreaves risked a glance. He wasn't far from the little speedboat now. The vessel was almost completely ashore as the tide flowed out. Only its stern rose gently with each new wave.

Kill the creep Riley first? Or use the boat as cover? He could cut the line and pull it into the water. Ten rounds left in his Glock if it came to a fight.

From the opposite end of the island, he heard the honk of a voice through a bullhorn. The words incomprehensible at this distance, but Hargreaves had the gist. Telling anyone still in the estate to come out. Police teams would be sweeping the island before long.

Decision made. Get to that boat. Leave this cursed place behind forever.

EIGHTY-THREE

Rain and trickling mud had made the bluff slick. Shaw descended slowly, testing each toehold before daring to move his hand down to the next spot that offered a grip. The sheer face was only twenty feet high, but it might have been a thousand for the caution Shaw had to give it. Slipping and busting his leg or worse on the beach would be the same as painting a fluorescent target on himself.

He reached the shore and dropped to crouch in the crook of the cliff wall. Water trickled from the crags above, giving thicker shape to the rain. The shooter, if he hadn't moved, would be fifteen long paces to Shaw's right. Hargreaves another twenty yards to the left, on the far side of the beached speedboat.

The two combatants at a standoff. Neither, Shaw thought, aware that he was crashing the party. He glided along the projections and hollows of the cliff face as though listening closely to the island's whispered secrets.

He saw the man's legs first. Extending from an especially deep shadow, toes of his boots almost straight up toward the sky. Shaw held very still. One of the legs turned an inch. The man was seated upright. Mostly upright. Slumped against the vertical wall. Arms down at his sides, loose. Left hand empty.

Shaw covered the last five yards in a rush. He pressed the muzzle of the Browning hard against the man's temple, forcing the head to one side, as he clamped his other hand down on the man's right forearm. A Colt pistol fell from the killer's loose fingers.

It was the other hitter, the snaky one with the eyeglasses. The left side of his neck and his shoulder so coated that the tinny blood smell wafted strong through the rain. His glasses were askew from the force of Shaw's gun against his head.

The killer's eyes turned to him, slowly, peering over the black frames.

"Hey," he breathed. "Look at you."

His lip curled up, maybe attempting a smile. The last of his air rasped out. His chest shuddered for an instant and then was still.

From the distance, past the boat and wherever Hargreaves hid on the shore, came the low drone of someone speaking through a bullhorn. The tac team, clearing the house and estate grounds.

Splashes. Against the glitter on the rolling waves, Shaw saw Hargreaves duck behind the body of the speedboat. A moment later the bowline fell limp to the beach and the boat began to slide backward into deeper water. Pulled by Hargreaves on his knees.

Shaw unslung the rifle from his shoulder. The glistening hull of the boat was the brightest thing in view. It turned, tugged by Hargreaves's unseen hand, until the bow pointed parallel to the shore. The boat tilted to port to show Shaw a portion of its white belly. Hargreaves, climbing aboard on the far side, his weight making the small boat list.

Shaw raised the rifle as the boat came back to center. Hargreaves now a ghostly gray shape just ahead of the outboard engine. An easy shot. The sniper rifle's supreme accuracy would counter the night and the boat's slow rise and fall on the waves. Shaw used the scope, breathing easy. Plenty of time to put the crosshairs right where he wanted them.

The speedboat's engine started with a buzzsaw roar. An instant of life before Shaw's .300 round hit it, shattering the plastic hood and half the works within. Shaw heard Hargreaves's cry of alarm as metal fragments and gasoline sprayed over the cockpit.

With the motor's abrupt silence, the island seemed even quieter than before. Even the rain had lessened.

"Toss the gun," Shaw shouted.

Hargreaves stood dazedly in the boat. A scarecrow figure, his suit torn and stained, shirt loose and transparent with wet. Fresh cuts on his forehead and cheek welled up, the blood caught immediately by raindrops and racing to drip from his brow and chin.

"Do it," Hargreaves called. More at the island than at Shaw, who remained cloaked in darkness.

The boat receded slightly with each wave, floating out toward the channel. Toward the great swells that rolled from the north. Without its engine and forward momentum, the little boat would be swamped within minutes. Its foam-and-fiberglass construction might not allow it to sink completely, but it would be hardly better than a floating log as it was borne out to sea. Along with anyone still clinging to it.

Hargreaves, apparently resigned to the fact that Shaw wasn't going to kill him outright, turned to look out at the horizon. There was nothing to see. Any islands in the distance, shrouded in rain clouds and night, might as well be another continent. Only the merciless straits awaited.

"Come on!" he yelled. The boat rose on an upsurge and settled again, another few feet farther from land.

Shaw waited. He believed that Hargreaves would accept a bullet. He was morbidly curious whether the covert spook could face a slower death.

A long moment passed. Hargreaves stepped onto the boat's rail and into the water. He swam and splashed his way to shore. His hands were empty.

From far up the beach, Shaw saw the glittering dots of flashlights. And a police launch, thundering at half throttle, coming from the same direction. He walked away from the cliff, the rifle trained on Hargreaves, who offered no resistance other than a look of hatred. The blood trickling from his face gave him a demon's visage.

"Fucking coward," he said to Shaw.

The beam of a searchlight on the police launch pierced the night. The light swept past them, reversed, pinned them like dragonflies to a corkboard.

"Every man his own courage," said Shaw.

EIGHTY-FOUR

They held Shaw for a month. The charges were felony escape and criminal trespass, but those were appetizers, the state prosecutor's office promised. More serious indictments would quickly follow if he refused to cooperate. Bail was an unlikely prospect, and given that three different law-enforcement agencies were demanding hours of his time every day for interviews and crafting what would become his sworn statement to the court, Shaw said to hell with it and stayed in the King County lockup. At least it spared him the commute.

Not that Ganz had been idle. Reenergized with Linda Edgemont's killer in custody, the attorney was out for blood.

He joined Shaw for every one of his meetings with cops and Feds of various ranks, not even delegating the rubber-stamp work of drafting motions for discovery to his firm's associates. He was just as active away from Shaw as well, working the phones and giving holy hell to any delay in attending to his client's legal rights and privileges. The duel with the lawyers of the other defendants had begun, fingers pointing in every direction.

Ganz passed news to Shaw as it developed. Jane Calloway, the erstwhile C.J., was denied bail as the states of Washington, Louisiana, and New York investigated her for multiple counts of homicide. Her MO had remained largely unchanged for some years. Now that detectives had a face and a name to match with unsolved murders committed with suppressed .22-caliber handguns, they were boring in.

Calloway, in turn, was rolling over like wood on a lathe on her boss, James Hargreaves. Looking to dodge the death penalty by tying other cold cases to the lethal pair of Taskine and Riley, about whose activities she knew far more than she had confessed to Shaw. Duplicitous to the end.

Every day seemed to bring a new line of investigation on James Hargreaves, and on his firm, Paragon. Ganz shared that the New York cops had essentially created a task force to grill all the intelligence firm's operatives. And Paragon's clients were scrambling to cover their asses. Given Hargreaves's shadowy background and uncertain level of influence, the cops had first kept him in isolation at County, only a floor or two away from Shaw. Then somebody whispered in somebody else's ear, and Hargreaves was quickly and quietly transferred to the federal detention center at SeaTac, where his former agency was probably listening in to every syllable he uttered, rights be damned.

Morton looked likely to get off scot-free. He'd cooperated with authorities, thanks to Karla Haiden's convincing him that any other decision would end with Hargreaves ensuring the chemist's permanent silence. And Morton's lawyer could make a reasonable case that his client was unaware of the full nature of the industrial theft from Avizda and the crimes committed as a result. Maybe it was even true.

Pollan had survived the havoc on the island. The FBI tactical team had found her hiding in one of the maintenance sheds. She was out on bail within days. Anders had told police that Kilbane's bunch had been brought in as bodyguards for himself and Sebastien Rohner, without knowing what the sale of the chemical involved.

The security woman wasn't the only person Anders was looking to protect. The Droma chief of staff had set himself up as the lightning rod for every charge aimed at his friend and employer, Sebastien Rohner. Anders claimed that he'd been behind the negotiations with Chen Li to give Droma access to the Chinese market, in exchange for Droma's assistance in securing the missing details of the stolen polymer. Anders also said he'd been the one to engage Paragon to infiltrate Avizda. He was emphatic that Sebastien Rohner had believed the entire affair was legal and aboveboard.

The fly in that particularly slick ointment, ironically, was Hargreaves. While the former spy himself was hiding behind his own phalanx of attorneys, he hadn't had a chance to delete all the voice recordings made of Anders's phone conversations or the conversations between Linda Edgemont and Edwin Chiarra, who was spilling every bean he could find in an effort to avoid prison. Anders was holding tight to his story, even as the recordings put the lie to it.

"Ever loyal," Shaw said to Ganz as they sat in the same county-jail interview room where Shaw had met Chiarra. He shook his head. "Hard to believe Anders would stick his neck out so far."

"They've been friends since school." Ganz shrugged. "Maybe once you get in the habit of looking after somebody, it's second nature."

"So what's the likely outcome?"

"For Rohner? He's remained in the United States—voluntarily, his lawyers keep shouting—for the past few weeks. But the pressure's on to either file charges or let him travel to attend to his business. Once he does"—Ganz made a flying gesture with one hand—"I think we're looking at a Polanski thing here. He's committed no crimes in Europe. He'll stay there as long as he can avoid extradition, which is forever."

"And Anders takes the whipping," said Shaw.

"What I hear, the prosecutor's not looking to tie Anders to any of the homicide charges that Hargreaves is facing. Or even the theft of the chemical sample from Avizda. That was all Chen Li, and we know he's in the wind. The most Anders will likely face is purchase of stolen property, maybe conspiracy to commit cybercrime and industrial espionage. He'll make a deal and serve a few years in minimum security. Rohner's got some top-flight attorneys running interference for him."

"None as good as you."

"Hold on the praise until I get you out of here," Ganz said. "And I'll do it. Least I can do after . . . you know. Linda. You got the filthy worms responsible."

"My pleasure."

Ganz smiled grimly. "I know you're not kidding when you say that. Sometimes I wish I coulda been there." He set his files into his briefcase and closed the latches. "But better I leave that kind of mayhem to you."

Shaw agreed.

It took three more days to get him sprung. Ganz made the ultimatum to the Justice Department that if they wanted Shaw's testimony on Anders and Hargreaves, they had to start treating him like a source instead of a suspect. The Feds subsequently swatted down any state intentions for Shaw. No one made a fuss. New York didn't give a damn about Shaw's break-in at Paragon, not when it had led them to a trove of bigger goodies.

Even Kanellis didn't seem to mind seeing Shaw go loose. The detective had his moment in the sun as the guy who'd turned Morton informant and brought the whole case to light. He'd even shaved properly for press appearances, a couple of which Shaw had caught on the communal room TV. Shaw suspected that Lieutenant Guerin had coached him some.

Shaw signed for his street clothes—a set that Addy had dropped off weeks before; the mud-covered gear he'd been wearing at the island was considered evidence—and left the jail via the main entrance on 5th Ave. He shielded his eyes from the sun as he walked past the odd chunks of artwork in green mosaic, sculptures that always reminded him of board-game pieces.

Hollis was waiting outside, sitting on a marble border by the steps. Karla Haiden stood beside him. She was dressed for the early-August heat in a soft turquoise skirt and white blouse. Her red hair had been cut since he'd last seen her. Tortoiseshell clips held the locks back on each side.

"Sorry for the surprise," she said.

"Speak for yourself," said Shaw. "It's good to see you."

"I'm going for coffee," Hollis said, standing and pointing a thumb uptown. "This place makes me nervous."

Karla and Shaw began to walk down James Street. Shaw had a feeling of unreality, seeing the sky after so many days of incarceration. He took a long breath. It was midmorning. The temperature still in the seventies but promising to creep up a degree every few minutes.

"How are you?" Karla said.

"Better. There are a lot of interviews and other court dates in my future. But it looks like I'll be on the right side of the courtroom."

"Me, too. I'm going back to New York. The DA's office wants me to give a statement about James and to tell what I know about some of the other Paragon operations."

"Any charges?"

"No. Not yet anyway." Karla sidestepped to let a dog walker with half a dozen canines straining in happy frenzy pass on the sidewalk. "Since I was the first of Paragon's people to come forward, that seems to have bought me some leeway. My attorney is making it official. State's evidence."

They reached the broad plaza that wrapped around the western side and corners of the county administration building. Karla angled left, and they strolled onto the plaza's tiles. The nine-story building had a honeycomb motif on its exterior walls, like a hive built by especially severe bees. They sat on one of the low, square benches. Karla folded her hands, almost primly.

"When do you leave?" said Shaw.

"Today. That's why I asked Hollis to bring me along. I just wanted to see you, even for a minute. Do you know what you'll do, after . . . ?" She motioned back toward the jail.

"Get on with work. Make my apologies where I have to."

"Like I'm doing now."

"I don't need any amends," he said. "Are you going to be able to keep your PI license?"

Karla tilted her head. "I'd have to fight for it." Her indecision clear.

"You're good at the job. The Abramses said so. Maybe they'd even help you get on your feet."

"I hadn't even thought of Ronald and Lorraine. God." She exhaled. "I'm not sure I could face them."

"One battle at a time," said Shaw.

"Battles." Karla leaned against his arm. "I heard most of the story about what happened on the island from my lawyer and what I could piece together from the news. It's horrific. I'm so glad you're okay."

"A visit I don't want to repeat. But unless Rohner rebuilds that damned pavilion, I won't have to worry about it."

Shaw joked, but more than one night during the past month he'd lurched awake in his cell, thinking the helicopter was crashing through the shattered spires once more. This time he could only stand and watch as it plunged toward him. He would stay awake after the dream, totaling the butcher's bill. The men on the island who'd died by his hand, directly or not, weighed against the crimes they had committed. It never came out even. He never expected it to. Living with whatever remorse he might feel was a learned skill.

"Will you come back?" he said.

"Yes. I want to." She smiled. "We can take another train ride. A better one this time."

"And you can catch me up on news from the Revolutionary War."

"All the latest dispatches. Just give me a little while to put my life in order. Then . . ."

"Who knows?"

"I like that," she said. "The potential of it. Who knows."

Karla stood up. When he did the same, she stayed close and tilted her head up. He kissed her, softly, with more warmth than heat.

"I'll see you again," she said, and walked out of the plaza to continue down the street. Shaw watched until she was no longer in sight. She hadn't looked back.

Probably the right idea, thought Shaw. When he left himself, a few minutes later, he kept his eyes on the road ahead.

EIGHTY-FIVE

Hollis and Addy had joined forces on a welcome-home celebration for Shaw. Perhaps guessing that he'd prefer calm to raucous, they kept the guest list highly selective. Half a dozen people aboard the *Francesca* as she made lazy circles off Golden Gardens Park, just outside the marina. The surface over the shallow fathoms tranquil enough even for Addy's touchy equilibrium.

Shaw took a spell at the helm on the open flybridge, freeing Hollis to usher everyone away from the galley. Addy and Paula Claybeck moved into the aft section, not pausing in their conversation. This was the first time the two women had met. They'd quickly discovered a shared love of midcentury jazz and were comparing which albums had gotten them started.

Wren stood at the bow with Cyndra. They leaned over the rail, watching the boat's prow slice gently through the water. Every few moments Cyn looked up to scan the bay. Earlier she'd seen a harbor seal poke its sleek head above the surface, and she was alert for a reappearance.

Wren saw Shaw looking and smiled. She said something to Cyndra and walked to the stern of the boat and up the steps to join him. She wrapped her arms around him from behind and rested her head against his back.

"That's good," said Shaw, reaching with the hand not on the helm to hold her wrist. "Let's just stay here for a century or two."

She hummed contently. "We'd get hungry after a while."

"Cyndra can throw us fish."

They stood, feeling each other breathe, as the *Francesca* completed another gentle circle. Shaw didn't have to move the wheel from ten degrees off center. He might have set the autopilot, but it was more enjoyable to do the work, such as it was, for himself. Peaceful.

"I thought I might lose you," Wren said. Her words almost submerged beneath the thrum of the engine.

"If I went to prison?" Shaw felt her nod against his shoulder. "You still wouldn't have lost me. But I get it. That's a long time to be apart."

"A terrible feeling. As though my heart was rehearsing for the time when you wouldn't be there anymore."

"I'm sorry."

"It would be devastating if you went to jail. But not only because you would be trapped." Wren moved to his side without releasing her arms from around him. He laid his own arm over her shoulders. "I'd feel just as sad if we were in different cities."

He looked at her, at the golden flecks in her eyes.

"You're staying?" he said.

"I'm staying. The herbalist puts down roots." She smiled. "Whatever happens with us happens. I know our relationship is unusual. No reason to make it more difficult by moving apart. At least not until you're sick of my company."

"We're talking centuries again," said Shaw.

He kissed her. The boat went off course. He let it.

"Besides," she said when they resurfaced, "I've always wanted my own house."

"Shame," he said. "I had six million dollars just a few weeks ago. The FBI made me give it back. We could have bought something with turrets."

"Darn your laws."

"Worth it to be here."

"Yes. Worth everything to be here." Wren grasped the helm. "You'll get plenty of me later. Go talk with Cyndra. She could use as much time as you can spare for a while."

"Yeah."

Shaw kissed her again. He stepped up on the dash and over the stubby windscreen to the cabin roof and in three quick bounds ran down the front slope of the cabin to Cyndra at the bow rail. Hollis's indignant shout thundered from the galley. Cyn grinned at the acrobatics.

"Spot any more seals?" he said.

"Nope. Some fish jumped over there. Why do they do that?"

"Hunting for food, mostly. Or trying not to become food."

"Weird. Like if we jumped into a lake and it spat us back out again." She scraped a fingernail on the rail. "Noah and I broke up."

Shaw knew Noah's name, barely. Hadn't known that Cyn was dating him, or for how long. Her pink dye job had grown out and faded, leaving her blond hair almost silver at the ends.

"You've had a tough summer," he said.

Cyn kept looking at the water, her profile to Shaw. She was wearing a life vest at Addy's insistence, one more suited for a full-grown adult, and it hung on her like a parka.

"Worse than mine, I think," said Shaw. "I had a portion of the blame and the responsibility. Some measure of control. You just had to go along with whatever happened."

She didn't answer. There was a splash from off the starboard side. Neither of them turned to see what had made the sound.

"When Dono went to prison, I was younger than you. You know that. He got out after a year or so, but it seemed like much longer." Shaw shrugged. "I was so mad and scared that I made this kind of shell around myself. I think there are still pieces of it left now. Maybe always."

He exhaled. "I was mad at Dono for getting busted and scared that I'd have to survive without him somehow. All shit I could have told anybody at the time, if anyone had asked. But what I was really frightened of was that Dono would forget about me. That even if he got out of prison, he'd be a different person by then and he wouldn't want some kid around anymore."

Cyndra's jaw twitched. Not quite a nod but getting there.

"That's not us," Shaw said. "Ever. Promising you I'll never get in trouble again would be false. You're too smart to believe it anyway. But you can be certain that whatever happens, I'm with you and Addy. For good. I'd be lost without you guys."

She turned, and he saw that she was crying after all. The tears had restricted themselves to her left eye, as if allowing her that privacy until she was ready.

"You okay?" he said, putting his arms around her.

"Uh-huh."

"You want to tell me anything?"

She held tight to him, which was plenty.

The boat had come around to face north again in its circle. Long past where Shaw could see, over many other landforms, was the island. Burned and scarred and patient. Waiting until the humans and their attempts at shaping it to their needs had gone, so it could return to what it truly was.

"You want food?" said Shaw after another few moments.

"Yeah." Cyndra wiped her eyes on the sleeve of her sweatshirt.

"Cool," Shaw said. "Go on below if you want. I'll keep an eye out for your seal buddy."

"I forgot. Hollis said I could go swimming tonight."

"It'll be freezing. Summer or not."

"I don't care. It's not too late, is it?"

Shaw looked out over the deep water, endless and powerful.

"Not from where I'm standing," he said.

ACKNOWLEDGMENTS

First and foremost, a sincere thanks to everyone who has read one of my previous Van Shaw novels and sent me words of encouragement via email or social media. I love meeting readers in person and on-line. So if you enjoy this book—or have a question—please shoot me an email at: Glen@GlenErikHamilton.com and say hello. You'll be among the first to know when my next work is coming out and receive other fun news and fan extras.

No one is an island. My love and gratitude to the people who helped me conquer *Island of Thieves*.

Lisa Erbach Vance of the Aaron Priest Literary Agency, for her unwavering support and astute advice.

Lyssa Keusch at William Morrow, whose editorial insights and enthusiasm make every page stronger.

Caspian Dennis of the Abner Stein Agency, our top op in the UK.

And the brilliant team at Morrow who makes it all possible: our publisher par excellence, Liate Stehlik, Kaitlin Harri, Amelia Wood, Sophie Normil, Maureen Sugden, Bob Castillo, David Palmer, Andrew Clark, Richard Aquan, Amy Halperin, Nancy Singer, and Mireya Chiriboga. It takes a lot of dedicated professionals to put a new novel on shelves both physical and virtual; it's my privilege to work with such talented people.

And appreciation to those who lent their time, knowledge, and advice. As ever, the cool stuff is theirs, any mistakes are mine.

Jessica Watts, CQA ASQ, for her invaluable guidance in the plot points involving molecular chemistry and research and innovations in that field. In the interest of speeding the story along, I had to distill some complex concepts. Jessica made sure that I didn't boil away the flavor along with the fat.

Christian Hockman, BCO 1/75 Ranger Regiment, for details on military life and tactics. Christian has always had my six when it comes to giving Van a soldier's mindset.

CDR Ed Weisbrod, USN, Ret., for keeping the book's helicopters in the air until the story demanded they come down to earth. Any pilot error is solely the fault of the characters in question.

Mark Pryor, author of the wonderful Hugo Marston mysteries, for lending his legal expertise as an assistant district attorney. Even Ephraim Ganz would think twice about facing off with Mark in a courtroom.

Jamie Mason, acclaimed author of *The Hidden Things* and other thrilling novels you should race to read, for her advance perusal of the manuscript and sound story advice.

Kristie Foss, friend and fellow conspirator, for her guided tour of the hidden side of Pike Place Market.

Amy, Mia, and Madeline: Even after a year and counting of quarantine—with a writer, no less—you're somehow still thriving and confident. Clearly you can accomplish anything. Thanks for bringing me along for the ride. I love you.

AUTHOR'S NOTE

My standard disclaimer: This novel is fiction, which means I get to make up anything and everything, including but not limited to businesses real or imagined, jurisdictions, history, or anything else that might keep the story moving, keep the lawyers bored, and keep potentially dangerous information where and with whom it belongs.

The most obvious fabrication herein involves the COVID-19 pandemic and its aftermath. *Island of Thieves* was written during the first eight months of the quarantine. I was overly optimistic in assuming that our lives would be largely back to normal by the following summer, when the book is set. But as I type these words we're still in the early stages of vaccinations across the world. Since mentions of the pandemic in the book are few, I hope readers will forgive my wishful thinking. Here's to all of us emerging from this terrible time stronger and wiser.

ABOUT THE AUTHOR

A native of Seattle, Glen Erik Hamilton was raised aboard a sailboat and grew up around the marinas and commercial docks and islands of the Pacific Northwest. His debut novel, *Past Crimes,* won the Anthony, Macavity, and Strand Critics awards and was also nominated for the Edgar, Barry, and Nero awards. After living for many years in Southern California, he and his family have recently returned to the Emerald City and its beautiful overcast skies.